SOMEONE
Has Taken My Place

Identity Theft, Insurance Fraud
& Criminal Activity

BASED ON A TRUE STORY

DAVID SNOW

ACKNOWLEDGEMENTS

cℐℛ

In writing this book I would like to acknowledge the assistance provided by my editor Aoife Barrett of Barrett Editing, who worked tirelessly on the editing of the manuscript and to Paul Williams, for the inspiration from his many true crime books. I also pay thanks to my many friends in An Garda Siochana, various law enforcement agencies within the United States of America and the International Association of Special Investigation Units.

I also acknowledge the support from my wife Jacinta and the individuals who have shared their experience and knowledge with me over the past 20 years, including Garda Chief Superintendent Michael Casey (Retired) and Derek Nally (Retired). Sandra Mara former President of the Institute of Irish Investigators, my many former Pinkerton colleagues and above all Shirley Sleator and Sam Carroll for opening the door in 1989.

Additionally I would like to acknowledge the sacrifices made by the United States of America in the pursuit of liberty, justice and freedom, following the horrific attacks of 9/11. In particular I would like to remember US Army Sgt Daniel Tallouzi who paid the ultimate sacrifice, and to recognise the brave and courageous efforts of his mother Mary Tallouzi with the Wounded Warrior Project.

There is no greater love than to lay down one's life for one's friends – John 15:13

First published in 2012
Copyright © 2012 David Snow
All rights reserved.

ISBN-10: 1480035483
ISBN:13: 9781480035485

A percentage of the sales of this book will be donated to A Little Lifetime Foundation, formally known as Irish Stillbirth and Neonatal Death Society (Isands) www.isands.ie

DEDICATION

This book is dedicated to the memory of my son Andrew Murray Snow, who was born and returned to the Lord on the 13 November, 2003, and to my cousin Mark Brooks and my Great Uncle William Brooks who chose to return home at their births. I also remember baby Ruth, Reece, Carol Anne Shaw and my school friend Garda Gareth Harmon, who paid the ultimate sacrifice for protecting the citizens of Ireland.

I also dedicate this book to my Mother and Father and thank you for giving me life. But most of all to my mother Mary for all the sacrifices you made in your life for the benefit of mine.

"All that I am, or hope to be, I owe to my angel mother."
—Abraham Lincoln

THE AUTHOR

∂∫∫

David Snow has been working in the private investigation arena since 1989. He was one of the first graduates and members of the Institute of Irish Investigators. He obtained the "youngest student award" from the Institute in 1989. He was employed by Sleator Carroll Insurance Investigators and then Pinkerton Security & Investigations, the world's oldest and largest private detective and security agency with operations on every continent. He joined Pinkerton in 1993 and became the General Manager of the Irish operation in 1996, leaving in 2001 to pursue a career within insurance fraud investigation.

Today he is employed as the Head of Special Investigations for the Irish operation of a multi-national insurance company. He is a member of the International Association of Special Investigation Units (IASIU), the Association of Certified Fraud Examiners (ACFE) and the Association of Irish Risk Management (AIRM) and is the current chairman of the Irish Insurance Fraud Investigators Group (IIFIG). He is a retained fraud lecturer for the Insurance Institute of Ireland and IASIU Europe. He is also a member of the Irish charity A Little Lifetime Foundation, formally known as Isands, obtaining an award in 2012 for his efforts in the prevention of the theft of the identities of dead Irish babies. He has also lectured extensively on insurance fraud in Ireland and Europe.

FOREWORD

This book examines the complexity involved in the investigation of insurance fraud and other financial crimes caused by identity theft. The horrific 9/11 terrorist attacks, an attack not just on the United States of America but on all countries that enjoy freedom and liberty, made it clear that in order to assist in counter-terrorism the Irish authorities need to ensure passports are not issued under false pretentions. Can you imagine if the 9/11 terrorists had carried Irish passports?

Identity Theft is relatively new to Ireland when compared to the United States. However it is a growing problem. Effectively identity theft is the ability to take somebody's identity and use it to commit fraud. The most common form of identity theft is obtaining credit card details and using them to purchase goods or services in that person's name. If you combine identity theft with the obtaining of insurance policies, opening false bank accounts and making fraudulent insurance claims, it makes the investigation of these crimes extremely complex and difficult. Identity theft of the dead is also a major problem in the United States. Sources there estimate that there were 800,000 attempts to steal dead people's identities in 2011 alone. The website of the US Federal Bureau of Investigation (FBI) states: "A stolen identity is a powerful cloak of anonymity for criminals and terrorist and a danger to national security and private citizens alike."

There is a clear need for the harmonisation of all investigators, so that insurance investigators like myself, can work together with law enforcement agencies, nationally and internationally to reduce fraud and crime, and to above all protect our citizen's identities and our national identity.

David Snow
2012
www.davidsnow.ie

CHAPTER 1

It was a cold day; snow was falling, a light dusting at first, dangerous to drive but not bad enough to stay at home. I was on a routine car theft investigation in Balbriggan, a town about 15 miles north of Dublin City. It was a small investigation, a car stolen 'without the keys' as we termed it. The car had a value of circa €10,000 so the pay out by the insurance company I worked for, Dallast, wouldn't be too big.

I was interviewing the insured, Mr. Charlie Gibson, in a hotel in Balbriggan. It was the usual story X cannot explain how his/her vehicle was stolen. Charlie still had the car keys, which was a little strange as nowadays most car thefts are carried out with the keys because modern cars are fitted with an electronic immobiliser, making it impossible to start the car without the factory supplied key.

Charlie and I sat at the open fire of the hotel, drinking coffee as he told me his version of events. He'd been away on holidays when his vehicle was stolen and had received a call in America telling him that his car had been found in a field, destroyed by fire. I was aware of this already as I had spoken to the police. Charlie's vehicle had been used in an armed robbery during a raid in a local Dublin bank.

I have interviewed hundreds of individuals over the years and heard all types of stories about supposed car thefts. In my experience, when a car is stolen 'without the keys' it was automatically a suspect case. Normally we do a little digging and find out that the insured is having financial difficulties, such as late payments on the vehicle finance, employment problems, or they are going through some personal difficulties, for instance a divorce. As an investigator you develop a sixth sense and quickly realise who is telling the truth. My instincts were telling me that Charlie might be guilty of fraud. Not that I would dream of mentioning it to him as I had no foundation for my gut feeling. In a litigious society like Ireland you cannot state, or write down your views anywhere, unless you have proof and I didn't have anything on him.

I have been a private and insurance investigator for the past 23 years, including five years with the American corporate giant Pinkerton. During this period of time I have investigated many interesting and complex files in Ireland, America and Europe. I recall one case that involved a man who worked in a bar who had been in a road traffic accident. He was knocked down and broke both his legs. It seemed a genuine and serious injury and he told us that he would never be able to work as a bartender again. But after an in-depth investigation I established that he had purchased a pub in Dresden, Germany, and was working there. He had failed to disclose this information and the case was eventually settled for very little money. A second case I particularly remember involved an American lady who had been in an accident in Ireland. The lady said she was living in New York and was unable to return to work after the accident. Our Pinkerton agent in New York was unable to find the lady at first, but he eventually traced her to Miami, Florida where the accident 'victim' was working as a Jet Ski instructor! As a result of our inspections, both cases were withdrawn from the courts.

Fraud investigation is complex and can require many hours of meticulous searching for facts, with full attention to all the specific details involved. However, even though committing fraud in all its many forms is a criminal activity perpetrated by individuals from all walks of life against both insurance companies and other financial institutions, private investigators and insurance fraud investigators operate in no-man's land in Ireland. They do not enjoy the statutory protection of any government agency. Effectively if you are a civilian investigator you are on your own. You rely on the generosity of others for assistance in obtaining intelligence and information, but their willingness to help is continuously tested by the ever tightening laws. This is not the case in other jurisdictions, such as the UK or the US, where there is legislation in place to support financial investigators.

It is difficult to place a cost on insurance fraud worldwide. Based on figures from the Federal Bureau of Investigation (FBI), insurance fraud in the United States is estimated at costing $40 billion, while in the UK the Insurance Fraud Bureau estimates a cost of Stg£2 billion. Australia is the latest country to co-ordinate industry efforts in combating insurance fraud. Like the UK, they have also set up an insurance fraud bureau. Australia estimates that insurance fraud is costing Aus$2 billion annually.

According to the Irish Insurance Federation (IIF) it is estimated that insurance fraud in Ireland costs €100 million per annum. However this figure was released in 2003 and, sadly, ten years on Ireland is a completely different place. At the moment there is an increase in fraud cases, which is related to the downturn in our economy. It would be reasonable to suggest that the cost of insurance fraud has doubled since 2003, to approximately €200 million each year.

It is important to ask yourself: who pays for insurance fraud? The answer is "You!" The cost of fraud is added to everybody's premiums. Insurance fraud is a crime against all citizens of the country as most Irish people have at least one insurance policy, be it motor, household, travel or public liability. The Insurance Fraud Bureau UK estimates that fraud adds Stg£44 to every policy of insurance. Fraud, and more particularly insurance fraud, is the crime where the ordinary decent citizen pays.

As I continued to interview Charlie I noticed that he never made direct eye contact and always shuffled when I asked him straight-forward questions. From interviewing many people you gain skills in the art of telling if somebody is lying: fast eye movements, excessive blinking or requiring the toilet are all suspect signs. When someone is trying to invent or construct a story they become nervous and it shows on their faces and in their body movements. I once interviewed a lady in my car and she wet the seat when I asked her if she was telling the truth.

I was suspicious of Charlie's claim and the statement he had given me, but that being said I liked him and felt that there was a certain amount of honesty in his case. He was friendly and I allowed my mind to drift as we started talking about America and the various holidays we'd both enjoyed there. Talking about the US always reminded me of my younger years, working for the Pinkerton Detective Agency in Los Angeles, California, and getting friendly with the local ladies.

My trip down memory lane was abruptly interrupted by my mobile phone which started vibrating on the coffee table. I tried to ignore it as I recognised the number – Head Office. It was not that I was intentionally ignoring my colleagues; it was that I did not want to be interrupted while I was interviewing Charlie. Also I was planning a short day: interview the insured, obtain a statement, talk to the cops again to confirm that the vehicle was reported stolen, as per the statement of factual evidence provided by Charlie, and then go home to work from my home office. Talking to Head Office was not part of the plan so I didn't take the call.

I finished the statement at about 11.30am and was ready to wrap up the meeting and drive to my home office, located near Balbriggan, when the phone rang again. This time it was our Insurance Liability Claims Manager, Dan Courtney. Dan was a very enthusiastic manager in his late fifties, of American background and well-liked by his multiple claims' teams. He was meticulous in dealing with facts and, due to his many years experience defending personal injury claims, he was well able to sniff out a file which was not all that it seemed.

"Excuse me Charlie; I need to take this call," I said as I stood up and walked outside.

"Where are you Andy?" Dan asked. "I need you to meet me in the office this afternoon."

"I am in Balbriggan; it's snowing fairly heavy so I was thinking of heading home and catching up on my emails from my home office."

"Negative, I need to see you."

Before I could respond the phone went dead.

I walked back over to Charlie, feeling irritated that I now had to drive 20 miles in the snow into our Dublin city office. The snow was getting heavier and I knew it was going to take me at least an hour to get there. I had planned to go home, set the fire and then get the dinner ready for my wife, Jackie, and my two daughters, Olivia and Sarah. Jackie used to work as a lawyer with me at Dallast Insurance but she was now in private practice.

But I had no choice. I knew by the tone of Dan's voice that it was important and that he was politely saying "Get your ass in here." My biggest problem was going to be coming home, leaving Dublin City at rush hour, sitting in gridlock, with the snow causing extra delays. The slightest amount of snow in Dublin brought the traffic to a standstill.

I thanked Charlie for his time and for meeting with me. I had obtained my standard two-page statement on the theft of his vehicle and was ready for the next step.

"We'll conclude our investigation within a week Charlie and I'll talk to the investigating police officer as well."

This was the polite way of saying I am going to verify your statement and confirm if you are telling the truth!

We stood up and shook hands: "Thank you for your time Charlie. I'll be in touch."

I returned to the car park, loaded my laptop and equipment into the boot and began my journey into the Dublin office.

As I drove I started pondering why Courtney, one of our Senior Managers, was looking for me. Most of the referrals to the Special Investigations Unit (SIU) were from claims handlers, underwriters, lawyers or loss adjusters. In the back of my mind it occurred to me that if Courtney was looking for me then it might just be an interesting case file and not the standard routine investigation, like poor Charlie Gibson and his stolen car.

Little did I realise that this was going to be the start of my journey into the most interesting case I have ever investigated — to date.

CHAPTER 2

The weather was appalling. It was -4°C and the snow appeared to be getting heavier. I was listening to my car radio when the news advised that Dublin Airport had been closed due to heavy snow. I immediately telephoned my wife.

"Hi Jackie, where are you?"

"I am in the Dublin High Court; the courts are being suspended due to the snow. You should head home Andy."

The Dublin High Court is located in the city centre, a short distance from my office. My wife is an independent high value defence litigation lawyer, who defends large institutions, such as insurance companies from claims.

"I can't Courtney is looking for me and wants to meet me this afternoon in the Dublin office"

"That's strange because when I left your office, senior management were allowing distance workers to go home. I wonder why Courtney is looking for you. The snow is not letting up, it's heavy in the city, so be careful driving and don't worry I will pick up the kids."

"I will; see you later at home."

I continued on towards Dublin, with the snow belting off my car window. It was going to be a slow drive to the office.

I arrived into the office just after 1.30pm. The Dublin office is the headquarters of the Irish operation, with a staff of 700, including senior management. All of the claims and large operations are covered from there. We also have offices in many other Irish cities: Cork, Limerick, Galway, Kilkenny and Waterford.

I met with John Denton, one of my colleagues within the SIU. John was a young investigator aged about 21, and eager to make a name for himself in the investigation business.

"What are you doing in with all the snow?"

"'I am here to see Courtney."

"Can I have a meeting with me before you leave the office?"

"Sure no problem."

I walked towards the rear of the claims department, passing at least 90 claims staff, who were all working hard at their desktops, trying to keep clients happy, paying claims, organising hire cars, dealing with lawyers and other contracted support staff.

I approached Courtney who being a manager had his own private office. He was in conversation with Tanya Sanderson, a new member of staff who had recently joined us from Norway. Ireland is a vibrant country which in recent years has seen a large influx of many nationalities including Polish, Russians, Chinese and Nigerians.

I waited for a break in the conversation and quickly said: "I am in and will be at my desk when you're ready."

"No hold on, this involves Tanya, it is one of her files. Pull up a seat Andrew."

I sat down beside Tanya and Courtney sat back in his comfortable, leather manager's chair.

"Andrew I have a file for you to investigate here — it's a big one; we're holding a reserve of €750,000."

Insurance companies place a financial reserve on all personal injury files, pending more details on the scale of the injury and the likely final costs involved. The reserve will include lawyer's fees, medical charges, any potential loss of earnings for the claimant, investigators fees and any other costs associated with the settlement of the claim. It was crucial that a technical manager reviewed the financial reserve set by the claims handler as it can be rather embarrassing having to increase a financial reserve during the life of the claim. I once worked on a case with a reserve of €50,000 which eventually settled for €150,000 as the loss of earnings had not been factored into the original calculation of claim costs. This can be embarrassing for the individual claims handler and manager as it affects the financial projections of the whole company.

I took out my police notebook, which had been given to me by a friend in the Gardaí, the Irish police force.

"OK give me the usual: name address, date of birth, accident details," I said.

"I have a name and an email address and that is it I am afraid," Tanya said.

I paused; how the hell was I going to investigate this?

"OK give me the story," I said.

"Our insured, a Polish citizen Nigel Boroski, was driving his car in The Curragh in Kildare and crashed into an American tourist," Tanya explained.

The Curragh was the training grounds for the Irish army, a large open field and park, consisting of over 200 acres.

"We are told that Nigel Boroski was in the area at 7.30am and was going to walk his dog. He stopped his car, looked down to change a CD then went to drive on and crashed into this American man who was out for a jog."

"When did it happen and who reported the accident?" I asked.

"We received a telephone call from the American man who got injured, a John Harrison, and the accident occurred on 5 December. Our insured obtained the insurance on the 18 November."

"John Harrison does not sound like an American name," I said.

"Andrew, his name is John Harrison — would it make a difference if his name was Tom Cruise?" Courtney asked.

I thought it best not to comment any further on the name and to just continue with the questions.

"What address do we have for the American?" I asked Tanya.

"We don't, just an email address. Oh and he is now in Liverpool in the UK. He contacted us by email and also by phone, complaining that he was in agony with his back and his right leg and that he had to go to hospital there."

I was trying to take notes and was also aware of Courtney, who just sat still, staring at me. Courtney was a firm but fair manager. If I could impress him with this case then just maybe I would get a higher payment in my annual bonus.

"What else do we know about him?"

"That's it on him but his wife is five months pregnant and is expecting a baby. They live in Louisiana, USA. We also got some medical reports from the doctors in Liverpool Hospital."

Tanya gave me a copy of the medical report, confirming that John Harrison had nasty back, right leg and shoulder injuries. The report also advised that he was not fit for travel on an airplane and that he would require back surgery to correct the damage caused to his facet joints. The doctor had noted that Harrison should be in hospital to minimise any strenuous movements of his spine.

"Not much to go on!" I said.

"Well that is what you are paid for Andrew; now go get me a result," Courtney said dismissively.

I exited his office and walked back towards the SIU desk.

Tanya caught up with me and said: "Andy I forgot, here this may help you."

She handed me an email which was from John Harrison.

I quickly read it and discovered he was going to be staying at his uncle's farm, Swan's View, located in Liverpool.

"If you have any more emails or contact from Harrison contact me at once will you Tanya? And don't make him suspicious of our investigation just handle the claim in a normal manner. At this stage we have nothing to go on. The UK doctors have told us he has nasty injuries and he's in pain, so this could be a genuine one."

"Will do Andy."

I returned to my desk and checked Harrison's name with Insurance Link. It's a database shared by all insurance companies operating in Ireland for the prevention and detection of fraud. Each insurance company inputs all data that they obtain on claimants, including their addresses. These claims can then be cross-checked by other insurers. Insurance Link was an excellent tool in combating fraudulent insurance claims and it has saved a huge amount of Euro and Dollars since it was established in 1992. Like all databases, however, it was only as good as the data inserted.

I got nothing in response to John Harrison so I decided to test our insured's name, Nigel Boroski. I checked the underwriting screen and nothing came up, other than that the insured was Polish and had a Polish driver's license.

Denton returned to the SIU desk and I noticed that he'd just brushed his hair, no doubt in the hopes that one of the many girls in Claims might express an interest.

"That guy Connolly was in looking for his cheque for the stolen Toyota Hiace again," he sighed.

Connolly was a nuisance to all insurance companies as he made multiple claims for similar accidents. I had dealt with his claim when his Toyota Hiace went on fire as he was driving. I had discovered that Connolly had forgotten to tell us that he had been convicted of drunk driving and should have been off the road at the time he took out his motor insurance policy. I'd found his conviction in the newspaper and voided his insurance policy. As a result his claim for €15,500 was denied.

"Was he looking for trouble?" I asked.

"You better watch it as Connolly is still trying to get your number," Denton said.

"Forget Connolly; I have a real case to investigate now," I said and briefed Denton about our new American case.

"John I need you to assist with our other investigations and in particular my case load as I need to give this case my full attention — OK?"

"Consider it done Andy."

I left the office that afternoon with my new case on my mind. I loved a good case, it's like getting your teeth into a good book, you know the sort of book you get on holidays and enjoy reading so much you forget to enjoy your break.

As I began the drive home, the traffic was heavy but moving. Thankfully the snow had stopped, but it was bitterly cold.

I managed to get home before Jackie, prepared dinner and had it ready for her and our two kids, as I played the new case over in my mind. I had a feeling I was going to need all the brownie points I could get from my wife in the near future as it looked like it was going to be a demanding file — I was soon proved to be correct.

CHAPTER 3

⚜

The following day I decided to stay at home and work from our small but convenient home office. I like working from home as you do not have to battle the Dublin rush hour traffic and there was nobody annoying me. It was just me, my emails, my mobile phone and my new case.

I started at the beginning and looked back over the time and date of the accident. On 5 December, 2008, at 07.30am, our insured Nigel Boroski had knocked down a pedestrian in The Curragh. Although I knew The Curragh was a popular park for walking, running and horse riding, I was immediately suspicious about an American tourist who was out for a walk by himself at 7.30am. At that time of the day The Curragh would be deserted. It was also a good distance from any houses, so an American jogging there on his own sounded most unusual.

I ran the names Harrison and Boroski through all my available databases and achieved nothing. Not a single record of information – just nothing. This was not unusual for Harrison, as he was an American tourist on vacation but as far as we knew our insured Nigel Boroski had been living and working in Ireland for a few years.

I opened the file and discovered that Tanya had instructed the services of a liability investigator, John Hayes of HTS & Associates. A liability investigator was engaged to independently determine the cause of the accident and who was at fault. The investigator would provide a detailed report, on occasion interviews witnesses and also provide contact details for the attending emergency services. It was more economical for us to outsource this service to local independent contractors, as they were based in every county in Ireland.

I found a copy of John Hayes' report and read that he had met with Boroski at the scene of the accident a week after it happened and obtained a brief statement. Boroski's statement was a standard document which briefly detailed: 'I was driving in The Curragh, stopped my car to change a CD and then continued on driving and crashed into a pedestrian. I got out of my car and helped the pedestrian stand up. The pedestrian was an American man whom I do not know and I gave him my insurance details.'

Our investigator had advised in his report: 'The insured is a Polish national, has a poor command of the English language and is returning to Poland tomorrow.'

I was thinking about what to do next when my phone rang. It was Dave Hendrick a loss adjuster based in Naas, Co. Kildare. A loss adjuster effectively acts on behalf of the insurance company when dealing with property claims. They investigate and determine the reason for the property loss and adjust the claims accordingly. A good loss adjuster was one of the most valuable assets an insurance company could employ in the prevention of fraud.

"Hi Andy, how's life?"

"Busy trying to keep everybody happy!"

"Do you want to meet for lunch in Naas? I'd like to show you the new office and introduce you to some of the new staff."

"That sounds good Dave. I will meet you later on, say about 1pm."

"Look forward to it Andy."

I decided to go ahead and meet Dave for lunch as I could take a drive by the location of the accident in The Curragh and also take a closer look at Nigel Boroski's home address in Naas. Hayes had stated that Boroski had returned to Poland but I thought it was worth double checking. I knew it was most likely he'd been renting the Irish house, but when investigating a suspect file you have to follow up on all leads, no matter how small or irrelevant the lead might appear to be. If I got lucky I might be able to talk to someone who knew him and get some local intelligence.

Traffic on the M50 was surprisingly good, moving fast as I drove along in my Toyota Avensis. It was a new car and I was trying out the various speeds, enjoying myself just like a little boy racer, only I was showing my age with my choice of music, *You can go your own way* by Fleetwood Mac.

It started to rain just as I was arriving in Naas. Dave saw me pull up and ran from his office to meet me. Dave was the best of the best, an excellent loss adjuster who had a real noise for sniffing out fraud. He was about 50 years of age and had been in the insurance business for some 30 years. I respected his view on matters.

"Nice wheels," Dave said, as he sat into the front passenger seat. "Must be nice to get a company car."

"Yes but don't forget the bloody benefit-in-kind tax."

"Yeah tell me about it, tax and more tax!"

As we drove to the local pub for some lunch I told Dave all about my new file.

"That sounds like a very interesting case. It's nice to get your hands on a juicy case from the beginning and not when it's halfway through the investigation," Dave said seriously.

"Well considering the American contacts I have from working over there I should be in a position to obtain some information."

Little did I know then how much my contacts were going to be tested.

After lunch I decided to take a drive to Boroski' address in Craddockstown, a respectable private housing estate located in Naas, Co. Kildare. I found the house where Nigel Boroski had told us he was living. It was a standard three bedroom, semi-detached.

I rang the doorbell but nobody answered. There was no car in the driveway so I decided to call to the neighbours. I tried the house on the left and also got no answer. From past experience I knew that it was always best to do cold calling in the early evening, as most people are away at work during the day.

I was preparing to leave when the lady from the next door house on the right opened her front door. She was in her early forties and wearing her pyjamas.

"This had better be good," she moaned, "as I am working nights."

"I'm sorry; I hope I did not wake you up."

"No I had to get up anyway. What do you want? You best not be selling anything!"

"No I am an insurance investigator and I am trying to get some information on the people who lived next door."

"Insurance! I don't want to buy any insurance."

"No I am not selling anything but I would appreciate your help. Any information you could give me on your neighbours would be great."

The lady took a cigarette from its packet, lit it and inhaled deeply. I could see the sense of satisfaction she derived from her cigarette addiction etched on her stony face.

"The people next door were a Polish couple I think but they moved out and have gone back to Poland."

"Do you recall their names?"

"Yes strange name, Borottski I think. They left in December; kept to themselves mainly but a bit noisy at times."

I thanked her and returned to my car. I was disappointed that she did not have more information, but then in these modern times how many of us know our neighbours?

I decided to drive to the scene of the alleged accident as it was only 20 minutes away. I always say alleged accident as my experiences in the insurance business have demonstrated the level that people were willing to go to, to extract money from insurance companies. In the old Wild West days the gang would rob the local bank or post office, but that has gotten too dangerous as the police are willing to use deadly force to stop armed robberies. Instead the criminals now rob insurance companies using false and exaggerated claims.

I arrived at The Curragh just after 4pm. The light was starting to fade but there was just enough left to take some photographs.

As I stood in the middle of the park I realised that we had absolutely no evidence or clues of any description to reject Harrison's claim. In the years before insurance companies had special investigation units his claim would have just been settled, even though there was no evidence or independent witnesses and the police had not been called to the scene of the accident. At least I could now try to find out if the claim was genuine or false but I was fully aware that we could still ended up paying this American almost €1 million.

By the time I finished the photographs it had started to rain. The only sign of life in the area was the sheep and they were not going to give me a statement of evidence. I decided I'd better make a move back home as the M50 traffic always got bad in the early evening.

As I was driving back towards Naas, I decided to check the house in Craddockstown again. It was hitting 6.30pm and I was starting to get tired and hungry. Hunger pains can be rather painful especially on a cold winter's night in Ireland but I ignored them and drove back to Boroski's last known address. This time a light was on in the front downstairs room and a blue, Dublin-registered Ford Mondeo was parked in the driveway.

I decided to take a direct approach and chance ringing the doorbell again in case Boroski was still living there. The claimant did not have a lawyer involved as yet so I didn't have to walk on egg shells. If Boroski was still in Ireland I needed to interview him, as just maybe he could provide some crucial evidence.

"Sorry for disturbing you,' I said as an elderly man answered. "I am an investigator with Dallast Insurance Company and I am trying to establish some information."

The man, who was Irish, asked: "How can I help you?"

"Do you own this house?"

"No we are renting and moved in a few weeks ago."

"Do you know anything about the former tenants? I believe their name was Boroski?" "Not really. I think they were Polish and have gone back to Poland."

"Did you ever get any post for them?"

"Yes we have received some post for someone with a Polish surname; I passed it on to the letting agent."

"Was the surname Boroski?"

"I am sorry I don't recall."

I thanked the man for his time and decided to try the house on the left again. I rang the doorbell and immediately heard a dog barking. I could tell by the sound of the bark that it was a large dog.

All the investigators or loss adjusters I knew who called to people's homes were well aware of the risk of an angry dog attacking them. I have learned that when visiting houses in rural parts of Ireland, it was always a good idea to leave your car door open. There have been a few occasions when I have simply had to run for it!

The front door opened and a lady in her early forties stood in the hallway. Thankfully there was no sign of the dog. She must have locked it in another room.

Once again I started with an apology: "I'm sorry for annoying you. I am with an insurance company and trying to obtain some information on your former neighbours."

"Insurance company! Don't talk to me about insurance, the price of car insurance is so expensive and I have never had a claim," she said aggressively.

I once again apologised, even though it wasn't exactly my fault that insurance was expensive!

"Well it's not your fault," she said, calming down, "who are you interested in?"

'There was a Polish family living next door to you…"

"Oh that bunch! They always played loud music at all hours of the night, no respect."

"Do you know how many people were living in the house?"

"How the hell do I know; let me see maybe five or six girls and two guys."

"Thank you for your time, sorry to hear you had trouble with them, maybe your new neighbours will be nicer," I said and started to walk back towards my car.

"Please God, anything would be quieter than the Polish and that bloody Yank," she shouted after me.

I immediately stopped in my tracks and turned back.

"What Yank?"

"I think one of the men was an American."

"How do you know he was American?"

"Well I never met him but I remember one of them had a John Wayne accent; he did not sound Polish anyway, that's for sure. Yes John Wayne."

I thanked her again and got back into my car.

Driving back home I was playing different scenarios over in my head. Did Nigel Boroski know the American he had knocked down? Was this a staged accident?

A staged accident was a term used in the insurance business for an accident that basically never happened. Usually it was a road traffic accident, in which there were multiple occupants in two vehicles. The first vehicle stopped and the second vehicle crashed into the back of it. The occupants of both vehicles then pretended to develop soft tissue injuries and claimed compensation from the second driver's insurance company. This compensation can be a lot when you consider the number of people involved, medical expenses, engineer fees and of course legal fees. A staged accident involving one claimant was less common but not unknown.

Had this accident been planned by Boroski and Harrison? Sometimes the supposed injury and damage to a person/vehicle was done prior to any alleged incident or sometimes there was no actual injury. However this case sounded different as Harrison had attended Liverpool Hospital and he definitely had serious injuries.

My mind was still working overtime the following day which can be good but I reminded myself that one of the best attributes an investigator could have was to keep an open mind. I arrived into our Dublin office and met with Tanya.

"John Harrison has contacted me again via email and is looking for more money. Courtney wants to meet you to discuss the case and plan tactics or possibly to settle the claim."

I was in the process of asking Tanya what she had said in the email, when Courtney tapped me on the shoulder.

"Hi Andrew come down to my office we need to discuss the Harrison file. Are you ready Tanya?"

"I'll be there in one minute," she agreed.

I sat down in Courtney's office and we were quickly joined by Tanya

"Well Andrew, you got anything?" he asked, drinking his coffee.

"No, nothing – I have searched all our databases and can find nothing."

"OK, I appreciate I only gave this file to you 48-hours ago but as you have found nothing I think we should move to settle the claim."

I was horrified that he wanted to settle a possible €1 million claim so fast. However I was aware that Courtney had a well-honed commercial sense and he was obviously anxious to settle the claim before it escalated out of control.

"Tanya you said Harrison has been in touch," I said. "What did he say?"

"It was another email. He's looking for another €5,000 and he said he does not want to have the surgery in the UK; he wants to go back to America."

"What do you mean another €5,000?" I asked, surprised.

"We gave him €5,000 to cover his out of pocket expenses while he is stuck in the UK. We gave it to his uncle," Tanya explained.

I thought that €5,000 was a very generous amount but Courtney was the boss. However one thing was troubling me.

"Why his uncle?" I asked.

Courtney was getting impatient with my questions and stood up.

"Andrew we made the cheque payable to his uncle as poor John Harrison does not have a bank account in the UK as he is a tourist. How could he cash the cheque?"

I didn't say anything as Courtney scratched his balding head; he looked frustrated with the whole situation.

"I have discussed the file with our Directors and we have clearance to organise an air ambulance for him to New York to have the surgery. They are not one bit pleased about this claim as it is going to cost us big time – maybe another €200,000 on top of the initial €700,000.

"Whoa, slow down your guys, what has happened to make you want to settle so quickly?" I asked

"From his last email I think he may accept an all in payment of €200,000, which would be a good … no a great result, we would save €700,000 or €800,000," Courtney explained.

"We got another medical report from Liverpool Hospital, which shows he needs surgery and will require 10 days in hospital,"Tanya said. "We'd be lucky if he accepted an offer of €200,000 to settle the claim."

A fast settlement sometimes permitted insurance companies to get a favourable result but I wasn't convinced we should pay the American any money at all.

"Can we slow down here and consider our options?" I asked.

"Options," Courtney growled. "What options? We have got an American tourist who was knocked down by our insured Nigel Boroski and who has got a serious back injury, which is backed up by medical reports. Our options are Andrew we try and settle the claim for €200,000 or we organise an air ambulance to NewYork, pay for surgery in America and compensation for loss of earnings, which comes in at somewhere around €1 million – either way this is going to cost us big time, but I like the sound of €200,000 a lot more than €1 million."

Even with my limited knowledge of surgery in America I realised that Courtney was right. The claim was going to cost us serious cash — unless of course it was fraudulent.

As Courtney continued to talk, I thought about what the lady in Naas had told me about an American being in Boroski's house. I knew this was only hearsay and may not have been the truth or indeed may just have been a Polish man with an American accent. I was uncertain about giving this information to Courtney at this early stage but I'd a strong feeling this claim wasn't right. My instincts were telling me to keep investigating.

"Harrison has not yet appointed a lawyer — don't you think that seems strange?" I queried. "And why did he travel to the UK with a back injury? Why not obtain treatment from an Irish hospital? I think this accident just doesn't add up."

"He travelled to the UK to see his relations, now he just wants to get back to his job in Louisiana and he wants his health back," Tanya explained.

"Look as all we have is an email address and a mobile phone number let me give him a call. After all he is more or less alone in Liverpool and maybe we should organise one of our UK people to meet him and make him more comfortable."

There was complete silence for a few moments.

"Andrew I don't want you to upset this guy as we have to presume he is genuine and we may still get out of this claim for €200,000," Courtney ordered. "Just don't piss him off."

"OK I will do my best."

I stood up and was leaving Courtney's office with Tanya, when he said: "Stone I am warning you, go gentle on this guy. It's on your head if you mess up and we end up paying more then we have to."

I returned to my desk and sat down. I felt pressurised and a bit fearful as I did not want to mess up. I wanted a good result for Courtney — and for myself.

"Tanya can you please give me all the recent emails and medical reports?"

"Sure Andy. Courtney has authorised me to pay another €5,000 to Harrison. I'm posting the cheque today."

She handed me the medical report and was walking away, when I shouted after her.

"Tanya what is his uncle's name?"

"We are making the cheque payable to Sean Moran."

Tanya dropped over the new material and I started reading. Normally I would get an entire information pack at the start of a case but this file was strangely different. The amount of money at risk meant that Courtney and the top brass were originally dealing with the claim before they had decided to pass it over to SIU.

I opened the medical report and was astonished by the list of injuries. They showed that this Harrison guy must be in agony. He was being prescribed serious painkillers and must be very uncomfortable. The emails from him explained that he was staying with his uncle, Sean Moran, at Swan's View Farm in Liverpool, UK. He also said his wife was expecting a baby back in Louisiana, USA, and he was missing out on the pregnancy. He just wanted his claim sorted as soon as possible so he could get home.

I decided to risk it and ring him — if he was genuine then he would appreciate a 'friendly' call offering assistance.

I dialled the long mobile number listed on his file and I was surprised when it rang with a foreign tone, like the one you hear if you are ringing Continental Europe and not somewhere in Ireland or the UK. After about three or four long ring tones the phone was answered.

"Hello."

"Is that John Harrison?"

There was a pause and then the voice at the other end of the phone said: "Yes."

"Hi my name is Andrew Stone. I am with the claims department of Dallast Insurance. I am trying to get some clarification on your injuries and to find out if we can make you more comfortable."

"Oh that sure is great as I am running low on money and need to get some more medication," Harrison said.

From my time living in America I could tell that his accent was from the South, possibly Texas.

"Are you still living with your uncle Sean Moran, at Swan's View Farm?"

"No, I moved out. My uncle was not happy with me staying there as I was a burden on them. I am now living in the city. I am renting a flat and it is costing me Stg£800 per month."

"I've got to ask you, why were you in Ireland?"

"Well I am Irish. I was born in Kildare and then the family travelled back to the United States. I was in Ireland visiting some friends when I got run over."

I started asking another question, but Harrison continued: "At the time I was run over I was in shock and I did not feel any pain. I then travelled via the boat to the UK to visit my uncle in Liverpool before flying back to Louisiana."

Again I tried to ask a question but Harrison was in full flow: "However I developed severe back pain on the boat and just about made it to Liverpool. I went to the local hospital emergency room and they kept me there for two days."

"How are you feeling now?"

"I am just scared and in real pain. I want to get home to my pregnant wife but I can't fly. What the hell am I gonna do?"

Harrison sounded in a bad way so I tried to change the topic.

"How long have you been married?"

"Not long and this is my first child so I want to get home."

"I completely understand. Mr. Harrison do you have a job there?"

"Yes Sir, I work for a tow-truck company in Louisiana. My boss is keeping my job open for me but I am not sure for how much longer. I really got to get home."

"It's a great country. I used to work and live in America," I said trying to relax the situation a bit.

"Really, whereabouts?" Harrison asked.

"Well I lived in Los Angeles; I just loved Long Beach and the boardwalk in Santa Monica. Have you ever been in California?"

"Yes Sir I sure have. Great bars and women in LA."

"Tell me Mr. Harrison…"

"Oh call me John," Harrison interrupted.

"OK John, can you tell me what you were doing in The Curragh at 07.30am?"

"I was out for a run as I was staying with some friends in Naas. I was jogging when I got run over by that car."

"John, can you describe to me what happened, with as much detail as possible?"

"Like I said I was running on the sidewalk, well there is no sidewalk just the grass beside the road, when I felt a sudden push or knock from behind and I fell over. I guess I must have blacked out."

"Did the driver stop?"

"Yes he did. I don't know the guy; he was a big, tall man and did not have much English. I think he may have been Polish. He wrote down his insurance details and gave me the registration of his car."

"Did you call the police or an ambulance?'

"No when I got run over I fell to the ground, next thing I remember the Polish driver of the car was helping me stand up. I had no pain but I was shocked."

"Do you know the driver of the car who knocked you down?"

Harrison categorically answered: "No, I told you I have never seen him before."

He appeared to get a little agitated after this question and ranted: "You know I am sitting here in the UK and I am stuck renting a room. I got no money, the US embassy will not assist me and I have got bad pain in my back. I really miss my wife and I have missed so much of her pregnancy because of this accident, but most of all I just want to get home."

I stayed silent for a moment to try to calm the conversation down.

"Your medical report states that you cannot fly as you have got to have surgery on your back," I said sympathetically.

"Yes I know. I can tell you man, there is no way I am having an operation with the NHS in the UK. I will have my op back in the USA, with real doctors. I don't want any Irish or UK doctor playing with my back."

"Is the pain bearable in your back?"

"The pain in my back is real bad, but the Doc has given me some drugs which help. My leg is also very painful and now I have erectile dysfunction and sometimes I wet myself."

Listening to Harrison's complaints and his description of the problems he was experiencing I knew that Courtney was right in placing a high reserve on this case. We would be very lucky if we got out of this claim for €200,000 – unless I could prove it was fraud.

To try to catch him off balance I asked: "John what way did you fly from Louisiana?"

"I flew British Airways from Baton Rouge to London Heathrow, then the boat to Ireland via Holyhead. Why are you asking me such a dumb question? I am here with pain in my back and you want to talk about airplanes."

"Yes you're right John it is a dumb question. Tell me would you be willing to meet one of our Dallast UK people to see if we could make you more comfortable?"

"Look I don't have a problem meeting people but I just want this sorted. I got €5,000 from you guys but that is almost gone with my medical bills. I am going to need another €5,000 ASAP to keep me going."

I found this all a little strange. If I was stuck in America I would take help from anybody or my family would get me sorted. Why did he leave his uncle's farm and rent a room? It sounded really suspicious.

"Thank You John for your time today. I am going to arrange for a representative from Dallast Insurance UK to contact you shortly.'

"Well OK I guess that would be fine with me."

"Goodbye John," I said and hung up.

I immediately started checking out his story, comparing the little information I had with the medical reports obtained from Liverpool Hospital. I had to leave before I could do more but I drove home listening to a CD recording of the phone call, asking myself: "What the hell was he doing in Ireland? Why would he leave his pregnant wife and travel to Ireland for a holiday?"

It did not make sense.

Back at my home office I played the call over and over, looking for a clue. As with all investigations, attention to detail was normally the thing that gave you a lead or a clue to work with. Harrison had told me that he flew direct from Baton Rouge to London Heathrow. I checked all airlines and it quickly became apparent that there were no direct flights on that route. It was only a small thing but I had found him out in a lie. Although only a small lie, it was still a lie and it further aroused my suspicions that the case was fraudulent. On that positive note I decided to call it a night.

As I walked into our Dublin office the following day, Tanya greeted me with a pleasant smile.

"Dan Courtney is looking for you; we got an email of complaint from Harrison."

"A complaint! Please email it to me Tanya."

"I already have."

I sat at my desk and started to read the email from Harrison. I'd just finished when Courtney appeared at my desk.

He stared at me, anger written all over his face.

"Stone, my office; I need a word — now."

I knew Courtney was pissed as I got up and followed him to his office. I felt like a puppy being taken for a walk by its owner.

Courtney sat down in his executive chair and glared at me.

"Well done Stone you screwed up. We could have got out of the claim for about €200K but because of you it's probably going to cost us at least €700K. Well what have you got to say for yourself?"

I knew Courtney was annoyed but I also knew that I was onto something. I could feel it. One of the best tools an investigator or detective has is his gut instinct

I looked Courtney in the eye and stated: "Dan this claim is a fraud."

Courtney sat back, looking a bit more relaxed and at the same time curious: "Well what have you got?"

I paused for a moment. I had nothing but I could not say this to Courtney. Instead I responded: "I want to get some assistance from Dallast Insurance UK and I would need to talk to some former contacts in Pinkerton North America as well."

There was an uncomfortable silence for a few moments.

"OK Stone let's do it your way. You have two weeks to investigate but keep me informed on your progress and keep the investigation costs down; you have clearance for €20,000 to investigate this claim."

This was a large amount of money to be given for a single investigation. We would normally have an allowance of about €5,000 and that would include medical fees and advice from the legal team. I was going to ask Courtney why the allowance was so big, but then when you were ahead why look back.

"Thanks. I am going to get in contact with Nigel in the UK and ask him to make contact with Harrison. I will also contact Jeff in North America and get him to run a few checks."

"Right go do what you do best — just get me a result," Courtney said.

I logged onto my computer, still thinking about the €20,000. I was lucky to have it now that the investigation was going international. I was aware that we had a new Claims Director, Thomas Hughes, who was interested in supporting the company's efforts in combating fraud. Perhaps he had sanctioned the €20,000? Or perhaps Courtney was now suspicious about the claim too? Anyhow, whatever the reason, I did not want to let him down.

I decided to take another look at the complaint email from Harrison, in case it contained a possible lead. It was more like a ransom note than an email complaining about our lack of assistance and my questions. In the last paragraph Harrison stated: 'I want no more contact from you guys. I will get my operation in the USA. Give me Stg£100,000 by Friday or else."

I suddenly realised that this was the reason Courtney had sanctioned the €20,000 for the investigation. Yes Courtney was pissed, but not at me — he was furious with John Harrison.

CHAPTER 4

ઝૌ

I telephoned Nigel, a specialist intelligence collator, who concentrates on putting evidence together. Nigel was a good talker, one of the tidiest people I've ever met, always on time and had a good eye for attention to detail. He was based in the London office of Dallast Insurance UK and worked within the British Special Investigations Unit. Nigel was also a specialist financial fraud investigator and was well known and respected in the UK insurance world. He was a member of various UK anti-fraud groups, including the British anti-terrorist training committee. He had also lectured on insurance and financial fraud within various organisations.

I phoned Nigel's mobile. As per normal within two rings he answered.

"Alright mate, how are things in Ireland? Top of the morning to you!"

"Less of the top of the mornings Nigel! All is fine but I need your assistance on a nice large case."

"You know me, always busy but willing to provide assistance or advice!"

"Glad to hear it! We have picked up this claim by an American named John Harrison. He was run over by a Polish man Nigel Boroski, who was our insured. Harrison then travelled to the UK and presented himself at Liverpool Hospital A&E,"

"John Harrison, OK," Nigel said. "What address have you got on him?"

"We don't have an Irish address. He was staying at Swan's View Farm and then moved into a flat in Liverpool, Anfield Road."

"And what about your insured guy?"

"We've been told he has gone back to Poland. Harrison has a wife expecting a baby in Louisiana so he needs to get home. Can you go and meet him?"

"Yes Liverpool is about a four hour drive for me, but it sounds like we need to get him some money and to look after him."

"We have already sent him two cheques, for €5,000 each, to cover his out of pocket expenses and medical costs."

"Two cheques! How did he cash them? If he's a tourist then he won't have a bank account in the UK."

"We made the cheques payable to his uncle, Sean Moran. Apparently he owns the farm."

I could hear Nigel's pen writing in the background as he took what I was sure were meticulous notes.

"Why has he moved from his uncle's farm to a flat?" he asked, sounding surprised.

"I am not sure. He said they had a disagreement. I will email you his contact and medical details. To be honest Nigel, I don't like this claim. It smells and I have a gut feeling it's not all that it seems."

"Well you do have a good nose for fraud Stony boy!" Nigel said. "But we don't have much to go on mate. Leave it with me and I'll drive to Liverpool, but just for you Stony.'

"Thanks Nigel, I'll buy you a pint of Guinness when you're next in Dublin."

"I'll hold you to that Andy, cheers!"

I typed a brief email, detailing Harrison's injury details, email address and telephone number, and sent it to Nigel. Just as I was about to leave the office my desk phone rang.

"Hi Andy, it's Nigel. I was thinking get an agent or better still get yourself down to Nigel Boroski's address and see what you can find out."

"I've already done that. According to the neighbours an American was staying with the Polish guys."

"And so the plot thickens Andy, you're telling me that a Polish and an American man who possibly know each other have a car accident in Ireland, very unusual!"

"It is a little strange but possible."

"Possible but unlikely Andy. This sounds like a staged accident. I will get to Liverpool as soon as possible. Cheers."

Next I decided to email the American branch of our insurance company, which is based in Philadelphia. I was aware that our Special Investigation Unit there was very good. Instead of just sending an email I decided to phone Jeff, who was the head investigator at Dallast North America.

The phone rang twice before I realised it was only about 05.30am in Philadelphia. I had forgotten the time difference! I was about to hang up when, to my surprise Jeff answered.

"Hi Jeff, it's Andy in Dublin, Ireland. I am really sorry; I just realised how early it is in Philadelphia."

"Hi Andy, not a problem. I am just leaving for work. How can I help you?"

I gave Jeff a brief rundown of the case.

"All I have to go on is a name," I concluded.

"Just a name, mmm … it's going to be difficult but let me see if I can get anything for you."

"Thanks Jeff, I will talk to you later."

Jeff was a real gentleman. He's an ex-United States Marine and was still in the army, although semi-retired. We had met at a company briefing in Berlin, Germany, and had drunk several beers together one evening. He'd served in the first Gulf war and I was surprised at his knowledge of European History and his genuine friendship towards me. I had met plenty of former US military personnel in my time at Pinkerton, but they always had a dark side — probably because they were aware of the ever present threat to American citizens. I'd discovered that most American military personnel/investigators/cops run a background check on you before a meeting. Jeff was different; he was friendly and had a genuine warmth about him. I really needed to find out everything about John Harrison — and Jeff was the man to do it.

I was also a member of the International Association of Special Investigation Units (IASIU) so I sent off a quick email to some of my American contacts. I was confident that they would find some interesting information for me if at all possible.

That afternoon I left the office early and headed out to Naas yet again. I'd decided to call to the letting agent in the hope that I might get some information on Boroski.

It was a small estate agency based in Kildare called Freeman Estates. The letting agent was friendly and invited me into her office as I quickly got down to business.

"Hi, I am Andy Stone, an investigator with Dallast Group insurance. I am trying to trace a man who may have some valuable information regarding an insurance claim. Would you be able to assist me?"

"An investigator! How can I help you?" she asked, looking as if the word investigator had impressed her.

"I am particularly interested in a tenant who rented a property from you, Nigel Boroski."

"What is the address?"

I was starting to feel as if I was going to obtain some information as I handed over the details.

"You know I am not supposed to do this, but I am just about to destroy the tenants' file so I'm sure it won't matter," she smiled. "What would you like to know?"

"Who was living in the house?"

"The house was rented by a number of Polish people. Nigel Boroski was one of the tenants there. I remember him: he was a tall, good-looking, fit man, friendly and charming."

"Was an American living there?"

"I have no record of any American living at the property. However it is possible that they sublet a room."

"Thank you for you kind assistance," I smiled as I left and started the long drive home across the M50.

I felt a little disappointed as I had hoped that maybe there would be a link to Harrison.

That evening I got home late and the kids had gone to bed. I decided to log onto my laptop and do some digging on the internet. I spent hours running through various Google websites, Facebook, Twitter and got nothing. The only John Harrison I could find was a musician in America. It was frustrating.

I tried to figure out a way of finding out more and started looking through my old business cards. I found one from a former Pinkerton colleague, Kelly O'Dwyer. I knew she was now a Special Agent with the Federal Bureau of Investigation, based out of Washington DC. I decided to give her a call to say hello and to see if she could provide me with any assistance. Unfortunately all I got was her answer phone. As I left a message, I was a bit worried she'd find it strange as I hadn't spoken to her in over ten years. I hoped she didn't mind that I was appearing out of the blue and as usual looking for some information, but hey what are friends for!

The following day I had to drive to Athlone on a routine investigation. Athlone was a town located in the heart of Ireland and it was a good two hour drive away. Another car had been stolen 'without the keys' and I needed to take a statement.

As I was driving along the motorway, my mobile rang. It was Nigel and he was excited to say the least!

"Andy, Andy, Andy – you have got a live one here! I drove to Liverpool and located the farm. I met with a very helpful lady, Sandra Hynes, who is the owner."

"But according to Harrison his uncle Sean Moran is the owner of Swan's View Farm."

"Well he's not! I had a long chat with Sandra – she rented a room to a man named Sean Moran who is an American citizen. She also knew him as Kenneth Smith. He left her farm about a month ago, with his pregnant wife who is Polish and is named Jenny."

I was shocked.

"But his pregnant wife is in Louisiana, in the States and who exactly is Kenneth Smith?"

"I bet you Sean Moran, Kenneth Smith and John Harrison are all the same person!"

"Maybe you're right – tell me more Nigel," I ordered.

Nigel was really excited and had decided to take a drive over to the second address in Anfield Street.

"It will take about 90 minutes. You know this guy borrowed Stg£300 from Sandra and then simply disappeared. According to her he was a really nice, friendly man who was attending medical specialists in London for a back injury. He borrowed the Stg£300 to attend the examination and then he was gone."

"Why would Harrison say that Sean Moran owned the farm?" I asked.

"It has to be because he needed the cheques paid in that name so he could cash them," Nigel replied.

"I will run a trace on the cheques to see what bank accounts they were lodged into."

"Good man Andy. It looks like you may be adding money laundering to the list."

Nigel's line crackled as I was in a poor reception area. He quickly said: "going to check the second address; will call you back later," and hung up.

I really hoped he'd get more information on the case.

I drove on to Athlone and met with the claimant. He provided me with a reasonably satisfactory story regarding the theft of his car. Being honest, all I could think about was the Harrison case.

I drove back to Dublin and got caught in traffic. I tuned my radio onto Newstalk 106 and listened to my radio friend George Hook. He was taking his usual stand against another corrupt Irish politician who had decided he must travel first class at the tax payer's expense. To this day I cannot understand how the Irish Prime Minister earns a salary greater than the President of the United States. George and I share the same view: Ireland is worth fighting for it's time for the dishonest politicians to face the public.

My mobile rang again. This time it was Jeff from America.

"Hey Andy, how are you doing?'

"Good Jeff, just sitting in the daily traffic. Have you had any luck at your end?"

"I have run some checks on your boy Harrison and we ain't come up with much. He does not appear to have any claims here in the United States. However he does appear in Texas and then seems to have moved to Arizona. Not too much on him, other than he had a problem with the Sheriff's department in a town in Texas. But this information may not be on your boy Andy, as John Harrison is a common name here in the USA."

I was all set to question him when the phone went dead. I tried to call him back but could not make contact. Although modern appliances like mobiles are great, I guess that sometimes they also have their problems.

I continued the drive home as Fleetwood Mac's *Tell me Lies* played on the radio. I knew Nigel was onto something in the UK and that the telephone interview I'd had with Harrison was like the song – pure lies!

I was looking forward to updating my wife with the new information. I was incredibly excited about this case as it was more than your usual stolen car, burglary or jewellery case. As any true investigator will tell you, you just know when you know, that a case feels wrong and that you are onto something good. Well I was sure now that this was one of those cases. .

My irritation with the traffic was vanishing as I thought of ways to obtain more intelligence. What would tomorrow bring? Hopefully more information from our American and UK operations so I could collate the data and provide Courtney with an interesting update!

The following morning Nigel telephoned me and said he had contacted the owner of the flat on Anfield Road, Liverpool.

"Andy you have got a serious fraud here and I think it involves identity theft."

I could feel my excitement building: "Go on Nigel — this sounds interesting."

"Well the owner of the flat is Nick Berry. According to him John Harrison rented it about a month ago and then left leaving rent outstanding. Nick gave me the key to the flat and I had a look around. I found some opened post in the bin, which included a letter from CCD Insurance UK requesting a Gary O'Neill to attend a medical examination in London, following a road traffic accident. I have the CCD claim number so I will make contact with their Special Investigation Unit and see what I can find out."

"Nigel I just know this guy isn't straight. And he's looking for €200,000 by the end of the week."

"According to Berry, John Harrison is an American and looks a little like the Irish actor Colin Farrell. I think it is possible that John Harrison, Kenneth Smith and Gary O'Neill are all the same person. Unfortunately this is only my theory Andy. It's now over to you to prove it."

"Nigel thanks very much for this. Let's both run some checks with our internal database and intelligence units and see what we can dig up. – I will call you tomorrow."

I logged onto my computer and ran the three names through Insurance Link to see if there was any information on claims made with those identities. However without an age or an address it was pointless. Looking at an Irish database for a man named Moran or O'Neill was like looking for a needle in a haystack.

I was wondering what Nigel would discover. He was an outstanding investigator and also an expert with I2. I2 was intelligence collating software used for displaying links between various individuals and organisations. In the UK they are a few steps ahead and have various systems, including Claims and Underwriting Exchange (CUE) and the Credit Industry Fraud Avoidance System (CIFAS), the UK's fraud prevention service, which operates the country's national fraud database. The Insurance Fraud Bureau UK, established by the British Insurance industry, was also an option. It was dedicated to combating insurance fraud and providing training and analytical intelligence. Unfortunately there was no Irish equivalent. I did check the Irish Insurance Federations Anti-Fraud Group and also Insurance Confidential (www .insuranceconfidential.ie), an internet hotline for reporting false insurance claims but nothing came up.

The following morning I arrived at the office early, about 07.30am. Courtney was sitting at his desk, reading a newspaper. He glanced up as I approached.

"Well Stony, you got something?"

Stony was another one of Courtney's names for me. He used it when he was frustrated.

"Yes, we have a live one here."

Courtney put the paper down.

"I think we are dealing with a serious case of insurance fraud and identity theft. We've discovered that John Harrison is also Gary O'Neill, Sean Moran and Kenneth Smith."

"I thought Sean Moran was his uncle who lives in that farm where Tanya sent the two cheques?"

"Nigel has interviewed the real owner of the farm and she has provided a statement that an American man, driving an Irish-registered car, rented a room from her in the name of Sean Moran. However she also knew him as Kenneth Smith."

Courtney leaned forward in his chair: "So you're telling me that John Harrison and Sean Moran are the same person."

"Exactly. We also think that Harrison is using the name Kenneth Smith and possibly Gary O'Neill. And he was staying at the farm with his wife – a Polish lady named Jenny."

"So you're telling me that Harrison, Moran and Smith and some other guy called O'Neill are all the same person and also that Harrison's wife is Polish and she is pregnant and staying with him in the UK."

I was impressed Courtney had said all of this without taking a breath.

"Yes, that is basically it."

Courtney starred directly at me. I felt as if I was giving evidence and was about to be cross-examined by a barrister in the High Court. "OK let's say your theory is correct ... then prove it."

"I will need more time."

"It sounds like a wild story Andy but I will trust you on this one. You appear to be doing a fair bit of digging on this file. Maybe it will pay off. So go get me some evidence and let's save a €1 million."

"Yes Dan, I will."

I left Courtney's office feeling a little intimidated. I had a challenge on my hands now. I needed solid evidence and I needed it fast. Hopefully Nigel would come up with something.

CHAPTER 5

✌️

One of the keys to being a good detective or investigator is to have good contacts in a variety of areas. In fact the more unusual the areas, the easier your job will be to investigate and obtain intelligence. One of the advantages of being a member of the International Association of Special Investigation Units (IASIU) was that I had gained access to a database of members across the globe. Some of these investigators I got to know personally from meetings at the annual European and American seminars. There was a type of creed or brotherhood between most of the members of IASIU. If you needed some advice or assistance, even if you were with a competitor when it came to fraud it didn't matter and everyone would help. It's only by standing together that we have a chance of defeating fraud.

I had also made some good contacts in my days working in Pinkerton. My FBI contact and friend Kelly had worked with me in the office in Los Angeles for two years when I'd lived in Long Beach, which is south of Los Angeles city. I envied Kelly for being accepted into the FBI. No matter how good a private detective I was with Pinkerton, I would never have been accepted as a basic FBI entry requirement is that you are an American citizen.

Using contacts like Jeff and Kelly, I was pretty certain I was going to be able to locate intelligence on Harrison but as it was possible that his real name was not John Harrison, I decided to name the file "Operation Cowboy" until his true identity was confirmed. In the world of financial fraud, identity theft was a major problem for insurers and other financial institutions. In Ireland and the rest of Europe, we have Data Protection legislation which is enforced by the Data Protection Commissioner's office. Data protection is important for the protection and safety of citizens and helps to prevent identity theft. Unfortunately it also protects criminals who use it as a cloak to hide their identities and to prevent information from banks, insurance companies and other financial institutions being released. An example of this would be a man who is banned from driving because he was under the influence of alcohol. This individual is a danger to the general public and other motorists but he can obtain car insurance by simply ticking the box on the insurance proposal form saying he has no previous convictions. If he is then involved in an accident, the investigating police officer cannot advise the insurance company of the driver's previous conviction for driving under the influence of alcohol, as this would be considered a breach of the Data Protection Act.

A second example would be if a woman takes out property insurance on her private house and ticks the box on the insurance policy claiming no previous criminal convictions. In reality there may have been several. I recall one situation where the insured had been sentenced for supplying drugs. She only told me about the previous convictions when I interviewed her as I was investigating her claim. The police were aware of the previous convictions but again the Data Protection laws meant that they could not provide the information to our insurance company. I agree that there is a need for Data Protection laws but there is also a need for financial investigators and police to share information on criminals and Operation Cowboy looked like it was going to be a case in point.

I ran another few checks on my computer system, the internet and our internal databases, however I could find nothing. I was getting frustrated as there was simply no information on John Harrison, Sean Moran, Kenneth Smith or Gary O'Neill.

The phone rang and it was Jeff from our North American office. He told me that he had sent one of his investigation teams out to the small town in Texas where Harrison's name had cropped up.

"The team met with the Sheriff's department Andy and Harrison was wanted for a minor offence but he skipped bail. I had hoped that the Sheriff's department would have a 'Wanted' photo, but unfortunately he was not photographed."

"I am not sure if John Harrison is his correct name as Nigel in the UK also thinks he is using the names Kenneth Smith, Sean Moran and Gary O'Neill."

"That sounds potentially complex Andy as identity issues are difficult to investigate. You got a date of birth on any of them?"

"Not yet, but we are waiting for an updated medical report, so we should get his date of birth. I will get back to you then."

"OK Andy I will run those other names through our systems, however without a date of birth, I don't think we will do so good."

"Thanks Jeff."

I started to feel a little low, especially considering that Courtney was on my case and was looking for a result. I wanted to give Nigel a call, but decided against it as I did not want him to think I was checking up on him.

I decided to talk to Tanya again.

"Tanya, would you do me a favour? Would you please check with the Liverpool Hospital and the medical expert who examined our Cowboy? I want to get a full description of what he looks like and also to get a date of birth from the medical reports."

"Sure Andy, I will do it right away."

Less than ten minutes later, Tanya walked over to my desk.

"According to the girls in the hospital, he is a good-looking Yankee, about 5ft 10ins, slim, athletic build, with very short dark hair; looks a little like the actor Colin Farrell!"

"Are you sure they said Colin Farrell?"

"Yes that is what the receptionist said — Colin Farrell."

I stood up, feeling energised.

"Colin Farrell is how Sandra Hynes, the owner of Swan's View Farm, described him."

I was now satisfied that John Harrison, Sean Moran, Kenneth Smith and Gary O'Neill were all the same person, but I still lacked physical evidence.

My desk phone rang just as I sat back down.

"Andy!" Nigel shouted down the phone, sounding excited.

"Hey Nigel, just to let you know, according to our medical people our Cowboy looks like Colin Farrell, which matches the description you got from Sandra Hynes."

"Yes he certainly does look like Colin Farrell."

"How do you know that?"

"Simple, I have a photograph of him."

"How? What? Where did you get it?" I asked.

"Our intelligence team found it on the internet. The District Attorney's office in Oklahoma is looking for him. There is also a 'Wanted' photograph. Andy got to go. I will talk to you later but check out this website."

I typed in the web address as he called it out and hit the enter key on my computer. I hung up the phone without even saying goodbye I was so eager to see Harrisons picture.

I quickly logged onto the website which read:

'Detective Mark Keating of the Oklahoma's District Attorney's office and Sheriff's Department requests the assistance of the public in tracking a John Harrison who has committed fraud and other crimes in the state of Oklahoma. John Harrison has a history of criminal activity and is also a known forgery expert. Any information as to the whereabouts of John Harrison should be passed to the Sheriff's Department of Oklahoma by ringing 123356789 or to any Sheriff's Department in the state of Oklahoma.'

I could not believe what I was looking at; there Harrison was in a perfect photo shot taken by the Oklahoma Police Department. I called Tanya over to my desk and showed it to her.

"Yes he does look like Colin Farrell!' she gasped. "Our Cowboy is a good looking guy."

I phoned Nigel back.

"Hello Andrew."

"Nigel!" I exclaimed. "That information was excellent. What's our next step your end?"

"I have sent a copy of the photograph to Sandra from Swan's View Farm and also to Nick Berry who rented Harrison the flat, just to confirm it is the same guy."

"It's great we now have a photo of Harrison. I'm going to call the detective from the Oklahoma District Attorney's office."

"You better hold off on making the call for a few hours Andy," Nigel laughed.

I had a quick look at my watch and realised it was only 11.00am so it would be 5am in America.

"You're right Nigel! Thanks again for your help. I'll update you when I made contact with the detective in Oklahoma."

"Great Andy while you are doing that I will check with the CCD insurance Special Investigations Unit and see what I can establish."

We hung up and I sat at my desk looking at my clock: 11.02am, 11.03am, 11.04am — each minute was passing as if it was an hour. I checked the internet and realised I would have to wait till 2.00pm Irish time before I could make the call to Oklahoma.

The time crawled by — I typed a short file note on the Athlone case and quickly emailed it to the Claims Handler, just to get it off my desk. All of my time, energy and thought processes were focussed on the Operation Cowboy case. I could feel that I was onto something good.

Denton was busy on the phone dealing with one of the many complaints we received. I sat and waited trying to think of other cases but my mind was too focused on Harrison.

At 1.30pm I couldn't wait any longer and telephoned the American number. The call was answered almost immediately.

"Good morning District Attorney's Office."

"Good morning, I am calling from Ireland and I would like to talk with a detective as I have some information regarding a person you guys are looking for!"

"One moment please," she responded.

A few minutes passed and then a man came on: "Hi I am Detective Keating. How can I help?"

"Hi my name is Andrew Stone and I am with the Special Investigations Unit at Dallast Group Insurance, Ireland. I have some information on a guy you are looking for, John Harrison."

"That is a name I have not heard of in a while, John Harrison. But hey … are you really calling from Ireland?"

"Yes, Ireland, Europe, the other side of the pond, and yes John Harrison is over here. Well he was in Ireland, then the UK and now he's possibly in Poland."

"That guy Harrison is a real pro. His speciality is what do you Europeans call it, oh yeah bouncing cheques. He's written a lot of bad paper over here in Oklahoma and also in Texas. We are looking for him as he is wanted for a specific fraud case here in Oklahoma."

I explained about the case and that Harrison was looking for a large payment from Dallast.

"No we only have a few small amounts of cash outstanding over here but I sure would love to catch up with that guy."

"Tell me Detective Keating do you have any further information on Harrison or would the FBI have an interest in his activities?"

"Well it is only small money on this side of the Atlantic; the FBI would require at least US$100,000 before they would take an interest in him. However I will talk to some of my colleagues and I have a good contact in the local FBI office, so let me see what I can find out. Give me a week and come back to me."

I thanked Detective Keating for his time and for the photograph which would be most useful in identifying Harrison.

I'd plenty of leads and I had a lot of information on Harrison but I was not sure how best to proceed. But I was now starting to believe that John Harrison was indeed the Cowboy's real name. I decided to phone Nigel and bring him up to speed.

Nigel as usual answered his phone immediately.

"Hi Andy, well what did the Yanks have to say about John Harrison?"

"I spoke to Detective Mark Keating himself and he told me that Harrison was wanted for bouncing cheques and other fraud related crimes in Oklahoma. Detective Keating is also going to try and establish if the FBI has an interest in Harrison and also what other US States have to say about the Cowboy's activities."

"Well at least we have a photo of him now. It will be interesting to see how things develop in the US. I am going to call back out to see Sandra at Swan's View Farm and also Nick Berry. They should have got the photographs by now and will hopefully verify that this is the same John Harrison as your claimant. I haven't heard anything back from CCD insurance yet so let's wait and see what they can dig up too."

"Nigel, Harrison has been emailing our claims handler Tanya Sanderson and is still looking for a fast cash settlement."

"Well he can't get any more cheques as we know he is no longer living in Liverpool."

"Maybe we can put some cash on his credit card for him!" I laughed. "Thanks for all the assistance Nigel, we will hold off making any further payments or dealings with Harrison until you came back with your updates."

I sat at my desk and decided to summarise the intelligence we had established to date:

1. The claimant's name is John Harrison and he is a citizen of the United States of America.

2. He was allegedly knocked down while walking in The Curragh area of County Kildare by a Polish national named Nigel Boroski.

3. According to Harrison his wife is expecting a baby in Louisiana, USA, yet according to Sandra Hynes, the owner of Swan's View Farm, his wife Jenny was with him at the farm in Liverpool, UK.

4. Swan's View Farm is not owned by Sean Moran, the man Harrison claimed was his uncle. According to Sandra, Sean Moran is another name used by Harrison.

5. We have paid €10,000 to Sean Moran, two cheques of €5,000 each, as Harrison said he did not have a bank account in the UK.

6. Harrison rented a flat in Anfield Road, Liverpool. Nigel found post at this address for a Gary O'Neill who was knocked down by a Kenneth Smith. A claim is pending against CCD Insurance UK.

7. Nigel discovered that John Harrison is wanted in Oklahoma on fraud charges. He also skipped bail in Texas.

8. There is possible information pending from my FBI contact Kelly and from Detective Keating in Oklahoma.

Harrison's case was unravelling before my eyes. Things were moving well but what was going to be the next stage of the investigation? I was sure we had only revealed the tip of the iceberg.

CHAPTER 6

❦

I'd booked a family holiday to Miami some time before the Harrison case started. I was so obsessed with the Cowboy I didn't want to go but I'd no choice. I kept an eye on my Gmail account while I was away and one morning a message arrived from Nigel, advising that there were no further developments in the case. I was impressed to read:

'I have also circulated the following warning on one of the UK insurance warning system databases Andy:

Warning Suspected Fraud:

John\ Harrison is a United States citizen but has travelled extensively in Ireland and the UK. It is known that he has also been travelling by car around Northern Europe. As a result of our investigation we believe that our insured Boroski and Harrison are connected and have staged a motor accident.

Harrison is known to have several aliases in the UK
and Ireland and is known to have filed two false personal injury insurance claims. There are outstanding
arrest warrants for Harrison in the United States.
Any information on his location or any claims presented in this name should be forwarded to Nigel at
Dallast Group UK.'

I was delighted that Nigel was taking the case seriously
and that the UK insurance companies would be in some way
warned and protected. Unfortunately in Ireland we were
not as advanced as the UK and did not have similar levels
of computer-based advanced warning systems. That being
said Ireland was a much smaller country and word of mouth
was a powerful weapon and we also had the Insurance Link
database.

After a most enjoyable holiday in Florida I drove back
into work the following Monday with the Irish weather being
its usual self — raining and cold. I was keen to get going again
so that I could stop Harrison's claim against my company and
also prevent him from ripping off other insurance companies,
banks and financial institutions in Ireland, across Europe and
possibly in America.

I entered the office and was greeted with the usual pile of
paperwork sitting on my desk, letters of complaint, solicitors
demanding payments and reports back from various experts.
There was also a small yellow sticky note from Caroline who
was a specialist claims handler from Poland. It simply said:
'Call me, Caroline.'

I was curious but decided to clear some of the backlog of
post and emails first. I got stuck into the usual claims letters
and the 432 emails which had accumulated while I was away.

"Great tan Andrew,"Tanya smiled, stopping at my desk.

"Thanks Tanya, any further developments with our Cowboy?"

"Nothing: no calls, no emails – no word at all."

"That's strange Tanya. You would think that somebody with such a serious injury, who is stuck in the UK, away from his pregnant wife and family, would be on the phone daily."

"I agree. Anyway I have to go, welcome back and maybe we can talk about it later."

I ploughed through my emails, finding nothing of interest. I was still stuck in Florida time and I was tired. The only reminders of my holiday were my tan and of course my credit card bill. I was so busy opening post and feeling jetlagged that I forgot to contact Caroline.

That afternoon my internal phone rang. It was Caroline.

"I am sorry for not ringing. I got your note, but I was just a little busy over here catching up with financial reports."

"No problem. Are you still interested in that American, John Harrison?"

I could feel a shiver of anticipation rage over my body.

"Yes," I said quickly.

"I think you should call over to my desk. I have something that will interest you."

I jumped out of my seat, knocking over my Starbucks coffee. It spilt all over my desk and the floor. I didn't care. I just ran, leaving the mess behind me.

Caroline's desk was on the far side of our claims' office. As I approached she was looking in my direction with a big smile.

"I have a photo of John for you."

"Is that all? I already have a photo that we got from the American cops."

"I am a member of a Polish website which is similar to Facebook and I have found something which I think will interest you."

She opened the webpage and showed me the photograph. My jaw dropped when I saw it! I was looking at John Harrison's wedding photograph. Standing beside him was his wife, in a beautiful white wedding gown. He was wearing a large Texan-styled cowboy hat and a dark suit with a cowboy neck tie. He looked as if he had just walked off a John Wayne Western movie.

The wording below stated 'our wedding in Hawaii'. I stared at the photograph again and asked: "How did you get this photo?"

"I found it on his wife's website, Jenny Boroski," Caroline smiled.

If this was his wife then more than likely Nigel Boroski was her brother. Now we were really starting to get somewhere with this file.

"Thanks Caroline — this will be a great help!"

"Wait, Andrew I have another photograph which may be of some assistance to your investigation."

She opened the second photograph which was of a jeep and two people in what looked like the Mourne Mountains. The caption stated: "Off-road Driving in Louth".

It was the man we knew as John Harrison and his wife Jenny Boroski. They were standing beside a jeep in a mountain area, surrounded by lush green grass. Only a jeep would have had the ability to navigate the terrain.

I was very happy to get the photographs and asked Caroline to email them to me.

I arrived back at my desk and quickly opened the two images. This was strong evidence and the break that we needed in the case. We now had the link or an indicator that

Harrison and our insured, Nigel Boroski, were brothers-in-law. I recalled my telephone interview with Harrison when he'd categorically stated that he did not know the driver of the car and that he was some tall, Polish man. This was clearly a lie. However in order to prove it I needed one vital piece of evidence — the marriage certificate.

I decided to try to contact my old friend Kelly O'Dwyer of the FBI again. I telephoned her but got no answer. I left a message and hoped she would return my call.

I then phoned Nigel.

"Hi Andy. You're back from sunny Florida then! Before you start I am still working on your Cowboy file and I am trying to get further information."

"Hold it Nigel, we've got more photographs. I'm emailing them to you now."

"Wow. Good photos Andy, nice job, how the hell did you get them?"

"Ah sure you know us Irish, friends in the right places! Nigel, they were married in Hawaii so I am going to try to obtain a copy of the marriage certificate from Honolulu. If I can get the certificate it will show that our insured, Nigel Boroski is Harrison's brother-in-law. That should be enough to prove this is a staged accident and we're dealing with major fraud."

"Good thinking Andrew, I could not have put it better myself. I am still trying to get information from CCD insurance. My contact is on holidays, so I will hopefully get the information on the claim for Gary O'Neill by the end of next week or as soon as I can get the information. Cheers!"

I had just put the desk phone down when my mobile rang.

"Hi is that Andrew Stone?" a lady with a strong American accent asked.

"Yes," I said, wondering was it my old friend.

"Andrew Stone! It's been a long time; this is Kelly O'Dwyer!"

"Kelly, how are you keeping?"

We made some small talk about the past and Kelly told me that she was now married to another FBI agent and that she was living in Dallas, Texas, with her two young girls. I then gave her a rundown on the case.

"Kelly I have obtained a photograph which looks like evidence that our claimant John Harrison was married to a Jenny Boroski, who is the sister of the man we insured, Nigel Boroski."

"Sounds like an insurance fraud to me, you been digging on the internet?"

"Yes we have. A colleague found the wedding photograph on the Web and ideally we would like to get a copy of the marriage certificate."

"I am currently on maternity leave Andy but I will run some checks with a few colleagues and see what intelligence I can get for you. Email me the photographs and I will have the metadata checked. Maybe it will throw up a useful date or something."

I took down her email and signed off. I sat back, feeling happy with the developments. The case was progressing at a nice pace and the new photographs and leads from the States and the UK were a big step forward. I always enjoyed dealing with United States' law enforcement. The agents in the FBI, police detectives or other agencies were really professional and were always willing to offer assistance, even when the successful conclusion for an investigator included criminal prosecutions in jurisdictions outside the United States.

I was looking forward to talking to Kelly again and was hoping she'd phone back the next day. But I decided not to update Courtney until I had some further information. I needed to be positive that the man in the photograph was the same man as the claimant John Harrison before I got my manager involved.

I decided to see if I could meet a friend who was a senior Garda detective in the National Bureau of Criminal Investigation (NBCI). We will call him Hugh as in order to protect his identity as I cannot reveal his name. Hugh was a real cop, the kind of officer who made a difference and all for the benefit of the public. Hugh was a highly-decorated officer and had served in many cities around Ireland, including some difficult parts of Dublin and Limerick.

I telephoned Hugh and he agreed to meet me 30 minutes later in a nearby hotel. As ever, we first chatted about current criminal activities, including an ongoing insurance fraud which we had both been investigating.

"Andy we got a result in that case involving the crashed UK BMWs."

"The one where all the cars were bought cheaply in the UK and then brought into Ireland via Northern Ireland and crashed?"

"That's the case Andy. These cars were all smuggled into Ireland, had their registration numbers changed to similar makes in Ireland, were insured with Irish insurance companies and then crashed."

"I know all about it Hugh. I heard of two Irish insurers that paid out the full amount on the BMWs as they did not know about the UK angle."

"Andy, there was one crashed BMW 320 convertible that was purchased in the UK for a €1,000. It was then smuggled into Ireland and had its plates changed to match a genuine BMW convertible here. The car was insured and then a few weeks later crashed. The Irish insurer was about to pay out €25,000 on that particular claim."

"Easy money, if you can get it!"

"Yes but there was a bigger picture Andy. The guy who was your insured was only small time. He was the front man for the organisation. We got an additional four arrests on that case, which involved the police in England and Northern Ireland. Andy I think the money from these false claims was being used to finance terrorism."

"So it that your way of saying thanks Hugh?"

"Don't get smart. I think you need me more then I need you!"

I was unsure if Hugh was serious, however he was right I did need him more.

As we sat in the pub drinking pints of Guinness, I could not help talking about the Cowboy file. One of my reasons for meeting up with Hugh was because my wife could not listen to me talking about Harrison any longer. I told him all about the case and explained about the false identities we'd heard about from Sandra at Swan's View Farm and how she knew Harrison as Sean Moran and Kenneth Smith and how Nigel had dug up Gary O'Neill as another possibility.

"So you're talking about identity theft Andy."

"Yes Hugh, I sure am."

"But how do you know his real name is John Harrison? Maybe that is also a fake identity."

"Well I have a FBI contact in the States doing some checks for me. I also know he was married in Honolulu, Hawaii, so I'm trying to get a copy of his marriage certificate and that should reveal his true identity."

"Identity theft is a big problem in the States, especially for the cops who are trying to establish a person's true identity."

"Do we have the same problem in Ireland?"

"It's a growing problem, mainly with credit card scams. Just be careful with this one."

We decided to call it a night and were leaving the bar when Hugh grabbed my arm.

"Andy, the best advice I can give you is this — keep an open mind, believe nothing unless you can prove it and remember be careful, these Yanks are handy with guns. Let me know if you need some protection."

He pulled back his coat and revealed his personal handgun, which is issued to Garda detectives.

"Thanks Hugh, but I think I will be OK."

When I was younger I did not think of my personal safety. However as I am now married my personal safety and that of my family was my utmost concern. My Garda and FBI contacts can protect themselves with their firearms, but civilian investigators are not permitted to carry guns in Ireland.

It had been a long day; I was tired and ready for bed when my phone rang.

"Hi Andy, it's Kelly."

I looked at my watch it was now 10.30pm, which was only about 2.30pm in Dallas. I had only spoken to Kelly a few hours earlier and here she was calling me back already; I was impressed!

"Hi Kelly, wow that was fast!"

"Andy, I don't have much information for you but I do have a contact for you in the Sheriff's Department in Honolulu, you need to call Sheriff Thomas Belling on 001 123 676767. He is an old timer, but he is good and will assist you with the marriage certificates."

"Thank you very much. I really appreciate it."

"Andy, law enforcement includes insurance fraud investigators in the United States so if I can help just call me. I will drop into our local field office next week and run some checks for you. Let me know some more information on Harrison, date of birth and anything else you have and I will see what I can establish

"Thanks again Kelly," I said as we hung up.

I dialled the number for Sheriff Belling immediately.

"Good afternoon, Sheriff's Department," a woman responded.

"Hello, I am looking to speak with Sheriff Belling."

"I am sorry Sheriff Belling is out on a call. Can one of his Deputies assist you?

"No I am calling from Ireland and need to talk to the Sheriff."

"Is that Ireland in Europe?"

"Yes that's right."

"My grandmother was from Ireland. It sure looks like a nice place. I would like to visit someday."

"Yes it is a nice place especially if you enjoy the rain," I laughed.

I gave her my number and she promised she'd ask the Sheriff to call me.

I headed to bed and fell into a deep sleep within minutes.

I was awoken in the middle of the night by the sound of my phone ringing. As I quickly answered before my wife woke up I glanced at my watch and saw it was 02.12am!

"Hello," I said softly.

"Hi, I am looking to speak with Andrew Stone," a man said in an American accent.

"You got him," I whispered.

"Hi Andrew, I am Sheriff Tom Belling."

I thanked the Sheriff and started to brief him on the case but he interrupted: "Hold on a minute Andrew, your FBI friend has told me all about the case. Now any friend of the

FBI is a friend of mine, even if you are on the other side of the world. What do you need me to do?"

"Well I would appreciate if somebody could check the marriage register in Honolulu to see when a John Harrison married a Jenny or Jennifer Boroski and if possible to get me a copy of the original marriage license. I tried searching on the internet but I was unable to get the correct information. Either way I will need a hard copy of the marriage certificate for evidence."

"Is that all? Consider it done Andrew. I will have a Deputy drop by the registry office to get the information tomorrow. Give me a couple of days to get back to you."

"Thanks again for your time Sheriff," I whispered and hung up the phone.

Unfortunately it was too late and the phone call had awoken my wife who was not very happy about it! I was now fully awake and hungry for more information on Harrison so I decided to go surf the internet. Just maybe I'd find out the Cowboy's current location — he could even be back in Ireland!

CHAPTER 7

❧

I had to stop off in Starbucks to get an extra big coffee the next day. I'd ended up spending a couple of hours on the Web without finding anything.

I sat down and took a few moments to evaluate the evidence. I'd found in the past that it was important to constantly review the gained intelligence and evidence when I was dealing with a complex investigation.

I looked at the notes on my laptop, deciding how to proceed. I was enjoying the coffee, feeling as relaxed as it's possible to get in our open-plan office environment, when Tanya approached.

"Andy, Courtney wants you in his office."

I was still gathering my notes, when I saw Courtney standing at his office door at the far end of the room. He pointed towards me and crooked his index finger in a come here gesture, like a parent calling a child. I tried to sort my notes which were a complete mess, as I walked towards his office. I would have to be one of the most untidy investigators in the country, which is not so good when you have to go to court and you need your files. Being organised, or better yet having a secretary to sort out your files, was crucial in my line of work.

I entered Courtney's office and closed the door.

He stood with his back to me looking out the window, which had a bird's eye view of Dublin City.

"Sit down Pebble."

When Courtney referred to me as Pebble he was normally in a good mood.

He turned around and asked: "How long are you in the insurance business?"

"Eight years Dan."

"And before that you were a Pinkerton?"

"Yes that's right," I said, wondering where this was going.

"You know I was born in Tucson, Arizona. My great-great-granddaddy served with the Confederates. Allan Pinkerton ... he sided with the Yankees during the war didn't he?"

"Yes that is true and the Yankees..."

I stopped mid-flow as I knew Courtney was not a man to be crossed. I'd been about to say and the Yankees won the war but I decided that there was no need to state the obvious.

"How old were you when you left America?" I asked instead.

I'd no idea why Courtney was hitting me with these questions but playing along until I found out seemed like the best idea.

"We left Tucson when I was eight years of age and went to live in San Francisco. We moved to Ireland when I was sixteen."

Courtney, who was now in his mid-fifties, still had an American accent, especially on simple words like "Hi" or "So long" which he still used instead of Hello and Goodbye. I'd heard him say soda in place of soft drink as well.

"Give me an update on the Harrison file."

The friendly conversation was obviously now over and it was back to business.

I shuffled to try and find a more comfortable seating position and said: "I believe that this case is fraudulent and that the accident was staged. I have obtained assistance from our UK operation and also called on a former Pinkerton colleague who is now in the FBI."

I told him about the photographs Caroline had found and my conversation with the Sheriff in Hawaii.

"Hopefully I will get a copy of Harrison's marriage certificate, proving the link between Nigel Boroski and our Cowboy."

"Do you need to head over to the States?" Courtney asked to my surprise.

"No, not at the moment, things are going fine."

"OK," Courtney nodded. "I like what you are doing with this case, keep me updated."

"Is that a compliment?" I asked as I stood up and opened the door.

"Don't push it Andy!"

I returned to my desk feeling a little more relaxed; the heat was off, at least for a while. I checked with Tanya to see if we had received any more emails from Harrison.

"No, nothing, it's all quiet, no calls or emails."

When I had spoken to Harrison he'd urgently needed money so he must have got spooked in the meantime. Maybe he knew we were on to him.

As I sat back down at my desk, I had one question on my mind — where was he now? I looked through the medical reports again and at the other intelligence I had received from America but there were no clues there. I decided to see if I could have lunch with Hugh, to give him the updates on the case and to get the views of a professional Garda.

I phoned and he answered almost immediately.

"Morning Andy"

"Are you in Dublin?"

"Yes I am in court today."

"Great, do you fancy meeting up for some lunch?"

"As long as you are buying!"

We agreed to meet at 12.30pm at a bar located near the Four Courts in the heart of Dublin City.

In the meantime I re-checked the details and information that I had on file and noted a date of birth, 28 May, 1975. It had been handwritten onto a report from one of the doctors who had examined the Cowboy in the UK. Looking at the photograph we had obtained from Oklahoma, it looked like Harrison was about 30-35 years of age so it was reasonable to assume that it was his date of birth.

I noted the date down in my notebook. I may be hopelessly untidy when it comes to my files, but I do maintain a notebook which I keep in my car or jacket. A former Garda Chief Superintendent, Michael Casey, who provided me with some training many years before, had told me to always keep good notes in a personal notebook. This was one of the most important lessons I ever learned as a valuable notebook can save you when you are being cross-examined on the witness stand. Former Chief Superintendent Michael Casey was an excellent Garda and also one of best investigators operating in private practice in Ireland. He was a true legend in Irish policing and investigation and, above all, a true gentleman. Unfortunately he has now retired and is enjoying life with his grandchildren.

I arrived early for my meeting with Hugh. To my surprise he was already sitting at a table having a coffee. He looked angry.

"What's up with you?" I asked as I walked over.

"I had a good case which has just fallen apart as my main witness has been intimidated. We spent hours on this case and now it has been destroyed — and the bastards have walked free."

Hugh was furious and understandably so. I was aware that he was close to retirement and a case like this could make him retire before his time, which would be a sad day for the Irish police.

"I am sure you will get your man in the end Hugh."

"I am in the Gardaí over 30 years Andy, maybe it's time for me to retire. I am fed up with a system that always sides with the criminal, it's making me sick."

Before I could respond Hugh asked: "How are you getting on with that American case?"

Although I felt bad for Hugh, I was happy that we had changed the subject.

"Not bad Hugh, some good information is now coming my way, plenty of leads to be followed up on."

To my surprise Hugh had ordered lunch for me. We were silent as we devoured the coffee and sandwiches that arrived.

After lunch I updated Hugh on the case and asked him what he thought I should do next. He looked at the photographs and wrote down the registration number of the vehicle from the picture that had been taken in the Mourne Mountains.

"I will check to see who is the owner of the vehicle and will come back to you. Looking at the amount of writing on it and the lights on the roof, it belongs to a commercial company, possible a security contractor."

"No shit Sherlock," I joked but looking at the expression on Hugh's face I realised he was in no mood for gags.

"Do you want me to check the registration or not?"

"Yes please that would be helpful and I would appreciate it."

"I am back in the station this afternoon," Hugh said, as we stood up. "I will run the registration and give you a call."

I thanked Hugh again and we went our separate ways.

I returned to the office and met Denton who was working on other general cases, including my cases as I had been given clearance to work solely on the Cowboy file. This was a tacit acknowledgement of the complexity of the case and the money involved. Most of the cases we investigate do not carry financial reserves as high as €1 million.

Denton was in a real happy mood. He was getting some quality cases, which he was enjoying and making some good savings.

"Andy, we have a large property fire in Limerick, would you mind if I investigated the file?"

Property fires were one of my favourite areas of business to investigate but I gritted my teeth and said: "Work away."

Denton looked a little surprised.

"Thanks," he said quickly and rushed off.

I decided to leave the office early and drive home. I needed to work out a game plan for the case. Insurance fraud investigation was like a game of chess and at this stage I could only anticipate Harrison's next move but I needed to make sure I was ready for it.

CHAPTER 8

I arrived back in the office early the following Monday morning. I had decided that we should try to trace the two cheques we had made payable to Sean Moran, the so-called uncle of John Harrison. I was about to start when my mobile rang.

"Morning Hugh you're up early."

"Sorry Andy, I completely forgot about checking that registration number you gave me on Friday. I have it now; you got a pen?"

"Yes, fire away."

"The vehicle is registered to Murray Towing Services Company and they're based at the Quays Bridge, Drogheda, Co. Louth."

"Thanks Hugh."

"I got to go Andy, there is somebody here to see me, talk soon."

Logging onto the web, I quickly found a website and a phone number. I looked at my watch. It was 08.15am, maybe a bit early but I decided to give them a call anyway.

To my surprise the phone was answered within a few seconds.

"Hello," a woman said.

She didn't say Murray Towing, so I thought I had dialled the wrong number.

"Is this Murray Towing Services?"

"Yes."

"I am sorry for troubling you. My name is Andrew Stone of Dallast Insurance. I am looking to talk to the manager or owner about a possible former employee"

"Is it a reference check? I am sorry but we don't give out information over the phone. Jerry Henderson is the owner and he will be here at 11.00am, but you would need to call down to see him."

"OK, I will call to your offices at 11.00am. Thanks for your help. See you then," I said and hung up

I took the photograph of Harrison and his wife standing beside the jeep from its folder. I had marked it as evidence exhibit AS3. It had obviously been taken by someone who was quite far away from the subjects so it was not possible to confirm if the man in the photograph was the same John Harrison as the man in the Oklahoma 'Wanted' picture. I placed the photo into my laptop case, along with a printed photo of the wedding, now marked evidence exhibit AS2 and the 'Wanted' picture from Oklahoma, which was marked evidence exhibit AS1. I then set off for Drogheda, Co. Louth, which was only about 45 minutes from our Dublin office.

At 10.15am I located the address of Murray Towing Services. It appeared to be a garage located to the side of a large private house. The house looked very well taken care of and there were a few cars in the driveway. Even though I was early I decided to call into the house.

A lady answered the door and I informed her that I was Andrew from Dallast Insurance.

"Hello Andrew, you spoke to me on the phone this morning. I am Linda Henderson, Jerry's wife. Please come in."

We shook hands and I followed her to an office located at the rear of the house.

A few moments later a man entered the room and shook my hand.

"I am Jerry Henderson, owner of Murray Towing, MT for short," he said as he handed me one of his company pens with the words *MT — Service you can trust* on it. "That's our company logo."

"Thank you Mr. Henderson for meeting me."

"Call me Jerry. How can we help you?"

We all sat down in his comfortable office.

"I will get straight to the point. Did you ever employ a man by the name of John Harrison?"

Without taking time to think he immediately responded: "No I have never heard that name. We are a small family business. I only employ four people and I have never employed or heard of John Harrison."

"Did you ever employ an American?"

"No only Irish here, sorry," he responded quickly.

I felt bitterly disappointed but I thought of the photograph of the jeep in my file and decided to double check. I quickly handed it to him.

He paused and then said: "Honey, pass me my glasses please."

She handed them to him and he looked down at the photograph and said: "Where the hell have they got my jeep?"

I felt the excitement building up inside me and asked: "Do you know the people in the photograph?"

"Yes that is Kenneth Smith and his girl Jenny."

"Who is Kenneth?" I asked.

Jerry was about to talk when his wife said: "Oh that guy!"

My eyes quickly turned to Linda as her tone of voice was interesting. It sounded as if she had a lot more to say about him.

"Linda, he wasn't that bad," Jerry smiled.

I once worked for an excellent female private investigator, Shirley Sleator, who said that you should always listen to a woman's instinct! Shirley has since written and published a great book, *My Years Undercover*.

"As you can tell Andrew, my wife did not like Kenneth that much!"

"It's not that I did not like him, it's just he was a bit creepy."

"Kenneth worked for me for a few months."

"Only a few months? Was there some type of problem? Was he looking for cash payments instead of being on the books maybe?"

"No way. I may be a small operator but all my guys are on the books, I don't pay cash," Jerry said in a stern, boss-like voice.

I apologised and said: "If it's the same guy he's American."

"No, he is Irish, but he lived in Canada or America for a long time."

"How do you know he is Irish?"

"He has an Irish passport; I have seen it as we travelled to Holyhead to pick up a car and he used his Irish passport for identification."

"Jerry would you mind taking another look at the photograph as I know this man as John Harrison?"

Jerry appeared to be a little insulted.

"Look, I am 100 per cent certain this is Kenneth Smith and his girlfriend Jenny. What bothers me more is where the hell did they take my jeep?"

"Do you know his wife's surname?"

"Sorry I don't. She is not Irish. I think she's Polish or maybe Latvian, but she has great English."

Linda looked at the photograph.

"Yes that's Kenneth and Jenny, no question about it."

"Do you have any details for him, an employment number or a photocopy of his driver's license maybe?"

"Linda looks after all my files and tax work; can you help him out honey?"

"He only worked with us for a few months," she said, walking over to a large filing cabinet. "I am sure I have some details on him, just give me a few moments."

"Why are you looking for Kenneth?" Jerry asked.

"I am dealing with a large insurance claim for a John Harrison. I think possibly Kenneth Smith was a name he was using."

Linda came back from the filing cabinet, holding a small file. It reminded me that I also had the wedding photograph and the 'Wanted' picture to show them. I passed them the wedding photograph first.

Linda looked at it and immediately said: "Yes that's Kenneth, he looks a bit heavier there and that's his Jenny. I didn't realise they were married."

Jerry nodded in agreement.

I showed them the 'Wanted' picture next.

Jerry looked at the photograph and immediately stood up, looking shocked and dismayed. He took off his glasses and gasped:

"How can this be? It says John Harrison, but he is Kenneth Smith. This cannot be right, it must be a mistake."

Jerry walked over to the fridge taking out a bottle of Miller beer.

"Would you like a cold beer Andrew?"

"No it's a little early in the day for me but thanks."

Linda picked up the 'Wanted' picture and looked at Jerry.

"I told you he was creepy, I just knew there was something wrong with him."

She opened the employee file which contained a few documents and handed me a sheet of paper with hand-writing on it.

Harrison had listed his bank account details for the bank branch in Naas and his date of birth.

"According to our records, we employed Kenneth Smith from 1 February, 2008 to 5 May, 2008."

"Why did he leave the company?"

I assumed they would say we fired him.

"Kenneth was only with us for a few weeks, but in that time he was a good no a great worker," Jerry said. "His time-keeping was not so good, but he did work hard. Unfortunately he was involved in a road traffic accident, when he got knocked down in North Dublin."

I could not believe my ears and I sat up in my seat.

"Do you know anything about the accident?"

"Yes, he was walking, I think in Blanchardstown Village, and he got run over. He was hurt really badly and he needed surgery," Jerry explained.

"A likely story!" I muttered.

"Do you not believe me? I have no reason to tell lies!" Jerry said aggressively.

"It seems like a very unfortunate accident, if it was genuine," I said.

"It was a genuine accident. Kenneth, I mean John or Kenneth or whatever his bloody name is, was hurt. He needed surgery on his back; sure I even brought him to the hospital."

At this stage I was a now confident that Kenneth Smith really was John Harrison and this was another fake accident but a good investigator should always question and re-question the evidence at hand.

"Which hospital did you bring him to? And can you give me some more details about the accident?"

"Well he showed up for work and told me he was in bad pain with his back. I drove him to Beaumont Hospital as we had been working in the area. I left him in the emergency department and he told me not to bother waiting. I did not witness the accident as it happened the day before."

"Are you aware of any other circumstances or any other information about that accident? Even if it appears irrelevant, it may just assist my case."

Jerry and Linda sat thinking for a few moments.

"I think Kenneth said a Polish lady knocked him down," Linda said slowly.

"Do you know the name of the lady or her insurance company?"

"I have no idea what her name was," Linda said. "I don't know what insurance company covered the claim either. I don't even know if there was an insurance claim."

I was sure there was an insurance claim. Hopefully I'd be able to locate it on Insurance Link.

"I really did not like that man," Linda said again.

"Why?"

"He just appeared suspicious; I cannot put my finger on it; just a feeling I had… "

"That accident was genuine enough though," Jerry interrupted.

I decided not to make any further comments on that and asked Linda and Jerry to take another look at all three photographs.

Linda looked at the photos again and said: "I am 100 per cent certain the man in these photos used to be employed by our company and is known to me as Kenneth Smith. The lady in the photograph is Jenny."

"I don't have to look at those photos again," Jerry said standing up. "I agree with Linda, that's Kenneth and Jenny."

I started gathering up my file.

"How can Kenneth be this John guy? Was he involved in something dodgy? Is this identity theft? I don't understand this," Jerry said.

"To be fair Jerry I don't understand it either, which is why I am investigating this matter. Thank you both very much for your time, you have been of great assistance."

Driving back towards the Dublin office, I'd a fairly good idea why John was also Kenneth, and Sean and most likely Gary too – it just gave him more opportunities for fraud and also for ways of beating the computer prevention systems. I have worked in fraud for so long, nothing would surprise me anymore.

At least I now knew for sure that Kenneth Smith was one of John Harrison's false identities.

CHAPTER 9

I arrived back at my desk and shifted through all my notes and the ever growing intelligence I was gaining on Harrison and his wife. Sandra Hynes also knew the Cowboy as Kenneth Smith and not John Harrison. So with Jerry and Linda Henderson's confirmation, that was three people who had stated that they knew John Harrison under a different identity.

"Any update on John?" Tanya asked.

"I am continuing to investigate the matter," I assured her. "We are possibly dealing with a case of identity theft."

"Identity theft, I have seen that on some movies and heard about people stealing credit card numbers to buy things, but surely nobody would be stealing identities in Ireland?"

"You're right Tanya it's a relatively new problem in Ireland and certainly not something I have much knowledge of, especially in the insurance business. But then again Tanya, as a fraud investigator the best way I can get knowledge is from experience."

"Yes I understand but how can you have identity theft in a personal injury insurance claim, especially with doctors, medical examinations and lawyers? How is Harrison doing it?"

"That is what I am trying to establish. Tanya this case is turning into a complex file. It's almost like trying to make a jigsaw in the dark."

"Well that's why we have you working in fraud Andrew. I am sure you will get a result. I am going to the canteen, you need anything?"

"Yes a black coffee with one brown sugar please," I shouted after her.

I decided to run the name Kenneth Smith, with the date of birth provided by Linda of Murray Towing through the Insurance Link database. Thankfully it had been updated in 2008 with a new special investigators search engine, which permitted me to carry out searches on a name and date of birth or approximate age and on an address. This has been of major benefit to the Irish insurance industry in the prevention of criminal activity.

I opened Insurance Link and as usual I had forgotten my password which is a well-known joke within the company. As we are dealing with the public's personal data it was important that we did all we could to protect the information so we all had individual access passwords. After a telephone call to Insurance Link and a few moments wait, I had obtained my new password: "Yankie25" and was ready for action.

Just as I logged onto the website, Denton walked into the office and over to my desk. As normal he was well turned out in crisp, white shirt, tie and trousers. His hair was perfect, gelled back with style and as he would say: "Ready for some action with the ladies." But I realised that he seemed agitated.

"What's wrong with you?" I asked.

"I am in the shit. I have got a house property fire in Wexford and I forgot to instruct forensics. Now we are going to have to settle the claim."

"How much is the reserve?"

"€200,000 — Courtney is going to kill me! I messed up again, what am I going to do?"

"Calm down and give me the claim number," I said.

"It's HF X553, what will I do Andy?"

"Just relax; go and get a coffee and I will see what I can do to fix it."

I felt sorry for the guy, as Denton is a good investigator but he lacks experience. I logged onto our claims management system and located the file. The adjuster who was dealing with the claim was my old friend Dave Hendrick.

Denton was in a real panic, standing beside me saying: "Courtney is going to kill me. I am a dead man walking."

"Go to the canteen and get a coffee now and that is an order!"

I watched Denton walk away from my desk and hurry into the Men's room — I was glad I was not in there!

I phoned Dave Hendrick but to my surprise he did not answer the phone. This was unusual for him as, like me, his mobile is glued to his hand. I then realised that I had called from my office phone. I decided to try him again on my mobile.

Within a couple of rings he answered: "Morning Andy."

"Dave I have got a problem!"

"What you done now? You need me to bail you out of jail?"

"No, not that serious! My colleague Denton is working on a property fire in Wexford with you the claim number is HF X3…"

"I know the file Andy," he cut in.

"Dave what are we dealing with?"

"A house fire, most suspect, possible multiple seats of fire and no forced entry."

"How do you know there are multiple seats of fire?"

"Forensic report from Bob."

"But according to Denton we did not appoint forensics."

"Ah yes Andy, but there are two houses in this fire, because they are attached. IXFP Insurance is covering the other house so they appointed Bob to do the forensics. I asked them to look at the two houses for the cause of fire ignition. I have agreed with IXFP Insurance that the report will be shared with your company for a 50/50 on the fee."

"Thanks for putting the arrangement in place Dave. Will you do me a favour please and keep a watchful eye on Denton? He's good but he needs experience."

"Consider it done Andy. Denton is a good guy and we work well together. Talk to you soon."

"Thanks Dave," I said and hung up.

Denton was running so scared I thought I'd better tell him about his Dave Hendrick safety net before he lost it.

"Denton, you're in the clear. Dave Hendrick appointed forensics on that file," I said quietly when I found him in the canteen.

"Ah Andy, thank God. Dave Hendrick has saved my neck."

"Don't thank me or God. Call Dave and thank him!"

To say Denton was relieved would be putting it mildly.

My mind turned back to the Insurance Link search I'd been about to carry out when Denton walked in. I logged onto to the database again, entering my new password. Opening the Special Investigation Unit screen, I keyed in the only information I had: name and DOB. Within a second of pressing the enter key I had a match:

Confidential Insurance Link Report:

Insurer: Mustang Insurance Ireland
Insured: Jenny Boroski
Address: Naas, Co. Kildare
Nationality: Polish citizen
Incident date: 5 May, 2008
Claim Type: Motor Accident
Claim No: SS232XX4
Claimant name: Kenneth Smith
Nationality: Irish-American
Claimant Address: 12 Pinebrooke Monaghan Town, Co. Monaghan
Date of Birth: 30 June, 1975

Mustang Insurance was a relatively small Irish insurance company and thankfully I knew the fraud manager, Pat Coops. My excitement was getting the better of me again as I struggled to locate his number on my mobile. I was lucky Ireland was a small place. I found the number and phoned him.

Pat answered with his traditional: "Well Andy!"

I immediately got into my reason for calling him and didn't even bother with the usual small talk.

"Hi Pat, I have a match on Insurance Link and I would appreciate if you could verify the specifics of the claim for me."

"No problem Andy — it sounds urgent."

"Yes it is!"

I gave Pat the claim number and heard him type it in.

"The claimant is a Kenneth Smith of 12 Pinebrooke, Monaghan Town, Co. Monaghan."

"Yes that's the claim Pat; what can you tell me?"

"What's there on screen is about it, straight-forward motor personal injury insurance claim. Our insured crashed into a pedestrian who sustained an injury to his back."

"How much did you pay out?"

"Give me a minute; we paid ... €55,000 plus his medical costs. There's not much else I can tell you Andy. I will have to call back the original file from storage."

I finished writing my notes and asked the killer question.

"Pat, can you confirm the name of your insured?"

"Jenny Boroski."

I could feel my pulse rate increase and my heart was beating against my chest with excitement.

"Got You!" I said

"What are you talking about Andy? This is a genuine claim, as the claimant was an American and the insured is Polish; they did not know each other. How could they know each other?"

"Pat, I am working on a large case and I am still collecting intelligence on this American guy, whom you know as Kenneth Smith. I don't want to give you false information but it would be great if you could retrieve your full file from storage as I will have further information for you shortly."

"OK Andy, I will call you when I retrieve the original file and you can tell me all about it then."

"Thanks Pat, talk to you soon."

Evidence was coming in at a good rate and we almost had enough to contradict John Harrison's claim but I wanted some solid proof. Nigel Boroski had knocked John Harrison down and I was satisfied that Nigel was Jenny Boroski's brother, making him the brother-in-law of John Harrison. I just needed the marriage certificate to prove it.

I was mindful that it was only a few days since I had spoken to Sheriff Belling in Hawaii but I desperately wanted to telephone him to see if he had obtained the certificate.

However I did not want to be a pain in the neck so I decided instead to give Kelly a call. It was 4.25pm which would make in about 10.25am in Dallas, Texas, an acceptable time to make a telephone call.

I dialled her number which rang with the usual long American tone. A man answered the phone with a sharp, New York accent.

"Hi can I talk to Kelly?"

"Is this Andy from Ireland?"

"Yes it is."

"Hi Andy, I am Steve, Kelly's husband. She has told me all about you and your Pinkerton party days!"

"Yeah it was a good time Steve. Is Kelly there? I need to talk to her about the contact she gave me in Hawaii."

"No Andy she has gone out with the kids ... is it Sheriff Belling you are talking about?"

"Yes that's the one. He was trying to get me some marriage documents."

"Well Belling is my contact. He is a great guy and will help you in any way that he can. Tell you what give me a few hours and I will call him and see what is happening and then get back to you."

"Thanks Steve and pass on my best regards to Kelly. Talk to you later."

That evening I left the office at 7.00pm. I would have worked later but security closes the building at this time.

As I drove home, I decided to treat myself to the Port Tunnel which only costs €3 after 7pm. At peak hours it's €10. I was driving along listening to Fleetwood Mac's *Rumours* album. *Second Hand News* started and the lead singer, Lindsey Buckingham, sang the words "someone has taken my place". It looked like somebody had taken the place of the real Kenneth Smith. At this stage I was pretty certain that John Harrison had in some way managed to obtain the identity of Kenneth Smith in Monaghan, to make a false insurance claim. The next question was who was the real Kenneth Smith? And did he know his identity had been stolen?

My phone rang just as I decided to go to Monaghan Town to find out.

"Hi Andy, sorry for not coming back to you sooner, I was dealing with some other issues."

It was Sheriff Tom Belling.

"No problem Tom and thank you again for your help."

"Well son I got your information, a John Harrison married a Jenny Boroski on the 25 September 2007, here in Honolulu, Hawaii."

I scrambled to find a pen to write down the information and stupidly asked: "Are you sure?"

"Of course I am sure. I am looking at the wedding certificate!"

"Thank you Sir. Can you please send me a copy?"

"Consider it done; just send your postal address to my email and I'll post it along. I will have Shirley in the office scan a copy and email it to you as well but the original will be in the regular post."

I was delighted as I thanked him again and said goodbye. I was sure that John Harrison would never have expected an Irish investigator to trace him halfway round the world to Hawaii.

I would have some real evidence in front of me shortly which I could show Courtney. The fact that John Harrison and Jenny Boroski were married and I had obtained the official wedding certificate would give us enough evidence to contradict his claim. I even had the audio recording of him denying that he knew the driver of the vehicle that had knocked him down when in fact I would soon be able to prove that John Harrison was actually married to the driver's sister! I had just saved the company a minimum of €200,000 and I'd beaten Harrison. It was a brilliant feeling, like scoring the winning goal in a football game.

CHAPTER 10

I decided to take a trip up to Monaghan to meet a loss adjuster I knew, Connor Spain. Connor, like Dave Hendrick, was an excellent loss adjuster, with a particular skill for dealing with fraudulent insurance claims.

I met with Connor in a local hotel and discussed another claim we had running, involving the theft of jewellery from a house. Monaghan is a moderate-sized town located on the border with Northern Ireland. It's about a two hour drive from our Dublin office. Monaghan had its difficulties in the past during the Troubles in Northern Ireland. Today it is a peaceful modern town that sadly suffers from high unemployment.

When I arrived Connor was sitting in the corner of the hotel with the file open in front of him.

"Coffee Andy? Black with one brown sugar?" he asked as I approached.

I was impressed but did not want to show it.

"Hello Mr. Spain!"

Connor briefed me on updates on the case involving a man who had purchased jewellery and other items on the internet which had then been stolen when his house was robbed. The Gardaí had recently arrested a man in the locality in possession of the stolen items. To my surprise it looked like it was a genuine claim after all!

"Connor, do you know a Kenneth Smith, living in Pinebrooke or maybe somewhere else in the town?"

"I don't but I will run the name through our database at the office to see if he's one of our customers.

He called the office and spoke with his assistant.

"Sorry Andy, we don't have any records of a Kenneth Smith or anybody living in the town by that name."

"Do you know Pinebrook?"

"Yes, it's a small housing estate, consisting of maybe 60 houses located at the north end of the town, beside the Texaco petrol station"

"Thanks Connor. I am sorry I don't have longer to talk but I have a lot on at the moment."

"That's you Andy. No problem we'll catch up soon."

I left the hotel and decided to call to the address I had for Kenneth Smith, 12 Pinebrooke, to see if the Insurance Link database had the correct one. I drove the short distance to the housing estate and eventually located the correct terraced, semi-detached house. I noticed that no cars were parked in the driveway or on the road outside.

I pulled up and opened the gate. I walked up to the front door and rang the doorbell. However nobody answered. The next-door neighbour was working on the engine of his car so I asked: "Is this number 12 Pinebrooke?"

"Yes it is."

"Does a Kenneth Smith live here?"

The man stood up and gave me a suspicious look.

"Who are you? Are you a Guard?"

I showed my company identification to the man, advising "I am looking for Kenneth, following an insurance claim."

The neighbour appeared more at ease and responded: "Yes this is Kenneth's house but he has not lived here in a few months. However he is still living in town."

"Can you describe what Kenneth looks like?"

"What he looks like?"

"Yes, does he look like Colin Farrell?"

The man started to laugh loudly: "Kenneth look like Colin Farrell! He wishes."

I remembered that I had the 'Wanted' photograph in the car so I quickly walked back and retrieved it from my file. The neighbour followed me.

I handed it to him, asking: "Is this Kenneth Smith?"

"No it does not look like him at all. Kevin has a small build, black hair and a fairer complexion."

"Have you ever heard of a man named John Harrison or a woman named Jenny Boroski?"

"No I am not familiar with either of those names. If you're looking for Kenneth, Tara who lives up the road there would have his telephone number."

"Thanks for your help. I'll try her."

I knocked on the door of number 22 and spoke to a lady who identified herself as Tara. She gave me a mobile number for Kenneth Smith. I thanked her and returned to my car.

I sat there and wondered should I chance telephoning the number and talking to Kenneth Smith. My worry was that he might be involved with Harrison and I'd tip him off. In the end I decided it would be of more benefit to the claim if I talked to him. I dialled the number feeling anxious.

"Hello," a man answered, with a strong Monaghan accent.

"Is this Kenneth Smith of 12 Pinebrooke Monaghan?"

"Yes."

"My name is Andrew Stone of Dallast Insurance. I am investigating an insurance claim and was wondering if you would meet me to answer some questions?"

"No thanks I don't want to make any insurance claims."

"No you misunderstood me, I'm looking at a particular file here and you may be able to provide me with some assistance."

"I don't have any insurance claims pending.

"You may be able to help me with some information," I said and quickly moved onto a question as Kenneth was starting to sound a little impatient. "Kenneth did you ever have an injury claim with Magnum Insurance?"

"Insurance claim? No I told you I did not. What's this all about?

"Kevin I could really do with meeting you. I have some information which may be of benefit to you."

"Look, I told you I don't have any insurance claims and I don't see why I should meet you."

"Look Kenneth I understand and just maybe the information I have is wrong but I really need to meet you to verify it."

"Well I am busy at the moment. I won't be able to meet you for about an hour. Tell you what if you're that desperate to meet me you can buy me my tea."

"No problem Kenneth. You know this area, where shall we meet?"

"There is a hotel on the main street, the Western Arms Hotel. I will meet you there."

"Thanks Kenneth, would you mind bringing some photo identification with you, such as a passport or your driver's license?"

"A driver's license, why do you need that?" he asked in a raised tone of voice.

"It's just for personal identification purposes," I said calmly.

"I will have to find my license. OK sure I will see you in an hour at the Arms."

"See you then. Thanks Kenneth."

As I had an hour to spare, I decided to call to the house of an old Pinkerton friend of mine who was living in Monaghan. I had not seen John from Pinkerton in a couple of years but he was still working in the security and investigation business and I was sure he would assist me if possible.

He opened the front door and greeted me as if he had only met me a few days previously.

"Well, look who it is!" he smiled.

"Hi John, good to see you."

John invited me into his house, leading me into a large country-styled kitchen.

"Will you have a cup of tea Andy, or sorry coffee as you're probably one of those city boy coffee drinkers now?"

"No thanks John. I don't have much time, rushing as usual. Could I run a local name past you?"

"Sure Andy, what have you got?"

"Do you know a local man by the name of Kenneth Smith, living in Pinebrooke?"

"I do indeed."

"What can tell me?"

"Is he in some kind of bother?"

"No nothing like that John. I am just dealing with an insurance claim and he may have information which will assist me. I am meeting him in about thirty minutes."

"Kenneth Smith, I used to play football with him when we were younger. Nice guy comes from a good family."

I pulled the 'Wanted' photograph of Harrison from my laptop bag and showed it to John: "Is this him?"

"No certainly not. He looks nothing like that guy."

"Have you ever heard of anybody by the name of John Harrison or Jenny Boroski?"

"Boroski, no never. I did know a Mike Harrison but he moved to London a few years ago. What is this all about?"

"I can't say at this stage John, as I am still investigating the file. Listen I've got to go but I will be in touch. Maybe we can catch up over a meal next time?"

"Sounds good, you take it easy Andy."

I arrived at the hotel at 6.45pm and sat in the lounge area drinking a coffee. I went over my file notes, feeling uneasy about my proposed meeting with Kenneth Smith. I really did not want to jeopardise the case. However I tried to reassure myself that a simple meeting would not create any problems. I was also afraid that he would not show up for the meeting as what would I do then? I sat back in the comfortable sofa and tried to relax.

I'd been there ten minutes when a man entered the reception area and looked around. I walked over to him and asked: "Are you Kenneth Smith?

"Yes are you Andrew from the insurance company?"

I nodded and we shook hands.

He followed me over to the sofa and I asked: "Would you like a drink, or maybe some food?"

"A coke would be great as I have eaten already. I was only joking about you buying my tea."

The waiter took my order for a coke and a black coffee and I relaxed a little. The Kenneth Smith who was sitting in front of me did not look anything like the photographs I had obtained of John Harrison.

"Thanks for coming Kenneth. I'm sure you must be wondering why I wanted to meet you?"

"I certainly am curious, have I won a prize or something?" he smiled.

"No I am afraid not. I have been investigating an insurance claim for the past few months which have raised serious concerns. Can I ask you some questions about the case?"

"What would I know about an insurance case?"

"Kenneth to be fair you may know nothing at all, but you may be able to assist me."

"OK Andrew, what would you like to know?"

I took a drink of coffee and then asked: "Kenneth have you ever had an insurance claim?"

"Let me think now, yes about five years ago I had a small water problem in my house and I claimed from my insurance company."

"Was it a large claim?"

"No, it was only small damage. I got about €200 from my insurance company to cover repair costs."

"Kevin, were you involved in a motor accident in Naas in 2008?"

"No, I have not been in Naas for over ten years."

I was not surprised with his answer, however just for the record I asked: "Are you sure?"

"Of course I am sure, what is all this about?"

"I am dealing with an injury insurance claim for a man named John Harrison. He has made this claim against my company and I am concerned about its validity. I have discovered that he may have been using the name Kenneth Smith to take out other insurance policies. A claim was made against Magnum Insurance, using your name and address in Monaghan."

"Hold on a minute, I do recall receiving some post from an insurance company some time ago. I can't remember the name of the company, but it was about a claim alright."

"What did you do with the letter?"

"I ignored it. I most likely put it in the bin."

I'd hoped that the real Kenneth Smith would have some information that could be traced back to Harrison.

"Were you ever employed by a company called Murray Towing Services?"

"No I have never worked for them. Who are they? I never heard of them. I am a builder by trade, although things are a little slack at the moment."

I was now unsure if I had the right man. I asked Kenneth if he had any identification with him. He pulled an Irish passport from his pocket and handed it to me. This surprised me as I could have been anybody and he had not asked to see my company identification card.

Examining the passport I was satisfied it was a genuine document. His name Kenneth Smith and the same date of birth, together with photograph, all appeared to be correct.

I handed it back to Kevin, fairly sure that Harrison must have stolen his identity.

"But how did the American get a hold of his details?" I muttered.

"Did you say American?"

"Yes, the guy I am interested in is American."

"Hold on a minute. I remember getting a call on my mobile from an American man. Let me remember, it was back in 2008. No hang on first I received several text messages and then a telephone call. The American told me that he was Irish-born but had lived in America for most of his life. He returned to Ireland a few years ago and went to claim his tax back. He checked my PPS number with me and he had the right one. He said he had been given the same number by the Irish tax office and that his name was also Kenneth Smith and that his mother's maiden name was Winter the same as my mother's name. I just took it that the tax office must have made a mistake and confused this American Kenneth Smith with me."

"Did you ever rent your house or have anybody staying in your home renting a room?"

"Other than some of my family no."

"Have you ever received any strange post or any unexpected queries from your bank or other financial institutions?"

"The bank gives me plenty of calls at the moment," Kenneth laughed. "Being serious though Andrew, the answer to your question is no, other than the letters from the insurance company."

"Are you sure?" I asked

"Yes … oh no hold on, I did receive some post a few months ago from a travel agency regarding a holiday in Florida. The travel agency told me I owed them €1,700 or thereabouts for the holiday."

"Have you ever been in Florida?"

"No, I would have loved to go to Florida but I never booked the holiday. The only place I have been on holiday was to Majorca a few years ago. Times are hard I couldn't afford an expensive holiday like that."

"What about calls from any credit card companies?"

"Yes somebody from a credit card company called to my house saying I owed them some money but I have never had a credit card so they went away."

I was now 100 per cent satisfied that this unfortunate man was the victim of identity theft.

"Kenneth, when we are finished I want you to go to the local police station and ask for a detective. Tell him that you met me and that your identity has been stolen."

"I have no idea what you mean Andrew. How has my identity been stolen? I would feel like a fool telling a Guard my identity has been stolen."

"I think that the American man I have been investigating has taken your identity, in other words he has pretended to be you to purchase items in your name, like that holiday in Florida."

"I don't like the sound of this at all,"

Kenneth was looking angry and somewhat shaken.

I handed him my company business card and told him to give it to the detective when he made his complaint. I felt genuinely sorry for Kenneth as he had no idea that he had been a victim of identity theft. I was sure his credit rating would have been badly affected by Harrison's actions.

"Kenneth thanks for your time and for the information you have given me. It really will be of benefit to my case."

I stood up and started to walk towards the hotel door. Kenneth was walking beside me looking a bit shell-shocked. He was muttering to himself. I could not understand what he was saying, something like "how did this happen to me."

"You know there was one other thing that I found strange Andrew. I was made unemployed a wee while ago and I went to sign on to get unemployment benefit. However I was told by the Social Welfare that I was already receiving it."

"Did you get it sorted?" I asked

"Eventually after a few meetings they gave it to me. Do you think that was also the American?"

"I have no doubt that it was him Kenneth. If you receive any more strange post or phone calls please call me. My mobile number is on the business card I gave you."

I couldn't believe Social Welfare had let the discrepancy go. What chance have insurance investigators got if a government office doesn't investigate these matters? If an investigation had been carried out then surely they would have established that they had two Kenneth Smiths with the same tax reference number, and the identity theft would have been discovered. Then John Harrison might not have got away with a fraudulent insurance claim for over €55,000.

I left Kevin and got back into my car. It was now just after 9pm. I knew my friends would think I was crazy working until 9pm on a Friday evening, when they were all out having a few beers but that was the price you paid in my line of work, sometimes the hours can be unsociable but it's all worthwhile if you get a positive result and it looked like I was on to something big.

Kenneth had signed a statement for me so I now had evidence that this particular case was not just about a single false insurance claim against my employer. It also involved a fraudulent insurance claim against another Irish company. My duty was to protect my employer but I was well aware that insurance fraud affects the whole industry. When I can assist other companies I do because if it's them today it could be us tomorrow.

After witnessing Kenneth Smith's shocked disbelief I felt a huge determination to continue to investigate the activities of John Harrison and to track down the other identities he'd stolen.

CHAPTER 11

I enjoyed my weekend break with my children and all too soon was sitting back at my desk in the office, early on a wet and windy Monday morning wondering why weekends went by so quickly. You are just starting to relax and enjoy the weekend when your wake-up alarm activates at 6am on a Monday morning and off to work you go!

Before getting stuck back into Operation Cowboy I started reviewing the new claims' statistics for the weekend. Generally any claim in excess of €100,000 was sent to my unit for review. We had also installed an automated referral system for files which might require closer attention.

To my surprise Denton was sitting down at his desk by 8.30am. This was most unusual for him, as he would rarely arrive into the office before 10am on a Monday morning.

"Not out partying last night?" I called over.

Denton looked at me and I noticed he had a large black eye.

"What the hell happened to you?"

"Got a smack during a football game on Saturday."

"Are you sure it wasn't one of those ladies you have been chasing?"

"No, it was my own fault," Denton laughed.

A few moments later my internal phone rang. Our receptionist told me that DHL had left something for me at reception. I get DHL packages all the time so I was not in any hurry to collect it.

"Thanks, I'll collect it later," I said and hung up.

I turned back to my computer and continued analysing the new claims. Looking through them I was glad to see there was nothing out of the ordinary and I'd be able to keep working on Harrison.

"Pebble you got any more evidence on the Cowboy file?" Courtney suddenly asked, walking by my desk.

I started to ramble on about the identity issue and that Kenneth Smith was also John Harrison. Courtney was a very experienced insurance manager but he did not have any background in dealing with criminal matters or fraud investigations. He fixed me with a management stare. We all know the look – when managers don't understand what you are saying and don't want to ask in case it would look like they did not understand.

"Are you finished the case now? You want to give me a full breakdown of your *evidence*?"

I noticed Courtney's emphasis on the word evidence. I knew he was correct to do so, as theory was irrelevant in court cases. All criminal and civil court cases were won or lost on the facts of the case and the amount of collated evidence placed before the court.

"Not yet, I need a little more time."

"Pebble you have been working on this case for almost three weeks now; how much more time do you need?"

I took a minute and thought of a few different answers, but I decided to be honest.

"I don't know."

"What do you mean you don't know?"

"I don't know Dan. This case is turning into a large spider's web. Every day I am uncovering new information," I said as I stood up. "When Elliot Ness was investigating Capone it took him over three years to get his conviction. I will need some more time."

Courtney walked away from my desk laughing.

"Pebble thinks he is one of The Untouchables; we will have to get him a new company ID card, Elliot Pebble Ness, ha, ha!"

I couldn't believe I'd said something so stupid; now I would be laughed out of it in the office.

We had recruited a new desktop investigator, Denise Elliot, who was a former claims handler promoted into working with the fraud team. I had personally selected Denise for the position as I could see a lot of me within her. Although she was about 15 years younger than me and was very highly qualified, I could see the same hunger to succeed as an investigator and an ambition to establish the truth in all cases.

Within the Special Investigations Unit (SIU) of an insurance company various levels and skills were required for each area of expertise. A desktop investigator was the starting point. It was a difficult job that required the person to have the ability to carry out investigations from behind a desk, using the internet to obtain intelligence for defending suspect claims, while also acting as the Unit's co-ordinator and directly supporting the field investigators. It was a multi-tasking role which required strong attention to detail and the ability to self-motivate, while keeping claims' staff and solicitors regularly informed of developments in particular investigations.

"Andy you don't look a bit like Kevin Costner in *The Untouchables!*" she laughed.

"Am I reviewing your salary pay grade next week?" I smiled.

Denise quickly lowered her head back down in front of her computer and pretended to look busy.

"Andy, are you coming down to the canteen for our 10am coffee break?" Denton asked.

"Yes I could do with a caffeine fix," I said as I stood up and started to walk away from my desk.

"Hold up guys, I am coming too," Denise said.

As we walked into the canteen Tanya and Caroline joined us.

Jim Brooks was sitting at a table, already tucking into a fresh scone. He was one of our most experienced and senior claims staff, who was only a year away from retirement. I often wondered why he'd stayed working for so long. He had been with the company for over 30 years so he had maximised his pension contributions. I think he just enjoyed it as he was also the local gossip and a great man for the news. You know the sort of guy that can tell you something a week before management even know what's happening. He was a real character and a very funny and witty man who always had a joke or two, no matter what was happening in the world.

"Hi Pebble. I hear you are changing your name to Elliott Ness!"

"Yeah, yeah, yeah," I said.

I hated been called Pebble instead of Stone or Andy and I was surprised how fast the joke had spread. But it was out there amongst my colleagues now and I thought I'd better play along.

We had the usual banter and chat at the table. Denise was telling us all about her new boyfriend while Denton was nursing his black eye and trying to comb his greasy, gelled hair. I think he had an eye for Tanya. Neither Tanya nor Caroline took any notice of Denton as they were too busy discussing the latest news.

I was laughing with Jim and as we say in Ireland "having the crack," with a bit of general chit-chat. I often wondered how Jim had ended up working in the insurance business as he would have been much better suited to journalism.

He started telling me about Courtney that he had lived in America for many years but that he had to leave for reasons unknown. It sounded quite mysterious and I wondered where Jim had got the information.

After our short break, I noticed that the red message light was flashing on my desk phone. The message was from Sheila in Reception reminding me of the DHL delivery.

I phoned and said that I would be down in a minute.

"No problem Andy. I have your envelope from America here on my desk whenever you want to collect it."

After hearing the word America I dropped the phone and ran towards Reception, taking the stairs six or seven steps at a time.

Sheila handed me the DHL envelope which had a Hawaii return address.

I quickly ripped it open as I walked back to my desk. The contents consisted of a note from Sheriff Tom Belling with the words: 'With compliments, Best Regards Sheriff T Belling.' There were also two official documents included: a marriage certificate for John Harrison and Jenny Boroski and an official marriage license certificate. This was a crucial piece of evidence which now officially showed that Harrison and Boroski were related. Effectively I now had enough to dismiss the claim against my company as fraudulent.

I walked over to Tanya's desk and showed her the documents and I also phoned Caroline and invited her to come and see them.

"Andy, this is fantastic. To think you got this document all the way from Hawaii."

"Well guys it was a team effort. If Caroline had not found the photo then none of this would have been possible."

"Maybe a team effort Andy but you did most of the work. Well done," Caroline smiled.

The wedding photograph and the other documentation supplied thanks to the assistance of Kelly and Sheriff Tom Belling were going to be of enormous benefit to the defence of the claim.

"So Andy when are you going to tell Courtney?" Tanya asked.

I immediately thought of Kenneth Smith and my vow to keep investigating Harrison.

"Let's hold off telling him yet as I want to continue looking at this guy John Harrison. I think there may be more going on here."

I'd only investigated the name Kenneth Smith but I wanted to find out about the other names the Cowboy was using. I would use any intelligence I gained as potential court exhibits when Courtney was looking for an update.

Both Tanya and Caroline agreed to keep quiet about the new information.

I carefully placed the certificates in the bulging Harrison file and decided that investigating Sean Moran should be my next move.

CHAPTER 12

Now that I'd established that Harrison had stolen Kenneth Smith's identity, scrutinising Sean Moran's life was the next step. But I also had other files to work on and financial reports to complete. This took most of my day, as my concentration levels for anything other than Harrison were low.

Later that afternoon, I was still working on some other files, trying to catch up, and to finish my monthly report for Courtney when I saw Tanya walking towards my desk.

"With all the excitement earlier I forgot to ask you were there any further updates on the Harrison file Andy?"

"Yes I met with the real Kenneth Smith and obtained a statement from him on Friday evening."

I gave her a printed copy of the statement and she sat on the edge of my desk and immediately started reading it.

"So you met the real man then!"

"Yes, I sure did. Nice guy lives in Co. Monaghan."

"You don't mind if I take a copy of this statement for my file?"

"Sure Tanya, just return the original to me as it will most likely be exhibited as evidence in court."

Tanya was about to walk away from my desk when I asked: "Tanya can you run a print out of all the payments we have made to Harrison so far under the claim?"

"Why that is very easy Andy. We have only made one payment to John Harrison, a cheque for Stg£5,000 that we cancelled as he does not have a bank account in the UK."

"But Tanya didn't we pay some cheques to Harrison to cover his out of pocket and medical expenses?"

"Yes but not directly. If you recall we paid his uncle, Sean Moran."

I quickly raced through my notes from Nigel and read his statement from Sandra Hynes again, the owner of Swan's View Farm. It was clear she had identified the man in the photograph as Sean Moran and he'd rented a room at her farm with his wife Jenny. He was also driving an Irish-registered red Alfa Romeo car.

"Tanya, this guy Sean Moran, can you run his name through our internal database and see if you can find any claims?"

"Sure," Tanya said, looking excited. She left the Kenneth Smith statement on my desk and I followed her over to her computer."

She logged onto our claims database system and keyed in the name Sean Moran, and about 200 claims popped up on the screen. They were all claims which had been registered over the past ten years. The claims included car theft, accidental damage, travel claims and property insurance claims.

I was surprised we only had about 200 claims as Sean Moran was a common name in Ireland but it was still going to be like looking for a needle in a haystack, as we only had the name to go on.

I walked back over to my desk and spoke to Denise.

"I need you to run the name Sean Moran through all available databases and in particular Insurance Link."

"What address and date of birth should I use?" she asked.

"We don't have that info."

"Andy we are looking for a claim by a man named Sean Moran and we have nothing else! You know this is going to be virtually impossible," Denise sighed.

"I know but we have got to try," I said. "Denise just do your best."

I sat back in my chair realising that Denise was correct and this was going to be almost impossible. I logged onto Insurance Link myself, and got access to the Special Investigations screen. I inputted the name Sean Moran and again over 200 claims came back as possible matches. I narrowed the search parameters by age, requesting a search for Sean Morans with an age of 30-40 years. This reduced the possible matches to less than 85 claims. It was still too many.

"This is hopeless," Tanya said as she walked back over to my desk.

"I agree with Tanya," Denise muttered.

I tried to sort out our options. I decided to examine the intelligence which we had obtained from the Kenneth Smith V Magnum Insurance claim. Kenneth, aka John, had supposedly been knocked down as a pedestrian while he was walking along the footpath. This was similar circumstances to the claim against us — our insured Nigel Boroski from Poland, had also allegedly knocked down a pedestrian. I decided to carry out a full search on the Insurance Link SIU database, this time using the following parameters:

Surname: Moran

First Name: Sean

Age: 30 years to 40 years

Type of Accident: Motor Personal Injury

I pressed 'Enter' and waited for no more than two to three seconds; it felt like an eternity. To my amazement only four claims came up matching my parameters. When I examined them I discovered that only one of them was as the result of a Sean Moran been knocked down by the driver of a car. I cross-checked the name of the insurance company and up popped Starling Insurance Ireland, with the relevant claim reference number. I noticed that the date of the accident was the 25 September, 2006. According to the notes, Sean Moran was a pedestrian who had allegedly been knocked down by a car driver, Sally Wall.

Starling Insurance Ireland was a small Irish insurance company that had recently been taken over by a multinational insurer. Luckily for me I was friendly with their fraud manager, Willie McCabe whom I played football with on a regular basis. Rather than e-mail Willie, which was the standard agreed protocol for sharing information, I decided to give him a quick call on his mobile. Willie was incredibly reliable and always answered his phone.

"Willie! Good morning; Andy here in Dallast Insurance. I have a match on one of your injury claims registered with Insurance Link. Will you see what you can establish for me?"

"No problem Andy, what do you need?"

I read out the claim number and I could hear Willie typing it in.

"OK, got it, our insured was Ms Sally Wall who was living in Newbridge, Co. Kildare. On 25 September 2006 she was driving her car when she crashed into a man who was walking in The Curragh area, no independent witnesses. It was a suspect claim, but we settled fast for €45,000."

"What was the name of the claimant?"

"A Sean Moran, date of birth 4 April, 1976. We have an address in Lucan, Co. Dublin ... I can't believe we paid this claim Andy, it looks all wrong."

"You can say that again Willie! I will fill you in after our football match on Saturday. But tell me did you have him medically examined?"

"Yes, it was a fast track claim as no lawyers were involved. The doctor was a Dr. Mohammad Yipsee in Kildare Town."

I then asked the crucial question.

"Willie do you have a record of Sean Moran's nationality?"

There was a pause for a few moments as Willie read the file.

"That's strange – on the medical report he is down as Canadian, yet on the claim form he is American."

"Willie that is powerful information. Please hold onto your file as I will need it for evidence."

"I will call it back from storage Andy."

"Thanks Willie."

I sat back in my chair delighted with the information I had obtained. It now looked like John Harrison had also obtained the identity of Sean Moran and was using it to make fraudulent insurance claims. The Cowboy was good — exceptionally good.

I called Tanya and Denise over to my desk.

"Well guys, I think we have just gotten another large piece of intelligence on John Harrison."

I quickly filled them in on the Insurance Link information and what Willie from Starling had told me.

"Andy you keep finding more insurance claims. How many more cases are there?" Tanya asked.

"That's why I like my job Tanya you never know what will happen next. It's like a good mystery novel."

This case was getting more and more interesting. Establishing more on the identities of Sean Moran and Sally Wall would be my priority after I found out everything I could on Kenneth Smith.

CHAPTER 13

૭૪૦

The following day, I arrived into the office at 7.15am. Security had just about opened the building. I always enjoy arriving early as it's very quiet and you have plenty of time to gather your thoughts for the day ahead. I unlocked my filing cabinet and pulled out the Harrison file which was growing larger by the day. Unfortunately the canteen was not yet open, so I had to do with a coffee from the machine and it was disgusting.

I logged onto my computer and retrieved my emails — the usual claim notifications, loss adjuster problems and requests to use private investigators. The last email I opened was from Nigel. He had obtained a formal statement from Sandra Hynes of Swan's View Farm and Nick Berry, the owner of the flat in Liverpool. Both statements made interesting reading and Nigel advised he would courier them over to me. The statements from Nigel were excellent and provided critical evidence which would be most valuable to the case and the potential presentation of evidence in court.

I decided to carry out a full collation of the evidence and intelligence I had obtained over the past few weeks of the investigation. As I sat looking at the file, Denise came in. It was just after 7.30am. This was a most unusual start time for her, but I was pleased to see her. She sat down and I noticed she looked a bit sad.

"What's wrong?"

"I had a bad fall in my horse riding competition last night."

"You look fine to me."

"I am fine, apart from the embarrassment of falling off my horse in public. It's Jessie my horse; she hurt her leg in the fall."

Denise was a keen horseperson and was considering entering the professional show jumping circuit. If Denise's horse was injured, maybe with a broken leg, then the horse might have to be destroyed. I was afraid to ask how badly injured Jessie was as I knew Denise loved her horse like a parent loves a child.

"The vet looked at him last night and took some X-rays of his leg. I am hoping it's not broken. I couldn't sleep, so I came into work early. I am going over to Starbucks, do you want a coffee?"

This sounded like music to my ears as I was too lazy to walk the 200 metres or so to the café.

"Black coffee with one brown sugar please and get yourself a coffee on me," I said as I took a €10 note from my pocket.

"Thanks Andy; it's tea I drink."

I put the rancid machine coffee straight into the bin, got a fresh notebook and pen and spent the next two hours listing the intelligence I had obtained on the claim. Running over the information and intelligence obtained gave me time to search for clues. I now had three accidents, with three different insurance companies, involving the American claimant:

Claim (1)
Insurer: Dallast Insurance Ireland
Insured: Nigel Boroski
Address: Craddockstown, Naas, Co. Kildare
Nationality: Polish citizen
Claimant: John Harrison
Nationality: American citizen
Date of Accident: 5 December, 2008
Accident Location: The Curragh, Co. Kildare
Accident Details: Pedestrian who was knocked down by a car.
Injuries: Back injury, leg and kidney problems.
Contact email: JHarr@hopmill.com
Financial Reserve: €750,000

Claim (2)
Insurer: Mustang Insurance Ireland
Insured: Jenny Boroski
Address: Naas, Co. Kildare
Nationality: Polish citizen
Claimant: Kenneth Smith
Nationality: Irish-American
Date of Birth: 30 June, 1975
Claimant Address: 12 Pinebrooke, Monaghan Town, Co. Monaghan
Date of Accident: 5 May, 2008
Accident Details: Pedestrian who was knocked down by a car.
Injuries: Back injury
Financial Payment: €55,000 plus medical costs

Claim (3)
Insurer: Starling Insurance Ireland
Insured: Sally Wall
Address: Newbridge, Co. Kildare
Nationality: Irish citizen
Claimant: Sean Moran
Date of Birth: 4 April, 1976
Nationality: American or Canadian citizen
Address: Lucan, Co. Dublin
Date of Accident: 25 September 2006
Accident Location: The Curragh, Co. Kildare
Accident Details: Pedestrian who was knocked down by a car.
Injury: Back injury
Financial Payment: €45,000

I've found that when you write down all the information you
have obtained during an investigation the common denomi-
nators quickly become apparent. The common factors of this
case where staring me in the face:

The claimant was either American or Canadian.

- All of the accidents had the same modus operandi.
- The claimant was a pedestrian who was knocked
  down by a car driven by a woman.
- There were no independent witnesses.
- The police or other emergency services had not
  been called.
- The claimant had sustained a back injury in all three
  accidents.
- The claimant looked for a fast settlement and never
  engaged the services of a lawyer.
- John Harrison had somehow obtained multiple iden-
  tities.

I pulled out Harrison's marriage certificate and examined it again. It was the most crucial piece of evidence I had as it showed that our insured was the brother-in-law of the claimant.

After the review there was no doubt in my mind that the case was clearly displaying all the hallmarks of fraud by way of staged accidents. My next move would normally be to bring in the police. I would prepare a file of civil evidence and findings and then present it to the Garda Bureau of Fraud Investigation (GBFI) for their consideration. I was contemplating this but something, perhaps the fact that I was an investigator at heart, was stopping me. I also did not want to pass my case onto a police detective who would possibly not give it the same treatment or attention. I had enough information to prevent any payment on the insurance claim against my company but something was driving me to keep going. I was sure there was more intelligence to be established. I decided to hold off on contacting the Gardaí and do a bit more digging myself.

In the three claims the respective insurance companies, including our own, had made payments by way of cheque. This meant we could put a trace on the cheques involved to see where they had been lodged. We had made two payments to Sean Moran in the UK which would most likely mean the cheques were lodged into a UK bank account so I put a call into Liz in our accounts department.

"Hi Liz. Andy here in SIU."

"Morning Andy, what can I do for you?"

"I need to place a trace on two cheques which we made payable to a claimant who was in the UK."

"Should not be a problem Andy. Did we make the payment in Sterling or Euro?"

"The payments were in Euro."

"Right, I have just emailed you the request sheet which you need to complete and send back to me."

As I was talking to Liz the email arrived. I opened the Microsoft Word attachment, expecting a large questionnaire. However there were only a couple of questions, including a request for the claim number, date of payment and the name on the cheque.

"Thank you Liz I have that document. How long will it take to obtain the information?"

"Not long Andy, get the document back to me as soon as you can and I will forward it to our bank."

"Thanks Liz!"

I'd just sent her the completed request sheet when Courtney called me over.

I walked into his office and thought he looked agitated.

"Sit down Andy and close the door. We have got a problem," he sighed.

I've found that the word we, when said by a senior manager, normally means they have got a problem and they are going to get some comfort by spreading the risk down the line.

"What's the problem?"

"Dallast Global has appointed a new Global Head of Fraud Operations. He's an American guy, a tough cookie and he won't take any prisoners. We need to review our position. Your target for fraud savings this year is €10,000,000, are you on target?"

The €10 million target was large but I thought it would be achievable as we had some potential large savings in the pipeline which I had not yet disclosed to Courtney.

"Not too bad, a little behind target but I am comfortable we will reach it by the end of the year," I said as calmly as possible.

"Well that's good news because I have worked with this new fraud guy before and I know he will want to make a name for himself, so expect at least another 20 per cent to be added to your target before the end of the year."

"20 per cent," I almost shouted, "but that's impossible; that's €12 million."

"Pebble, you may have to make it possible. I hear you are doing good work on the Harrison file. Keep on digging and get me a result. We are all going to need the saving from that file."

Courtney undocked his laptop and placed it in his bag.

"Are you finished for the day?"

"Yes, you got a problem with that?"

"No, not at all Dan," I said quickly. "It's just you're normally here till late in the evening or should I say early night."

"Not today Andy, I have got some business to take care of."

"Thanks for the information on our new Global Head of Fraud," I said and left.

I walked back to my desk and decided that as soon as Courtney left the office I would be right behind him. I had been putting in some long hours and I wanted to take full advantage of his early exit.

I needed the win on the Harrison case more than ever now. Not just a simple win, but a good strike out of the claim which would give me a large saving. A criminal conviction for fraud against Harrison would also be very nice for my reputation, especially with the new Global Head of Fraud to pacify. It would get my name known for the right reasons.

As I spent the next 70 minutes battling the traffic to drive the 15 miles to my home, I was trying to work out how Harrison had opened a bank account in the UK under the name of Sean Moran. Hopefully Liz would come back with something tomorrow.

CHAPTER 14

❧

I was still playing my game of chess with Harrison as I investigated his insurance frauds — I was contemplating his every move and becoming more aware of the potential risks at stake. At this stage I was still gathering intelligence on my adversary John Harrison but I was also considering a more direct approach.

Our accounts side were pursuing the cheque angle and there were plenty of other loose ends to be followed up. I still could not understand how Harrison had managed to open bank accounts in the different names without having identification. It is a requirement of money laundering legislation that in order to open a bank account you must present photographic identification, such as a passport or driver's license. I wondered if Harrison had managed to get a copy of a driver's license. I realised the only way I could establish this information would be with the assistance of a confidential source. Unfortunately I did not have any contacts in the local banks so this was going to be difficult. At present there is no legal way for an Irish investigator to obtain information from banks. Instead I decided trying my contacts in the US and the UK would be a good idea as they might be able to assist me.

I phoned Nigel who, to my amazement, failed to answer his mobile. He always answered his phone so I left a message asking if anything was wrong and requesting that he contact me.

I decided to drive back to Naas, Co. Kildare. I had another case in the area and I wanted to go back to Nigel Boroski's house and see if I could find out any more information.

I arrived there just after 10am. I rang the front door and got no answer. Two young boys were playing football on the green outside the house and one of them shouted over: "Mister they're gone to work and won't be back till late tonight."

As I was looking at the house I noticed the line of buildings located to the rear so I decided to walk around and call into the houses there.

I worked out the house that was directly behind the Boroski's and rang the doorbell.

A lady in her late fifties answered.

"Hello and sorry for disturbing you. I am a fraud investigator with Dallast Insurance. I am trying to locate an American man who may have been living in the house behind you."

"What bank are you working for?"

"No I am with Dallast Insurance."

"Well that makes a change," she smiled.

"Excuse me?" I asked, feeling a little bit excited.

"I have had several people from banks and credit card companies calling here, looking to speak to an American who used to live in that house."

"What bank were they from?"

"I am not sure but I do recall it happened on four or five occasions."

"Do you remember the name of the American the bank people were looking for?"

"His name? Let me see ... well it wasn't Bill Clinton!"

"Please, this could be really important."

She thought for a few seconds, while I prayed she would come up with something.

"No I can't remember."

I was really disappointed.

"Did you ever meet the American guy?" I asked, without much hope.

The lady shook her head saying: "No I am sorry ... though wait a minute ... yes I shouted at him once from my bedroom window. I told him to turn down the music."

"What did he look like?"

"I didn't get to see him up close; I just remember that stupid cowboy hat."

Maybe it was him!

"Can you hold on for a minute while I run back to my car to get a photograph to show you?"

"OK," she agreed.

I had parked outside Boroski's house which was only a short walk away but it felt as if it took ages to get there. I quickly grabbed the wedding photograph and raced back around the corner.

"Is this the man?" I asked as I handed her the photograph.

She looked at it and immediately said: "I don't know. I never got to meet him, but ... I am sure that is the hat, a cowboy hat like the one JR Ewing wore in *Dallas*; yes that is the hat I am sure."

I handed her my business card, thanked her for the assistance and asked her to give my phone number to any bank employees who called to her home in the future.

I returned to my car happy with the additional information. The next-door neighbour had previously told me an American was living at the address and now I had a second witness. I didn't think it was worthwhile obtaining a statement from her as she could not remember what the American looked like, but she did remember the hat which was a strong indicator. So now I had tenuous proof that our insured, Nigel Boroski, was living with John Harrison, even though they claimed not to know each other.

As I was driving back to Dublin my mobile rang — it was Nigel.

"Hi Nigel, how are things?"

"Great Andy and I have some interesting news for you. I spoke to my contact in CCD Insurance UK about that claim from Gary O'Neill from the apartment on Anfield Road, Liverpool. They've now decided the claim is suspect and it has been referred to their SIU. I can't get much more information at this stage, just give me some more time."

I quickly brought Nigel up-to-date on the developments on my side of the Irish Sea.

"Yep it looks like you went fishing Andy and caught Jaws!"

A short while later I arrived back into the Dublin office. I waited for my e-mail to open, hoping that there might be an update from accounts. It was business as usual for everyone else. Denise was busy working at her desk and Denton was out at an investigation in North Dublin. I decided not to ask Denise about her horse as she still looked a bit upset.

My email finally downloaded and there was a message from accounts. I quickly opened it and read that the two cheques we had paid to Sean Moran had been presented and lodged at a Lloyds bank branch in the UK. The details retrieved included the account number and bank sort code where the cheques had been lodged. I quickly dialled Nigel's mobile and gave him the new information.

"Good man Andy. I'll make a formal application to the bank under Section 29 of the British Data Protection Act."

"Thanks Nigel. That would be great."

Section 29 allows for certain information to be released in the UK for the detection and or prevention of a crime. I was glad the cheques had been lodged in the UK because the Data Protection Act in Ireland was somewhat confusing. Although it reads the same as the British equivalent, the request for more information can only be signed off by a senior ranking police office or army officer. I think this is wrong as the people who need access to the information are financial investigators who are at the sharp end, investigating financial criminal activity as it is happening. The Gardaí and other law enforcement agencies do their very best, but because of funding and resource issues they cannot cover all suspected fraud cases in a timely manner. The Irish Data Protection legislation gives the criminals a direct advantage over the financial investigators.

With Nigel on board I was now very excited at the prospect of establishing how Sean Moran, aka John Harrison, had managed to open a bank account in the UK. It was possible that we were not only looking at insurance fraud, but other financial crimes which would be covered under the Irish Fraud and Theft Offences Act. As an investigator I found it strange that identity theft is not actually a criminal offence under the terms of the Act. It's the deception for unlawful financial advantage that is obtained from using somebody's identity that is the criminal act.

"How did you get on with the Waters claim in Naas?" Denise suddenly asked.

I was stunned. I had completely forgotten about my other case in Naas. Rather than give her a lame excuse I decided to tell the truth.

"Denise, with all the developments on the Harrison file, I completely forgot about the Waters claim."

Denise looked shocked.

"It's a simple case that only requires a standard signed statement. Why don't you go and get it?" I suggested, holding out my car keys.

"Is this a joke?" she asked, obviously unsure whether or not I was serious as intelligence investigators did not generally leave the office.

"You want to be a field investigator don't you?" I asked, as I placed the keys on her desk. "Well go out and get the statement."

"Are you serious?"

"Just be back by lunchtime as I will need my car."

She did not need a third invitation and practically ran out of the office.

I was working at my desk updating other files and carrying out some financial reporting, when my mobile rang.

"Nigel that was fast!"

"I have some information for you Andy, with more to follow. I made contact with one of the senior fraud managers at Lloyds who has agreed to provide some information. The cheques were lodged into a branch current account in Liverpool."

"I know the cheques were lodged into Lloyd's Nigel, our accounts gave me the details."

"Yes Andy but what you don't know is that after that just over €10,000 was transferred to a bank in Warsaw Poland.

The current account is now overdrawn and Lloyds have suspended all transactions from it."

"This is great information Nigel; so do we have an address for the bank in Warsaw?"

"Unfortunately we don't Andy."

I had a horrible, empty feeling in my stomach.

"Nigel, we know his wife is pregnant and is Polish, so obviously they have gone to Poland to have the baby. They might never come back to Ireland."

"Yes I know, but we don't have any more addresses. We are at a loss Andy."

"Shit!" I said loudly, causing a few of the staff to look in my direction. "Do you have any contacts in Warsaw?"

"Sorry mate can't help you with this one … Andy we don't even know if the money was lodged into a Lloyd's bank account in Poland."

"There must be over two million people living in Warsaw, this will be impossible," I said bitterly and sighed.

"I know, but even though we have drawn a blank on the Polish situation I am hopeful I will get some more information from my contact in CCD Insurance so perhaps that will help. Talk to you soon Andy."

"Cheers Nigel," I said and hung up.

I was really disappointed as it looked like the case had hit a brick wall.

CHAPTER 15

D enise returned to the office and handed me my car keys.
"Hi Denise, did you enjoy your trip out of the office?"

"Yes and I got a great statement which will really help the
case … you know what they say Andy, if you want a job done
properly, get a woman to do it!"

I threw an empty paper coffee cup at her, just as Courtney walked by. To my surprise he didn't stop but just growled:
"Kindergarten!"

I was still disappointed about the dead end on Operation
Cowboy. The case had gone international now. I wondered
if Harrison was in Warsaw or had he transferred the money
to another account in Poland or somewhere else in Europe? I
was fairly sure that he was not in the UK or Ireland and was
most likely in Poland, but I knew he could have gone back to
the US. I really needed some assistance in tracing him and it
sounded like a job for the FBI.

I decided to give Kelly O'Dwyer a call to thank her for the assistance she had given me on the marriage certificate.

"Good morning Kelly. It's Andy, how are you?"

"Oh hi Andy, how are you doing? Did you get the documents from Sheriff Belling?"

"I did Kelly and thank you so very much for the assistance."

"Oh, you're welcome Andy. I am glad that the FBI could be of some help. How are you getting on with your case? Did you get that Harrison guy yet?"

"No I think he has gone to Poland. He transferred some money into an account in Warsaw but we can't trace the money any further."

"Why not?"

"Because I have no contacts in Poland."

"I may be able to help you out again Andy, as my husband was stationed in Berlin, Germany, at our FBI field office in the Embassy. He may know somebody that can help you in Poland."

I sat up straight in surprise.

"Kelly that would be great. I would really appreciate it."

"Leave it with me for a few hours and I will call you back."

I hung up and began to feel excited at the prospect of getting a lead on Harrison. Courtney would be really impressed if I could trace the Cowboy to an address in Warsaw and then get some photographs of him. It would be crucial evidence and would link Harrison to his Polish wife and incriminate him for using the false identity of Sean Moran and for opening a bank account in a false name.

If Kelly got me some information on Harrison's location in Poland, I wondered if I should go there myself. It had been a long time since I'd worked undercover. I'd done it many times in my Pinkerton days but now I didn't even know where my surveillance camera had ended up. The budget wouldn't be a problem as I still had approval for €20,000 to investigate the case. I didn't know of any good Polish private investigators but perhaps Kelly knew someone.

I decided to send an email to the European Chapter of the International Association of Special Investigations Units (IASIU). I had recently met with a German investigator through IASIU Europe and I was fairly sure he would have a contact in Poland who could provide me with the necessary surveillance service.

Having sent the email I then met with Denton to discuss a case about a fire investigation and how it was developing. Thankfully the forensics report was showing some good information which was starting to develop into evidence. The house had been destroyed by a fire which at first had appeared to have been caused by a gas leak. However our fire forensic investigators had established that the cooker had been left on and that a gas pipe appeared to have been cut before the fire occurred. Although this was not enough to prove that our insured had caused the fire it was a significant development.

"What else should I do?"

"Have you interviewed the neighbours?"

"No."

"I would go and talk to them and to try and obtain more statements. Are there any signs of forced entry to the house?"

"The roof is gone, so maybe they came in that way!" he laughed.

"Denton this is a serious matter. You need to keep an open mind and consider all the options."

"Sorry Andy, yes you're right it is serious. I am just not sure what to do next."

"Contact the emergency services control room. Try to find out who dialled the emergency services. Find this person as they may have some valuable information and get a formal statement of fact from them."

"I did that already, it's on the file," Denton smiled.

"That statement is rubbish; there is no attention to detail. Go back to the insured and ask him who had access to the property and who was living there at the time of the fire. On the access you also need to establish who had keys to the house and was the front or rear door left open."

This was crucial information as according to our forensic investigators the fire was arson. For an insurance company proving arson is not enough; to stop the payment of the claim, the insurance company needs to prove arson by the insured.

"That's going to be difficult," he said. "But I'll see what I can find out."

I eagerly checked my email after the short meeting and as expected my IASIU contact had responded quickly. He had suggested four firms of private investigators who could carry out surveillance on Harrison in Poland. It was just a matter of agreeing the fee and expenses. My only problem now was that I did not know the Cowboy's current location.

I decided to look back through my notes and reports. The words of retired Garda Chief Superintendent Michael Casey were in my mind: "Look at the smallest of details and you will find the answer." Michael had also said that sometimes you have an important lead which you may have missed: "Keep on examining your reports and above all keep a notebook of your findings."

I read Sandra Hynes' statement again, hoping I'd missed something. I double-checked she'd rented a room to a Sean Moran, aka Kenneth Smith. Sandra had also advised that he was staying at her place with his pregnant Polish wife. I suddenly realised that I had some significant information that I had missed. Our man John Harrison had been driving a red Irish-registered Alfa Romeo 156. I decided to give Sandra a call to confirm it.

Luckily she picked up immediately.

"Hi Sandra, I am with Dallast Insurance in Ireland. You met with my colleague Nigel at your home address of Swan's View Farm, Liverpool."

"Oh, are you an investigator from Ireland?"

"Yes I am based in Dublin."

I could tell she was a bit surprised to hear from me but she sounded friendly.

"How can I help you Andy?"

"I am currently trying to trace a man known to you as Sean Moran."

"Oh him! He has gone to Poland with his pregnant wife, as she wants to have the baby in Poland."

"By any chance do you have an address for them in Poland?"

"No, sorry."

"Just one further question, can you remember the make of the car he was driving?"

"Yes it was a red or maybe pink-coloured Alfa Romeo with an Irish registration number."

"Pink are you sure?"

"Well I think it was originally red, but the colour has faded and now it's a pinkie-red."

"Can you remember the number plate?"

"No I am sorry … I cannot remember the number but it was a strange registration plate as it only had a single letter, a D I think, and then some numbers."

"Thanks Sandra that's a great help. I'll let you know if there are any developments," I said as I hung up.

Irish vehicle registration numbers have two numbers for the year, then one or two letters to identity the county where the vehicle was registered and then more numbers. For example a vehicle registered in Dublin in 2012, may read 12 D 12345. The information Sandra had given me was important as I was now satisfied Harrison was in Poland with his pregnant wife and he had not gone back to America. I also knew he was driving an Alfa Romeo with a Dublin registration plate. If I could locate the Polish town he was staying in then an American driving a pinkie-red Irish-registered Alfa Romeo should be easy to locate!

I left the office at 5.30pm and began the journey home. The Presenter George Hook was on the radio talking to Michael O'Leary of Ryanair. I enjoy listening to George as he talks straight and says it how it is. O'Leary was talking about the poor state of our National Health Service. I knew exactly what he meant as my Grandmother had recently died, having spent three nights on a trolley in the Accident and Emergency Department of a Dublin Hospital. Just as George was getting to the interesting part of the conversation my mobile rang.

I answered and someone with an American accent asked: "Is this Andy Stone?"

"Yes it is," I said quickly.

There was a pause and then the voice said: "You are looking for somebody in Poland."

"Yes, who is this?"

"You do not need to know my name but I will get you the information you need on Harrison's Polish address. Can you catch a flight to Warsaw?"

I was so obsessed with the case I answered without even thinking about it.

"Yes."

"OK organise a flight for next Tuesday and I will meet you in Warsaw Airport."

The phone went dead before I could ask any more questions.

I turned off my radio and dialled Kelly's number. She failed to answer so I left a message asking that she call me urgently.

At this stage I could only assume that the American guy at the other end of the phone was a contact of Kelly's or one of her FBI friends.

I arrived home and walked straight into the office, without even saying hello to the wife and kids. I quickly logged onto the Aer Lingus website and located a flight to Warsaw for Tuesday morning. It was the only direct flight from Dublin to Warsaw that day so I was sure it was the right one. I scrambled through my wallet for my credit card and booked the flight with an open return ticket. It was costly, but then I was uncertain when I was going to be flying back.

To say my wife was annoyed when I told her was putting it mildly. Here I was going off to meet a man with an American accent, whose name I did not know, or who I knew nothing else about, other than the fact that he would meet me in Warsaw Airport. Jackie gave me the silent treatment for a few hours which was well-deserved as I was putting myself at personal risk. I was fairly sure Courtney was not going to sanction the trip either as it would be considered too risky for an insurance company employee. However nobody was going to stop me going, even if I had to take an annual leave day.

The following day I arrived at the office late because one of my children was sick. I was about to sit down at my desk when Courtney signalled for me to come to his office.

"Give me the developments on the Harrison file," Courtney ordered, as I sat down.

I took a deep breath and started talking about the different names and identities and the fact that Harrison was now possibly in Poland driving a red, Irish-registered Alfa Romeo.

"Now tell me something I don't know," Courtney said.

"How do you know this information?"

"While you have been out chasing your tail on this case, Tanya and Denise have given me a full update on the developments ... well Andy you're doing a good job."

I was surprised as it was unusual go get a compliment from him.

"So Harrison is in Poland ... interesting."

I was not sure if I should tell Courtney that I'd booked a trip to Poland as I was certain he would object. I decided to stay silent.

"Well that is where his wife is from and we are told she wanted to have the baby in Poland."

"I reckon Harrison has got an idea you are on to him."

"Why's that Dan?"

"Well we have not heard from him in a while so maybe he thinks you are looking for him."

"Perhaps he does."

"Well you did a good job on this file and I think we've got enough to prevent payment so close it."

"Close the file," I repeated, feeling dismayed.

"Yes, it's time for you to move on to another case."

This was not what I'd expected or wanted to hear.

"With respect Sir, I think we have got a big fraudster here and I... "

"...cut the Sir shit Andy, what do you want?"

"I need some more time to complete my full case which includes possible false claims against other insurance companies."

"I don't much care about other insurance companies. I know you think you're one of *The Untouchables* Andy but not on my dime... " Courtney smiled, sounding more American than usual.

"No I am just trying to do my job, and yes you are correct we could close our file now, but just give me a little more time ... please Dan."

"How long?"

"I need another month."

"OK you have two weeks and that is it; after that close the damn file."

I nodded and left his office at top speed. Thank God I hadn't told him about my trip to Warsaw.

It was Friday afternoon so I decided to leave early as I had planned to take my wife out for dinner to try to convince her that the trip to Poland was safe. I was a bit creative with the information I gave her and said that I was meeting with a Polish police detective who was fluent in English and knew Harrison's current location. Thankfully this information appeared to satisfy her.

As usual the weekend passed too quickly and I was back sitting at my home office desk on Monday morning. My mobile rang just before lunch — it was Kelly.

"Hi Kelly."

"Andy how are you doing?"

"Not bad just looking out the window at the Irish rain"

"Oh how pretty it sounds!"

"Pretty is not a word I would associate with the Irish weather," I laughed.

"You know Andy when you have lived in a desert you really get to appreciate the rain," Kelly laughed.

"Nobody in Ireland appreciates the rain! Anyway thank you so much Kelly. Your contact phoned me about the meeting in Warsaw."

"What contact?"

"A man with a strong American accent rang me and agreed to meet me in Warsaw Airport tomorrow, to try to find Harrison's location in Poland."

There was a silence at the other end of the phone.

"Andy I was calling you to say I could not help you with Poland, as I checked with my husband and we don't have any contacts there anymore."

My heart started to race, not with excitement but with fear. Who was going to meet me in Warsaw Airport the following day?

"Are you sure?"

"I can't help you with this one Andy, any contacts we had have moved back to the States. Andy you're not considering making the trip are you?"

"Well I need to get more intelligence on Harrison."

"How do you know it's not a trap?"

"Come on Kelly, this is insurance fraud not the stuff you Feds are dealing with every day."

"Crime is crime Andy. I wouldn't go without having some local back-up."

I thanked Kelly for her concern and hung up without committing myself either way.

For the first time in my long career investigating insurance fraud I felt scared. Maybe I should pull out of the meeting in Warsaw? Just who had I talked to on the phone? I was aware they were American and male, but that was all the information I had. I played back the recording of the telephone conversation I'd had with Harrison just in case he was setting me up. But as I listened I was sure Harrison's American accent was completely different. My anonymous caller had sounded like he was from somewhere in the north of America.

I spent the rest of the night wondering if I should pull out. But at 6.00am the following morning I was sitting in the Departures' lounge of Dublin Airport waiting to board my flight to Warsaw. Rather than feeling excited about my trip I was sitting there biting my nails. Should I chance the meeting in Warsaw or just stay in Ireland? Perhaps Courtney was correct and I should just close the file.

I sat considering my options and started to feel really agitated. I had bitten my nails to the point that they were hurting my fingers. I was thinking of the British SAS motto 'he who dares wins' as the first passengers moved towards the boarding gate.

I was still deliberating when the Hostess announced: "Will the last remaining passengers travelling on Aer Lingus flight EI 362 please board, as the aircraft is waiting to depart."

I decided what the hell and jumped up. I could go to Warsaw Airport and stay in a public area. If I ran into problems I was sure that the Polish airport police would assist me. I quickly presented my boarding card and entered the aircraft.

The flight to Warsaw was uneventful. We landed bang on time, at 11.15am. I was surprised at how modern the airport looked. I had been half-expecting a 'Cold War' style, like I'd seen in old war movies.

I collected my bag, was quickly processed through immigration and was in the Arrivals all within minutes. It was not very busy and there were only a few people holding cards displaying printed names. I checked the cards but my name wasn't there. I started to feel uneasy as the hall quickly emptied, leaving me and a few people who had arrived on another flight.

After another 15 minutes waiting I walked over to the information desk and asked if anybody was expecting an Andy Stone from Ireland. The lady sitting behind the desk shook her head. No help there.

I was aware that the only flight back to Dublin that day would be leaving in one hour. I decided to stay for one night in Warsaw Airport and if nobody contacted me I would travel back the following day. I went over to the Aer Lingus ticket desk to reserve a seat with my flexible return ticket.

"Let me check the system Sir. Yes there is good availability on the Dublin flight tomorrow. Would you like me to reserve you a seat?"

"No thank you. I just needed to check availability"

"You should have no problem. Just contact me in the morning if you need to take the flight."

"Thank you."

I started to feel disappointed as I walked back to the information desk to get a recommendation for a hotel. Coming over to Poland was looking like a complete waste of time and money.

I placed my bag on the floor just as a woman with a British accent asked: "Mr. Stone?"

I turned and saw a beautiful, young blonde standing in front of me. We shook hands as she said: "Mr. Stone my name is Elaine."

"Pleased to meet you," I mumbled.

"Please come with me; I have a car waiting for you outside."

I started to feel a little uneasy but I walked along with her.

"Are you British?" I asked.

"No I am German but I learned English in London so I guess I have a British accent."

We walked outside the terminal and she ushered me into the rear of a black BMW. It was a high-end five series, with full leather interior. I was unable to get the registration number but I decided to get into the car anyway. Elaine got into the driver's seat and accelerated hard as we quickly left the airport behind.

The situation felt surreal — here I was leaving Warsaw Airport, in a top of the range BMW, been driven by a beautiful, young blonde lady who spoke excellent English. Although I was still feeling uneasy I was starting to think that I was on Ashton Kutcher's *Punk'd* show.

We were driving along a motorway at speeds of 90mph.

"Elaine, are you not worried about the police?" I asked, leaning forward.

"I am the police … well sort of police," she laughed.

"What do you mean sort of police?"

"Yes to police, but maybe not police in this country."

I sat back feeling reassured.

"Where are we going Elaine?"

"You needed some information so I am taking you to get that information."

She glanced in the mirror and could obviously see I was a little on edge because she added: "Mr. Stone relax. We will be at our destination shortly."

"Elaine please stop calling me Mr. Stone — call me Andy."

She nodded her head and smiled.

After about 30 minutes we arrived in a small town which looked more like the Poland I was expecting. It appeared run down and old-fashioned, as if it was still in the 1940s.

We parked outside a small coffee shop.

"Come on Andy let's go."

I followed Elaine inside as she greeted the man serving behind the counter, speaking in Polish.

"Andy come and sit at that small table at the back."

I walked over and Elaine sat down beside me.

The man from behind the counter came over with three coffees.

"Who are we waiting for?" I asked Elaine.

The man who was serving the coffee said in perfect English: "You are waiting for me." He then walked over and locked the door. I started to feel nervous again, which must have been obvious because Elaine reached out and gripped my hand.

"Relax Andy, it's OK."

The man sat down and, in a strong American accent, said: "Welcome to Poland Andrew Stone."

"Who are you?"

"We are your friends; my name is Fred."

Feeling a little braver I said: "Yes and my name is George Bush!"

"It's best if you do not know our real names so you will call me Fred and this is Elaine."

"How do you know me?"

"A friend put us in contact with you."

"What friend?"

"Andy there are some things you need to know and some you don't. All you need to know is that you are safe and we will assist you. When is your flight home?"

"I have an open ticket."

"You will go home on the Thursday flight," Fred ordered.

I felt more relaxed when I heard there was a plan for me to return to Ireland.

"OK well how can you guys help me?"

"You are interested in an American citizen named John Harrison," Fred said, as he stood up.

"Yes I am trying to find him."

"He is living in a small town about a five hour drive from here called Kostrzyn," Fred said calmly.

I couldn't believe it – they'd found him. I could feel my heart starting to race with excitement.

"How do you know this?"

"An American driving a red Irish car in Poland, this is very easy," Elaine laughed and Fred joined in.

"We do not have an interest in Mr. Harrison; although we will keep an eye on him. We are more interested in knowing his associates. Harrison would only be considered an amateur at our level," he said.

"Your level? What are you guys? CIA or Interpol?"

"It does not matter. Now Elaine will drive you to Kostryzn and will assist with your surveillance. Do you need any equipment?"

"I don't have any equipment with me, other than my new Blackberry," I replied.

"Not an issue," Fred said and turned to Elaine: "Use the Nikon and take the 300mm lens that should be fine."

She nodded in agreement and stood up. I got up too and Fred put out his hand: "May the best of Irish good luck be with you Andy."

"Thank you ... Fred," I said shaking his hand

I got back into the rear of the BMW as Elaine said: "Make yourself comfortable. We have got a long drive ahead of us."

As we were driving along at what seemed crazy speeds to me, I tried to make some small talk. I realised I should have sat in the front instead of been driven around like some politician but it was too late to change that now. I'd just have to make the best of it.

"Have you ever been in Poland before Andy?"

"No, but it looks like a place worth visiting."

"Poland is a beautiful country which has a sad history," Elaine nodded, "most recently because of what Nazi Germany did in World War II."

"Yes I know that but I feel a bit ignorant as my only education on Poland and on mainland Europe in general is from movies and the History Channel."

"So you do not travel abroad on vacations in Ireland?"

"Yes we do but I have spent many holidays in America and the Caribbean."

"Do you like America?"

"I love America, in particular Texas, Arizona and California. I just love flying into an American airport, picking up a Ford Mustang and heading off. There is such freedom there. I don't book hotels, just my flight and car and away I go."

I thought back to my single days travelling around America when I worked for Pinkerton but Elaine brought me back to reality by asking: "You got any kids?"

"Yes two beautiful girls, aged 6 and 3, and a great wife who is very supportive," I smiled.

"Ah that is nice, and in particular it is so no nice to hear a man speak openly of his wife. Most of the assholes I know are married but seem to forget that when they are away from home."

She accelerated hard as we passed a VW Golf and muttered something in what sounded like German.

"What is the speed limit in Poland?" I asked smiling.

"I don't know … maybe 60 mph … relax Andy you are very tense."

I laughed as I caught her eye in the rear view mirror: "Relax! Elaine, here I am somewhere in the middle of Poland, been driven by an amazing looking woman at crazy speeds, who works with a man called Fred who seems to be a gangster or something like that. I have never met either of you before and you want me to relax!"

She started to laugh too.

"We are not gangsters or terrorists. We are your friends; if you like America then we will like you too."

These words did make me relax a little, maybe Fred and Elaine were FBI or more likely CIA. Over the years I'd had many dealings with the FBI, United States Secret Service and other police forces but never the CIA.

Elaine turned on the radio and I must have drifted off for a few hours as it was late afternoon when I woke up again. Elaine slowed down a little and we turned off the motorway.

"I hope you enjoyed your snooze. We will be in Kostrzyn in about 20 minutes. We only have a window of 24hrs as I have another operation to work on and you need to catch your flight back to Dublin."

I was happy that Elaine had mentioned my flight home again but I still wondered why they had contacted me and who had given them my name and number? What was John

Harrison to them? Should I ask Elaine? I decided to stay silent on the subject until I knew more.

We arrived in Kostrzyn and Elaine turned the car into a large hotel car park.

"You are booked into this hotel under the name of David Jones. Go and check-in and I will see you in reception in one hour."

"But where are you going?"

"I will be back shortly, now go and check-in!"

"I don't have a credit card in the name of David Jones."

"Don't worry all will be fine, now please check-in."

I entered the hotel and was greeted by a friendly receptionist. I identified myself as David Jones and she handed me a key.

"Mr. Jones you are in Room 401, on the fourth floor."

I found it strange that I was not asked for a copy of a credit card or my passport for identification. Maybe she knew Fred.

The hotel was very pleasant and appeared to have been refurbished recently. I decided to take a shower but quickly changed my mind when I saw the Jacuzzi bath tub. Now I was starting to truly feel a little like James Bond. All I was missing was the glass of champagne.

As I sat in the bath tub I laughed to myself: "This is the life!" But then I suddenly wondered how I was going to explain the cost of the hotel to Courtney!

Having changed I walked to the reception and met with Elaine who was sitting in the bar drinking a glass of wine.

"What would you like to drink Andy?"

"I would love an American beer but I would settle for a glass of wine," I smiled.

Elaine called the waiter and spoke in Polish. The only word I recognised was Budweiser.

"Budweiser in Poland?"

"Yes we drink it too or would you prefer a glass of Guinness?"

"No Budweiser is just fine but Elaine how am I going to pay for this hotel as my credit card is not in the name of David Jones?"

"Not a problem — your bill is covered."

"Who is paying my bill?"

"A friend," Elaine said, obviously closing the discussion. "Now we need to talk about the surveillance operation."

"A friend, what friend?"

"It does not matter, all will be revealed in time."

I clearly wasn't going to get anything else out of her so I re-focused on the reason I was in Poland — to locate John Harrison and to arrange some surveillance.

"Igor is late," Elaine said, looking at her watch.

"Who is Igor?"

"Igor is one of our operatives based here in Poland. He is ex-Russian army intelligence and is excellent at surveillance."

"Russian intelligence? Is that like the KGB?"

"Yes that is correct — KGB."

KGB! This was getting stranger and stranger. I couldn't believe I was going to be working on a surveillance job with a former KGB agent in Poland.

As a man entered the hotel reception Elaine called out something in what had to be Russian. He was about 6ft 10ins tall and had a build like an American footballer.

Elaine stood up and greeted him with a kiss on the cheek.

"Andy this is Igor."

Igor put out his hand which was about twice the size of mine and we shook.

"Nice to meet you Andy Stone," Igor said.

We all sat down and Igor said quietly: "John Harrison is living a short distance from here in a large house."

"Tell me more, please," I said immediately.

"There is not much more to tell. He drives a red Alfa Romeo car with an Irish registration plate and his wife is pregnant."

Igor pulled a mobile from his pocket and showed me a photograph: "This is your man Harrison; I took this photograph today."

I looked at photograph on the phone and from the pictures I had on file I knew it was definitely John Harrison.

"Andy, Igor will look after you tomorrow and will get some photographs of Harrison for you," Elaine said, standing up. "I will see you on Thursday before your flight back to Dublin."

Igor also stood up.

"Mr. Stone you should get some sleep as I will collect you at 8.00am."

"Good night," I said as Igor and Elaine left the hotel together.

I would never have thought I'd be somewhere in the middle of Poland, working with former KGB agents and CIA operatives – it was definitely a story for the grandchildren.

I decided to go watch some TV in my room but I did not sleep well that night. I was too full of anticipation at the thoughts of finally locating Harrison the following day.

CHAPTER 16

The following morning my alarm woke me at 7am. I was surprised I had slept through the night. I felt a sense of trepidation of what was to come that day. Would the surveillance operation go according to plan? Would John Harrison spot us?

After a quick shower I put on my surveillance clothes: black Levi jeans, dark shirt and shoes. It was always best to wear dark clothing, as it made you less conspicuous. Surveillance was one area where I had plenty of experience. I had been trained well and by the best. My mentor in the art of surveillance was Sam Carroll a true covert specialist. One of the exciting parts to a surveillance operation was that you didn't know where your subject was going to take you. I recall carrying out an early morning surveillance operation in the leafy suburbs of South Dublin. The subject was a successful businessman who had told his insurer that he was no longer in a position to work, following an injury. However within a period of one hour I had followed him from his beautiful upmarket house to a building site. As a single surveillance operative I had to adapt and fit into the environment without having time to change my clothes. Fortunately Sam Carroll had taught me that wearing dark, inconspicuous clothing was important as you never knew when you'd need to simply vanish like a sniper. Shoes were also important during surveillance. The term "Gumshoe" comes from when detectives used to place chewing gum on their shoes to make their footsteps silent if they were following a suspect.

The breakfast was fantastic: and I realised again that the impression I had of Poland was completely wrong. I sat in Reception waiting for Igor to arrive, reading *USA Today*. Igor arrived at exactly 8.00am.

"Morning Mr. Stone."

"Igor please my name is Andy; nobody calls me Mr. Stone."

"OK Andy — my car is outside."

As we walked outside the hotel I expected another BMW or maybe a Mercedes but I was wrong — Igor was driving an old VW Passatt. Then again a BMW or Mercedes would not be suitable for surveillance.

He drove a short distance, no more than five miles. We stopped outside a large house that was surrounded by a large chain fence and security gates. There were a few cars parked at the front of the house and then I saw the red Alfa Romeo. Unfortunately it was parked too far away for me to obtain the registration. Even with the telephoto lens it was not possible to read the plate.

"He is not up to much. I had a look at him yesterday. He only went to a bank and then returned back to this address."

"It must be hard on him being in Poland and unable to speak the language."

"Yes that is true and Kostrzyn is not a cosmopolitan city, few people speak English; German would be the second language."

I looked at my watch. It was only 9.10am.

"He will not get active until about 11.00am … but we need to have the surveillance in place, just in case he moves early."

I nodded remembering a corporate investigation case in Pinkerton involving an employee committing fraud when the subject was due to attend a meeting at 1pm. We placed his house under surveillance from 7am, not expecting any movement. However shortly after we arrived he left the house and met with a person he'd said he did not know. This simple observation provided enough evidence for our client to show collusion between an employee and a competitor. The employee was providing confidential tender pricing information, permitting the competitor to undercut the company's quotations for jobs. The case was successful, but it would have failed if we had not set up the early morning surveillance.

As we sat there I tried to make some general conversation, which was not easy. What did I have in common with a former KGB agent? I'd never had any dealings with these guys and I was suspicious of him.

There was an uneasy silence in the car but then Igor turned to me and asked: "Do you like music?"

"Yes I do, mainly American music."

"Good," he smiled and switched on his CD player. It was U2. *I still haven't found what I am looking for* blasted out and Igor started to sing; his voice was terrible. It was a surreal moment – there I was sitting in a car in Poland with a former Russian KGB agent listening to U2. It was certainly another story to tell the grandchildren.

By 11.45am I was starting to get bored. Igor was staring non-stop at the car but I was trying not to drift off. It must have been his many years of training and maybe plenty of practice in the KGB. Surveillance was very tedious no matter who or what you have under observation. Dealing with basic human requirements such as eating or going to the toilet also caused problems. It's 'Murphy's Law' that as soon as you go to the toilet or to get some food, something happens. Hours of surveillance sitting outside a house can be destroyed by just taking a few minutes break. The police normally carry out surveillance in pairs; however in the world of private investigation, due to cost factors set out by the paying client, it was normally just one investigator. I suddenly shot upright as I wondered who was going to cover the fee for Igor and Elaine. Courtney had no idea I was over in Poland and I was most likely looking at a fee of at least €5,000. How was I going to get Courtney to sign it off? I was still trying to figure it out when the Alfa Romeo started to move. I jumped and Igor put out his hand to calm me.

"OK, the subject of your investigation is driving the car."

"Harrison," I muttered.

"Yes," Igor replied.

Harrison turned left as he drove from the house. I got a good view of him as he opened the driver's window while he was passing our car. He didn't look like the man in the photos I had obtained from the Web. He looked heavier and his hair was longer.

"I don't think that is Harrison!" I said.

"Yes it is John Harrison; we will follow him at a distance."

Igor followed Harrison as he drove along the outskirts of Kostrzyn. He turned left again and continued on towards the town centre. Igor was a real professional and I was impressed by his skill.

Harrison turned right and parked at the side of the street. As he got out of his car my heart was beating fast.

After spending the past few months tracking the Cowboy it was exciting to see my foe at last.

We parked our car and walked after Harrison. He entered a small bar, more of a coffee shop, and sat at a window seat.

"Let's enter the bar, I fancy a coffee," Igor said.

I sat close enough to Harrison to get a good eye shot of him. Igor sat beside me saying very little in a low voice. Everybody else was speaking Polish and German.

A waitress approached our table and Igor requested two coffees in Polish, handing over the money.

Harrison had some documents and three mobile phones in front of him on the table. Igor handed me a Polish newspaper and I pretended to read it as I watched Harrison shifting through his papers while drinking a glass of coke. I wanted to get a look at the documents in front of him but it was far too risky.

A phone rang and Harrison pulled a fourth mobile from his coat pocket. He spoke in English, with a strong American accent. All the other customers in the bar looked towards him as he said: "Yes darling, I will be back shortly and I will get the milk."

It sounded like he was talking to his wife.

Harrison pushed his papers into a large brown envelope that he placed inside his coat. Igor got up and walked from the bar, leaving me sitting at the table. I was a little concerned in case somebody asked me something in Polish so I kept my head down.

The waitress placed two black coffees on our table and tried to hand me some change. I waved at her to keep it. She nodded saying "Dziekuje," which I can only assume means thank you.

Out of the corner of my eye I saw Harrison pick up his mobile phones, wave at the waitress and leave the café. After a few moments I stood up and walked out. Igor had moved the car and was now outside the café. He nodded his head forwards and I saw Harrison entering a small shop. I decided to get back into the car as it would have been too obvious if

I'd followed him. I was also worried somebody would try to talk to me in Polish and my cover would be blown.

"I have not got any good photographs yet but I will get him coming out of the shop."

A few moments later Harrison walked from the shop, holding a small plastic bag. Igor raised his camera and zoomed in with the telephoto lens. I heard that sweet sound — click click — as the electronic motor of the camera captured some quality photographs.

Harrison glanced in our direction as he walked past our car and Igor quickly put the camera out of sight. To my surprise Igor wound down the window and called out to him: "Excuse me, excuse me, do you speak English?"

Harrison walked over to the window saying: "Yes."

"Oh good. I am looking for the main road to get me towards the German border – do you know it?"

"No, sorry man I am an American. I am only here on vacation."

"OK thank you."

I was surprised as normally when I was carrying out covert surveillance I would not expose myself to the subject. As this surveillance operation had a limited timeframe, I was fairly sure Igor was simply showing off. On the other hand I was now totally satisfied that the subject was indeed John Harrison.

Harrison walked on and I said to Igor: "I will follow him on foot."

"No need he is walking to his car."

After a few seconds Igor started his car and drove in the opposite direction.

"Igor we are going to lose him," I gasped.

"This is a one-way street, he will have to drive past our car," Igor smiled.

Sure enough within a few moments, Harrison drove past our car and turned back in the direction of his house. We followed him at a safe distance and we were fairly sure he did not detect our presence. I was certain that Harrison had let his guard down as he probably did not think he would be under surveillance in Poland. After all he had told us that he was trying to get back to his wife in Louisiana, USA, so why would we think he was in Poland?

Harrison turned right and stopped outside the security gates at his house. He got out and opened the gates which turned out not to be electronic. Igor clicked away, getting more excellent shots which could later be used in evidence. We did not really need these extra shots but it was safer to have them as a back-up. Harrison got back into his car, drove in, closed the gates and parked his car out of view.

"Job done," Igor smiled. "Let's go to your hotel for lunch and look at the photographs."

We arrived back at the hotel and sat in Reception, ordering coffee and sandwiches. I collected my laptop from my room and Igor installed the SD memory card from his camera on it. I copied the photographs onto my computer hard drive. In total there were 26 photographs, 16 of such excellent quality I could clearly read the registration number of Harrison's car.

As we sat eating, I tried to make some further conversation with Igor.

"Thanks for your assistance today Igor, you were a true professional"

"It is not a problem, by the way Andy do you have my change from the coffee shop earlier?"

"I told the waitress to keep the change."

"What! You gave her a €15 tip."

"Sorry, I didn't realise," I groaned, reaching for my wallet.

Igor's mobile phone rang and he stood up and walked away to take the call. I could hear him talking in what I presumed was Russian. He knew I couldn't speak it so I figured he was just being security conscious. The only language I can speak was English, which was embarrassing at conferences when most of the other Europeans have a second or third language.

"That was Fred," Igor said, walking back over. "He will collect you in 15 minutes. You are flying home tonight from Berlin."

"Tonight ... Berlin ... but my ticket is from Warsaw?"

"Berlin Airport is only 90 minutes from here. You need to quickly pack your things and check out of your room."

"I don't have a ticket from Berlin," I said, standing up.

"It's not a problem, now hurry."

I quickly packed my bag and returned to Reception.

"Thank you Mr. Jones, we hope to see you again soon," the receptionist said.

"What about my bill?"

"It is paid."

Igor yelled at me to hurry out the door and I said a quick goodbye.

When I walked outside Fred was standing beside a black Audi A4 Quattro. He shook my hand saying: "Igor says it all went well?"

"Yes very well."

I turned to say goodbye to Igor but he was gone.

This time I decided to sit in the front seat. Fred accelerated hard and there was a roar of power from the Audi engine. I felt myself being pushed back in the seat of the car as we gathered speed.

"What is it about you guys and speed?" I laughed.

"We have so much to do and so little time. I am sorry but I need you to fly home tonight as I have a lot of work to do tomorrow."

Fred pulled an airline ticket from his coat pocket.

"Take this; it has your booking reference number. I am sorry I could not get you a direct flight to Dublin; you are going via London Heathrow."

"Thank you but what about your fee and the cost for the ticket and the hotel?"

"Do not worry, we have mutual friends; there is no fee amongst friends."

I was happy to hear this as now I wouldn't have to try to get Courtney to sign off on the fee but I wanted to hear more about these friends.

We were travelling very fast along back country the Polish roads as I tried to figure out the best way to approach it. We were almost there when Fred broke the silence.

"Again I must apologise for my poor manners and hospitality Andy, but we are so very busy. Did Igor get you everything you needed?"

"Yes, he was great."

"Excellent, he is one of my best agents."

"Agents, so you guys are like the CIA?"

Fred looked at me and said: "No, not like – we are the CIA."

I sank back into the leather seat of the Audi, not sure what to say next. If I could phrase my questions right I might finally get some answers!

"So you do know Kelly?"

"Kelly? Who is Kelly?"

"Kelly is a FBI agent in the States."

Fred appeared to think for a few moments and then said: "No I do not know a Kelly in the FBI."

"Well how the hell did you get my contact details and phone number?" I asked as Fred pulled up outside Departures in Berlin Airport.

He shook my hand and said: "Good luck Andy."

"You still have not answered my question. How did you get my phone number?" I asked as I got out of the car.

Fred handed me my bag and winked: "You are the investigator you figure it out. Goodbye Andy."

"Thanks Fred," I shouted as he jumped back into his car and sped away.

I walked into Departures and found the desk for the Lufthansa flight to London Heathrow. The steward greeted me and examined my booking.

"Mr. Stone, you are seated in seat 1A Business Class to Heathrow and BMI seat 1A, business class to Dublin."

"Business Class," I repeated, "can you tell me who made my booking?"

She checked the system: "I am sorry that information is not available, but please hurry as you are boarding at gate B17 in ten minutes."

I thanked her and ran for the boarding gate.

The journey back to Dublin was uneventful, with the Lufthansa and BMI flights both on time. I felt a real sense of achievement as I sat looking at the photographs on my laptop, while drinking a glass of champagne — if only Dan could see me! The evidence I had obtained with Igor's assistance was crucial to the defence of the claim. I was sure that the time was now right to prepare a file for the Garda Bureau of Fraud Investigation (GBFI).

CHAPTER 17

I arrived back in the Dublin office late on the Thursday morning.

"Morning Denise. Any news?" I asked casually, wondering if Courtney had been looking for me. This was going to be delicate as I needed to work out how I was going to explain my Poland trip to him.

"Morning Andy. No all quiet, Denton is out trying to clear up his cases as he is off for two weeks on Friday."

"OK, thanks Denise. How is Courtney?"

"I don't know as I don't have that much to do with him. He was looking for you on Monday but I have not seen him in a few days."

I booted up my laptop, excited at displaying the evidence I had obtained in Poland, but also worried as Courtney had not sanctioned my trip. I looked at the various photographs of Harrison and decided not to show them to anybody else until I briefed Courtney. This would be difficult as Tanya had sent me an email wanting an update on the file.

I saw her coming in and quickly walked over to Courtney's office but it was empty. Brenda, his assistant, was busy typing away at her computer.

"Excuse me Brenda do you know if Dan is in the office today?"

"He is at a meeting upstairs, but will be back later, maybe after lunch."

"Thanks Brenda, please tell him that I need to see him."

I walked back to my desk and could see Tanya waiting for me. I greeted her with the usual: "Hi Tanya" but she was keyed up about the case and anxiously replied "Well what is happening with the John Harrison file?"

She was as committed to the file as me.

"Tanya I have some good news but we must keep it confidential for the moment or until I talk to Courtney."

"Tell me!"

I could see Tanya's eyes widening with the potential excitement of a development in the case.

"Well I flew to Warsaw, met up with some CIA guys, who drove me to a town not far from the German border. We then put Harrison under surveillance, obtained some photographic evidence and then I flew home via Heathrow."

"You have lost it now Stone! You in Poland with the CIA, ha, ha, ha," she laughed as she strolled back to her desk.

I was surprised but decided not to comment or challenge her. It was easier if she did not believe me as it gave me more time to talk to Courtney.

I was looking through the various photographs again when it dawned on me that I had another lead staring me in the face. Who was the registered owner of the Alfa Romeo? And more importantly who was the insurance company?

I rang Hughie and was relieved when he answered.

"You in work Hugh?"

"Yep what do you need?"

"I am still working on this American case and I need to check a registration number with you."

"No problem Andy, shout it out."

I called it out, hearing the keys clicking away as he typed it into the system."

"One moment Andy … is your database open?"

"Yeah, what do you need?"

"Type that reg you just gave me into your search screen."

I started to feel embarrassed as I knew what was coming next!

"Sorry Hugh … so we insure the car."

"Yes Andy it's insured with you guys," Hugh laughed.

"Thanks Hugh. I should have checked our system first."

"Don't worry about it; even for us hardened detectives sometimes the lead is already in our notes – you just got to open your eyes!"

"Thanks again Hugh," I muttered and hung up quickly.

I immediately ran through the insurance policy details. The Alfa Romeo was insured to Kenneth Smith, aka Harrison, with a date of birth of the 30 June 1975, at an address in Naas, Co. Kildare. The account had been set up with direct debit payments from a local Irish bank. The policy of insurance had been taken out on the 1 June, 2008 and suspended by the insured a few months later.

I decided to chance my arm and contact the fraud manager at the local Bank B. To my surprise he was more than helpful and agreed with me that financial institutions need to work closer together in order to combat fraud. Unfortunately Data Protection would not share the same view. It is well-known in the financial fraud prevention industry that the best tool the criminal has in his arsenal is not the gun but laws like Data Protection.

The fraud manager confirmed that the account number was in the name of Kenneth Smith and that they could see direct debit payments had been forwarded to Dallast Insurance. He also advised they were looking for Kenneth Smith as the bank account was overdrawn. Under money laundering legislation you must produce photographic identification and a copy of a household bill to open a bank account. He told me that the account had been opened with an Irish passport in the name of Kenneth Smith and gave me the passport number.

"The proof of the address was an invoice from Dallast Insurance and a copy of a motor insurance policy."

"He used Dallast Insurance paperwork for proof of his address?"

"Yes that is what I said," he replied.

"Thanks for your assistance. Please keep your file to hand as I think the Gardaí will need it shortly."

"Why? What has this guy done?"

"I can't go into detail just yet, but thanks again for your help."

The fraud manager had been really co-operative and I was tempted to give him some more details on the Cowboy but I decided to hold off as it was an ongoing investigating.

I thought back to my meetings with Smith's employers and my interview with the real Kenneth Smith in Monaghan Town. I was now certain that the Kenneth Smith we had insured was really John Harrison.

I phoned the Irish passport office in order to verify if the passport number the fraud manager had given me was listed for Kenneth Smith.

"I'm afraid I cannot release any information because of Data Protection," the lady at the other end of the phone advised.

"I understand, but I am about to release a large cheque to a gentleman who has presented a passport as proof of identity and it looks as if it has been through a washing machine," I improvised quickly.

"Well I tell you what I will do, if you read me out the details that you have I can confirm if they are correct."

"I have a copy of a passport for a Kenneth Smith, passport number X123456E."

"What date of birth do you have?"

"30 June, 1975."

She paused and then said: "Yes that information is correct."

"This is a legitimate passport?"

I was shocked.

"Yes the passport is totally legitimate."

I thanked her and hung up.

How the hell had Harrison got a real passport? I was bewildered and could not understand how two Kenneth Smiths could have a passport under the same name and date of birth.

I sat back, trying to decide what to do next. I was contemplating phoning Kenneth Smith in Monaghan, but was unsure what additional information could be obtained from him.

"Andy there is a KGB agent looking for you in the reception," Tanya laughed, as she passed my desk on her way to lunch.

I laughed but I was also a bit concerned. If Tanya did not believe me about what had happened in Poland, what chance would I have with Courtney?

I went back over my notes and files and decided to phone the real Kenneth Smith. I thought about double checking that he'd never had a car policy with us but I didn't want to worry him and I was sure the Alfa Romeo policy was Harrison.

"Hi Kenneth it's Andy here from Dallast Insurance," I said as he answered the phone.

"Well Andy. How are you?"

"I am fine Kenneth. I'm just following up on our meeting. Have you gone to the Guards yet?"

"Yes I went to the station and a Garda took my details and wrote it up in the book. I also gave her your name."

"Good, that's what I wanted to hear Kenneth. You know the passport you showed me, is that the only one you own?"

"Yes it's my only passport."

"When is it due for renewal?"

"Give me a few minutes till I find it … got it … now it's due to expire in four months."

"Thanks Kenneth, have you had any more contact from the American?"

"No nothing Andy. What is happening?"

"I am still investigating but unfortunately I cannot discuss the case with you."

"Am I in some sort of trouble?"

"No you have logged your complaint and details with the Gardaí so you will be fine"

"OK thanks Andy. Will I still phone you if the American contacts me again?"

"Yes please do and try to get his phone number. Thanks Kenneth, I will talk to you soon."

I was about to leave my desk to head for the canteen for lunch when Hugh phoned.

"Andy, I ran the vehicle registration you gave me for that red Alfa Romeo through our Pulse system."

Pulse is the Irish Police IT database system. It is used for logging details on individuals and vehicles, such as criminal convictions and intelligence. It also records accidents and other incidents involving members of the public were a police officer has attended or intervened.

"Did you find something?"

"It turns out we stopped him a few months back for speeding near Naas."

"Who stopped him?"

"One of our traffic officers. The Alfa Romeo was travelling at 100mph in a 60mph zone, a dangerous speed to be travelling. The driver gave the name Kenneth Smith with an address in Naas and was issued with a speeding ticket. He was told to produce his driver's license and proof of insurance at the local station but he never showed up."

"Thanks Hugh that is very interesting."

"Andy can you post me a print of the photograph? I will send it to the traffic officer as she may remember him."

"No problem Hugh I will post it today or I could email it to you?"

"No you best print the photo and send it to me. It will make it easier."

"Thanks Hugh; talk to you soon."

Hopefully the traffic officer who'd stopped Harrison for speeding while he was using the name Kenneth Smith would remember him when she saw the Cowboy's wedding photographs and the 'Wanted' image. If she did it would confirm the identity theft.

CHAPTER 18

I was getting my coat when I realised that Courtney was standing behind me.

"Hello Dan," I said.

"I hear you have been busy Stone."

"Yes very busy, working on this Harrison file."

"Good. Meet me in Brady's bar in ten minutes and you can give me an update."

I agreed but wondered why he wanted to meet in the local pub as his office was only a short walk away from my desk. It was only 4pm in the afternoon, a little early in my reckoning for having a beer.

He walked off and I quickly gathered my documents and disconnected my laptop from its docking station. I was half-way to the staff exit when I realised I didn't have my notebook. I rushed back and quickly grappled with my untidy desk. I had to locate it, as it contained all my notes on info from sources and developments, not only on the Harrison case but on all my investigations over the past year. If there was a fire in the building, it was the only item I would take with me as it contained so much valuable information. In court an investigator or police officer is entitled to refer to their personal notebooks when providing evidence and I knew I would need to refer to mine for my meeting with Courtney!

I found it and rushed over to Brady's, which was only a short walk from our office. Courtney wasn't there so I set up my laptop and opened some of the photographs I had obtained from the Polish surveillance. I was ready for the probing questions which I had no doubt would be coming.

The photographs I had obtained from the Polish surveillance looked great, clear and well-focused. Igor was a true professional with a camera.

About five minutes later Courtney walked into the bar and ordered two bottles of Miller and a Jack Daniels whiskey.

"Andy, let's walk to the back of the bar. It's less busy there so we can talk."

I looked around the bar in surprise. There were two men sitting at the counter drinking and a barman. The pub was very quiet. It was a bit strange that Courtney wanted me to move to the rear of the pub but I wasn't going to have an argument about it.

"You're the boss Dan."

I picked up my belongings and laptop and followed him to a dimly-lit and very private seat. I sat at a small table and Courtney sat down opposite me, facing the room. Just as I was about to say something the barman approached, carrying the drinks on a tray.

"Now Sirs, two bottles of Miller and a Jack Daniels. Would you like me to turn on the lights?" he asked.

"No we are just fine, here you go and keep the change and we don't want to be disturbed," Courtney said as he handed the barman a €20 note.

"Thank you sir," the barman replied and walked away.

I was a bit confused — it was not normal management practise in Dallast to socialise with the staff. What was going on?

"We need to talk in private Andy," he said looking serious.

"OK Dan," I replied, deciding to humour him.

There was an uneasy silence until he said: "Do you trust me Andy?"

"Yes of course I trust you — you're the boss Dan."

I answered this without thinking much about it as the truth was I didn't trust Courtney. I felt he always had an ulterior motive. But then he was the boss and I was not going to tell him how I truly felt.

"Cut the shit Andy; I am not talking to you as a manager now. I am talking to you as an investigator."

"An investigator? With respect Dan you are an insurance man not an investigator."

"No we are both investigators," he insisted.

"But you're an insurance claims manager Dan," I said again.

I felt a little annoyed as there was a distinction between an investigator and an insurance claims person. They are completely different positions which require different levels of experience.

"How old do you think I am?"

That was a strange question.

"At a guess I would say 55," I said, trying to be kind. I was genuinely uncertain of his age.

"Must be all the good living," Courtney laughed. "I am 65 years old. I will retire at the end of the year."

I was surprised at this as Courtney was a fit man. He ran marathons with good finish times and looked like he was in really good condition.

"65 … no way, you are fitter then most of the young guys."

My end of year appraisal was not that far away and my final score, as decided by Courtney, would affect my bonus payment, so a few compliments seemed like a good idea. It was a really strange situation to be sitting in a bar with Courtney talking about his age and his retirement plans. In the past I had only had minimal dealings with him and it was very much an employee/manager relationship.

"Tell me Andy what do you know about me?" he asked.

"I don't know that much Dan, other than you told me you lived in San Francisco and Arizona in the United States.

"Huh San Francisco," Dan said with a grin. "I like you Andy, you and me are alike in more ways than one. What I am about to tell you is between you and me, do you understand? Not a fucking word."

I was shocked to hear Courtney cursing as he was always the perfect gentleman, tough at times but always the gentleman. I was not used to him sounding like an angry American either. I just nodded, as I was intrigued about what was coming next.

"I am not Dan Courtney; my real name is Edmund Roberts," he said softly, leaning towards me. "I was born in El Paso, Texas in 1945. My mother was Irish and my father was from Texas. I joined the United States Marine Corps (USMC) aged 17 in 1962. I was shipped to Vietnam where I did my tour. I saw some real shit out there and yes before you ask I have killed many people, with guns, knives and even my fucking hands."

As I looked at Courtney I could see a change in his eyes — a madness. I was unsure what to say so I kept quiet.

The decision was made for me as Courtney continued: "Vietnam was hell on earth. I lost so many of my buddies, good men ripped apart and for fucking what? A country nobody is interested in, that is 20 hours flying time from America. Yeah Vietnam was a real shithole."

"Why did you change your name?"

"Let me continue. I got hit in the leg and picked up shrapnel wounds from a grenade." Courtney stood up and pulled up his right trouser leg. His right calf muscle was more or less missing. There was also a large amount of scar tissue, which was difficult to see in the low light of the bar.

"That's incredible Dan. How do you run the marathons with such a bad leg?"

"I do it as I need to prove to myself that I am still a full man, that's why I do all the training."

I was stunned.

"So how did you end up in Ireland?" I asked finally.

"My mother was born here. Since my days in Vietnam I have been tormented by the memories. The only place that gives me rest and peace is Ireland."

Just as I was about to offer some words of comfort, Courtney looked up and said: "I have not been Edmund Roberts since 1977."

"Why did you …"

Courtney cut in.

"… after I got wounded in Nam I shipped back home to recover … not that you recover from Nam, you just learn to live with it. The memories are always there. I wanted to get back over to my men but the army would not let me go back; fuckers wanted me to leave the Marines. I was not going out that easy."

"So what happened then?"

"I refused to leave so I was made a Gunnery Sergeant at the training camp. I did it for a few months but I hated training those young guys to become killers."

"Then you left the Marines?"

"No the CIA needed a tough guy like me so I was recruited by them, then I went back to Vietnam as a Co-ordinating Intelligence Officer, great name for a shit job."

"So what did it involve?"

"As I was experienced in the field, in particular at burning those endless tunnels, I would assist the interrogation officer who would basically interview captured prisoners."

"Interviewing prisoners sounds easy enough," I said naively.

Courtney looked at me incredulously.

"Easy job! Covert missions working behind enemy lines, on your own with no back up — easy job my ass. Working with the intelligence team was horrific; I saw firsthand the effects of napalm on those people. We always aimed for the army but sometimes innocent people got hit. Working behind enemy lines I remember seeing napalm hit a village. Those poor people burned to death in agony. All I could do was look on in shame. What we did was inexcusable. I know it was accidental and the pilots would have been aiming for the Vietcong but when you see the effects of napalm on children well you will never forget it."

I could see Dan's eyes starting to fill with water.

I felt a bit stupid but asked: "So you were in the intelligence team. Is that like full CIA membership?"

"Yes we were the CIA."

That's when it dawned on me.

"So you organised the Polish guys — Fred, Elaine and Igor?"

"Fred … is that what he is calling himself now?" Courtney smiled. "Yes Fred was with me. He is like my brother and we are still good friends. Did he look after you in Poland?"

"Yes — they all took good care of me."

"Elaine is Fred's daughter, very intelligent girl. You know she is fluent in about five languages?

"Wow, five languages, I can only speak English. She's an amazing looking girl and friendly too."

"Yes and good looking," Courtney smiled and sipped the Jack Daniels.

The atmosphere was now much more relaxed. Courtney appeared to have almost enjoyed telling me his life history. I felt a little like a priest must feel after a confession but there was still that burning question to ask: "So why did you have to change your name?"

"I left Vietnam in 1980, long after the war had finished. I was transferred back to the United States and I served in the CIA for another two years, basically sorting our documents and looking for American soldiers who were missing in action in Vietnam. I had seen so much shit in the war and was tied up with so much crap from the CIA that I had no choice but to get out. But I'd witnessed a lot of things so I needed to get a new identity as so many people wanted to see me dead. So Edmund Roberts died and Dan Courtney was born. I needed some time to myself to try and regain my life …"

"So you moved to Ireland," I interrupted.

"No not initially. I moved to Barbados in the Caribbean, where I opened a small surf bar and hotel. I stayed there for four years and met Mary who was on holidays, fell in love, married her and moved to Ireland.

"Your wife Mary, is she aware of all this?"

"Yes she knows about Nam. She has witnessed me waking up screaming in the middle of the night from bad dreams often enough."

"What about your family in America? How did you get your new identity?"

"My parents are dead and I was an only child, so making me disappear or die was easy. Edmund Roberts was killed on active duty in Vietnam. You can check the records. Changing my identity, well when you are part of the United States Government you can change anything you want and the CIA is a Federal agency."

"What did you do for money?"

"Well that's the one thing Uncle Sam was good for. I was well taken care of … I don't really have to work now but I would go mad sitting at home."

"I don't think I will ever look at you in the same way again," I said, feeling dismayed but yet honoured that Courtney had told me his story.

"Well you won't have to. I am leaving at Christmas. I'm going to move back to Barbados with Mary. The heat is good for my aching bones and the old wounds."

"Do you want me to brief you on my activities in Poland?"

"Fred has already given me a report. Just show me the photos you got."

As we finished up Courtney said: "Stone don't ever leave the country again without telling me where you are going."

I nodded in agreement.

We finished our drinks and walked from the bar. I was shocked by what he'd told me but I was relieved that Courtney knew about Poland as it had been bothering me.

I drove home without turning on the radio as my mind was full of Dan Courtney's revelations. This information was going no further. I even decided not to discuss it with my wife. Staying silent was sometimes the easiest and safest option.

CHAPTER 19

It was a beautiful Monday morning, the sun was shining and the traffic on the M50 was moving well. I had just enjoyed a great weekend but I'd found it really difficult not to discuss what Courtney had told me with my wife, however I had given him my word. I was saddened by his story and I wondered how he survived living with such bad memories.

I was on my way to Naas, Co. Kildare, in order to locate the address I had obtained from 'Kenneth Smith's' insurance policy on the Alfa Romeo, 50 Terun View. I eventually found it. The apartment was in a private complex, located in its own grounds, with car parking in front. To enter the car park and apartments you needed to pass through an electronic security gate which was controlled by a code – which I didn't have. As I was wondering what to do the gates opened. A small truck drove out and I quickly drove in before the gates closed. As I parked my car I was feeling a little trapped but I was sure I'd be able to get out. In the meantime I decided to take a walk around the grounds and locate his apartment block.

I walked up to the door which was locked and had an intercom system, with a number listed for each apartment. I also noticed that each individual apartment had a mail box outside the front door. I pressed the intercom button to number 50 but nobody answered. I also checked the letterbox, however it was locked. No joy there. I was disappointed and also aware that people were probably watching me. I felt a little like a bird in a cage, especially as I didn't know the key code for the security gate.

I decided to try his neighbour in 51 and pressed the intercom button.

"Hello," a lady answered.

"Hi. I'm looking for Kenneth from number 50."

"I don't know a Kenneth in number 50. They are all foreigners and they work, so you will need to call back after 6pm."

"What nationality are they?"

"I am not sure. I think they are Polish or maybe from Russia. Now I have to go."

"Thanks for your help. Do you know if one of them is American or Canadian?" I quickly asked.

"What is this all about?" asked the lady

"I am just trying to find a witness to a road accident."

"I see. No I don't think there is an American living there as they do not speak English."

"Thanks very much for your help," I said and returned to my car. I drove towards the security gate just as a man walked over and entered a key code. It was 5050 and it opened the main gates. I quickly noted the number in my notebook and exited the car park after him.

As I drove from the complex, I realised that the address we had for Nigel Boroski was only about 500 metres from the new address obtained for Kenneth Smith. I decided to give Tanya a call to get her to check the new information I had obtained.

"Hello Mr. KGB," she laughed.

"Yes, yes, yes," I said, "now enough of that rubbish. I am in Naas and need you to check some addresses for me on the internal system."

"No problem Andy. What do you want me to check?"

"Run the address of 50 Terun View through the various systems and databases and see what you can find. Also run the three names we have, John Harrison, Kenneth Smith and Sean Moran, and see if we can obtain any more leads or strands for further investigation."

"OK Andy, I will ring you back in 20 minutes."

While I was waiting I decided call into my friend Dave Hendrick to see if he wanted to buy me a coffee!

Just as I drove into his car park my mobile rang; it was Tanya.

"Andy, are you aware that John Harrison requested us to insure an Alfa Romeo a year ago?"

"No ... what address did he use?"

"It's the same John Harrison date of birth 28 May 1975, red Alfa Romeo, The Stables in Sallins Co. Kildare.

I hung up the phone without saying goodbye I was so excited. My tyres actually screeched as I drove out of Hendrick's car park and raced towards Sallins, a small town, located about five miles from Naas.

When I arrived there, I had to ask for directions to The Stables. It turned out to be an estate of new townhouses. I located the house Harrison had listed, but nobody was home. I called to the next-door neighbours who told me that a foreign family were living there for a while but that they had moved out and the house was now vacant.

"Was there an American or Canadian living in the house?"

"No I think they were Russian, not American," the neighbour, who was also a foreigner, replied.

I walked back to my car, disappointed that I had come up with a blank. I decided to telephone Dave but his phone was diverted to his secretary because he was on a few days holiday.

As I drove out of The Stables, I noticed a local café and I decided to get a coffee and some lunch. I sat reading the paper and drinking my coffee listening to an elderly lady who was having an issue with one of the employees.

"I want to see an Irish person, I want to complain to an Irish person," she sighed. "I am sick of all these foreigners."

I felt sorry for her but her words suddenly made me think of Harrison's Polish wife. I had a brainwave and asked to see the manager.

One of the employees directed me to a small office at the rear and I was introduced to the Manager, Jim Doyle.

"Hi Jim, I'm a financial investigator and I am trying to track somebody down," I said.

"What can I do to help?"

"Do you employ many Polish people?"

"Yes, the Polish are good workers."

"Did you ever employ a lady called Jenny Boroski?"

"Yes I remember her; she was an excellent worker."

I could not believe my ears. I was sure that the excitement was showing on my face. Investigators need lady luck on their side as much as possible.

"How long was she with you and when did she leave?"

"Hey! What is this all about?" Jim asked.

"I am investigating what I believe is a fraudulent insurance claim"

"Fraud! I don't like the sound of that. I can't imagine Jenny getting involved in that sort of thing."

"Well it's not Jenny that I am really interested in, I think she might be related to somebody involved in fraud."

"OK, well she was with me for about five or six months and left about six months ago as she became pregnant. I think she went back to Poland to have the baby."

"Did you know her partner or husband?"

"Yes, the American — was he married to her? He was a strange fellow, used to be always hanging around the place, getting in the way. I think he went out drinking with a few of the lads here."

"Did they live in Sallins?"

"Yes they used to have a place here, then they went to live with her brother in Naas and then I think they moved to an apartment over a shop, just down the road. Listen Jenny, was a really nice girl. I don't want to get her into any trouble."

"It's not Jenny I am interested in. It's her husband,"

"OK, I suppose," Jim said and escorted me to the door, pointing me in the right direction.

"Thanks for your help," I said and handed him my business card. "Could you contact me if either Jenny or the American gets in touch with you?"

"Look, fraud is a serious matter. I don't want to get involved."

"I understand and I can assure you I am only interested in talking to the American guy, not Jenny."

Jim reluctantly accepted my card.

I left the shop excited with the developments and drove down the road to the shop he'd pointed out. There were private apartments located above it.

I made enquires in the shop and was told to walk around the back and ring the bell for Apartment 1 as the landlady lived there.

I located the intercom and pressed number one.

"I'll be with you in a few moments," a woman advised.

I waited at another electric security gate, but there was no mail box this time. As I waited I realised that this would be an excellent place to live if you were a fraudster. You could hide your car around the back and nobody could get at you without first passing through the security gate. I knew from previous experience that surveillance operations on addresses like these were virtually impossible.

"How can I help you?" a lady asked, walking out from behind the security gate.

"Hi, are you the landlady?"

"Yes but if you are looking to rent an apartment I am afraid they are all taken."

"No I am a financial investigator and I am trying to trace somebody who used to rent an apartment from you."

"Oh that sounds interesting."

"Can you tell me did you rent an apartment to a John Harrison?"

"No, I don't know that name."

"Did you rent an apartment to an American and his Polish wife maybe?"

"Him! I knew there was something wrong with him but I can't remember his name. Let me think... "

"Would it have been Kenneth Smith or Sean Moran?"

"Yes Kenneth that's it and his wife was Jenny. She's Polish. They rented an apartment for a short time, maybe two months and then they left leaving us short on the rent. He borrowed my husband's Sat Nav which was expensive at the time. Kenneth said they were going to Poland for a holiday and we haven't seen them since."

"So you have had no further contact from them?"

"No ... I remember her brother who was Polish lived in Naas., He used to be with them most of the time, but no I have not seen them."

I pulled out the 'Wanted' photograph from the District Attorney's office in Oklahoma.

She took one look at the photograph and said: "Yes that is Kenneth. I am certain that's him."

I handed her my business card.

"If either Jenny or Kenneth contact you, please will you call me?"

"Is there a reward for information?"

"No I am afraid not, thank you for your time."

I was happy with the new developments in the case. If necessary, Jim and the landlady could be interviewed by the police and used as potential witnesses in court.

I decided to chance calling back to The Stables but nobody was home. I looked through the window and saw that there was little or no furniture. I called to the neighbour on the other side and she was there.

"I do recall a man with a kind of an American accent. He was living in the house with a few other people."

I pulled the photograph from my pocket however the lady was unable to confirm if it was the same man who had lived in the house.

"No I've no idea who owns that place. It's had several different occupants living there over the past few years."

It looked like The Stables address was a dead end but as I updated my notebook I felt a sense of satisfaction.

I drove the short distance back to Naas, checking the other addresses I had for John Harrison. I was not sure what I was looking for as I knew he was in Poland with his wife. I just wanted to get a sense of where Harrison had been living. When a detective is at a crime scene they use their senses to try and pick up a lead or information. I guess this was what I was doing by visiting Harrison's previous residences.

I called into the local Garda Station. I approached the officer who was standing behind the counter completing paperwork.

"Excuse me Garda."

"Yes, how can I help you?"

"I am with Dallast Insurance and I am trying to locate some people involved in an accident. Would you ever have come across a Polish man named Nigel Boroski or an American John Harrison?"

"Insurance!" he growled. "I only deal with serious crime."

"Well it's a case of identity theft and insurance fraud," I explained

"Well then get a detective."

"Please can you just tell me if you have ever come across either of them?"

"No I haven't. Now please, I have work to do."

"Thanks Garda."

"It's Sergeant, can you not see the stripes?" he shouted at me as I exited the station.

As I left the station I thought it was bizarre that insurance fraud and identity theft were still not considered to be a serious problem in Ireland. If this was the attitude of a local police officer then what chance had I got? How was I supposed to solve the case and possibly obtain a criminal conviction if I'd no support from the police?

Feeling a bit annoyed with the officer's attitude I decided to drive home. As I drove I was thinking of the case and pondering what to do next. After Poland I had started to prepare the file for the Garda Bureau of Fraud Investigation (GBFI) but I was well aware that once they got involved I would have to back off. I decided to hold back for another few days as I wanted to follow up on a few more leads first. I was hoping I'd hear back from Hugh about the traffic officer before I had to pass everything over. I was also interested in talking to Sally Wall as she would have some information on Sean Moran. At this stage I had exhausted all avenues of investigation into Kenneth Smith and it was time for me to move onto investigating the identity of Sean Moran.

CHAPTER 20

That night I could not sleep as I kept thinking about the case. Before Operation Cowboy I would usually come home from work, switch off, watch TV or catch up with some friends, but the hunt for Harrison had changed that. Eventually at 2.15am I got up and went downstairs. I checked my Facebook account for messages and then started having a look around on the Web.

I entered the words John Harrison again but as per my previous searches nothing of any interest or significance appeared. I was sitting glaring at my computer, while my dog Ben was looking at me with his ever-affectionate eyes. My other dog Sue was asleep in her bed.

"Looks like it's just you and me tonight Ben!" I laughed quietly.

I opened YouTube and watched some scenes from the TV show *Cops*; just the usual stuff — cops chasing and catching the bad guys. It made me think of the staged accidents and I decided to do a little research on Sally Wall, the insured who had supposedly knocked Sean Moran down. Normally in an insurance claim you look at the claimant and not the insured, however, with Harrison I needed to look at all parties.

I switched back to Google and entered the words 'Sally Wall John Harrison' and up popped the following page:

American and Irish Girl Rob Cash before Fleeing Ireland

'A young Irish woman, infatuated by an American who was living in Ireland, robbed €10,000 from her employer a court heard on Monday.

Sally Wall, aged 19 from Boyle, Co. Roscommon, and her American fled Ireland with money she took from The Market Hotel, Carrick-on-Shannon, Co. Leitrim.

Judge Nicole Daly heard how after stealing the money, the pair drove to Dun Laoghaire in Dublin, took the ferry to Wales and travelled, via the Channel Tunnel, to Holland, and then flew to Mexico.

They tried to enter the USA by crossing the Mexican border but as an illegal, Wall was held by US immigration in Texas before being sent back to Ireland.

The court heard that Sally Wall fell for the Cowboy, John Harrison, after she travelled to Arizona to work on a ranch. Harrison was an employee at the ranch and told Wall that he would come to live with her in Ireland. While living in Ireland, Harrison spent his time walking around the town of Boyle in cowboy boots and a large white cowboy hat.

The Detective Garda giving evidence described Harrison as a professional scam artist.

Sally Wall's mother told the court that John Harrison had ruined her daughter's life. Harrison had panicked when he was routinely stopped by Gardaí and told Sally that he was going to be deported and he needed money. He persuaded her to rob the cash from her employer.

Judge Daly felt sorry for the young and naive Sally Wall and gave her six months to pay back the money or face jail. The judge also ordered her to contact the police if John Harrison made contact with her again.'

I could not believe what I was reading. This had to be the same John Harrison. I read and re-read the article, feeling excited – there was no chance of me going back to sleep now. I had to trace Sally Wall, interview her and try to establish what connection she still had to Harrison.

I tried to print off the document; however Olivia had used up all the ink on photographs of Justin Bieber. I saved the information instead and also emailed the website link to my work email address. Then I continued checking the internet for clues or other links which might assist the investigation. Detective work has changed so much since the Pinkerton agents were trying to track down Jessie James and the Younger gangs or Butch Cassidy and the Sundance Kid. I once read how the Pinkerton agents would place 'Wanted' posters in all the small towns around the various States. All they had back then was word of mouth and tip-offs from local Sheriffs and Deputies. With the evolution of email and the internet it's now so much easier to gather and obtain intelligence on individuals. You can even do it without leaving the comfort of your house!

At 6.00am I heard my wife getting up.

"Jackie, I have been working on the Harrison file, look what I found last night."

"That's great, now when are you going to paint the hall?"

"Yeah I will get the paint at the weekend, but take a look at this article."

My wife quickly glanced at the computer screen.

"Fascinating," she said sarcastically. "I think you need to see a doctor Andy as this Harrison guy is taking over your life."

She was a lawyer and they have a certain way of thinking but perhaps she was correct. I had completed the insurance investigation and had enough information and intelligence to close the file and make a huge saving for Dallast.

"You've done your job Andy – why can't you just let it go?"

"I don't know why. I just know there is more to this guy. I just feel I have to keep digging into Harrison's background."

She walked off in disgust but I knew I just could not stop myself. There was something driving me, even if I had wanted to stop investigating I simply couldn't do it.

That morning I drove the children to school and arrived at the office just before 8.00am. It was reasonably empty with only a few staff around.

I spotted Tanya sitting at her desk and decided to give her a full update on the information I had established. I hoped she was no longer laughing about the KGB contacts.

"Morning Tanya. Any news?"

"Hi Andy, no news," she said, looking up. "Strangely I have not had anything from Harrison since we received his 'Ransom note'."

"You will have no more contact from Harrison. His claim is gone ...anyway he is in Poland now."

"I will close the file then."

"No, hold off on closing the file, until I have fully briefed Courtney."

"OK Andy. Do we have any proof he is in Poland?"

I opened my case and placed two photographs Igor had taken of Harrison in Poland.

"Told you I was in Poland!"

"Are you serious?"

"Yes Tanya and here take a look at this. I found it on the internet last night."

Tanya looked at the newspaper cutting, quickly reading the first few lines.

"I don't believe it … is this the same John Harrison?"

"I would bet you 50 bucks it's the same guy but I need to trace Sally Wall, which will be difficult as she may not want to be found."

Tanya's phone rang before she could reply and I walked back to my desk as she took the call.

Denise arrived in next and she was in such a good mood I asked: "What has you so happy?"

"My horse is fine; no broken bones just a few bruises, a few weeks rest and he will be as good as new."

"That's great news Denise; tell me do you need any investigating done in the West, in particular around Galway, Mayo or Sligo?"

I was hoping she would say she did as I needed a reason to call to Sally Wall's home in Roscommon. According to the newspaper she lived in Boyle, about a two-hour drive from Dublin.

"Give me a minute Andy! I am only in the door; at least let me take my coat off," Denise smiled.

"Would you like me to get you a cup of tea?"

"Yes please, you go get the tea and I will check the data-base for files in the West."

As I walked away from my desk Denise shouted after me: "Get me a Starbucks tea, none of that canteen rubbish."

"Starbucks it is Denise!"

I walked back into the office, carrying a Starbucks coffee and a tea.

"Thanks Dave," she said, looking impressed as I sat back at my desk.

"You're welcome. So any cases in the West?"

"Why are you so interested in going there?"

I handed her a copy of the article from the Web. Denise read the full newspaper article and then laughed: "I knew you would not be travelling that far just for one of my cases!"

"Denise that is not fair, we are a team!"

"Yes sure we are ... when it suits you, we are a team! But anyway I do have a file in Sligo which you could do for me."

"How much is the financial reserve?" I asked, deciding to ignore her comments.

"€40,000, it's a BMW stolen without the keys."

"Thanks Denise that will do nicely!"

She gave me the full details of the insurance claim, which involved the theft of a BMW from outside a business address at 11.00am. This was unusual and warranted an investigation. I was glad as it was not really economical for me to drive all that way just for Sally Wall, especially considering we had already obtained enough evidence to close the file. Now the journey would be more justifiable.

That afternoon I decided to telephone Michael Conlon, one of our motor engineers, who was based in Mayo. He covered the West of Ireland and inspected vehicles which were involved in road traffic accidents in the area. Michael, a native of Roscommon, knew many people in the county.

"Do you know a Sally Wall from Boyle?"

"Sally Wall … em … no …. I do know a Harry Wall but he does not live in that area. Leave it with me and I will see what I can find out for you."

I thanked Michael and hung up. I left soon afterwards as I would have to leave the house early the next day to drive to Sligo and Roscommon. As I was driving home Michael phoned.

"Andy I can't find any information on a Sally Wall, however there is an Ann Wall who is living in the town. That could be her mother or maybe a sister."

"Thanks Michael, I owe you one."

"Have you any idea what this lady has done?"

I did not want to go into details with him so I just said: "She could be a witness and may have some valuable information regarding an ongoing claim."

"OK I will do a little more digging and talk to you tomorrow," he said.

The following morning I left the house at 6.00am and began the three hour drive to Sligo. Travelling at that hour of the morning was enjoyable as there was so little traffic on the roads. The weather was also fantastic, warm, with a clear blue sky, which was unusual for Ireland.

I arrived in Boyle and called to the local post office, asking for Ann Wall. The post lady directed me to a house a short walk away on the Main Street. I was lucky Boyle was a quiet country town where the locals all knew each other.

I found the house and knocked on the door. I was taken aback and disappointed when a man of about 40 years of age answered it.

"Is this the home of Sally Wall?"

"No, Sally moved from here a long time ago."

"Do you know an Ann Wall?"

"Yes I do; she is Sally's mother," the man said looking cautious. "What is this about?"

"It's a private matter, but it's very important that I locate Sally or Ann Wall."

"Are you police?"

"No and I am not a tax inspector."

The man laughed: "Those bastards have us all fleeced."

I nodded in agreement.

"Now let's see; it's Ann Wall you are looking for, well now she moved from here a few years ago, but wait I have a phone number for her new home," he said walking back into the house.

I stayed at the front door waiting impatiently. A few moments later he handed me a scrap of paper.

"Here you are son, that's Ann's phone number."

"Thanks, that's great," I said and walked back to my car.

I telephoned the number and a woman answered.

"Is this Ann Wall?" I asked.

"Yes Ann Wall speaking."

"I am sorry for troubling you. My name is Andy Stone. I am a financial investigator and I am trying to get in contact with a Sally Wall."

The phone went dead.

"Oh shit," I said. I would have to try a second time.

I telephoned the number again and the same woman said: "Leave us alone, I have nothing to say."

The phone went dead again.

I was unsure what to do. I was disappointed but I was determined to get her to talk to me. Looking at the number I recognised that it was a local one, possibly in the town of Boyle itself.

I decided to drive onto Sligo first and carry out Denise's investigation. As I drove along the country roads I couldn't help thinking that I had messed up and maybe I should have tried a different approach. I needed a new angle or maybe she just needed some time or perhaps I could try to locate her home, for a direct, face-to-face, call to the front door.

I arrived in Sligo and located the business where the BMW had been stolen. I viewed the CCTV footage which clearly showed an individual breaking into the BMW and driving away. I was satisfied that this was a genuine theft and had no problem signing off on the €40,000 pay out.

I got back into my car and headed back to Boyle, determined to work out some way of interviewing Ann Wall.

CHAPTER 21

A s I was driving out of Sligo, my mobile rang.
"Is this Andy Stone?" a lady asked.

"Yes it is."

"This is Ann Wall; what do you want with my daughter Sally?"

"Thank you for calling me Mrs. Wall," I said quickly, surprised she'd phoned. "First let me apologise if I have caused you any upset."

There was silence and then she said: "You still haven't answered my question: what do you want with my daughter Sally?"

"Mrs. Wall I am not really interested in your daughter, it is a former acquaintance of hers that I am trying to find."

"I'm not sure if I can help you as Sally no longer lives in Ireland."

I decided to just go for it and ask the direct question: "Do you know an American named John Harrison?"

"That's a name I don't want to hear again! Don't talk to me about that man! He destroyed my daughter's life," she shouted. I could hear a quiver in her voice she was so upset.

I was now more interested than ever in hearing her side of the story.

"Would it be possible to meet with you as you may be able to assist me with the defence of a large insurance claim?"

"I don't want to get involved with that man again. He has caused so much pain and hurt to my family."

"Mrs. Wall you may be able to give me some information that will put him behind bars."

"Mmm ... OK, I will meet you but only if you keep my daughter out of this. Sally has a new life with a good husband and a family. She does not need that man coming back into her life. He brought her nothing but trouble."

"I am only interested in the activities of John Harrison," I assured her.

"OK when would you like to meet?"

"Well I am leaving Sligo now, heading back towards Dublin, could I meet you in an hour?"

"You must be very anxious to meet me!"

"Yes I am."

"Well it's sudden but I will meet you in the Landmark Hotel, in Carrick-on-Shannon."

"Thanks Mrs. Wall, I will see you then."

"How will I know you?"

"I am wearing a white shirt and navy trousers, keep your phone on and call me if you cannot find be. I will be in reception"

"OK," she said and hung up.

I had been on the go since early morning but I was fully charged on nervous energy, excited about the new information I was going to obtain on John Harrison.

I arrived at the hotel just after 5pm and sat in Reception, drinking a coke. It was quiet, with only a handful of customers drinking in the bar area.

At exactly 5:15pm a lady walked in and caught my eye. She was in her early fifties and wearing a grey business suit

"Are you Andy?" she muttered in a Dublin accent.

"Yes, are you Mrs. Wall?"

She nodded and I invited her to sit down.

"Would you like some tea?" I asked.

"Yes please."

I placed our order and returned to my seat.

"First of all let me thank you Mrs. Wall for coming to meet with me."

"Andy, please call me Ann. I don't like been referred to as Mrs. Wall. It makes me feel older than my years."

"Sure Ann, that's what my own mother says."

"What is her name?"

"Mary, Mary Stone."

"Mary, that's a good Irish name."

"Well Ann thanks for coming to see me especially at such short notice. Your accent does not sound like you're from the West of Ireland. Are you a Dublin woman?" I asked trying to make some small talk so she'd relax.

"Yes I was born in Dublin, raised in Tallaght and moved here a few years ago."

"I suppose it's much nicer down here, than living in the big city?"

"Yes it is. The people are very friendly and I enjoy horse riding, so living here is much easier on me than Dublin."

"Do you miss Dublin?"

"I miss my friends."

Ann seemed a little more relaxed now so I decided to go for it.

"Ann, I am currently investigating a large insurance claim against my company by an American man named John Harrison, anything you can tell me about him would be much appreciated. No matter how small or insignificant it may be to you, it could be crucial evidence and may assist the defence of the claim."

"Andy, everything is wrong about John Harrison and I would not believe a word that comes out of his mouth," Ann said, sitting up and sounding angry. "But before I talk to you about him, you have got to promise me that you will keep my daughter out of this."

"Ann, I can assure you I have no interest in your daughter."

"OK Andy if I have you word … John Harrison … call it a mother's intuition, but from the moment I met him, I knew there was going to be trouble. You know I reported him to the police in Tallaght, but they did nothing."

"Ann please, let's go back to the start, to when you first met him. Tell me your story. I am really interested in this guy."

"How long have you got?" she asked, half-joking.

"Ann I have got all night if needs be."

"OK Andy but you had better make yourself comfortable as this is going to take some time."

"I am not in any rush," I said as I sat back in the plush sofa.

Ann took a drink of tea and then started talking.

"My daughter Sally was studying to be a doctor at Trinity College, Dublin, in 2000. She'd repeated her Leaving Certificate to get enough points to be accepted into college. Anyway having completed two of her three years she decided to go to America to work on a ranch for a few months. You see like me Sally loves horse riding. She applied for a position advertised on the Web. It was at a ranch near a small town called Tombstone in Arizona."

"Tombstone? Wasn't that the location of the famous shootout at the OK Corral with Wyatt Earp?"

"Wyatt who?"

Obviously Ann's interest in the American Wild West was not the same as mine.

"It doesn't matter please continue."

"However she could not get a work visa, so she did a deal with the owner of the ranch. Sally agreed to work there for the summer without any payment, but they'd give her a room and cover her food costs and any other associated bills. I think they even covered her flight."

"What was the name of the ranch and also can you remember the manager's name?"

"The manager's name was Laura Quinn. I can't remember the name of the ranch but it will come back to me."

I was writing notes as we talked. I'd decided not to use a Dictaphone as I was afraid it would make Ann feel uncomfortable.

"We drove Sally to Shannon Airport and she got a flight to Phoenix Arizona, via New York or maybe it was Chicago. Sally loved working in Arizona and in particular staying on the ranch with the horses but it was there that she met *him*."

"Him being John Harrison?"

"Yes, he destroyed my baby's life. When I think what he has put us through, it makes me so sad."

I noticed her eyes had filled up. She took a tissue from her pocket and wiped away a tear.

"Ann would you like to stop and we can do this another time?"

"No, this is good for me. I want to clear my head," Ann said, as she leaned forwards and grasped my right hand. "Andy, whatever John has done, I want you to promise me that you will do all that you can to put him in front of a judge."

"Ann I can assure you I will do all that I can to ensure that justice prevails."

"Thank you Andy ... that is all I can ask ... now let me continue."

Ann took another drink of tea. She looked as determined as a witness who was about to testify in a criminal court.

"We used to keep in contact with Sally on the phone and she was always telling us stories. I remember her telling me that it was so hot one day that she got into the horses' drinking water to cool off. Every two or three days, Sally would phone and we would call her back," Ann said, with a slight laugh. "It cost us a bloody fortune. We also emailed and Sally sent us some amazing photographs; Arizona looks so beautiful."

"I am sure it is beautiful and perhaps someday you will visit it."

"No I don't think so, I do like America but I need to forget that part of Sally's life. One day, about two weeks before Sally was due to return home to Ireland, she called and asked if John could stay with us for a week. John and his then girlfriend Laura wanted to move to Ireland to open a ranch or horse training arena."

Ann stopped and started to smile: "We agreed to put John up in our house for a week and went to collect him at Shannon Airport. It makes me smile Andy, to remember John when he walked into the Arrivals Hall of Shannon, wearing blue dungarees. He looked like John Boy Walton. And as for that stupid cowboy hat ... he just looked ridiculous."

"Hang on a second Ann," I said and started searching my laptop bag. I pulled the wedding photograph out and showed it to Ann.

"Yes that's the stupid hat and that is John; who is the poor unfortunate girl?"

"It does not matter … so you picked him up at Shannon Airport. Tell me how was he physically, did he look fit?"

"He looked slim and yes maybe fit, but how could he be fit when he was injured?"

"Injured, what injury?" I asked, sitting up.

"I don't know how the injury occurred. His right leg was in a bandage or maybe a support. He walked with a bad limp and he was on painkillers for his back. He complained of having terrible pain there. I remember him taking painkillers like sweets."

"You have no idea how the accident occurred?"

"No I don't."

"Ann this information is vital. Are you sure you don't know anything about the accident?"

"I have no idea Andy. He arrived in Shannon Airport looking like that."

"Would Sally have an idea?"

"No, I don't want Sally involved," Ann said, standing up. "Now I think I better go. Sally has moved on with her life and does not need John coming back into it."

"OK Ann, no problem," I said, as I stood up. "I understand this is causing you difficulty, remembering what happened. If you want to call it a night then that is fine with me but what you tell me could help to convict Harrison."

Ann calmed down and asked for another cup of tea. I summoned the waiter and requested a tea and a coffee.

"I am sorry, it's just these memories are difficult for me."

"I understand Ann. I really appreciate you talking to me."

"Now let me remember, we collected them from Shannon Airport and drove back to our home. Our eldest son, Shane, was away in England working so we let John stay in his bedroom. At first he was fine, polite and a real charmer with the ladies and the locals, especially with his sexy American drawl. Hold a minute, now I remember, the name of the ranch in Tombstone was the Mustang Stallion Ranch."

I quickly wrote it down.

"So did John stay long?"

"Yes, when I think how stupid I was back then. Not only did we let him stay in our house but I washed and ironed his clothes. I cleaned his room and cooked him his meals. In a way I felt sorry for him as he appeared to be in pain, with his leg and back. He had a lot of medication with him."

I was most interested in Harrison's injury to his back and leg and was curious how it had occurred. Perhaps it had happened from a previous car accident. If I could find out it would be crucial information.

"Andy, one thing I found strange was when I was hoovering his bedroom one afternoon, his passport was on the bedside locker and I knocked it onto the floor. I picked it up and, to be honest, I was curious as I had never previously seen an American passport before. I opened it and looked at the photograph page where there was a good photograph of John. However the name on the passport was Luke Wilson. I put it back on the locker and left the room. I told my husband and we agreed to say nothing. I know I should have said it to Sally. There was something odd going on and I did nothing."

I was amazed. Was it also possible that Harrison had obtained a United States passport in the name of Luke Wilson? Who was Luke Wilson? Did he live in Tombstone? I was going to leave this meeting with more questions and leads than ever.

"Who is Luke Wilson, is he John Harrison?" she asked.

"Ann I honestly don't know. I have never heard of Luke Wilson before today. Have you ever heard the names Sean Moran or Kenneth Smith?"

Ann thought for a few moments.

"No, I do know a family by the name of Moran, however that is Charles and Janet Moran and they live in Dublin … no I have never heard of a Kenneth Smith or Sean Moran."

"OK, please continue."

"John stayed with us for about a week. We brought him out to the local pub on a couple of nights and I did notice that he never once bought anybody a drink."

"So what happened next Ann?"

"Not much. He used to stay in his room most of the day and then go out drinking at night. A week later I drove him to Shannon Airport again and we met Laura and Sally. I was so embarrassed when Laura and John kissed passionately, right there in the Arrivals Hall and he must have been 20 years younger than her; it was disgusting. However I was delighted to see Sally who was excited to be home. I was glad when John and Laura went their way. I think they rented a car in Shannon Airport and Sally and I drove back home. Sally was talking all about her trip to America and how she wanted to return to Arizona. She must have spent a week talking about her trip – it was constantly, America, America, America… "

"So that was all you had to do with John and Laura?"

"I wish," Ann sighed. "About two weeks later, John arrived at our home with Laura and they collected the rest of his belongings. I drove Sally back to Dublin as she was returning to college to complete her degree; all appeared well and we got back to normal with our lives."

Ann seemed to be getting upset again. Perhaps it was time for some food.

"Ann would you like something to eat?" I asked suddenly.

It was getting late and we had been talking for about two hours.

"There is a time for eating and a time for talking and this is no time to be eating, now let me continue."

It was 9pm and I was starving, but my quest for information on Harrison got the better of me and I nodded.

"I can't remember the exact date, but it was October 2001 when Sally phoned me one evening and told me she was now in a relationship with John as Laura and he had separated. Laura had gone back to America. This took me by surprise Andy, but a week or so later Sally phoned me again telling me that she had dropped out of college. It broke my heart. She was a really good student and would have made an excellent doctor. In November 2001, Sally and John moved into a small rented house here in Carrick-on-Shannon. I found it strange as John always appeared to have money, even though he was not working. It made me feel uneasy. He had also bought a red Jeep-styled thing that was maybe four or five years old. We wondered how he afforded it. I remember one time he went out and bought a double oven for the house. I know these things are expensive and he also bought Sally some jewellery. Sally was totally taken by him. She had fallen in love with John and nothing else appeared to matter to her."

I knew how it felt to be obsessed with someone, only I was obsessed with getting enough evidence to refer John Harrison to the Gardaí for a criminal trial.

"They appeared to be happy living together in that small house. Then Sally got a job as a receptionist in the Market Hotel in Carrick-on-Shannon. The money was not great but it was a job and Sally worked long hours. One of them had to get a job and John was still complaining of pain in his back and leg so she had to work. I remember John was very protective of Sally, not in a nice way, more of a jealous way. He used to drive her to work and collect her every day. Then late in 2001, possibly December, he was stopped for drink driving by the police and had to produce his passport. I found out later that John did not have a passport and he'd entered

Ireland under the name of Luke Wilson. The Gardaí stopping him is where it all went wrong."

"Ann how did you find out he entered Ireland as Luke Wilson?"

"Will you give me a minute, I am trying to tell you the full story," Ann said, sounding anxious.

"Sorry Ann," I said.

Ann looked sad and took a deep breath.

"Have you seen the newspaper cutting, *Cowboy and Irish Girl?*"

I nodded.

"He was told to produce his passport and driving license at the local station. How could he, as he did not have any identification in his own name? So he panicked and Sally, who was in love with him, listened to every word he said, as if she was in a trance. I am not making excuses for Sally, but she was young, had never been in trouble with the police and she had fallen for the Texan," Ann said.

She took a drink of some tea and then continued: "What I am telling you are painful memories Andy but in some ways I am glad to be telling you all this if it will assist you in getting Harrison into a court room."

"I can't promise anything but I will do my best," I said crossing my fingers.

"It was on the 3 January 2002, early in the morning, maybe 8am. There was a knock at my front door, which was unusual as it was so early. When I opened it there were two police detectives and a uniformed policewoman standing in my porch. They walked into the house saying they were look-ing for Sally. I told them she was living with John at the old cottage in Carrick-on-Shannon. The detectives were aggres-sive and kept questioning me and my husband about Sally. It's strange when I think back to that first meeting as those two detectives became good friends and in the long run were very good to Sally and my family. But at the time I had no idea what had happened or why the police were looking for her. I did have a feeling it was something to do with John Harrison. If anyone had brought trouble to my door I just knew it was him. One of the detectives told me that money had been stolen, that €10,000 had gone missing from the safe of the Market Hotel. They were looking for Sally as she had the keys to the hotel and safe and she had also locked up the previous evening. Apparently there was no sign of any forced entry and nothing was damaged so whoever had taken the money had a key and knew the code to the safe. The Manager had come into the hotel early in the morning and found the safe open and the money gone. She then tried to contact Sally but her mobile was turned off. It was then that the Manager called the police and they arrived at my house," Ann said, teary-eyed. "Please give me a few moments Andy."

"Of course," I said as Ann stood up and walked over to the ladies.

I understood that this was painful for Ann, but I was engrossed in the story and hoped she would finish it.

I took the opportunity to call my wife and told her that I would be late home. It was now just after 10.30pm. I read my notes, in excess of ten pages and growing, and then headed to the men's room.

When I returned Ann was in the process of pouring some fresh tea.

"Ann, are you OK? Would you like to finish?"

"No I am fine and I really want to continue talking. It's kind of a release for me."

"OK please carry on when you are ready."

"I remember a day or possibly a few days passed and then I received a telephone call from Sally who told me that they had taken the money and not to worry as she was fine. The phone then went dead. I passed this information on to the detectives. About a week passed and there was no word and I was so worried for Sally. One of the detectives called to my house and told me that Sally had been arrested in Houston Airport, Texas. She did not have a return ticket from the United States so she was put into a holding area for a few weeks. Eventually the police told me she was to be deported and that she would arrive in Shannon Airport on an Aer Lingus flight, accompanied by United States Air Marshals. The Gardaí were very good and permitted me to meet Sally in the airport and to bring her home before they interviewed her. I was shocked and in bits when Sally admitted that they had taken the money from the hotel safe and fled. Apparently he first drove to Belfast but was too nervous to go through the city, I don't know why, maybe he was thinking of the IRA, who knows? So they drove to Dublin and took the ferry to Wales and then drove through England and took the Channel Tunnel to France. Sally told me she was scared and knew that what she had done was wrong. They drove through France all the way to Holland. Then they ditched the car and flew to Mexico. I am not sure what city they flew from, possibly Amsterdam. On landing in Mexico they split up and tried to cross the border into America. Sally got a flight to Houston, Texas, and this is where she got stopped by United States Immigration. I tell you Andy she cried nonstop for a couple of days. I know Sally did wrong, but she is a good person who got carried away with him and his Texan charms. I just knew he was wrong from the first time I met him. He always had money yet I never remember him working."

I looked down at all my notes as Ann stopped speaking. I was trying to think of any questions I'd forgotten to ask her.

"Ann, there's one other thing. Could I get a formal statement from you? It's so late now maybe we could meet again in a week or two.

"No, if you want the statement you take it now, while my blood is still boiling."

I ignored my tiredness and started to type on my laptop:

The Statement I took from Ann was brief in comparison to the usual statements I took as I had all the information I needed in my notebook. I obtained some crucial points formally in the statement knowing that if a criminal prosecution was to take place then it would be required by the Gardaí. From my point of view, the most important point covered in the statement was that Harrison had arrived in Shannon Airport suffering with leg and back problems. This information was crucial to the defence of the claim he'd submitted against Dallast. Now I finally knew the genesis of the back and other injuries which had no doubt led to the medical information we'd received from Liverpool Hospital.

I checked the last lines: 'As far as I know Sally is working and trying to pay off the money she took from the Hotel. My daughter has since made a new life for herself. I confirm this is a true statement.'

On completion of the Statement of Fact I asked Ann to review and then sign and date it.

It was now extremely late and I had to drive back to Dublin.

"Ann, thank you so much for talking to me and for all the information."

"Just promise me you will keep Sally out of this"

"I promise you I will. Is she in Ireland?" I asked inquisitively. "Is she still in contact with John?"

"She had better not be or she will have me to deal with," Ann growled. "After the court case Sally moved out to the

Midlands. We kept in touch but lost contact for a time. I don't know if she was in touch with John then."

"I ask because I am aware of an insurance claim where a Sally Wall knocked down a pedestrian named Sean Moran. I hate to tell you this but Sean Moran is a name used by John Harrison."

"When was this accident?"

"September 2006, in Co. Kildare."

Ann looked upset and asked: "Are you sure?"

I nodded.

"I knew she was in contact with him! Call it a mother's intuition. Is there likely to be a prosecution for that?"

"No I don't think so. I am not investigating that claim and it is finished and closed. I am investigating another matter. However at this stage I have so much information I will need to collate all of the data and gained intelligence before passing it on to the Gardaí. Ann I cannot thank you enough for the information you have given me, especially as I understand the pain Harrison has caused you and your family."

"Andy just promise me you will do all that you can to get him to court."

"Ann, my ultimate goal is to get him behind bars!"

I assured her I would do my best and we said goodbye. I started the drive home more determined than ever to nail John Harrison after hearing what he had done to the young and innocent Sally Wall.

CHAPTER 22

The following morning I arrived into the office late, after midday. I justified the extra few hours in bed in my head as I had been working the night before in Mayo.

Nobody noticed me as I slipped into my seat and logged on to my laptop. Denise had left a note on my computer screen: 'Hi Andy, gone to Wicklow on the John O'Brien job. See you tomorrow!'

I was impressed that Denise had managed to get Denton to drive her to Wicklow on another case. It was good for both of them, as my long-term plan was to get Denise on the road as a field investigator. She had already displayed a good grasp and knowledge of investigation procedures and just needed experience to boost her confidence.

My desk phone rang as I logged onto my work computer.

"Hi Andy!"

"Nigel any news? How are you doing?"

"Oh yes Andy, I have loads of news for you; tell me are you sitting down?"

"You know me Nigel, always sitting on my ass."

"Never a truer word said Mr. Stone!"

"So Nigel, what have you got?"

"Andy, do you remember the CCD claim letter I told you about, the letter I found in the apartment in Liverpool?"

"Yes, I remember — the Kenneth Smith one."

"Yes, that's the one Andy; well I've got a bit more information on it from their investigations unit. The bare bones are that a Kenneth Smith hired a car from Hertz in Liverpool Airport. Apparently as he was driving along he knocked down a pedestrian named Gary O'Neill. O'Neill is claiming against the CCD insurance policy issued to Kenneth Smith by Hertz. CCD Insurance is still holding a large financial reserve as apparently Gary O'Neill has, you'll never guess it ... hurt his lower back but they are sure the claim is suspect."

"That is very interesting Nigel; I just wish I could find something on Gary O'Neill."

"I will tell you what I think has happened here Andy, Gary O'Neill, Kenneth Smith and John Harrison are all the same person. I think that Harrison hired a car from Hertz in the name of Kenneth Smith and then knocked himself down, entering a claim in the name of Gary O'Neill. It sounds complex, but in reality it's really very simple. There are no independent witnesses of the accident because the accident never happened — it's your classic staged set-up. There is no accident, no injury, no car with any damage on it — it's all lies, but there is a pile of cash at the end paid out by the unfortunate insurance company."

"So Harrison has a third alias — we've Sean Moran, Kenneth Smith and now Gary O'Neill. Are you sure about O'Neill Nigel?"

"Well I can't be 100 per cent certain, but I would bet my bottom dollar it is our Cowboy."

"I agree Nigel but the only thing is we have to prove it. Do you have a date of birth for Gary O'Neill?"

"Yes according to CCD it's 11 September, 1975." said Nigel.

"That's very close to John Harrison's date of birth, 28 May 1975."

"I know Andy and if you check Kenneth Smith's date of birth and the date of birth of that other name you gave me, Sean Moran, that will also be within a year. Why I ask you?"

"Because it's the same person."

"Well done Sherlock," Nigel laughed. "Andy, I will compile a report for you. I think you should get the Irish police involved now. Have you finished the file?"

"I agree Nigel and I'm nearly there on the file but let's hold off for a few days. I want to run some checks on Gary O'Neill before we call them in. Thanks Nigel, I will call you back shortly."

I hung up and ran Gary O'Neill, with his date of birth, through our internal claims database. But there were no matches for previous claims. I also ran the name through some financial databases and again found no matches. Finally I entered the name and date of birth into the Insurance Link database. The database was running unusually slowly, which was more than likely down to the internet traffic. I waited a few seconds more and then I struck gold. I got an exact match against Mustang Insurance.

Confidential Insurance Link Report:
Insurer: Mustang Insurance Ireland
Incident date: 9 February 2005
Claim Type: Employer's Liability
Claim No: X123HI

Claimant name: Gary O'Neill
Claimant Address: 315 River Valley Vale, Swords, Co. Dublin
Date of Birth: 11 September 1975

As I read down through the claim information I thought it looked promising but I was concerned as it was a claim for employer's liability. This basically meant that an employee had sustained an injury at work and was claiming against the employer. All the other claims were personal injury claims from motor accidents involving a pedestrian. This claim was different. I needed to find out more about it as maybe it wasn't Harrison.

I telephoned my contact in Mustang but unfortunately he had just gone on a two week vacation. However I was able to find out that the claim had been handled quickly and that a payment of €25,000 was made to Gary O'Neill, who had allegedly injured his back. According to Amy, the lady I ended up talking to, O'Neill said he was lifting a wheel for his employer when he had felt a sudden pain in his back. O'Neill attended a medical examiner and provided medical evidence of a back injury. Magnum Insurance had felt that the claim was genuine and made a fast settlement. No more information was on file other than that Gary O'Neill had represented himself. There were no witnesses to the accident and he was described as being a Canadian citizen. On hearing the words "Canadian citizen" I just knew it was Harrison. It was essentially the same fraud, just with a different modus operandi. Somehow John Harrison had assumed the identity of Gary O'Neill. I had no idea how he'd done it but I was more determined than ever to find out.

I thanked Amy and suggested that she place an electronic trace on the cheque which had been paid directly to Gary O'Neill.

"I'll do that Andy. It will take about a week and I'll contact you when I have further information."

The address in Swords, Co. Dublin was only about a 30 minute drive from the office. I printed the Insurance Link report, grabbed my file, the precious notebook and ran out of the office, almost knocking over Tanya.

I left the car park so quickly the exit barrier brushed off my roof as I drove off. I was on a mission — I needed to find the address in Swords and get confirmation of the identity of the man who was living there. Although I was 99.9 per cent certain that this was also John Harrison, I knew I could assume nothing and had to prove it. Having a hunch was useless, unless I could back it up with factual evidence. Providing evidence in court would not be a very enjoyable experience without proof.

The traffic was particularly light and I located 315 River Valley Vale with relative ease. It was located in the middle of a housing estate and looked poorly maintained. It would certainly have benefited from a coat of paint.

I walked up to the front door and rang the doorbell. However nobody appeared to be at home. I turned around and saw the next door neighbour taking her shopping from the boot of her car and carrying it into her house. She obviously did not hear me walking up behind her as I startled her so much she jumped. Not the best beginning for trying to get information from a stranger!

"Oh, I am so sorry for startling you," I quickly apologised.

"That's OK. I should not be so nervous."

"Can I ask you a few questions? I am not selling anything and I am also not a politician looking for your vote."

"Well then make yourself useful and help me carry this shopping into the house," she said, handing me three bags. "Here put these in the kitchen."

I thought she must be a relaxed type of person to invite a complete stranger into her house so I was hoping she might have talked with the neighbours. I left the bags on the kitchen table and walked out towards the car again. I met her in the hallway.

"That's all the bags, thanks ... now how can I help you?"

"I am investigating an insurance claim and I am interested in some people who lived in the house next door."

"That house is rented out. I don't know how many people are staying there."

Just then a man appeared at the open front door and walked in.

"This is my husband John," she said. "John this is ... I am sorry I don't know your name."

I put out my hand and shook John's saying: "Hi, I am Andrew Stone of Dallast Insurance's fraud unit."

"Pleased to meet you; this is my wife Linda. What is this about?"

"It's nothing to do with you guys," I said quickly as he was looking a bit worried. "I'm just trying to follow up a lead on a man who possibly lived next door, and I would really appreciate your assistance."

"Look we keep to ourselves, we don't want any problems. We live a quiet life," John said.

"Anything you say to me is off the record unless you want to put it in writing. I am just trying to locate a man and solve a possible insurance fraud against my company and probably another insurance company."

"Insurance fraud!" John groaned. "Do you know how much it costs me to insure my car? It's crazy money. What do you need to know?"

"Do you know the people who live next door?"

"I would know a few of them to see. I think there are about five or six people living there at the moment. I don't think any of them are Irish."

"Have you any idea who is the owner of the property?"

"Yes," Linda said. "The McGuirks own it. I have their phone number. I'll write it down for you."

"Thank you Linda that is great I will give them a call."

"So who are you looking for?" John asked, as she went upstairs.

"I am trying to locate an American or Canadian man who possibly lived there about four years ago."

"An American … hmmm, what did he look like?"

"He looked a little like the actor Colin Farrell."

"That sounds like that Texan man," Linda said as she came back with the number. "I remember he was in the garden one time without his shirt on — a real American poser."

"Yes, he is a Texan," I said feeling excited.

"I didn't meet him but I do remember Linda talking about him," John said.

"Linda, how did you know he was from Texas?"

"He had a white cowboy hat that he used to wear all the time and he told me he was from Texas. He was bragging," she smiled.

"Give me a moment," I said and ran out to my car. I pulled the wedding photograph from my file and ran back into the house with it. I showed it to Linda without saying anything.

She held it in her right hand and studied it.

"Yes that's him and that's the cowboy hat."

"Are you sure Linda?"

"Yes I am 100 per cent certain that is the man," she said, handing it back.

"Well I'll be dammed, you're very good John Harrison," I said.

"Sorry?" Linda queried.

"Oh, I was just thinking out loud. Linda, John thank you very much for your assistance, you have been very helpful."

I returned to my car feeling delighted but also a bit concerned. How was John Harrison doing it? How had he managed to change his identity on so many occasions?

While I was driving back to the office I telephoned the McGuirks. Unfortunately the phone was turned off and it was not possible to leave a message.

I arrived back at the office late in the afternoon. Most of the staff had finished for the day with the exception of a few dedicated individuals and of course the management team.

I logged onto my computer and checked my emails, which had built up during the day. Having dealt with the urgent ones I decided to try the number Linda had given me for the McGuirks again.

The phone was answered by a man with a Dublin accent.

"Hello is that Joe McGuirk?" I asked.

"Yes this is Joe."

"Hi Joe, my name is Andrew Stone from Dallast Insurance. I was wondering if you could assist me with some information."

"Dallast Insurance… I was insured with you guys for many years. Insurance is gone so expensive. Thank God I don't need to insure anything."

"No you misunderstood me I am not trying to sell you anything. I am trying to get some information on a man who used to rent your house."

"Rent a house? I have a few houses rented out – which one was it?"

"It's in River Valley Vale, Swords, Co. Dublin."

"Yes that is one of my houses, but that house is rented as four independent rooms, so basically I have four tenants staying at that house, foreigners. I think they are Indian or maybe Pakistani."

"The man I am interested in is American," I said, and held my breath.

There was a silence on the phone for a few seconds which felt more like minutes to me. Would he be able to give me another lead?

"I think I know who you are talking about; what does he look like?"

"He looks a bit like Colin Farrell, the actor."

"Yeah that sounds right; he was a good lucking dude from Texas, always in cowboy boots and hat."

"Joe what colour was the cowboy hat?"

"White or cream I think."

I was satisfied that this was John Harrison but I needed verification.

"Do you have an email address I could send a picture to Joe? It would be very helpful if you could verify if this is the guy who rented the room – OK?"

"Yes, hold on, I'll call it out."

I typed the address in and thanked him for his help. I quickly attached the wedding photograph, and with the touch of a button, the email was gone.

I was anxious and hoped he'd get back to me soon. The tenant sounded like Harrison but it would be better if Joe could ID him from the photograph. It was so different from the old days. I still found it odd that it was now possible to take a photograph on your Blackberry and email it directly to someone for identification purposes. It really assisted me in surveillance operations.

I was so hungry my stomach was gurgling. I decided to take a walk over to the local coffee shop to get a sandwich while I was waiting but it started pouring rain. I grabbed a chocolate bar from the vending machine instead and had a cup of very bad coffee. It gave me the burst of energy I needed as I returned to my desk and checked my email. To my surprise Joe had responded already with a simple email: 'Yes, that is him. Do you know his current location as he owes me some money?'

It was another positive result. I was curious to find out about the money that was owed to Joe and decided to give him a quick call.

"Hi Joe; it's Andy from Dallast Insurance again. Are you certain sure this is the man who rented the room?"

"That's the guy — he owes me two weeks' rent. He rented a room for about four months a few years ago, maybe 2005 and then he disappeared without paying me. It's the same guy, wearing that stupid cowboy hat."

"Can you remember if he had any injuries? Did he have a problem with his back or his legs?"

"I think he did now and again but he was only there for a couple of months.

"Thanks Joe, I appreciate your assistance," I said and we hung up.

I was getting a picture of Harrison's life in Ireland. It was interesting that in 2005 he was still suffering from back pain. Ann Wall had mentioned that Harrison had problems with his back when she collected him at Shannon Airport in 2001. This had to be the original injury he was using to manipulate payments from insurance companies for the staged accidents.

I was hopeful that the Gardaí would be able to discover the truth when I handed over my presentation of evidence for discussion with them. I knew it might be a challenge to get the GBFI to take on the Harrison case as so many files were referred to them from financial institutions. Would they be willing to take on an investigation into an American citizen?

CHAPTER 23

I telephoned Hugh, my main detective contact, the following morning.

There is a protocol in place between insurance companies operating in Ireland and An Garda Siochana. It is applied to the referral of suspected insurance fraud cases to the Garda Bureau of Fraud Investigation (GBFI) for possible criminal investigation and prosecution. There is a duty on financial institutions to first carry out a full investigation into the matter before contacting the GBFI. Like Dallast insurance, most financial institutions have an Internal Investigations Unit (IIU) or Special Investigations Unit (SIU) who will do this. Essentially files should only be forwarded to the GBFI when there is strong evidence of fraud and, above all, a good chance of achieving a criminal prosecution. As with all State agencies there are restrictions on budgets and stringent cost control so investigators should only refer quality files for further investigation.

Within the GBFI there is an Assessment Unit, whose members have the difficult task of assessing the files and cases which are referred from insurance companies, banks and other financial institutions, members of the Gardaí and on occasion, the general public, via local police stations. The unit has a Detective Sergeant and six detectives whose function is to consider which files should be forwarded to the different teams within the GBFI for further investigation and which should be rejected. The GBFI has a specialist financial fraud unit which is headed up by a Detective Inspector, with a Detective Sergeant and an additional team of detectives. However, in order to get your file viewed by this team, you must first pass the Assessment Unit. The complexity of the Harrison case, with the many different identities involved, along with the potential values of the claims, should make the GBFI accept it but I was hoping Hugh could give me an extra edge.

"What do you need Andy?"

"Well hello to you too Hughie."

"Andy, you're a good friend, but you normally only phone me when you need one of your little favours."

"I know Hugh, and to be fair that is true!"

"Well what do you need?"

"I need to hand over my American case to the Fraud Squad as I can do no more from my end. Any advice?"

"Is this the American with the different identities?"

"Yes; I have exhausted all my lines of investigation. I have collated buckets of evidence and now I need to hand it over to your lads but I want to make sure they take it on."

In one way I couldn't believe what I was saying, handing over my file was going to be difficult for me. It was like the feeling I'd got leaving Olivia off for her first day of school but I knew I could do no more with the investigation and I had certainly gone beyond the requirements of an insurance investigator. It was now time to send in the cavalry.

"Andy, from what you have told me about the file, it seems rather complex and confusing, especially with all those insurance terms."

"You're right Hugh; it is a bit on the complex side, so I was wondering if you could put a word in with your contacts?"

"Andy it won't be a problem. I am sure the guys will accept your file. Do you remember that excellent Detective Sergeant I was telling you about who was based with the GBFI? She would be the ideal detective for Operation Cowboy. When you're talking to them be sure to emphasise the money and the different passports as that will get them interested."

"Money and passports, OK Hugh."

"Look Andy don't worry I will have a word with one of my contacts and there will be no problem."

"Thanks Hugh."

I added my notes on Gary O'Neill, Harrison's fourth identity, to the presentation. I emphasised that the identity thefts were my main reason for handing the file to the police as I needed them to look at bank accounts and criminal records. This avenue was not open to financial investigators and was effectively against the law.

After getting the low down from Hugh I also decided I needed to have a conversation with Nigel.

"Hi Nigel, it's Andy. I am preparing that file for the police. I think that there are so much evidence and leads that I will prepare a presentation for them. If I set up a date with them I would need you to come over to Ireland to cover your UK investigations — is that OK?"

"Ireland — yeah OK. Try and make the meeting on a Friday or Monday and we will make it a weekend trip. Just organise my ticket and I will be there Andy. I am running late for a meeting so call me later."

The Dublin office would need to cover the cost of his ticket and expenses. This should not have been a problem however, as with most large organisations there were restrictions on costs and in particular on airline tickets. It was a strange restriction when it was possible to book a Ryanair ticket for as low as €50 return from London to Dublin, but I would have to get approval from Courtney if I didn't want any trouble. But before I booked anything I first needed to confirm that I could present my findings to the GBFI and I needed to get a date to meet them.

It was time to try the direct approach. I phoned the Assessment Unit and spoke to 'Ray', an experienced detective who I'd had some dealings with on past cases. They had ended with successful criminal prosecutions but they were not of the same magnitude as the Harrison file.

The conversation went something like this:

"Good Morning, Garda Bureau of Fraud Investigation, 'Ray' speaking."

"Morning Ray, this is Andrew Stone in Dallast Insurance."

"Hi Andy, have not spoken to you in a while. How are you doing?"

"Not bad Ray. I think I have a large case for you here, serious money involved and potentially serious fraud."

"How much are you talking Andy?"

"Ray at this stage I am looking at about €500,000."

"That is serious money Andy, what have you got?"

"I have so much evidence and so many leads I am not sure where to start. This case involves serious fraud, multiple identity thefts, various insurance claims and the fraudulent use of Irish passports."

"You mean somebody is copying Irish passports?"

"No Ray, not copies or forged Irish passports. These are real passports which seem to have been obtained using false identities."

"Hold on a minute Andy," he said and put me on hold.

I started to feel a bit nervous. I was putting my professional reputation on the line with the suggestion of false passports but I had the Kenneth Smith details to hand in case Ray requested further information.

After no more then a minute, Ray was back.

"Andy, do you want to call over to our office?"

I breathed a sigh of relief as it looked like I had the Assessment Unit interested which was a good start.

"Ray, I appreciate the offer of calling over but with the amount of evidence I have obtained, which involves Dallast UK investigators and surveillance in Poland, would it be possible for you to come to my office and I will give you a full presentation?"

"Wait a minute," Ray answered, and once again put me on hold.

This time I was only holding for about 20 seconds but it felt like an hour as the time passed so slowly.

"OK Andy, I will call over to your office with the Detective Inspector. When do you propose meeting?"

I already had a date planned in my head.

"How about next Tuesday, the 14th at 11.00am?"

"That is fine with me Andy. I will let you know if there are any changes from our end."

"Ray, I will have a colleague flying in from the UK, so please try to hold the meeting to this date."

"OK Andy, it should be fine. I will see you next Tuesday."

As soon as I hung up I telephoned Nigel, hoping that he would be available on the 14th. Thankfully he could make it; his only request was that I book him a ticket from Heathrow Airport. Unfortunately this meant it would be a bit more expensive. As time was not on my side, I decided to ignore company procedure and instead I immediately purchased a ticket online, Heathrow – Dublin return, at a cost of €155, using my own credit card. I did manage to get a receipt so there was a chance I would be able to claim the cost back but I didn't care much as I was so focused on the meeting. I needed to provide the GBFI detectives with enough strong evidence to get them to pass the file onto their financial investigation team.

I knew it was time to bring Courtney up to speed with the developments, now that I was getting the police involved so I sent him a quick email:

> 'Hi Dan,
> I have nearly completed the investigation on the American and did not need to use the entire €20,000 for the investigation costs. I have been in contact with the GBFI who have agreed to call to the office on the 14th. I will draft a full presentation of evidence and Nigel from the UK office is also attending. I have booked a ticket for him to fly in from London. Nigel will draft a presentation and will provide an information chart of evidence for the detectives. I will also ask Tanya to attend, just in case there are any technical insurance related questions.
>
> Talk to you soon,
> Regards
> Andy'

Almost immediately a response came from Dan's Blackberry: 'Good Job….. Dan'

Trying to put together a presentation of evidence at my desk with the many interruptions and the noise of a busy claims department in the background was difficult. I had plenty of annual leave left and decided to take the Friday off as a holiday. I didn't even want to work from home as per normal as I wanted to be able to switch off my phone. Finalising my presentation of evidence for the GBFI was going to take time and I needed it to be accurate as eventually it could end up as evidence in court.

That Friday morning I brought my file, which was now a large box, from the boot of my car and set up my laptop computer to begin the presentation. It was a beautiful summer morning and I was ready and free to concentrate fully on summarising the case.

I began to work my way through the file and gradually realised that the presentation of evidence to the GBFI could eventually be used as a part of an insurance fraud training manual or presentation for the Insurance Institute there was so much there. As I started on the origins of the case, with details of the alleged accident, the insured, John Harrison and so on it was hard to believe I'd only been investigating him for about 12 weeks. I gave a broad outline of the UK side and was glad Nigel would be able to present his evidence with me. I also included a base slide on the information I had obtained from our operation in North America, including the information and photographs obtained from Detective Mark Keating in Oklahoma. I covered Harrison's wedding in Hawaii, the wedding license and photograph.

I moved on to his other identity, Kenneth Smith and double-checked the photographs obtained of the jeep in the Mourne Mountains and detailed the interview with Harrison's former employer at Murray Towing Services in

Drogheda, Co. Louth. I also included the financial payments made to Kenneth Smith by Mustang Insurance and the links to Sean Moran and his payment from Starling Insurance.

As I wrote about my time in Poland carrying out surveillance it sounded like a scene from a James Bond movie. I attached Igor's photographs and the details of the red Alfa Romeo, insured and registered to Kenneth Smith.

I went through the facts and photographs again, double-checking my spelling and making sure it looked good. It had taken me over eight hours to collate all the evidence and I had completely forgotten to eat or drink. I guess I was working on adrenalin.

The following Monday morning the traffic was really bad as I drove past Dublin Airport. I was enjoying listening to Newstalk 106, as Ivan Yates the broadcaster was giving some politician a good verbal bashing over the poor state of the finances of Ireland.

As I drove along, my mobile rang. It was Ray from the GBFI.

"Morning Andy, just to confirm are we still OK for 11am tomorrow morning?"

I relaxed as I'd been afraid he was cancelling or postponing the meeting.

"Perfect Ray, I will see you at 11am."

I could start to feel the excitement building in me at the thought of the meeting the next day.

After I arrived in the office I quickly went to work on my emails, clearing as many as possible. One of the emails was from the fraud manager of Bank B where Harrison had held an account under the name Kenneth Smith.

The manager was suggesting we meet for lunch to have a chat about cross-industry fraud. I was going to email back that

I was too busy to meet him for a few days but then I thought it might be an opportunity to discuss the bank account John Harrison had set-up as Sean Moran.

I searched through my file for the details of Sean Moran's €45,000 claim against Starling Insurance and found Willie McCabe's phone number.

"Hi Willie. It's Andy in Dallast."

"Hi Andy, how can I help you?"

"Willie remember I spoke to you about a claim and the claimant was Sean Moran?"

"Yes, I have the file in front of me."

"By any chance, did you put a trace on the cheque you made payable to Sean Moran?"

"I am one step ahead of you Andy. I have the full account number here and the sort code."

I took the numbers down as he called them out. I was delighted as "Bank B" was the fraud manager's bank. It would be worth meeting him for that lunch.

"Thanks Willie, you are a star!"

I immediately telephoned 'John', the fraud manager at Bank B.

"Hi John, it's Andy in Dallast."

"Hi Andy, did you get my email?"

"I did John and yes I would love to meet you for lunch. However before we meet I need a favour."

"What can I do for you?"

"If I gave you a bank account number and sort code would you be able to check and see how the account was opened?"

"Yes but as we talked about Data Protection will not permit me to share this information with you."

"Yes I know and understand, but do you recall I asked you to check an account on a Kenneth Smith a few months back?"

"Yes, I gave you the passport number. In fact I still have a photocopy of the Kenneth Smith passport in my drawer."

"OK John, please just take a look at this other account. Can you just confirm if it was opened with an Irish passport?"

"I will only be able to tell you limited information but go ahead."

"Thanks John!"

I gave him the account number and sort code and heard him type them in.

"What proof of identity was used to open the account?" I asked eagerly.

"Give me a minute!"

I could hear him clicking away as I waiting impatiently.

"Now the account was opened with an Irish passport, I have the number here ... hold a minute that's strange."

"What? What's strange?"

"Very strange; no it cannot be possible... "

"John, please tell me what is strange? Come on please."

John eventually answered: "The photographs in the two passports are very alike, but it couldn't be right. How could Sean Moran be Kenneth Smith? It must be a mistake."

"John this is no mistake; this is identity theft. Do you want to meet for that lunch and I'll tell you about it?"

"I will meet you in the coffee shop in Stephen's Green Shopping Centre in twenty minutes," he said and we signed off.

I ran to my car and rushed to the Stephen's Green' car park. I barely made it to the coffee shop in time. It was easy to spot John. He looked like a typical banker, standing outside holding a black brief case. As I greeted him, he opened his case and handed me a brown envelope.

"You didn't get these from me. I am sure it will assist your investigation, thanks for the offer of lunch but I don't have time!"

And with that John quickly walked away. It was as if we had just done a drug deal!

I returned to the car and opened the envelope — inside there were two photocopies of the passports in the names of Kenneth Smith and Sean Moran. I was not trained in the examination of documents and photographs, but it looked like the man in both passport photographs was John Harrison.

I drove back to the office, delighted with the new evidence. I really wanted to know how Harrison had obtained the passports. Hopefully the GBFI would be able to satisfy my curiosity.

I awoke early the following morning. I had slept for only a few hours as I was too nervous about presenting the evidence to senior detectives from the Fraud unit to relax.

I left the house early and drove to Dublin Airport, parking in the car park at 7.30am. Nigel's flight was not due to arrive from Heathrow until 8.30am but I wanted everything to go according to plan and was glad I was early.

I walked into the Arrivals Hall which was busy with business passengers arriving from mainland Europe and the US. Nigel's flight was running ten minutes late, but that was fine as we had plenty of time.

I purchased a coffee and sat waiting. The wait reminded me of difficult surveillance operations I'd run in various airports for Pinkerton. I had gained a lot of experience over the past 22 years of investigating but trying to pick up a passenger who had just arrived in the airport could still be a difficult task. On one occasion I needed to place surveillance on an Irishman who was flying into Dublin from JFK Airport, New York. All I had was a good physical description and his mobile phone number. I was lucky on that particular operation as the target arrived and the description was perfect. I also phoned his mobile which gave me confirmation of his identity.

I was thinking about how lucky I was to be living and working in Ireland as so many of my friends have had to emigrate to America, the UK and Australia, when somebody poked me on the shoulder. I turned around and to my surprise it was Nigel.

"How the hell, did you get here? Your flight is not due to land for another 40 minutes?"

"I was at Heathrow early and Aer Lingus permitted me to fly on the earlier flight, so here I am."

"How did you recognise me?" I asked, as we began to walk towards my car. "You have only met me once before."

"I always remember an ugly face!"

We left the airport and had an uneventful drive into the office. Using the Dublin Port tunnel allowed me to get us there in just under 30 minutes. I had booked our Directors' boardroom for the day as it was the best room in the office, with comfortable leather chairs and top quality computer and projector equipment.

We were so early we had ample opportunity to set up all our computer equipment and to run through our presentations and Nigel's professional looking intelligence chart. It was excellent as it showed the possible connections and also the actual connections in the case. For example the possible connections' list included all the different mobile phone numbers that Harrison had used when contacting insurance companies in the UK and Ireland. He'd illustrated the actual connections with red lines, such as the marriage certificate to Harrison's wife, obtained from Hawaii and the links between the different bank account numbers.

By 11.10am, all was looking good. The IT equipment was working and I was ready to give the performance of my life. The words of William Shakespeare's *As you like it* 'All the world's a stage and all men and women merely players,' raced through my mind.

"I nearly forgot. I have something to show you Nigel."

With that I opened the brown envelope 'John' from Bank B had given to me and showed Nigel the two photocopies of Irish passports in the names of Sean Moran and Kenneth Smith.

"Good God, this guy is bloody good, these forged passports are excellent."

"Nigel I am sure they are not forged. I'm almost 100 per cent positive they are genuine Irish passports. I know for a fact the Kenneth Smith passport is a genuine document and I am sure that the Sean Moran passport is as well."

"But it's the same face in the photograph on each passport, they must be forged!"

"You're right it is the same person in the photograph, however they are genuine Irish passports. I just don't know how he did it."

"This is amazing Andy."

"Yes it is Nigel. We have done a good job with this case!"

"It's a bloody marvellous job Andy."

"We still need to get the police to accept the case. They just have to accept the file."

"They will Andy; they will. If Harrison has these two passports there is possibly another passport in the name Gary O'Neill."

"We will need to make the police aware of that. They will be able to check with the passport office."

I was really proud of this case and what we'd established, not just for my employer but also as a citizen of Ireland. Preventing financial fraud was one thing, but preventing an international fraudster from obtaining official Irish passports, well that was a matter of National Security.

Just as Nigel was about to talk the internal phone rang.

"There are two detectives in reception looking for you," Ciara advised.

"Thanks I'll be right down. They're here," I said and stood up. "You ready?"

"Ready as I will ever be!"

I left the room and walked towards reception. The play was about to commence.

I was greeted by 'Ray' as I walked into reception. He was accompanied by a Detective Inspector 'Sweeney'. To get a Detective Inspector from the GBFI to attend your office was an achievement. I could feel a bead of sweat trickling down my back with anticipation.

As we walked towards the Conference room I thanked them for coming to the office and for taking such an interest in the file.

"This is our job Andrew," Det. Insp. Sweeney advised. "Ray tells me you have an interesting file, involving possible identity theft and false passports; we take these matters very seriously."

We walked into the conference room and I introduced Nigel and Tanya, who had also joined the meeting.

Everybody settled in and I wasted no time starting my presentation. The detectives sat staring at the computer screen and it was difficult to tell if they were genuinely interested in the file.

I sat down and Nigel stood up. He talked us through what he had discovered including the information about Harrison's claim against CCD Insurance, using his alter egos Gary O'Neill and Sean Moran.

As Nigel was talking Det. Insp. Sweeney interrupted: "This is all very interesting but we are only interested in what has happened in Ireland."

"I understand," I intervened quickly. "But we need to provide you with information on Harrison' activities in the UK and North America as well because it is all linked to Ireland."

"OK, please continue."

The inspector sat back with his arms folded.

Nigel completed his presentation and sat down. There was a loaded silence in the room.

"Would anybody like some tea or coffee?" Tanya asked.

Before anybody could answer Tanya, I stood up and continued with the American angle. Det. Insp. Sweeney and Ray sat up straight when they saw the information obtained from the District Attorney's office in Oklahoma and the wedding photographs from Hawaii.

"Andrew this is an excellent investigation, especially considering you are not a police officer. I congratulate you on a great job. Ray I think our boys could learn a trick or two from Andy's investigation."

Ray nodded in agreement.

I was sorry Courtney was not there to hear this praise coming from a GBFI Detective Inspector!

"Are you ready for some tea or coffee now?" I asked.

"No thank you we are fine," Det. Insp. Sweeney said.

I quickly talked them through the various claim payments made to Sean Moran and the evidence from the surveillance I had obtained in Poland.

"We have got a serial identity thief in our midst," Det. Insp. Sweeney said seriously. "Ray get on to the passport office and run the name and dates of birth. We'll have to get to the bottom of how this Harrison boy got so many of our Irish passports."

I could not resist the temptation and produced 'John's' brown envelope. I handed it over saying: "I think you need to see these documents."

I was going out on a ledge here. As these documents had been obtained unofficially, I was unsure how Sweeney was going to react. Tanya stayed silent as she did not know what was in the envelope but I heard a muffled gasp from Nigel and his eyes were fixed on the envelope.

The Detective Inspector opened it up and took a quick look at the photocopies of the two passports. He stood up, still holding the envelope. Ray also stood up as if he was a soldier standing in front of his commanding officer. I sunk lower in my seat, wondering what was coming next.

"This is serious Andy."

"I am sorry. I know I should not have obtained these passports and I understand it is against Data Protection."

"Yes it is, but in life there is the greater good. This is a matter of National Security. Andrew you have done an amazing job for your company and also your country. You should get a medal for your investigation. I salute you."

I felt totally exonerated.

"Ray you need to work with Andy on this file," Det. Insp. Sweeney said as he stood up.

"Inspector the only request I have is that you keep me updated on any developments with this case."

"I think you will be updating us Andy," he smiled. "Please give a full printout of all this evidence to Ray. So do you know Harrison's current location?"

"Possibly — we believe he is still in Poland, as his wife was pregnant."

"I bet he will return to Ireland," Ray said, following Det. Insp. Sweeney to the door. "It is just a question of when."

I escorted the detectives back to their car as Tanya and Nigel started clearing up the presentation.

"What do you need me to do next?" I asked.

Ray learned over from the driver's seat of the car.

"Print out the evidence Andy and call me in a few days as we need to put our heads together."

"What if he does not return to Ireland?" I asked the Inspector.

"It is not if Andy it is when ... we need to be prepared. Work with Ray and we will be in contact shortly."

They drove off and I returned to Nigel who was still in the conference room.

"That was bloody marvellous old chap; well done," Nigel said in his British accent.

"I couldn't have done it without you Nigel and you too Tanya. It was a team effort."

"Rubbish," Tanya replied. "It is you who will get him Andy. I need to get back to my emails!"

I drove Nigel back to the airport, where we enjoyed a quick beer and then I returned home. I was exhausted but happy with my performance. I had achieved my objective — the GBFI was now involved. All we had to do next was to get Harrison to come back to Ireland and then we could nail him.

CHAPTER 24

I took a few days annual leave to try to get my mind off the case for a while. I was driving back from a relaxing two night break in the K Club hotel in Kildare with my wife, when I could not resist taking a quick detour. I wanted to check out the addresses we had for Harrison in Naas and Sallins again, just in case he had returned to Ireland.

"You don't mind honey, if I take a drive past the addresses I have for Harrison on the way home?"

"Do you ever switch off? Andy I don't think he will come back to Ireland. If he has not made any further contact with your office, then he must know you are onto him. I think he will stay in Poland with his wife until she has the baby and then they will all return to America."

"You may be right, but I think because he has been so successful with his fraud activity here and he has got substantial payments from various insurance companies, he will return. Eventually his money is going to run out. When it does he will be back for more cash."

I was sure in my mind that he was going to return to Ireland. As Det. Insp. Sweeney had said the question was when, not if. From the surveillance operation in Poland I was certain that Harrison was not so comfortable living there. Poland was a beautiful modern European country, however if you cannot speak the language you will clearly be at a loss. I was sure that a Texan boy living in Poland would stick out even more than if he was living in Ireland.

"Or perhaps he will not return to Ireland but he will definitely return to an English-speaking country, maybe the UK or as he is so adventurous, possibly Australia or South Africa."

"Yes you're right," she said. "It would be difficult to live in a country if you did not speak the language."

We arrived in the Naas area and I drove past both the addresses I had for Harrison. I also drove past the additional addresses in Sallins, Co. Kildare, however all looked quiet and there was no sign of Harrison. Unfortunately he wasn't out playing football with the children!

Just in case we got lucky I took out my new 10.1 mega pixel Nikon camera. I was only an amateur photographer but I had recently purchased this basic model in case I found Harrison as I would need proof. Over the weekend, I had taken some nice photographs of my wife in the beautiful grounds of the K Club and she was more than happy with them – which was a relief as trying to please a woman with a photograph can be a difficult task!

"Look out for a faded red Alfa Romeo car. It is the car he was driving in Poland when I had him under surveillance."

"An Alfa Romeo? Nice car."

If I wanted to have any chance of locating him in Ireland, I would have to find the car, which should be parked outside one of his many addresses.

After half an hour we called it a day and drove home.

"Are you putting these photos on Facebook?" she asked, looking at the images.

"Yeah maybe. Any you like?"

"I have a few, but make sure I see them before you put them up there."

The tone of her voice suggested she was serious.

"You are really into this American case aren't you?" she enquired affectionately.

"Yes just a little!" I laughed.

"I remember when I was fresh out of law school I loved to get my teeth into a good case," my wife smiled. "Have you exhausted all avenues in the investigation?"

"Yes, I think so … although I would like to get some more information from Texas, Oklahoma and Arizona. Maybe we could take a trip over there?"

"What about the kids?"

"Yeah no Disneyland in Dallas, Texas; they would prefer Florida, but it would be nice for just the two of us to travel to Dallas. You know I was there before — in 1998/99 at an American security conference with Pinkerton."

"Would I like Dallas?"

"You would love Dallas; all those shops."

I was thinking I could drop my wife off at one of the many shopping malls and I could go talk to the local police.

"Andy I never heard you say we could go shopping on a holiday before."

"Not me dear, you. I could talk to people on the ground over there, find out about what John Harrison was up to in the United States."

"So we just need somebody to mind the kids for a few days."

"Yes, I wonder would the grandparents help out?"

"I'll check with them. Did you search the internet for information on your American?"

"Yes I searched Google and we found the link for that 'Wanted' picture of him in Oklahoma."

"That was good solid information but did you search Facebook?"

I was so stunned I stayed quiet for a few moments. Why hadn't I thought of Harrison and Facebook? It was so obvious a place to look, especially for an American travelling in Europe.

"Why the hell did I not think of checking Facebook? More than half the population of the planet are on it. Well done you!" I said.

We arrived home 20 minutes later and I couldn't wait to get onto the computer.

Jackie had taken my car to go and collect the kids from my mother's house, so that gave me at least an hour to hunt on the computer. I was obsessed with finding fresh information on Harrison.

I logged onto our computer and accessed my own Facebook account. I went into the search mode and input John Harrison. Within a couple of seconds about twenty or so John Harrisons popped up on the screen in front of me.

I tried filtering the information, entering the State of Texas, which resulted in no matches. I quickly tried Poland, Europe – again no matches. Then I gave Dublin, Ireland and Naas, Kildare, Ireland a go – again nothing.

I tried some of the other names he had used – Sean Moran, Kenneth Smith, Gary O'Neill but no positive matches were posted.

I was at a loss.

I decided to leave the computer running and went into the sitting-room, joining my wife who had returned home with the kids and was now watching a movie. I was uneasy and kept fidgeting which started to annoy her.

"Will you stop fidgeting, what is wrong with you?"

"I can't find Harrison on Facebook."

"Well I am sure there are more than a few John Harrisons on Facebook. You won't find him sitting here watching TV with me."

I nodded in agreement and once again logged onto Facebook. I searched the names again but had no luck. I was sure that John Harrison was his real name – his true identity – and that he would most likely be using it to keep in contact with his friends and family back in the US but I couldn't find him.

It was 1.07am and I decided it was time for bed. I was about to switch off my computer when suddenly I thought of searching under the email address we had for him. I keyed it in and was stunned – the Facebook website for John Harrison popped up immediately. I could not believe my eyes. I was looking at a photograph of him that matched the photographs I had obtained in Poland. To my amazement his Facebook website was not locked; no security had been applied to the site.

"You slipped up there John!" I smiled to myself.

I eagerly scanned down the page. According to the current info, he was employed by a company called Silver Diamond International and was living in Paris, France. His date of birth was the 28 May, 1975 and his hometown was set as Dallas, Texas, USA. This astonished me. I was amazed that a professional scam artist would reveal his true date or birth and home address on Facebook, especially considering his account had no security settings in place. Even my kids know not to input personal details onto the internet. He had 72 friends attached to the site. Looking at the list of friends most of them were in Texas. Two of the friends were based in

Ireland and a couple of them were Polish. His wife Jenny was also listed as a friend.

I could see from his Facebook wall that he was a regular user of the site and was constantly updating his information. Reading down through the wall notes one of his friends had commented that he had done well in securing a job at Silver Diamond International. I could not help laughing. Usually I don't like reading other people's correspondence as it's intrusive, however, this guy was not an average person and he'd left the information out there for anybody to read. I also had a very good reason to try to find out more about him. What Ann Wall had told me was playing on my mind. I was determined to get justice for her. I had given her my word that I would do my best.

There were also some photographs of Harrison with his wife in Poland. I wasn't sure of the location, but they were swimming in what looked like the Mediterranean Sea. I copied the photographs and I was satisfied that it was the same man I had come to know as John Harrison.

The following morning I arrived into the office late. It was after 10.00am and most of the staff were busy working away on their computers. I don't like arriving this late as even though I was technically working until after 1am, it always looked strange. I felt I had a guilty look on my face as Denton greeted me with the usual nod of his head, almost like a cowboy tipping his hat in the old Wild West.

"Courtney was looking for you earlier. I think he is in his office," Denton said as I turned on my computer.

"How is he today?"

"His normal gruff self Andy."

I walked towards Courtney's office and peered in the door. He was sitting at his desk.

"Come in Andy and sit down," he requested, without even looking up.

I could see he was busy working on a document. His computer was switched off and the mouse was hanging over the monitor. I knew that he hated computers and much preferred using pen and paper to email.

"Andy you have done a very good job on that American case I gave you," he said after a minute.

"Thank you Dan."

"I hear you had the GBFI officers in with you, are they any good?"

"Yes they are good. I have worked with Ray before; don't know Inspector Sweeney but he seems interested in the case. However we simply do not know Harrison's current location. I'd say he is most likely still in Poland."

"You need the boys to go take a look at him again?" Courtney asked, sitting back.

"Not at the moment. I found him on Facebook and will monitor his activity from there."

"Facebook! Are you telling me he is that stupid?"

"I found him last night Dan, or should I say earlier this morning, about 1.00am. I have full access as he has not locked his security, so effectively anybody can look at his page."

"Well I think we can safely say that you have saved the company a considerable amount of cash on this one. Let's hope the GBFI catch up with him and he will face some Irish justice— well done."

"Thank you Dan. Yes the case is more or less solved and we can close our insurance file, however, I would like to assist the GBFI with their investigation."

"I don't have a problem with that as that guy Harrison needs to be behind bars, but remember who pays your wages. You work for Dallast Insurance and I am sure you have plenty of fresh files waiting for you to investigate. Don't neglect them over this."

"I'll get back on those right away!" I smiled and made a fast exit.

I was delighted that Courtney had cleared me to work alongside the GBFI officers. However he was correct, I had a mounting amount of files and Denton could only do so much. I needed to start working on some new case investigations.

Thanks to our IT security, access to the Web was limited to some basic sites and Facebook was certainly not permitted. I gave it a quick try anyway as I sat back at my desk but no luck. I'd have to monitor Harrison's page using my home PC. It was annoying as Nigel was permitted full access because our UK operation had a more relaxed view. They'd have to get us up to speed in Ireland soon as times were changing and the internet was now one of the best tools available for a fraud investigator.

Until I got home I decided to play along with Courtney's request. I would do my other work, investigate the cases and hopefully obtain financial savings from fraud, but I would continue to investigate Harrison in my own time. I understood where Courtney was coming from. I had completed the investigation for Dallast, had saved the company money and it was now a police matter. However I was far too interested in the case to let it go. I still had plenty of questions that I needed to answer: Who was the real Gary O'Neill? How did Harrison obtain the passports? Were there more identities and fraudulent insurance claims waiting to be detected? The insurance investigation may have been completed, but I had to keep on digging.

CHAPTER 25

A few days had passed since Courtney had told me to call off my investigation. I was working on some new cases but I still had the Harrison file in my head. It was strange as I never dream and I was now having dreams about the case. I couldn't get the images of the passports of Kenneth Smith and Sean Moran out of my mind. I was keeping the Harrison Facebook page under observation – maybe if he was coming back to Ireland I'd get lucky and he would mention it.

I was sitting at the breakfast table trying to read the Sunday papers and at the same time thinking of my dream the previous night. It was the same dream I'd had a few days before: I was standing in an airport holding a passport with the name Sean Moran. The man in front of me had a passport in the name of Kenneth Smith, however the photograph in the passport was the same as the photograph in my passport, yet it was not me or the man in front of me. I could not understand what the meaning was behind the dream or perhaps there was no meaning at all.

My daughters, Olivia and Sarah, were playing, running around the kitchen. Olivia, my eldest, was pulling at my hand wanting me to go and play with her in the garden.

"Olivia, go and play with Sarah. I want to read my paper."

"Dad can we go and see Andrew today?" she asked suddenly.

"Why do you want to go to Andrew's grave?"

It was a strange request to come from a six-year-old. Andrew was my son, Olivia's older brother, who had died at birth ten years before.

"We have been talking about life and death in school."

This must have triggered the idea in Olivia's head.

"But why do you want to go to his grave. You know he is not there."

"Well I know he is in Heaven with Jesus, but I would like to go and place a flower and a toy on his grave, so the angels can take it to him."

"That is a very nice idea Olivia. We will go and buy him a toy in the shop and then you can give it to him."

"No Dad. I already have the toy he wants — it's the blue police car that I have."

"OK Olivia we will place that on his grave this afternoon."

"Thanks Dad," Olivia said, running off.

I hadn't been at my son's grave in a while so I guessed it would be nice to visit with Olivia.

That afternoon Olivia and myself went to Dardistown Cemetery beside Dublin Airport. It's so close it's almost as if you can reach out and touch the airplanes as they fly directly overhead. Andrew's grave was located near Veronica Guerin's grave, the Irish journalist who investigated dangerous criminals and caused so many problems for their criminal empire that she was assassinated. As a direct result of her murder the

Government passed new legislation in Ireland to form the Criminal Assets Bureau (CAB), a specialist unit of the Gardaí that target assets criminals have purchased using illegally obtained money. As an investigator I find her work inspiring. She was one truly, brave lady. I enjoyed reading the accounts of the investigation into her death and the formation of the CAB, which have been covered by Paul Williams, the journalist and author, in his excellent books *Evil Empire* and *The Untouchables*.

Olivia placed the small toy car on Andrew's grave and kissed his headstone. I was moved to tears by her actions. It is difficult to ever come to terms with the death of a child or a baby.

We both paused and stood in front of the grave for a few moments, with Olivia holding my hand. The only noise was the roar from a Delta Airlines' jet that flew over our heads on its final approach into Dublin Airport.

We returned to the car and I drove home. Olivia was soon happily playing in the garden and I decided to do some more research into Harrison and to check his Facebook page. I logged onto my account and found his site – which still had virtually no security.

"Harrison would want to be careful, maybe his identity would be stolen by somebody accessing his Facebook page," I laughed to myself.

There wasn't much activity on his page, other than he was comparing himself to an infamous American outlaw. Ironically Allan Pinkerton, the founder of the Pinkerton's Detective Agency had been instrumental in tracking down the bandit. I wondered if Allan Pinkerton was laughing down at me, a former Pinkerton detective who, over 150 years later, was trying to locate an American who considered himself a modern day outlaw.

I glanced out the window at my girls who were running around the garden, enjoying the little sunshine we get in Ireland. I was thinking of what might have been with my son Andrew. Maybe he would even have been a Garda detective. As I sat looking at my daughters I thought about my surname and wondered who would carry on the name.

I opened the folder on my computer which contained photographs taken of Andrew when he was born. He was 9lb 2oz which was a good weight and was perfect in every way except for a mark on his neck. It had been caused by the umbilical cord. It was ironic that the cord that had nourished him and kept him alive while he was in the womb had also killed him.

I looked at the photographs as I listened to my children playing and it was as if something flashed in my head — a moment of genius or maybe an idea that had been placed there. I quickly opened my case file and found the photocopies of the passports for Sean Moran and Kenneth Smith which had been given to me by 'John' from Bank B. I knew that the real Kenneth Smith was living in Monaghan Town and that the identity theft had occurred by way of Harrison's phone call. I was still amazed that Kenneth had passed his personal information over the phone to a complete stranger. But what about Sean Moran? Who was the real Sean Moran and how was his identity stolen? Harrison did it so well that he had successfully taken €45,000 from Starling Insurance. I had tried following up leads on Sean Moran but there was nothing. The police and other sources had no information on a Sean Moran who was born on 4 April, 1976 either, but he must live somewhere. I had gone over and over my notes and covered all aspects but could find no evidence of his existence. Sean Moran was born in 1976 and then his life was a blank. But as I'd looked at the photographs of my son Andrew it had suddenly hit me — what if Sean Moran was born in 1976 and then died as a baby? His birth would still have been registered and maybe that was how Harrison had stolen his identity and managed to get an illegal passport.

I was outraged and disgusted that somebody might have done this to an innocent baby who had died over 30 years before. But there was only one way to find out if I was right. I would have to carry out a long search in the office of Births Deaths and Marriages, on Lombard Street in Central Dublin.

I looked at my watch — it was just after 4pm. Even though it was a Sunday afternoon, I decided to chance giving Ray a quick call on his mobile.

"Hi Ray, it's Andy Stone here. Sorry for calling you on a Sunday," I said quickly.

"Not a problem Andy. I am working today. How can I help you?"

"I have been doing some work on the Harrison file and I was wondering if you have had any developments at your end?"

"Andy your investigation was excellent and we are currently planning tactics for the investigation. I'll let you know when we need you to assist us with some insurance information."

"Ray I will help you in any way possible, you know that goes without saying. However I'd really like to be kept updated on your developments. Is that possible?"

"Most companies pass the file to us and don't want any more involvement but updates will not be a problem Andy. The Superintendent has Okayed your involvement, especially with the way things are looking with our scarce resources!"

I was relieved to hear this as, despite their assurances at the meeting, I was still concerned that the GBFI would take the file and then leave me in the dark.

"Have you taken a look at Sean Moran yet?"

"Let me check my notes … yes nothing on him just a birth certificate, born on 4 April, 1976."

"Have you checked the areas that I can't look at, such as social welfare and tax details?"

"Ha! That is the first place police always check Andy, pity you don't have access as they have a wealth of information on people."

"Yeah I know Ray. Could you imagine if insurance, banks, police and social welfare could share information? We would save the country millions!"

"You're right there Andy. We don't even have enough people to investigate all the suspect social welfare claims."

"Ray, I am going to check with Births, Deaths and Marriages office tomorrow. Do you know Sean Moran's mother's maiden name?"

"It's Brady," Ray said after a pause.

"Thanks Ray. I will talk to you tomorrow," I said and hung up before he could ask me any questions.

I wanted the name because I was determined to go to the office of Births Deaths and Marriages the following morning. Sadly I would be looking for a death certificate.

The following morning I drove into Dublin city centre. As I was driving I was listening to Newstalk 106 again where the interviewer was taking another government Minister to task on his expenses and the poor state of our country. Insurance claims were on the rise in line with the recession and fraudsters like Harrison were contributing to the country's problems. What we needed now were some honest, hard-working politicians to lead us out of the financial mess Ireland was in.

I found a parking space almost directly outside the office of Births Deaths and Marriages. I was expecting a large amount of people to be standing in line, with a few civil servants trying to manage the flow. To my delight I was wrong. I was greeted by a friendly security officer who welcomed me and handed me some documentation. He explained how the system worked and told me what documents would be available and how to obtain a death certificate.

I walked into the main waiting area and completed the request form for a Death Certificate in the name of Sean Moran. I inserted as many details as possible, including the date of birth and mother's maiden name. I then handed the document into the hatch. I sat down again and expected to be there for some time. Yet again I was wrong. Within a few minutes I was called back to the desk and handed a copy of Sean Moran's death certificate.

"That will be €10 please," the lady said.

I handed her a €10 note and walked away, completely forgetting my manners I was so immersed in reading the death certificate. The last time I had seen such a document was after Andrew's death. It took me a few moments to come to terms with holding one again as it made me recall the precious few hours I had spent in the presence of my son's body.

Losing a baby is a horrific experience and I would not wish it on anybody, especially losing your first-born. All your plans, the turning of a bedroom into a nursery, purchasing push chairs, baby clothes, dreams of going to Disneyland, are all destroyed as the doctor says those words: "I am sorry but your baby has died."

How do you associate the birth of your firstborn child with those awful words from the doctor? As a parent you are expecting to have created a life, to be able to hold your baby, not to be dealing with your child's immediate death.

For the mother it is even worse as she has carried the baby for nine months and has felt the kicking, the movements and the life within her. It is put simply a traumatic event, which you do not ever come to terms with, but in time, if you are lucky, you do learn to live with the loss.

I sat in my car and analysed the document. I was aware that I was holding a valuable piece of evidence — a large part of the jigsaw. An Irish passport had been issued to a Sean Moran who in reality was John Harrison. The real Sean Moran had died a few weeks after his birth.

As I was deciding what to do next, my mobile rang.

"Morning Ray. Any luck with your contacts?"

"Hi Andy. No nothing yet but I have some questions on those insurance policies — are you around?"

"Yes I am about 20 minutes from your office. Will I call over to you?"

"Sounds good Andy, see you then."

Ray worked in the GBFI offices in Harcourt Terrace, Central Dublin. It is the head office for Ireland's specialised police units, including the Criminal Assets Bureau (CAB) and the National Bureau of Criminal Investigation (NBCI). Unfortunately locating a parking space around Harcourt Terrace can be difficult and spaces were always charged at a premium rate. On this occasion I was lucky and managed to park on the road nearby.

I phoned Ray when I was outside and he accompanied me into his office. There was strong security and access was only permitted to a few individuals. Ray had some basic queries on some of the insurance policies which I answered without any difficulties.

"How's the case going?" I asked, sitting back. "Anything new?"

"Not yet Andy. We have some other investigations which are taking priority for now and we are still collating data on Harrison's activities."

"Did you get any further information on Sean Moran?"

"It's really strange Andy; all we have is a birth certificate and that passport with who we believe to be Harrison in the photograph. It's like I was saying to you yesterday I have checked with all the many sources available to me and have found no records for Sean Moran. Maybe he emigrated?"

I slowly pulled the death certificate from my case.

"The reason you have no records for Sean Moran is because he is dead," I said as I handed it over.

"My God Andy — Sean Moran died as a baby. This is a major development."

"Not bad for a civilian investigator!" I grinned. "Ray we know Kenneth Smith is alive and is living in Monaghan, but I wonder just who is Gary O'Neill and did Harrison use more names to get passports?"

"We need the name Harrison used when he entered Ireland. I will check with Immigration."

My memory flashed back to my meeting with Ann Wall.

"He entered Ireland on an American Passport, under the name Luke Wilson!"

"How do you know that?"

I explained to Ray about what Ann Wall had told me about the Luke Wilson passport with a photograph of Harrison in it.

"How did he get the passport and who is Luke Wilson?"

"I don't know at this stage but I am going to find out."

"Andy relax, even if you establish that Harrison is Wilson, we don't have his passport and without that we have no chance of proving the case and remember we have no idea of his current location."

"If he was in Ireland would you arrest him?" I asked as I stood up.

"Yes of course, but we need to build a case."

"Then let's build the case. I will call you when I have further information," I said as Ray escorted me out.

I walked back to my car, thinking hard. I realised that if I went into the office I would not be in a position to work on the Harrison case, so I decided to go and work from my home office. I reassured myself that I was a diligent, loyal employee and I was not dossing off work as I was working on a large file which was now a criminal investigation. It was also my civic duty as an Irish citizen to protect the integrity of our citizen's passports. But most of all I was feeling motivated by my son Andrew. This was a strange feeling as I had not felt this close to him since he had died. Now I was on a mission — Harrison was stealing the identity of Irish babies who had died at birth and I was going to stop him.

As I was driving back home I kept glancing at the Harrison file on the front passenger seat. It now included several folders of information. I remembered what my old mentor Michael Casey, the former Garda Chief Superintendent, had always said: "The attention is in the detail; take good notes and read your file." His words echoed in my brain, almost like a Jedi knight talking to a student in *Star Wars*. Michael was correct. I needed to examine my file again. I also needed somebody to review the file with me and to give me some new direction. I decided to give my old employer and former mentor, Shirley Sleator, a call.

Shirley was the Managing Director of Sleator Carroll Ireland, a professional private investigation agency which she operated with her partner from 1980–1996. I had worked for Shirley as a junior investigator, effectively serving as an apprentice under her guidance. Although I gained much experience from my time working with Pinkerton, I learned the most from Shirley, especially how to carry out background investigations and to profile your subject. I also credit her business partner Sam Carroll with teaching me the art of covert surveillance. When I started with Sleator Carroll, I had a basic knowledge of investigation and surveillance from my time with the Institute of Irish Investigators where I had completed a three year Diploma on Investigation Studies. But it was Shirley and Sam who taught me the practical side of private investigation.

"Hi Shirley, Andy here, how are you?"

"I am good Andy, enjoying my retirement. I've just returned from France and I am planning on writing my next book."

"No doubt it will be as successful as your first one! Shirley I need some assistance with my case, can I call over to you?"

"I presume it's with your American case Andy?"

"Yes it sure is Shirley."

"Right I will have the coffee ready; you pick up some donuts on the way."

"Thanks Shirley – see you in 20 minutes."

I had discussed the case with Shirley before and she was clearly interested in the ongoing developments.

I arrived at Shirley's house just after 2.00pm and handed her a bag of fresh donuts.

"Hi Andy, come on in. I am interested to hear how you are getting on."

I carried in my files, laptop and my ever-increasing notebooks which contained snippets of information.

Shirley had the coffee ready. We chatted about our personal lives, caught up on recent developments and discussed the poor state of the Irish economy.

"OK let's get down to work," Shirley then said, all business. "Give me a look at your file notes."

Shirley's change in tone brought back memories of her commanding the surveillance teams and giving orders to Sam on what we needed to do to get 'the catch'. Private investigators use the term 'the catch' when carrying out surveillance. Put simply it means obtaining good video or photographic footage of a subject which can ultimately be used as evidence of wrong-doing. I had one case where we trailed a guy who was pursuing a claim with an insurance company, saying that he couldn't work. We carried out surveillance and got some great evidence of him painting a house – this was 'the catch' that I needed to contradict the fake medical evidence the claimant had supplied.

Shirley read through the files, scribbling some notes on a pad. There was a silence in the room as she analysed the documents. I was sorry I had not bought a newspaper as I had nothing to do, other than sit and wait.

"Make yourself useful, get me a fresh coffee," Shirley said, as she looked up.

I was delighted to be asked to do something and quickly made a fresh pot, pouring it into two mugs.

Shirley stopped reading and took a sip. She then took off her glasses, placed them on the table and rubbed her eyes.

"Nice job Andy, you certainly are putting long hours into this file."

"Thanks Shirley but what should I do next? The cops are investigating but I just know there is more to be done."

"Yes it's good that you have the professionals involved but I think you can certainly do more investigation in the background. I have a few ideas:

1. Go and talk to Ann Wall again and see if you can find out more information on Harrison's activities in the West of Ireland. If he entered Ireland using an

American passport under the name of Luke Wilson then maybe Irish immigration have a record.

2. Check with your contacts in the bank or ask the cops to do that. Did Harrison open a bank account in Ireland using the American passport?

3. Talk to your Pinkerton friends and contacts in North America, establish what else Harrison was up to on that side of the Atlantic.

"Thanks Shirley."

"Good Luck Andy and keep me posted on developments!"

I'd start with Ann Wall but I needed a reason to drive back to the West of Ireland in order to meet with her again. Maybe a phone call would suffice, but being a people person I much prefer eye-balling someone when I'm looking for information. And if she had anything more to tell me about the Wilson passport I'd a feeling it would be worth the drive.

CHAPTER 26

❧

That evening I could not sleep so I stayed up late working at my computer, trying to complete a management report for Courtney on our financial savings from detected fraud investigations. The report was due in the morning and I was rechecking my mathematical calculations, which were not my strongest point. I kept getting distracted, thinking about Shirley's observations and comments on Operation Cowboy. She was right — I needed to talk to Ann Wall again to see what other information I could establish about Harrison's life in North America.

I finally finished the report and logged onto Google. I was surfing through various websites and decided to search the State of Arizona and in particular to take a closer look at the town of Tombstone. It turned out Tombstone was a small old western town located at the southern end of Arizona, near the border with Mexico. The drive time was about four hours from Phoenix Airport.

Harrison had originated from Dallas, Texas so I opened an American map online and calculated that a drive from there to Tombstone, Arizona would take a good 14–16 hours. For an American that might not be a long drive but for an Irishman it would be a considerable journey. It only takes about three hours to drive across Ireland. In order to drive from Dallas to Tombstone, I would have to drive across Texas, into New Mexico and then Arizona. It made me think of the old Pinkerton stories of detectives chasing Butch Cassidy, the Sundance Kid and Jessie James across State lines—they must have spent a lot of time on horseback.

I checked my notes from my meeting with Ann Wall and confirmed that Harrison had met Sally Wall at the Mustang Stallion Ranch in Tombstone. I Googled it and found a telephone number. Should I dial it? I checked my watch; it was now 11.30pm in Ireland. I figured that Arizona would be about eight hours behind us. The problem with calling an unknown number was that the person who answered could be a friend or relative of the subject of the investigation. I remember phoning a number one time and the man who answered turned out to be the brother of the fraudster I was tracking. Thankfully I had a false story prepared and I managed to talk myself out of the awkward situation.

It was a risk phoning the ranch but I decided to go ahead and make the call. The phone was answered almost immediately.

"Hello," a man with a strong American accent said. He sounded southern, possibly Texan.

I stayed silent for a moment wondering if I should just hang-up. Had I just made a huge mistake?

"Hello," the man again said.

I decided to gamble.

"Hello, I am calling from Dublin, Ireland, can you hear me?"

"Yes Sir, I can. What can I do for you?"

"I am an insurance investigator and I am dealing with a case involving a Texan whom I understand was working or living at your ranch."

"What's his name?"

"His name is John Harrison."

There was silence for a couple of seconds. I was beginning to get worried. I had no idea what relationship this man might have with Harrison.

"That's a name I have not heard in a long time. What has he done now?"

It was looking good.

"I am dealing with a large insurance claim that he is pursuing against the company I work for."

"I see, well take it from me that the claim is all wrong. I sure don't want to go into much detail but I would not give that guy a cent."

"Can you tell me anything about him?"

Again there was a silence. It was only a few moments but it felt like an eternity.

"Well now let me see. He was in a partnership with our then manager a Laura Quinn and they left the ranch together. I think the local cops may have been looking to talk to him. I don't recall much more. My wife may have some more information."

"Is Laura Quinn still living there?"

"I don't know. You had best talk to my wife Stacey. She will be back tomorrow."

"Thank you Sir. I will call back then," I said and hung up feeling relieved.

Stacey sounded promising as I have found that women are generally a great source for information. I had a sense of renewed enthusiasm and decided to call it a night while the going was good.

The following morning it was my turn to drop the children to school. I arrived in the office just after 8am. Denton was working away at his desk.

"Morning Denton, how are you doing?"

"Grunt."

"Sorry what did you say?"

"Don't mind me Andy. I was on the beer last night; I'm not feeling great."

"Chasing the ladies again Denton?"

"No, just out for beers with the guys, just had one too many."

"Don't let Courtney know you were out, you know his attitude to hangovers!"

"Tanya told me he is gone on holidays."

Courtney taking a vacation was a surprise to me. I had planned to complete the management report and to carry out an audit and review of our injury claims files. However, I decided to take full advantage his absence and press ahead with meeting Ann Wall again.

I immediately telephoned her but only got her message service. I left a request for her to return my call. I knew that she might be avoiding me after our marathon session in the hotel, but I needed more information on Harrison's activities whilst he was living in the West of Ireland. She had been so helpful in the past I was sure that she would continue to assist me in the investigation as she too wanted him brought to justice.

I was relaxing at my desk, going through my notes and the suggestions I had obtained from Shirley, when my mobile rang —it was Ann Wall.

"Good morning Ann, thanks for calling me back and for acting so fast."

"Hi Andy. Any news on Harrison, did you get him yet?"

"No Ann, not yet. I am still working on the case. These things take time."

"I guess so. It's not like the movies, but you will get him won't you?"

"Ann I promise I will certainly do my best, actually you may be able to help me with some more information. Can I meet you again?"

"I think I have told you all that I know Andy and I'm going off on holidays today."

"Oh OK we obviously can't meet then but do you have time for a quick chat?"

"Yes, go on."

". I am trying to get some further information on what Harrison was doing when he lived in the West. Do you remember you said you think he had an American passport under the name of Luke Wilson? Do you know if he used it for any formal identification purposes, such as with the police or opening a bank account?"

"I don't think he had a passport under the name of Luke Wilson Andy — I know he had a passport under that name, as I saw it with my own eyes."

"Are you 100 per cent sure?"

"Of course I am sure," Ann said angrily. "I can testify that I saw his photograph on an American passport under the name of Luke Wilson. I will swear on the Bible if you want me to."

"OK; OK, I believe you Ann, but you have to understand I have not seen the passport."

"I understand. You know that man will never the see the inside of a courtroom," she sighed.

"Well the Garda Bureau of Fraud is actively investigating the file. I am also still working on the case. Do you know if he opened a bank account with the American passport?"

"I am not sure Andy. He may have had a bank account in Roscommon under that name. You should talk to a Detective John Foley in Boyle, County Roscommon. He may be able to assist you further."

"Thanks for your help Ann. I really do appreciate all that you have done. Before you go, do you remember you told me that you drove Harrison to Shannon Airport to meet his then partner Laura Quinn? Well do you know what happened to her?"

"I have no idea what happened to her after they broke up. I think she may have gone back to America."

"Thanks. I will let you know any developments. Have a good holiday."

I was about to hang up when Ann said: "Please Andy, do your best to get him. He really needs to be taken to court. He deserves jail for all that he has done to my daughter."

"Ann I promise you I will do my best and who knows maybe we will have a glass of champagne when I get him."

I felt sorry for Ann and her daughter. Ann's information had been really helpful to my investigation and I was sure I could confirm that Luke Wilson was another stolen identity that John Harrison was using.

I was curious to know more about Laura Quinn. I was aware that she was American, from Tucson or Tombstone, Arizona, and that she had worked at the Mustang Stallion Ranch. I was also aware she had travelled to Ireland in order to meet up with her then partner Harrison. Other than that I had no further information on her. I would have to try to follow this lead up with my contacts in Arizona.

I also now needed to talk to Detective John Foley in Boyle, County Roscommon. I didn't really have time to drive over there but I knew from previous experience that talking to cops over the phone was not as good as talking to them face-to-face, especially when dealing with sensitive information.

I telephoned Boyle Garda Station and asked to speak to Detective Foley. I was told he would not be on duty until 2.00pm. It was now only 10.15am. As Courtney was not in the office I decided to take full advantage of the freedom. If I left immediately, I would make Boyle in plenty of time to meet with Detective Foley at the start of his shift.

As I was packing up my things, Denton looked up.

"You out for the day?" he asked.

"Yes I have an important call to attend; do you need anything?" I asked.

"No you're fine – good hunting," he said with a wink.

Denton was a good guy and dedicated to his job but I was certain with both me and Courtney out of the office, he was going to take full advantage and leave early. This didn't concern me as he looked rough from the previous night's drinking and I knew he'd make up the time.

I arrived in Boyle at 12.30pm. I was hungry and could hear my stomach talking so I found a small pub and had a quick lunch. After I'd finished I was hungry for something else – intelligence on Harrison's activities.

I walked into Boyle Garda Station at 1.45pm and approached the counter.

"May I help you?" a polite young officer asked.

"Yes, please my name is Andrew Stone and I am looking to speak to Detective John Foley."

"He is out on a call, but should be back in about twenty minutes. Take a seat if you like."

"Thanks."

I sat down on a small wooden bench in the public waiting area. It was quiet, just a few people getting forms signed. While I was impatiently marking time a young man wearing a tracksuit and grey hoodie entered the station and walked up to the counter.

"I am here to sign the bail book," he said loudly.

The Garda placed a large book on the counter and handed over a pen.

The young guy tried to use the pen but it didn't work.

"Give me a fucking pen that works!" he shouted.

"Watch your manners Jimmy," the Garda said.

With that Jimmy, hocked up phlegm from deep within his throat and spat onto the book, shouting: "Fuck you, yaw pig!" He turned to walk out of the station as the Garda came around the counter to grab him. Unfortunately the young Garda was caught off balance and Jimmy punched him in the face.

I immediately jumped up and was about to assist when Jimmy pulled a knife from his pocket.

"Mind your own fucking business."

I stopped dead when I saw the knife. Jimmy inched towards the door, keeping his eyes fixed on me and holding the knife in his right hand. He did not see another man calmly standing just inside the door. As the young thug walked forward the man smashed him in the face with the butt of a radio.

Jimmy's face burst into a bloody mess with the impact and he fell to the floor. I helped the young Garda to his feet. He was more embarrassed than physically hurt.

"Thanks for your help. Now allow me to introduce you to Detective John Foley — this is Andrew Stone, Sir."

"Well, pleased to meet you Detective Foley; that was some entrance!"

"We get all types down here. People think that the thugs are only in the big cities."

We shook hands and Detective Foley ushered me towards his office, as two uniformed Gardaí appeared, picked up Jimmy and called an ambulance.

"Well Andrew, welcome to Boyle and thanks for your assistance in the reception; nobody was seriously injured anyway."

"I didn't do anything," I said, following him into his office.

"Sit down. Will you have tea or coffee?"

"Coffee please."

He poured out two coffees and then asked: "So what brings you to Roscommon?"

"Well I am employed by Dallast Insurance as a fraud investigator. I have been working on a case for the past few months and I understand you may also have had an interest in the individual concerned."

"What's his name?"

"John Harrison."

"Yes I remember him — an American; he got involved with young Sally Wall," he said, sitting back.

I could feel the excitement building up inside me.

"Yes that's him. What can you tell me about him?"

"We nicknamed him Huckleberry Finn," Detective Foley said, as he stood up and opened a large filing cabinet.

"I have a file in here on the guy, that robbery case is still open. I think we are still looking for him ... yes here we are."

He pulled a small, brown file from the cabinet and sat back down.

"You know I should not be showing you this, but if it helps you defend your case and possibly catch John Harrison... "

I kept quiet as the detective started to shuffle through the pages of the file.

"Sally Wall was convicted of the theft from the hotel and we are still looking to talk to Harrison about the matter. Do you know his location? Is he in Ireland?"

"No I think he is in Poland, but I can't be certain. Your colleagues at the GBFI are investigating the fraud aspect of the insurance claims along with passport identity theft."

"The GBFI — those guys are too busy to be talking to us country detectives, now let me see what I have. I don't know much more about the guy. Is there anything in particular I can assist you with?"

I thought of Shirley's suggestions and Ann talking about the American passport.

"I think he used a false name when he was here… "

"Luke Wilson… " Detective Foley interrupted.

"Yes that's the name!"

"He opened a bank account under that name with a local bank. He used an American passport as identification. I have a copy of his bankcard here."

Detective Foley passed over the photocopy of the card and I studied it. This was crucial Irish evidence linking John Harrison to Luke Wilson. It was a strange feeling holding an ATM bank card with the name Luke Wilson printed on it.

"I don't have a photocopy of the American passport but the bank may have one. That said I'm not sure if they would give you it, with the laws."

"I am sure they would pass a copy to the GBFI," I said.

"Yes that should be fine. Take a note of the bank account details from the ATM card and pass it to the GBFI. They will be able to request details about the passport or whatever proof of identity he used to open the bank account."

"Thanks for your help Detective Foley."

"Call me John and keep me posted on developments. It would be great if you could get that guy."

I nodded and stood up. We shook hands and I returned to my car feeling very satisfied. I had confirmed that Luke Wilson was another name used by Harrison. Obtaining an American passport under a false name would be considered a serious crime against the Federal government of the United States. If Harrison was prosecuted in the United States for obtaining an official American passport whilst using a false identity, then he would be looking at ten years in prison. If he had used the passport for fraudulent gain, such as opening a bank account, he would then be looking at about twenty years in jail. Opening a bank account using a false identity could also be considered money laundering. In the United

States offences of this nature are considered 'Felony Federal offences against the country, which are far more serious than breaking individual County or State laws.

I arrived home late to an empty house. My wife and the children had gone to Nice, France to visit their auntie. I was planning to catch up on some TV and to enjoy a few bottles of beer when my mobile rang. I could see it was an American number.

"Hello," I said.

"Is that Andy Stone?" a lady with an American accent asked.

"Yes."

"Hello Andy, my name is Stacey. You were talking to my husband Charles at the Mustang Stallion Ranch near Tombstone, Arizona."

"Yes hello Stacey. Thank you for calling me back."

"I hear you're interested in John Harrison and Laura Quinn."

"Yes, any information you have could assist my investigation."

"OK then, Laura was the manager here and then she left to go live in Ireland with John. She came back to Tombstone on her own but then went back to live in Ireland again. I think she may have remarried an Irishman, named Dunne, but that is only local talk."

"That is very interesting. I wonder where she's living over here. Tell me did you know Mr. Quinn?"

"No Sir. I didn't know him. Laura was also married to a Harry Wilson but he died a few years back."

I had my link and possibly I'd got 'the catch' as well.

"Did they have a son named Luke?"

"I am not sure. They were from Phoenix, Arizona originally but I am from Houston, Texas and only moved here when we got the opportunity to run the ranch."

I suddenly remembered Ann Wall, telling me that Harrison had arrived in Ireland with his leg was in a cast or a sort of plaster.

"Stacey do you know if John had any accidents or did he sustain any injuries while he was living in Arizona?"

"Well, I do recall a good few years back, before he went over to Ireland, he fell from a horse and that horse fell on top of him. I think he was hurt real bad, maybe his leg and his back. I am not so sure but I recall he went to hospital."

This information was music to my ears, as according to the doctors in Liverpool Hospital, Harrison did have a genuine back injury and problems with degenerative discs. If the horse fell on him in 2001, the discs must have deteriorated over the last seven years, leading to his current situation.

"Stacey, you are a star. Thank you so much for the information."

"You sure are welcome Sir. I am sure there is more I could tell y'all but you would really need to come and visit Tombstone so the local Sheriff here could help you out."

"Thanks Stacey I might just do that!"

I said goodbye and sat looking at my dog Ben, who was hoping that I would take him for a walk. I was thinking about how enjoyable a trip to Texas and Arizona would be and the amount of information I might obtain. I was only daydreaming as a trip of that magnitude would be expensive and Courtney was certainly not going to cover the cost. All the same I wondered if Jackie had asked the grandparents about it. She'd lived in Long Island and, like me, loved the United States of America.

I opened the back door and let Ben out to take himself for a walk around our garden. I returned to the computer and started to Google the names and words — Luke Wilson

— Laura Quinn — Tombstone — Arizona. However nothing of any interest came up. One thing which did pop up was that I was right and the shoot out at the OK Corral with the famous lawman Wyatt Earp had taken place in Tombstone, Arizona, in 1881.

I checked my notes from the conversation with Stacey. I had written down: 'Harry Wilson died a few years back?' I entered his name and death into Google, along with the word Arizona. This time the search engine responded with a notice of death from the *Tombstone Herald Newspaper*. The article advised that Harry Wilson had died in March 1995 and that he was survived by a son Luke. It also stated that he was married to a Laura of Tombstone, Arizona in the 1970s and that they had since divorced. I wondered if this was the same Laura as Laura Quinn.

It was interesting information but of no real issue to the defence of my insurance claim. However I would continue digging just to build up the case and provide information to the Gardaí to find anything that might assist in the eventual arrest and prosecution of John Harrison.

Operation Cowboy was no longer about insurance fraud. I was determined that Harrison was going to pay for stealing the identities of dead Irish babies and for using illegal Irish passports — I was going to see justice served.

CHAPTER 27

There are two types of cops: the officer who does it by the book and will not bend the rules; and the cop who gets results by taking chances and not following the rules. The second type is the one who puts criminals behind bars and is an achiever. I've been lucky as most of the detectives that I've dealt with are real cops who've had no problem bending the rules or working with fraud investigators in order to reduce criminal activity — in particular white collar crime, the crime for which the ordinary decent citizen pays.

Detective Ray Harding was definitely a real cop — hardworking, decent and he made plenty of arrests. I was writing up my notes on the new information about Luke Wilson when he phoned the following day.

"Hi Andy, can you drop over to me? I need to run some things by you."

"Ray no problem. I will be with you in an hour."

"Make it 11.00am Andy."

I drove to Harcourt Square, where parking was as manic as ever. There was nowhere to park at all. Then I noticed that the barrier was open to the Garda car park. I drove in and there were several spaces available. I parked in a space a short distance from the entrance door, phoned Ray and told him I was in the car park.

"How the hell did you get in here Andy?" Ray asked as he met me in the car park.

"The barrier was open and there was nowhere else to park!"

"This parking area is only for senior ranking officers. Ah Hell sure we won't be long, come on up to the office."

Ray advised that he was having some difficulties identifying Harrison as there were no records of him entering Ireland.

"What about the FBI, could they not assist you?"

"No not at this stage as we would need his fingerprints. Ideally we would need to have him arrested and in custody in order to get that information. To tell you the truth Andy, how do we know he is John Harrison?"

"Well according to the detective in Oklahoma he is John Harrison and the photographs are identical. And there's the Facebook account."

"Yes that may be true but until I see some identification… "

"Like what – a passport or driver's license?" I interrupted.

"Yeah Andy, we need to get some correct identification. Immigration has no record of him entering Ireland. I am not sure what information to pass to Interpol. I need to verify he is John Harrison before I submit a request to Interpol for information on him."

"Irish Immigration won't have any records on him entering Ireland."

"Why not?" asked Ray

"Because he entered Ireland under the name of Luke Wilson, on an American passport and then he opened a bank account using that name."

"How did you find that out? No don't answer; it's best I don't know."

Ray walked over to his computer and entered the name Luke Wilson.

"I will run it through our criminal database,' he said, quickly typing it in. "There is nothing; no information is showing up on that name, so even if he did enter Ireland using Luke Wilson he did not come to our attention. I will check with the bank and see what I can establish as he might have used the passport for proof of identity."

"Yes that's a good idea. By the way I think you should make contact with Detective John Foley of Boyle Garda Station."

"Why?"

"Detective Foley has had dealings with Harrison. I think you should talk to him. I am certain the Cowboy used an American passport in Luke Wilson's name to open a bank account."

"I am pretty sure he did too. I will chase that aspect up with the bank … but we'll do it officially Andy, right?" Ray said sarcastically.

I nodded in agreement but I wondered who I could contact in America that could access the information. Much as I had faith in Ray there was no harm in having a back-up plan.

"I was running some checks on Harrison's other alias, Gary O'Neill. It appears that he has also got a passport in that name," Ray said, as he pulled a photocopy of a passport from his file. "I did not show you this Andy but take a look at the picture and the signature."

I stared at the photograph of John Harrison. The signature was almost identical to the one on the other passports.

"This guy is good Andy; he is a real threat to our National Security. If he can get passports for himself this easily, then who else is he getting passports for? How many more illegal passports are out there?"

"What are you saying Ray?"

"Well it's possible Andy that Harrison is supplying Irish passports to terrorist organisations."

"Like the IRA?"

"No, more like foreign terrorist organisations."

I could tell by the tone of Ray's voice that he had real concerns about this possibility.

"So did you run Gary O'Neill through your criminal databases?"

"Yeah Andy, nothing came up."

"Sounds like Gary O'Neill might be another baby who died at birth. Did you talk to the Births Deaths and Marriages office?"

"I put in the request, so we'll wait and see what comes back."

Ray walked back over to his desk and shuffled through some papers.

"Let's review what we have Andy. We know Harrison is an American, from Dallas, Texas and that he possibly has an American passport in the name of Luke Wilson. We know that he has Irish passports in the names of Kenneth Smith, Sean Moran and Gary O'Neill. More than likely they were obtained from stealing the identities of dead babies, with the exception of Kenneth Smith."

"I suppose they are only the ones that we know of Ray. How many more identities do you think he has stolen?"

"We just don't know at this stage. The question is will he come back to Ireland?"

"Looking at his Facebook site, I think he is still in Poland and possibly still has the Irish-registered Alfa Romeo, which is insured under the name of Kenneth Smith."

"If he comes back to Ireland he may take the boat so he can use the car when he's here," Ray said. "I will alert the Harbour Police to look out for it."

"I don't think he'd bring the car. If he comes back surely he would fly into Dublin Airport — maybe you should alert the airport police and immigration control?" I suggested.

"But Andy under what name will he travel? He has so many identities and passports it would make it impossible to locate him. I will give the names that we know of to border security and we'll see what happens."

We both sat for a few moments thinking about how to advance the investigation further.

"I will make contact with Social Welfare and try to establish if he is in receipt of any benefit payments. Chances are if he is into insurance fraud then he will also have a go in other areas," Ray said.

This information was not available to private investigators but the Gardaí can check these government databases. All they need is an official request for information letter, signed off by a senior ranking officer.

"You can bet your bottom dollar Ray that he is claiming benefits under his multiple identities — this might be the breakthrough lead we need!" I smiled.

Ray nodded in agreement.

"Yeah, I will get onto it right away."

It is well known that professional fraudsters and scam artists will operate in multiple areas. The criminal who is committing social welfare fraud is the same individual who will try their hand at insurance fraud and other banking or credit card fraud. But unfortunately financial investigators' hands are tied when it comes to sharing information on suspected criminals and fraudsters. One senior and well-respected detective once said to me: "Fighting fraud in the private sector in Ireland is like the Irish rugby team going up against the New Zealand All Blacks, with one arm tied behind their backs. The laws are on the side of the criminal."

I could tell that Ray was excited about the case and that he was giving it his full attention and the commitment that it deserved. However, in order for the case to succeed, we would need a Superintendent to take an interest in the file to sign off on his request for information. But I knew I could leave that to Ray.

I shook Ray's hand, asking him to keep me posted on any developments and left his office. As I approached my car, I could see a man with a red face shouting at a uniformed police officer and pointing at it. As I walked over he confronted me.

"Who are you? How dare you park in my space?"

"Sorry, I did not realise it was your space."

"I asked you a question who are you?"

"I am Andrew Stone of Dallast Insurance."

"This is my parking space. It is not a public car park, now get out of here."

I quickly excited the car park. Thankfully the entrance barrier opened when I approached.

I decided to stay out of the office. I wanted to see if I could locate an American source to provide information on the passport under the name of Luke Wilson. I returned to my home office and checked through my collection of business cards and looked at the other contacts I'd made through the years. I found a few names. First off I decided to give my FBI contact Kelly O'Dwyer a call. Unfortunately her phone rang out with no answer. I then tried another old friend, Joe Peleg, who was also a fellow former Pinkerton. He worked for the United States Secret Service and was based at the US Embassy in London.

"Hi this is Joe," he answered quickly.

Although we were connected on the internet site LinkedIn I had not spoken to Joe in about ten years so this was going to be interesting.

"Hi Joe, this is a former Pinkerton calling — it's Andy Stone in Ireland."

"Andy Stone, how are you doing? I have not spoken to you in a long time."

"I am doing good Joe. When did you leave Pinkerton?"

"I left in 1998 and went to work in Atlanta, Georgia, before moving to London to work with the Embassy. Andy, do you remember Liz who worked in Reception?"

"Yes, the good looking, blonde girl."

"Well she's my wife now. We married in '99 and live just outside London."

"That's great Joe. I am very happy for you guys. Please pass on my congratulations to Liz."

"Thanks Andy but I know you didn't ring me up out of the blue for a bit of chitchat. You must be looking for something."

"You're right Joe. I am after a bit of information. Do you have any contacts in the American passports' office?"

"What you got Andy? What's this about?"

I briefed Joe on my file, and explained about the possible issuing of an American passport in the name of Luke Wilson to a John Harrison.

"Can you help Joe?"

"OK Andy, I will do some checks on this," he said, sounding concerned. "You have any idea about Luke Wilson's age and what State he's from?"

"Well a source told me he might be from Tucson or Tombstone Arizona but you'd need to check out the whole State maybe. However John Harrison is from Texas. He would have been born in or around 1972—1976 or thereabouts."

"Give me a few days and I will come back to you."

"Thanks Joe, any assistance is much appreciated. Make sure and tell Liz I was asking after her."

"I will Andy; good talking to you."

My mind was racing with thoughts on the possible next developments on the Harrison case as I headed back to the office. Working on other files was impossible but they had stated to build up in my in-tray. If Courtney was aware of all the hours I was still spending on the Harrison case he would kick my ass!

Just as I was about to get going on an urgent file my mobile phone rang. It was Detective Ray Harding.

"Hi Andy, I thought you'd like to know you were correct. We got the death certificate for Gary O'Neill. He died at birth. Looks like Harrison took Gary's identity to obtain an Irish passport."

"Thanks for the information Ray. It's another identity theft then?"

"Yes."

I could feel a sense of hatred building against Harrison; first Sean Moran and now Gary O'Neill — those poor families.

"Hold on Andy there is more. It looks like Harrison also got another Irish passport in the name of Thomas Taylor."

"Who is Thomas Taylor? I don't know that name?"

"Thomas Taylor is a name he used to get a passport a long time ago. We got the name from a source. Can you run it through your Insurance Link database and see if there are any claims registered?"

"Sure Ray no problem; what is the date of birth?"

"Give me a minute … it's 10 April, 1975 and the date of death is the 11 April 1975."

"OK Ray, I will run the check and call you back," I said and hung up.

I logged onto Insurance Link, entering the details on Thomas Taylor, however there were no available matches. I re-checked the system but nothing came up on the name. I also ran the name through our internal systems and checked our financial judgements and there were no matches.

I quickly phoned Ray and gave him the news.

"Thanks for trying Andy. To be honest I was dreading more paperwork and documents. You insurance guys love your documentation!"

I laughed as I hung up the phone but I felt disappointed.

The case was moving forward but every corner we turned brought new avenues of investigation, like Thomas Taylor and we were no closer to nailing Harrison. Hopefully Joe or Ray would turn something good up soon.

Later that afternoon when I was out investigating a car theft case, I received a call from Denton.

"Andy, Courtney is looking for you pronto."

"What did you tell him?"

"I told him you were out working on the Texas case."

"You're an asshole Denton," I said and hung up the phone.

I packed up my laptop and files and drove back to the office. It was after 3.00pm but if Courtney was angry it was better to head him off as I'd learnt in the past that attack is the best form of defence.

I arrived into the office 40 minutes later and dumped my laptop on my desk.

"Sorry Andy," Denton said as he looked up. "I think I landed you in the shit."

I ignored him and walked over to Courtney's office. He looked up and I could see he was angry.

"Come in and close the door. Have a seat, make yourself at home; would you like a drink or maybe a cigar?" he asked sarcastically.

"Hello Dan."

I closed the door and sat down in front of Courtney.

"What did I tell you to do Andy?"

"To stay away from the Harrison file," I muttered.

"So when I ask Denton your location and what you are doing why does he tell me you're out working on the Cowboy file?"

"I have been working on the file Dan, working many hours, but a lot of them were personal hours."

"Did you not understand my instructions?" Courtney asked, as he sat back in his chair.

"Yes I did understand your instructions, so I am still working on the file but it's on my own time. Now you can suspend me or even sack me if you want, but I will continue to work on the file and I *will* see Harrison convicted in court.

"Why are you so interested in this one file?" Courtney growled, standing over me. "Why?"

I sat back and tried to keep calm.

"Do you remember I had a son who died at birth in 2003?" I asked.

Courtney immediately looked uncomfortable.

"Yes, you called him Andrew."

"Yes Andrew is his name. Well how do you think Harrison is obtaining the Irish passports?"

"It's something to do with children dying a birth is it?" Courtney asked, as he sat back down.

"I have been working closely with the GBFI detectives, providing them with information on insurance related terms and conditions of policies, you know the usual, but we have also proved that on at least two occasions Harrison obtained legitimate Irish passports using the identities of Irish babies who died, in or around the time of their births."

"The dirty bastard," Courtney said grimly. "So he finds a baby who died at birth and then obtains a birth certificate in that baby's name?"

"Yes Dan, that is correct. He then makes an application for a passport in the dead baby's name and away he goes with a fresh identity and an official Irish passport."

"Those poor parents, if they ever found out it would be very difficult for them."

I nodded in agreement and there was silence for a few moments.

"Now I understand why it is so personal for you Andy — you should have told me sooner."

"I only made the connection a few days ago."

"OK well, what do you need to get this guy?"

"I just need some more time, to finish the file. It's a Gardaí matter now and to be fair the detectives are doing a good job. I just want to see Harrison brought to justice and then I can get some closure on the file."

"I understand Andy. Do what you need to do and I'll clear it."

"Thanks Dan, for being so understanding."

I left his office wiping the sweat off my face. That was a close one.

I returned to my desk hoping to talk to Denton but he had left for the evening. I was not surprised. To be fair he had only told the truth. It was not his fault. I gave him a quick call on his mobile and updated him on the developments and reassured him that Courtney was no longer on the war path.

"Andy, if there is anything I can do, just let me know."

"Yes, there is. I need you to cover some of my files."

"No problem, just leave them on my desk."

"Thanks Denton."

I switched on my computer and shuffled through my emails, thankfully there were only a few with nothing that needed my immediate attention.

"I think you should take a look at this Andy," Courtney suddenly said. I was so engrossed I hadn't realised he was standing behind me. "It is today's newspaper and may be of interest to you. Don't forget to switch off the lights when you leave."

"Thanks," I said, looking at my watch. It was 6.30pm and there was only a few staff still working in the office.

I opened the newspaper as Courtney walked off. I couldn't believe it. Russian spies had been caught with six Irish passports and Special Branch officers were investigating how it had happened. Apparently they were questioning people in the passport office. I wondered if Harrison had been involved.

It seemed that the personal details of six Irish citizens had been used by the Russians to get Irish passports. It sounded like Harrison's kind of operation as it was just like what had happened to Kenneth Smith. Even if he wasn't involved it clearly showed that Ray was right. The type of fraud he was committing was a National Security risk. It was also a risk to Aviation Security, as just maybe terrorists could get their hands on Irish passports.

The FBI had detected the Russian operation and the spies had been expelled from the United States. The Irish involvement must have been really embarrassing for the government. They'd already expelled a Russian diplomat from the local embassy and had vowed to investigate further.

I continued on searching on Google and found a photograph of one of the female spies. She looked like something out of a James Bond movie. The Russian spies had been using Irish passports, but they were forgeries. I smiled grimly thinking that the spies should have gone to Harrison as his passports were authentic Irish passports, just issued by way of identity theft.

Ray had told me that the Irish passport would be the passport of choice for any international spy or secret service agent. Ireland is a neutral country within the European Union, friendly with the United States, where English is spoken, with citizens who are free to travel around the globe and generally receive a good reception. I knew that the Israeli Secret Service had also used Irish passports on occasion. I decided to give Ray a call to see what he thought about the Russians and the Irish passports.

"Hi Ray, Andy here. Did you read today's newspapers about the Russian spies with the Irish passports?"

"Yes."

"Well what do you think?"

"It's very interesting."

"Is that all? Do you think John Harrison is involved?"

"It's a possibility."

"A possibility, is that a yes or a no?"

"Look Andy, this is serious police business. I can't discuss this aspect of the case with you. All I can say is that we are keeping an open mind. I've got to go."

The phone went dead.

CHAPTER 28

The following morning I was driving into the office when I received a call from one of my Dallast colleagues.

"Hi Andy, it's Nancy Smith here in customer relations."

Normally when somebody from customer relations contacts me it's about a complaint.

"Hello Nancy, what's the problem today?"

"Andy, there is no complaint. I have a note on one of our motor policies to contact you if there is any contact from our customer."

"Sounds interesting Nancy; what are the details?"

I assumed it was going to be a general query on a convicted fraudster or a well-known criminal trying to obtain an insurance policy.

"The motor insurance policy is with a Kenneth Smith on a red Alfa Romeo."

As she called out the registration, I nearly crashed into the car in front of me I was so surprised.

"Nancy who called you?"

"The insured, Kenneth Smith — he was wondering if he could get a rebate on his car policy."

"What did you say to him Nancy and when did he call?" I shouted. "Tell me everything you said in the conversation as it could be very important!"

"Take it easy Andy," Nancy said sounding surprised and a bit annoyed. "He called about ten minutes ago, enquiring about the rebate and I told him there is a small amount, about €50, that he would be entitled too. He told me that he was still staying at the address listed on the policy, in 50 Terun View, Naas. He also told me he had been out of the country working for a few months and asked for a quote to renew his insurance policy on the same car. What's going on?"

"Nancy, this is a major fraud. I won't go into details as it's a complex case and it would take at least an hour to explain the details. All you need to know is that this file has been with me in Special Investigations for a few months and is under investigation with the police."

"Sounds serious Andy."

"It is; tell me did you agree to send him a rebate cheque for the €50?"

"I told him I would have to get clearance from my manager before I could issue it. He told me to post it and the quotation."

"Nancy is the phone call recorded?"

"Yes, I will email you the MP3 file."

"That's brilliant. Please can you send it to me as soon as possible? Oh and sorry for being a little abrupt with you."

"Don't worry about it. I will send you the file straight away."

The Dublin city traffic was almost at a standstill so I decided to drive to the address in Naas instead. I quickly did a U-turn, ignoring the deafening sound of various car horns. I did not care; if I was a cop, my blue roof light would have been switched on. John Harrison was back in Ireland and I needed to get to Naas and fast. As I drove I considered whether or not to call Ray. However I decided to hold off as I wanted to see the red Alfa Romeo myself before I got the GBFI involved. Once I found his car I would call them.

I eventually got onto the main Naas road and accelerated hard. The speed limit on this road is 60mph and I had a very hard time sticking to it. But I knew the road was well-patrolled by traffic cops, who generally do not have an interest in fraud investigation: you break the speed limit – you get the ticket and pay the fine.

I arrived in Naas and quickly located 50 Terun View again. The security gate into the car park was closed but luckily I remembered the code and the gates opened as I keyed it into the electronic lock.

There were several cars in the car park however the red Alfa Romeo was not there. I parked in a space near the front gate. My surveillance experience had taught me to park close to a gate or to stand beside a door, just in case a fast exit was required!

Having secured my car I walked over to the block of apartments. The front door was locked. To the side were a number of intercoms and several letterboxes, metal boxes secured to the main concrete structure of the apartments. I located number 50 which was open and not secured. When I'd visited this address before, the letterbox was locked. I wondered if Harrison was only using the address and he had broken into the letterbox to retrieve his mail. There was nothing left inside it, other than advertisement leaflets for some local restaurants.

I decided to try calling number 50 and pressed the intercom bell. The buzzer sounded but nobody answered.

It was 9.05am, so perhaps the person who lived there had gone to work. As I was walking back towards my car, a woman walked out of the apartment block.

"Excuse me do you know who lives in number 50?"

"Nobody is living in 50 at the moment. They moved out about two weeks ago, a Polish couple."

I took a breath and asked the crucial question.

"Do you know if there was an American staying there?"

"No I do not remember an American; they were Polish."

I thanked her and returned to my car feeling a little disappointed.

I sat in my car for another few minutes but I was too conspicuous within the enclosed compound and I decided to leave. I entered the key code and stopped around the corner. I was uncertain what to do next. I considered calling to the other addresses I had located for him in the area but instead I decided to give Ray a call.

"Hi Andy, what's up?" Ray answered immediately.

"Hi Ray we have a development. We received a call at Dallast from Kenneth Smith aka Harrison early this morning, looking for a rebate on his policy for the red Alfa Romeo."

"Excellent stuff, Andy. What address did he give you?"

"He gave the address that is on the policy of insurance, 50 Terun View, in Naas. I am down here at the moment Ray."

"Did you call to the address?" Ray asked. It was obvious that he was a little annoyed with me for being there at all, as this was now a GBFI investigation.

"No," I answered

"Hold on a minute Andy," he said and put me on hold.

A few moments later he was back.

"All we have is the car but if we find the car we might find Harrison so we need to be careful Andy. That address of 50 Terun View may be just a postal address for him. I will make some enquires and come back to you. Andy I suggest you get out of there and leave this to me."

"OK Ray but let me know what happens."

Ray was correct the only way we were going to find Harrison was the car, especially as it was not a popular car in Ireland. I remember being on surveillance with Sam from Sleator Carroll Investigations and he always used to say: "If you lose your subject, check the area and keep your eyes open; you might just get lucky and find the car."

I checked through my notes and found the addresses that I had for Harrison in Naas. There was the one in Craddockstown, which was walking distance from 50 Terun View. I was aware that Ray had told me to back off, but then a drive around the area was not really getting involved.

I decided to walk past the house to try to find the Alfa Romeo car and within a few moments I was outside the address. However there were no cars in the driveway or parked outside.

I just had to find that Alfa Romeo. I walked back to my car and drove around checking all of the shopping centre car parks in Naas town centre and had soon exhausted all options.

I pulled in and rechecked my notes and drove on to the address in Sallins, about two miles away. It was worth a shot.

I checked the address which Harrison had previously used in The Stables Sallins. Nobody was home. A lady who lived a few doors down was cleaning her windows and I decided to risk questioning her.

"Sorry to disturb you. I am trying to get in contact with your neighbours."

"Nobody has lived there for some time."

"Do you know if there was an American man living there?"

"No only a young man. I think he was Polish or Russian maybe. He kept to himself and left a few months ago — what is this about?"

"Sorry I think I may have the wrong address. Thanks anyway."

I continued checking shop car parks as I drove along the Main Street in Sallins. It was a short street so I drove into the first car park I found. It was rather busy but there it was— the red Alfa Romeo, with the correct registration. It was neatly reversed into a car park space.

My heart was pounding with excitement. I felt as if I had won the lottery. I parked my car in the only space available which unfortunately was directly opposite his car. I felt a little conspicuous sitting in the driver's seat so I quickly changed to the passenger seat. This was another one of Sam Carroll's tips in the art of covert surveillance: a person sitting in the passenger seat of a car looks less conspicuous and blends into the shopping environment; if anybody noticed me, it would look like I was waiting for somebody.

I had my camera with me and considered obtaining some photographs of him as he got back into his car. However I decided this would be too risky and I already had Igor's photographs from Poland. I reminded myself that it was Ray's operation and all I could do was to follow Harrison to wherever he was living.

An hour later I was feeling a bit bored. I couldn't read as I'd been trained to keep my eyes fixed firmly on the subject or target — in this case the car. A former detective once told me that surveillance was the most boring aspect of an investigation, especially if you had to wait for hours and nothing happened. Worse still I knew it was when your mind drifts or you take your eyes of the subject that you lose them. At least nowadays we have comfortable cars in which to base ourselves. In the days of the Wild West Pinkerton detectives must have had some tough times on surveillance operations, when they were following suspected criminals to a hide out.

I was starting to feel stiff when a man walked out of the shop. It was Harrison. I couldn't believe my luck. He was carrying some shopping bags and wearing a black, long coat and dark blue jeans. He also wore a baseball cap that covered his face. He walked casually over to the car and got into the driver's side.

My heart was beating double time with the tension and excitement. Harrison started his car and drove from the car park.

I quickly jumped into the driver's seat of my car and followed him. I was in a good spot as there was one car in between our two cars which is ideal for mobile vehicle surveillance. Harrison turned right onto the Main Street of Sallins and drove over the bridge. The traffic lights changed and I got stuck at a red light. I was afraid I was going to lose him. As soon as Harrison's car was out of sight I carefully drove after him, even though the traffic light was still red. Thankfully there were no cars coming.

I drove over the Sallins Bridge and was just in time to observe him turning left into another housing estate, Sallins Woods. I knew it was a dead end so I parked on the Main Street, grabbed my jacket and quickly walked into the estate.

I was worried this was a stupid move as the housing estate was a big one. However I was lucky as Harrison was parking his car on the road about 200 metres in front of me. I slowed down and observed him getting out of his car. Harrison was still about 150 metres in front of me which was ideal for foot surveillance. As he walked he held the shopping bags in his right hand and crossed over the road onto the other pedestrian foot path. He then walked over a green patch of grass and into the driveway of a corner house. I kept walking as he took a key from his coat pocket and entered the house.

I continued walking for a couple of minutes, then turned around and headed back towards my car. I pulled my mobile from my pocket and phoned Ray.

"Hello Andy."

"Ray, I'm just outside Sallins Woods' housing estate in Sallins."

"What are you doing there?"

"I located Harrison's car in Sallins and I followed him to this address."

"Andy, I told you to back off"

"I know, I know, but I just happened to be in the area and spotted his car."

There was a pause and I wondered if Ray was going to lose it because I hadn't backed off but then I'd got 'the catch' so what could he say?

"Just in the area indeed ... well good job Andy. Back off now and we will take over the surveillance."

I agreed and signed off. I was more than happy to withdraw from the surveillance operation. I knew that any further involvement from me could jeopardise the criminal investigation.

I checked my watch; it was 12.30pm. It was more than time for me to return to the office. Courtney understood my motives for staying with the case but I didn't want to push my luck.

I'd just have to wait and check in with Ray later – maybe this would be the day we arrested the Cowboy. I was pretty sure that a result was imminent. I was hoping for Harrison's arrest and eventual prosecution. The cogs of law moved slowly, but at least they were moving. I was confident probably over-confident, but I had faith in Detective Ray Harding. He always got a good result. It had been difficult handing over the case but Ray was a smooth operator and a great detective.

The term investigator was more suited to a civilian detective like me. An investigator's main objective, be it a private investigator or insurance/financial investigator, was to investigate on behalf of their employer/client and then present the findings and evidence to a court. I had gone to the limit, and well beyond, of my responsibility and duty with this particular investigation and I was glad a detective of Ray's calibre was pursuing the criminal angle. I knew I had to move on to other cases but I called Ray first. His phone went to its message minder so I left a message asking that he call me back.

Ray did not return my call that day which was unusual as he always got back to me within a few hours. I arrived into the office early the following morning, eager for news. Denton had asked for an early meeting to discuss some files. He was tired, clearly hung over and in no mood for work so I sent him off to get some coffee and decided to call Ray. To my surprise he again did not answer his phone. I left a message asking him to give me a call when he got a chance. I wondered why he hadn't answered or returned my call from the previous day. Maybe he was on the surveillance operation?

Denton was busy talking about some young lady he had met in a Dublin night-club and I was trying to concentrate on my emails and requests for investigations. It was difficult as my mind was focused on the Harrison case. I was wondering if the police had arrested him and what information he had provided when questioned.

My mobile rang and I quickly answered, hoping it was Ray. However it was my good friend Dave Hendrick.

"Hi Andy, you still working on that American case?"

"No ... well not really; the police are now dealing with the case as he is back in Ireland."

"Have they arrested him yet?"

"I don't know," I said, wishing Ray would call.

"We are meeting up for a game of golf in Druid's Glen on Friday and then a few pints afterwards, are you interested?"

"Dave you know my feelings towards golf. I hate the game, but I will certainly meet you guys afterwards."

Golf was the last thing on my mind, as was meeting up with the guys for a few drinks but I had to keep occupied or I'd end up back in Sallins. I was engrossed in this case and would have loved to have been a Garda detective working on the file. Unfortunately I would have had to pass Irish in my Leaving Certificate exam in order to become a member of the Gardaí. There was more chance of me obtaining a job as an astronaut with NASA than passing the Irish exam. I was far too busy reading detective books and magazines to waste my time studying Irish. It was not that I had anything against Irish and I was glad it was the official first language of Ireland, but, I could not see the point in speaking a language that less than 100,000 people speak on a daily basis.

The day in the office passed slowly and I was really tempted to phone Ray again. I was hungry for information on the case and how it was developing. I wanted to know if they had arrested Harrison and raided the addresses. But I did not want to be a pain in the neck. Operation Cowboy was just one of Ray's many cases even if to me it was more than just an insurance and criminal investigation, it was personal. The idea of somebody using my dead son's identity for fraud and other criminal activity was horrible and beyond justification.

Early the following morning as I was driving into the Dublin office Ray rang. I dropped my phone I was so anxious to talk to him and had to pull in and rummage around on the floor looking for it. For some strange reason the Bluetooth had not connected on my hands' free. Eventually I grabbed it.

"Ray! What is happening? Is he in custody? What did he say?"

"Hold your horses Andy, this is not *CSI* and we do not want to arrest him just yet anyway."

"Why not arrest him? And what is happening with the case? What can you tell me?"

"OK, OK, we have him under surveillance at the moment as we are interested in observing his activities and seeing who else he is possibly involved with, especially considering the different passports."

"Do you really think he is involved with terrorists?"

I'd been wondering about this aspect ever since reading the newspaper article on Russian spies and Irish passports.

"I don't think so, however, he is using anti-surveillance techniques, such as driving around a roundabout a few times, or driving into a dead end, waiting to see if he is followed and then continuing on driving so he's definitely a professional."

"So what happens next? Are you going to search the addresses in Naas or Sallins?"

"We don't think he is staying at the Naas address. We think 50 Terun View is just a postal address that he uses. It looks like he is staying at the Sallins Woods address you gave us. We know it is rented out to some Polish people. We don't want to do anything to scare him off so we will just watch him over the next few days and establish what he is doing and who he is in contact with in Ireland."

"Thanks Ray, please keep me posted."

It was good of Ray to keep me updated on the case. I could tell he knew how important it was to me.

The week passed slowly. I tried to get my head off the case and started working on some long overdue files. On Friday evening I joined Dave Hendrick and the guys in Druid's Glenn for a few beers. I did not play golf as my golf skills are about as good as my Irish language skills. Getting out with the guys helped me to relax and stop thinking about the investigation, if only for a few hours.

The following Monday morning I received a call from Ray. It was not what I was expecting.

"Andy, Ray here."

"Hi Ray, what is happening?"

"He's been under continuous surveillance over the past few days and he has not been up to much, other than doing a lot of driving."

"So have you got a date for taking him into custody?"

"No Andy and I'm not going to bullshit you – we lost him!"

There was a pause as I bit back my first reaction.

"You lost him? How?"

"Due to budget restrictions, we could not cover him at night-time. We know he returned to the house on Saturday evening but when our surveillance team arrived early yesterday morning the car was gone. I was not looking forward to calling you, but you deserve the truth."

"Thanks Ray. Maybe he will be back; maybe he went down the country for a few days?"

"Yes that's possible but we don't have the budget to keep the house under surveillance anymore."

I felt disappointed. It was not Ray's fault and I could tell that he was feeling frustrated. I understood that night-time or silent-hour surveillance was a costly exercise and normally a waste of time. It must be a nightmare for the Gardaí working within budgets. Ray had assured me that he would work with me on the case and that he would do everything in his power to assist in the investigation as long as it was in Ireland and I knew he was serious.

"Look Andy, we have put out alerts looking for the red Alfa Romeo, that's our link to him. We've said it before but if we can find the car then we will find him or if he contacts you guys again let us know, as this time we will arrest him. We have enough now to take him in for questioning."

"I'll put a note on his file Ray. Thanks for letting me know," I said and hung up.

I was bitterly disappointed. After all that hard work Harrison was gone. I sat at my desk and felt like crying. He could be anywhere. Was he still in Ireland? Had he returned to Poland, gone somewhere else in Europe or was he back in the UK? Or worse had he gone back to the US? I was satisfied that I had not spooked him but maybe the Garda surveillance unit had alerted him to their presence somehow or perhaps he had been tipped-off?

It was a blow and I needed to take some time to decide my next move in the investigation. The one thing I knew was that it was far from over.

CHAPTER 29

I spent most of the weekend trying to come up with new leads on the case. There was no point pursuing the Poland side as I had completed that aspect of the investigation. The best angle for me to pursue seemed to be using my international contacts if I got the chance. This was one area where I had an advantage over the Gardaí. Ray, as a Garda detective, would have no legal right to work outside Ireland without getting formal permission to work in a particular country or jurisdiction whereas I could deal directly with my contacts. I was sure that if Harrison had been caught with illegal passports in the United States of America the FBI would have taken over the case and they would simply not stop until they captured him. But in Ireland, no one Garda unit was directly responsible. The GBFI could look for assistance from Interpol but they seemed to be concentrating their efforts on drugs and people trafficking. I was sure a case of identity theft and fraud would not be on their priority list — unless of course there was a connection to the Russian spies.

But I had to be careful as I did not want to jeopardise the Gardai's investigation. Ray had asked me to back off and I needed to respect his request. I decided the only way I could safely assist in the investigation at this stage was from behind a desk, locally in Ireland, following up on the addresses I had for Harrison.

I now had four addresses for Harrison, three in County Kildare, and one in County Roscommon. I was pretty sure that Ann Wall would spot him and contact me if he returned to Roscommon. Ray had told me that during the surveillance operation, they did not see Harrison's wife or child. I thought it was likely that the Cowboy had come over to Ireland for a specific reason and had then returned to Poland. The question was why did he come back?

I was still trying to figure it out as I logged onto my computer. Denise had been promoted to a full field investigator, specialising in motor theft. She was working hard on some large files and now spent over 80 per cent of her time on the road, investigating suspect files. To fill her previous role, we had a new person, Lesley Cantwell, joining the team. She was a specialist in intelligence gathering and had been transferred from our UK operation. Denise was giving her a formal handover.

"Nice to see you Andy, we seem to be always missing each other, are you avoiding me?" Denise asked sarcastically. "Have you met your new intelligence officer Leslie Cantwell?"

Leslie had been working in the office for two days and this was my first time meeting her.

I ignored Denise's comments and said: "Leslie, pleasure to meet you, sorry but I have been rather busy. Welcome to the team; your former UK manager speaks very highly about you and your work."

"Thanks Andy, Denise told me all about your Texan case. It sounds very interesting."

"It's certainly time consuming," I smiled.

I tried to block out the sound of their voices as I was still thinking about the American and his current location. I decided to pull all my notes together and to run through the various pieces of evidence and observations I had made during the course of my investigation. As Harrison was a nomadic person, and usually stayed with Polish people who were only renting in Ireland it was going to be very difficult to trace him. As before the key to his location was the car.

Denise headed out on the road and Leslie asked me about the case. I told her about the car and the importance of locating it.

"It's a pity you did not have a tracking device fitted to the vehicle," she said.

"A pity is right!" I groaned.

"Did you try running the registration with the police?"

"Yes, that is how we found out about Kenneth Smith and his previous insurance claim, and about the identity theft of the real Kenneth Smith."

"Did you try doing an Internet search on the registration number?"

"What would that show me? It'd just be the same address in Sallins."

"Give me the registration number and I will see what I can establish for you."

I called it out not feeling very hopeful.

After less than five minutes Lesley walked over to my desk and handed me a printout. I could not believe it. From entering the registration into Google she had discovered that the car was for sale.

I was impressed.

"This is excellent, why didn't I think of this? Well done!"

The advertisement stated that the Alfa Romeo was for sale with an asking price of €3,950. The car was described as being in excellent condition, with 90,000 miles on the clock. Under the description I found the following information:

'I have changed my employer and now have a company car. Therefore I am selling my current car. The car is in good condition and well-maintained and fully-serviced. New tyres have been fitted. I added a Sony stereo system and speakers that will be sold with the car.'

Harrison had provided an email address and an international phone number, with the Polish code 0048.

This was an excellent piece of evidence. We now had further proof of a link between the name Kenneth Smith, the car and John Harrison. The email address was more proof. It was the same email address that Harrison had used in his correspondence with Dallast on the insurance claim.

I was considering phoning the number but I did not want to spook him. I knew I should inform Ray of the developments however the temptation to call the number was too much. I dialled and a man answered with a strong American accent. I made an excuse and quickly hung up. I was now satisfied that Harrison was back in Poland.

More importantly I knew that he would be returning to Ireland in order to sell his car.

I quickly telephoned Ray.

"Ray, I have some news for you."

"I thought I told you… "

"I know Ray but just hear me out," I interrupted before he could finish. "We did a Google search on the registration number of the red Alfa Romeo. There is a for sale advertisement on the internet with a Polish telephone number."

"Good stuff Andy."

"I think he will definitely return to Ireland to sell the car."

"You're spot on there Andy. I will alert the Harbour Police to look out for the car on both sides of the border. But Andy do I need to tell you again to keep out of the investigation?"

"No worries Ray."

"Good man and good job Andy."

"Ray, before you go, is it OK with you if I do the occasional drive-by of the various addresses in an effort to spot the car."

"On one condition Andy, you spot the car or Harrison you phone me on my mobile, day or night you hear?"

"Absolutely and understood!" I said and hung up before he changed his mind.

I was not convinced that the car had left the country. It was possible that it had been parked in a car park in Ireland and Harrison could have got a flight back to Poland. I had three addresses in Co. Kildare for him, so a few drive-by, spot checks might just develop the case.

That evening I headed to Co. Kildare. It took me the usual hour to get there. I don't like working at night but it was the best time to try to locate a vehicle.

I arrived in Terun View at 01.10am and entered the code into the security gate. I drove around the car park but was unable to locate the car. I also checked the letterbox to number 50 which was still open and unsecured. Other than the same few restaurant advertisements, there was no post.

I drove out and continued to the address in Craddockstown. However there were no cars in the driveway or parked on the road outside the house.

From there I drove onto the address in The Stables Sallins, but there was no sign of the car. I also checked the most recent address in Sallins Woods but again no Alfa Romeo.

I drove home, back along the M50 feeling as if I had wasted my valuable time. I could have been at home tucked up in a warm bed. Lindsey Buckingham's song *Never going back again* was playing on the radio. I hoped that this was not the case with Harrison and that he would be returning to Ireland.

Over the next few weeks I took occasional drives to Co. Kildare and checked the various addresses however there was no sign of the car. While I was in Sallins one evening I called into a local shop to buy some chewing-gum and noticed that several foreign people worked there.

"Did you ever employ an American man here?" I asked without thinking. A split second later I knew this was a risky question as perhaps they knew John Harrison and would tip him off.

"No, I do not know any Americans."

A young man who was sweeping the floor asked: "This American is his name John?"

I nearly choked on my chewing-gum.

"Yes, do you know him?"

The young man stopped sweeping.

"Yes I know him; his wife is a Polish woman."

"What else can you tell me?"

"Not much, he used to hang around the shop and drive some of the Polish girls home, strange man."

"What do you mean by strange?"

"Well he never said much, only played games on his mobile phone."

"Do you know where he was living?"

"He used to live with a Polish guy in Craddockstown and then he moved to an apartment over a shop down the road, on the way to Clane."

This sounded like the address the man in the local café had given me previously but I decided to wait and see.

"How far is this shop?"

"It's only about a mile down the road, on the left-hand side. You cannot miss it."

"Thanks for that. When was the last time you saw him?"

"I am not sure ... maybe two years ago. Why do you want to know? Is he in trouble?"

I quickly thanked him and exited the shop.

I drove the short distance and confirmed it was the same address. Feeling a sense of disappointment I decided to call it a day and I drove home.

A few days later I received bad news. Ray phoned me telling me that the red Alfa Romeo had been registered to a new owner.

"Oh no Ray, that is bad news, what happened?"

"I checked the registration details. It was registered to a new owner a week ago in Athlone, Co. Westmeath. He told me that he purchased the car from an American about a month ago and had not registered the car until now."

"Thanks for letting me know Ray."

This was a devastating development in the case. Now our only Irish connection to Harrison was gone. It looked like the Cowboy was finished with Ireland and had moved on to committing fraud in other countries. Perhaps he would be settling in Poland with his wife and family. I tried to accept that it was unlikely that Harrison would ever see the inside of an Irish court — but I was not prepared to give up just yet.

CHAPTER 30

The weeks and months passed and there was little or no movement on the case. There had been no contact from Harrison regarding the outstanding money that was due to him on the car insurance policy either. At this stage I assumed that he was on to our investigation as we had heard nothing further from him about the original claim either. I was sure he would not risk getting caught over a €50 rebate.

I kept in contact with Detective Ray Harding but he had moved onto other criminal investigations which was understandable. I was also working on other cases and had a few good successful investigations. I usually got a good result for Dallast. All of the civil investigations which I had referred to the police, mainly the Garda Bureau of Fraud Investigation and the National Bureau of Criminal Investigation, had been successful. I was proud of my record and achievements but Operation Cowboy was still on my mind. I had put so much time into the investigation, mainly for personal reasons and it had been running for almost two years — two years since the alleged accident in The Curragh, Co. Kildare. I had traced Harrison to England, Poland, Oklahoma, Arizona, Hawaii and Texas and I was still hungry for a result.

I was banned from talking about the file at work. Dan Courtney had moved to another department and our new head had no interest in fraud, only figures. The new manager, Noel Kenny, had been a commercial accountant before he started working in insurance. In fact his placement with Dallast was his first job in the insurance industry. He had no interest in the personal story behind the investigation, just the financial results. He had no people management skills either and seemed focused only on achieving big savings and sucking up to his superiors. Every company or business has a manager like him.

Our claims investigations and financial results were performing so well we had even expanded. We were now ahead of our targets and Denton was also now a manager. He had two junior investigators working for him. Denise was training to be a lawyer and Leslie the new intelligence officer was pretty much running the investigation unit. Although I was still the overall head of the unit I was tied up with court cases and large fire investigations. I spent a lot of my time sitting in the Dublin courts waiting for cases to commence trial. Some cases get heard and some put back for a few months. It's basically a lottery system — you can be lucky and get your case heard or unlucky and have to wait for months. The American system is much better. You get a date and time and that is pretty much it, unless something occurs, like the judge calls in sick.

Every now and again I would review the Cowboy file and just hope that maybe someday Harrison would return to Ireland. There was no activity on his Facebook page and he had fixed his security settings, so there was now minimal information publically available. It was as if he had simply vanished.

Whenever possible I would drive past the addresses in Kildare, just for the sake of it. As the Alfa Romeo was gone, I was not sure what I was looking for. I just hoped that maybe one day I would see him walking along the street. I knew in my mind that this was highly unlikely. The Fleetwood Mac song *Never going back again* was starting to haunt me.

A few weeks later I was out working on a new claim file in Wexford, when I received a telephone call from Ann Wall. I had not spoken to her in a long time.

"Hello Andy," she said, sounding excited. "John is on Facebook."

"Hi Ann. I know about that but he has now secured his Facebook page so you cannot view his site without being a friend."

"I know – my daughter is a friend."

This was music to my ears.

"Is she in contact with him? Would she be willing to assist us?"

"She may not assist you Andy, but she will damn well assist me. What do you need to know?"

Ann sounded like a true mother, in control and ready to dispense her wrath on Harrison. Clearly she still wanted justice for her family.

I paused a moment – I had so many questions.

First things first: "Is he still in Poland?"

"Yes with his wife and new baby, but he was on a holiday in Australia. I think he may have got some surgery on his back while he was down under."

I wondered why he'd gone to Australia but it explained why things had been so quiet.

"Has he any plans to return to Ireland?"

"I don't know. Would you like me to find out?"

"Only if it does not alert him because if he returns to Ireland the Gardaí have enough evidence to arrest him and Ann I do not want to put your daughter in harm's ways."

"Don't you worry about my daughter; sure she is now living in San Diego, California."

"OK Ann, that would be great but your daughter needs to make sure he doesn't get suspicious about the questions she asks him."

"Don't worry, we'll do it. I'll contact you when I have some news."

I was excited by the development. However when I took a moment to think about it, I realised I would have to rely on others to act which was not a great place to be when dealing with an investigation. The chance of Harrison returning to Ireland was minimal. I decided not to inform Detective Ray Harding as at this stage I was unsure if Ann's plan would work. I was in contact with him on a weekly basis and he was still a little embarrassed about Harrison evading their surveillance and getting out of the country. I knew the detective badly wanted to arrest Harrison so I didn't want to give him false hope. Ray had also told me that Interpol had been alerted to the false Irish passports. He had assured me that as soon as the Cowboy stepped foot in Ireland again he would be arrested and taken into custody for questioning. Ray wanted a result as much as I did, so I'd wait until I'd something concrete for him.

I had a good feeling about it as there was nothing like a mother's anger. Harrison had done some serious damage to Ann Wall's daughter and at the very least he'd an unhealthy influence over her. Ann was obviously still raging that Harrison had got her daughter involved with the wrong side of the law.

For the remainder of the day I continued on with my investigation in County Wexford. I found it hard to concentrate as my mind was back on the Harrison file.

A week or so passed and I was dealing with year-end financial reports, important but boring work. My desktop phone rang which was unusual as aside from internal calls, most of my contact with people was by mobile.

"Is that Andy Stone?"

"Yes… "

"Andy it's Ann Wall, why are you not answering your mobile?"

I'd forgotten I'd given her my direct line. I checked my mobile as I said: "Hi Ann, sorry I just realised my phone is on silent."

"I have news for you … John is coming back to Ireland."

"When? How do you know?"

"He told my daughter, I am uncertain of the date, possibly later on this month."

"Are you sure?"

"Yes, I am sure — just not certain of the date."

"Do you know how he is travelling? Is he taking the boat or flying?"

"I think he is flying, he may be travelling from Poland or possibly via the UK."

"Can you tell me what email address he is using?"

"Hold on for a few minutes and I will check."

The few minutes felt more like fifteen. I could hear her tapping away on a keyboard.

"His email address is a Gmail one."

"Thank you so much Ann," I said, writing it down. "This is really helpful. If you get any more information, no matter how insignificant it may seem to you, then please let me know."

I said goodbye to Ann, picked up my mobile and telephoned Ray Harding.

"Ray I got a tip-off that Harrison is coming back to Ireland."

"Yes I know."

"How do you know?"

"Emm ... I can't tell you at this stage Andy. We have been working in the background with Interpol and yes we are aware he is coming back to Ireland."

Ray always said "we" when he was with somebody.

"Andy, I will give you a call later on."

"OK thanks Ray."

I was now certain that Ray had a senior ranking officer beside him and could not talk freely.

I was excited, but I was also feeling nervous. If all worked as planned, Harrison would arrive in Dublin and he'd be arrested. But, as I knew from the surveillance operation, there could be a hiccup along the way. I made sure my mobile was no longer on silent and tried to get back to work.

The day was drawing to a close and I was preparing to go home when my mobile rang.

"Andy, Ray here; Harrison is arriving in Dublin on the 17 January, from London on a Ryanair flight."

"How do you know that Ray?"

"I will tell you some other time Andy. Now I'm sure I don't have to remind you that what I've just told you is confidential, as we are planning a major surveillance operation involving six detectives."

"Are you sure that will be enough?" I asked.

"Yes more than enough, we are not going to lose him on this occasion."

"How did you know Ray?" I asked again.

"Interpol."

"Interpol! Is that because of the international spies using Irish passports?" I responded

"I cannot comment further. Now Andy not a word, this is confidential."

"I know Ray and thanks, I appreciate you letting me know."

"I will be in contact with you closer to the time but remember not a word Andy."

I drove home in a daze. Although Ray was aware that anything he told me would not go any further I knew this information was particularly sensitive to the overall operation. I decided not to write down any notes about the call, as there was no need and it could jeopardise my relationship with Ray.

I had nine days to kill until Harrison arrived. I was curious about how Ray had obtained the information on Harrison's flight details and under which name the Cowboy was travelling. As far as I knew Harrison did not have an American passport in his own name so maybe he was using the Luke Wilson passport again.

I was sitting at my desk the following day when my mobile rang, it was Ray again.

"Ah Andy, can you call over to our office for 2.00pm today and I will give you a briefing?"

"2.00pm today, see you then Ray."

Our new manager Noel Kenny also wanted to have a meeting at 2.00pm so this was going to be difficult. If I told Kenny I was meeting with the cops about the Harrison file, then most likely I would be instructed to stay away from the investigation. I decided to ask Denton for help.

"Denton I need a favour."

"Sure, Andy what can I do for you?"

"I have a meeting with Noel Kenny at 2.00pm today. It clashes with a meeting with the cops. Can you attend the meeting with Kenny?"

"Tell me this is not about John Harrison, have you not forgotten about him?"

"It is, I can't tell you much about it but I feel his arrest is imminent."

"That sounds promising, but have you not been here before?"

"Yes, but things are different now," or so I hoped!

"Alright Andy, but you owe me one."

"Thanks Denton, I will certainly remember this."

I arrived in Ray's office just before 2.00pm and was escorted to a large meeting room. I wondered why I was not going into his normal office, but decided not to ask any questions and just go with the flow. In the room I was introduced to the Detective Superintendent, a Detective Inspector and Detective Sergeant Sinead Guerin who was leading the field investigation and surveillance at the airport. There were another three Detective Gardaí in the room and of course my friend Detective Ray Harding.

After the introductions the Detective Superintendent congratulated me.

"This is a fine investigation, well-planned. Your file was of major support to our team. This is not just a fraud against your company, it's national fraud against our country; well done lad."

"Thank you, Sir."

"Team we need this Harrison man stopped. We cannot rest until justice has been served. Do you understand me?" the Detective Superintendent asked.

"Yes Sir," everybody, including me, responded.

The Detective Superintendent then shook my hand and left the room with the Detective Inspector.

"Nice report Andy," Detective Sergeant Guerin said. "Have you got any experience at surveillance?"

"Yes plenty," I said confidently.

"Would you care to expand on plenty?" she enquired.

"Well I trained in Ireland and was also with Pinkerton in North America. I have been involved in surveillance operations in Miami, Los Angeles and Ireland, including Dublin Airport."

"Wow, a real life *Magnum PI*," she responded.

Everybody in the room laughed. Perhaps I'd sounded as if I was bragging, which was not my intention.

"Ray says you want to be involved in the operation at the airport, I have a problem with that as civilians usually get in the way. However I will make an exception as long as you agree to observe only and don't get involved."

I was unsure what to say so I just nodded.

"You can partner up with Ray and watch from a distance," she continued. "We will pick Harrison up at the airport and see where he goes. Guys listen up, it's important we do not lose him as we only get one chance at this operation."

Det. Sgt. Guerin impressed me. She was well able to give orders, seemed completely in control and I had previously heard her name mentioned as a cop who got good results.

After the meeting I returned to the office. I wanted to tell my Special Investigation Unit colleagues about the operation, however I was sworn to secrecy and I also did not want to let the detectives down. Most importantly I did not want to jeopardise the case. It had taken me two years to investigate and, at last, Harrison was within our sights. Hopefully he would be in range for arrest within a few days.

For the rest of the day all I could think about was getting justice for the parents and babies whose identities Harrison had stolen. As a parent of a baby who had died at birth, I would have been totally devastated if his identity had been stolen. I needed a result and I'd a feeling Det. Sgt. Guerin was going to get me one.

CHAPTER 31

※

Surveillance is difficult, especially for private investigators like me who spend many hours sitting in cars and other public places, simply watching. It is also a costly exercise for a client. Surveillance with police detectives is entirely different, as they are the law and have the power to go almost anywhere. For instance they can drive through red traffic lights as long as it's safe. I can recall countless times when, after hours of surveillance, I have lost the subject at a red traffic light.

I had prepared myself for the police surveillance operation. I got my dark clothes ready, with the airport public environment in mind. I checked my camera equipment, making sure it was fully charged and working. I had also purchased a new 4GB Scandisk memory card just in case. Then again I assumed that the cops would have all the equipment we would need, but as my old mentor Sam Carroll used to say "prepare for all eventualities". The possibilities of not knowing what was coming next and where you would end up were what made surveillance exciting and paid off all the long hours of sitting still.

The morning of the 17 January arrived. I was feeling excited, yet with a sense of caution about what the day might bring. I met with Ray and Det. Sgt. in the car park of Kealy's pub, just outside the perimeter grounds of Dublin Airport. Two other detectives joined us.

Ray handed round a large photograph of Harrison's face.

"This is our target; let's refresh our memories on what he looks like."

I didn't need to look at Harrison's photograph. I had his face well placed within my memory.

Det. Sgt. Guerin introduced me: "Andy this is Detective Billy Carrick and Detective Martin Bourke. They are with the National Surveillance Unit (NSU). As I am the senior officer, I will take the lead on the operation however this is very much a team effort. We will have two cars and will use the closed signal Motorola radio system."

Ray handed me a radio instructing: "Put this in your pocket and put the ear plug in your ear."

The ear plug was a small wireless speaker that was connected to the radio in my pocket. I was impressed with the equipment.

"Carrick, are you carrying?" Det. Sgt. Guerin asked.

"No, but Martin is so he can't go airside."

"OK Bourkie you stay landside and watch the exits. Andy and Ray you guys are with me, airside beside Customs. This is where we will pick him up. Billy will be working undercover as a baggage loader out at the aircraft and will hopefully identify him as he walks from the aircraft. He's flying Ryanair so we don't know where he's sitting. Once Billy gives us the nod we will take it from there. Andy we're relying on you to spot him if Billy can't find him."

"Me?" I responded feeling worried

"Yes, you, after all you are the only one who has seen him in person."

Hearing the Sgt. say this, in her strong commanding voice, made me realise that I was not simply along for the ride. It made me feel nervous but it also gave me a sense of achievement, knowing that I was accepted by the GBFI as a professional investigator even if I was still a civilian.

"What if he gets into a taxi or gets collected from Arrivals, how will we follow him?" I asked her, feeling a bit stupid but too intent on catching Harrison to care.

"We will have two cars parked outside, a blue Ford Focus and a grey Ford Mondeo. The Focus will have a clamp on the wheel so it looks like it's immobile."

I decided to stay quiet and not ask any more questions, as it was obvious that Det. Sgt. Guerin was in control and had planned for all eventualities.

"Is everybody ready? Any more questions?"

We all shook our heads.

"Then let's go and take our positions. The flight is due to land in 40 minutes."

Det. Sgt. Guerin drove all five of us to the main entrance of the airport. We got out and a uniformed Garda drove the vehicle away. Det. Sgt. Guerin then did a radio check and we left Detective Bourke in position at the exits.

I walked into the Arrivals Hall feeling excited, like when you are about to fly away on a long distance holiday. It was just after 2.00pm, a quiet time in the airport which does not get busy again until around 6.00pm, when the business flights return from London and the rest of Europe.

Det. Sgt. Guerin showed her ID to an airport police officer, who nodded and we walked into the baggage collection area. Airside was a highly sensitive security area which made the surveillance operation difficult.

A few moments passed as we waited and then Det. Sgt. Guerin did a second radio check.

"Are you all in position? Call in. Over."

"I am in position on the stand of the aircraft, which I am told is on time. Over."

"Roger Carrick, got that. Over," she responded. "Bourkie are you receiving? Over."

"Roger Sgt., in position observing the exits. Over."

I checked my watch again it was now almost 2.28pm. The flight was due to land at 2:40pm. I stood beside Ray in the baggage area, trying to look like I was waiting for a bag to arrive. Det. Sgt. Guerin was standing beside a baggage carousel across the way, also pretending she was waiting for her bag.

A few moments later Detective Carrick called in: "The Eagle has landed, will be on stand in a few moments. Over."

It was 2.34pm, the Ryanair flight was six minutes early.

"We know there are 98 passengers on the flight and they will be exiting from two doors of the Boeing 737 aircraft so keep your eyes peeled Carrick. Over," Det. Sgt Guerin ordered.

"Roger!"

A few moments later he said: "Doors open. Over."

"Let's do this. Over." Det. Sgt. Guerin said.

I could feel my pulse racing. Every second we had to wait felt like a minute, every minute an hour.

Finally Detective Carrick radioed in.

"Possible target in sight, leaving aircraft now; subject is wearing black coat, dark blue jeans and a black baseball cap, about 5ft 11ins in height. Over."

"Stay with the aircraft, it may not be him. Over." Det. Sgt. Guerin responded.

To me it sounded like Harrison, but she was running the operation.

"Ray, he will be with you in six minutes twenty-five seconds, keep your eyes open. Over." she ordered.

"Six minutes 25 seconds," I said, "isn't that a little precise?"

"She walked the distance this morning; that's how long it took her."

I was really impressed with her surveillance skill and attention to detail.

"Andy, go and stand over by the Ryanair desk, you will get a better view of him from there. Over."

I stood at the desk trying to avoid the attention of the staff member who was working there.

After six minutes and fifteen seconds the subject came into view. It looked like Harrison but I could not be sure. I shook my head very slightly to let Ray know.

Sgt Guerin was out of my line of sight so she called over the radio.

"Andy is it the subject? Over."

"I am not sure. I can't get a look at his face; the baseball cap is blocking my view. Over."

With that the Ryanair girl asked: "Can I help you Sir?"

"No I am just waiting for somebody."

She continued to look in my direction. I could tell that she was not satisfied with my answer and thought I looked suspicious. With my luck she would probably call the Airport Police.

Det. Sgt. Guerin called out on the radio: "Ray, code amber!"

On hearing these words Ray immediately walked over to the possible subject and asked: "Excuse me do you have the time?"

"Sorry I don't have a watch," the guy replied in a strong Dublin accent.

"That is not the subject. Over," Ray said, walking back.

"Carrick here, I think all the passengers are off the aircraft. Over."

"Everybody stay in your positions. Over," Det. Sgt Guerin ordered.

I started to feel worried that we had missed him or maybe the information was wrong or, worse still, maybe he was aware of the operation and had decided not to travel.

Another few moments passed and Ray called Det. Sgt. Guerin.

"What now Sgt.? Over."

"Everybody stay in position. Over."

The Ryanair girl was still looking in my direction and I decided to walk back towards Ray.

Carrick radioed: "Guys the subject is in the baggage reclaim, carousel number 4, wearing a long black coat and dark jeans. Over."

I looked towards baggage carousel number 4 and there he was picking up a small bag — Harrison. I had to stop myself from shouting with excitement. Finally he was back in Ireland and he was going to be arrested.

"Bourkie he is on his way out to you, don't stop him. Let's see what he gets up to. Over," Det. Sgt. Guerin radioed.

I turned to follow Ray, and saw two Airport police officers talking to the Ryanair attendant who was pointing in my direction. The two officers started walking towards me. This was going to be disastrous. If Harrison saw me talking to the uniformed Airport police officers my cover would be blown and the Cowboy might try to run for it.

I hurried towards Ray who was now about ten feet in front of me.

I heard the police officers call after me.

"Excuse me Sir?" a voice said and I turned to face two rather tall Airport Police officers.

Just as I was about to start talking Det. Sgt. Guerin appeared, flashed her Garda identification and said: "He is with me."

We quickly walked after Ray who was now out of sight.

When we walked into Arrivals Ray was standing near the main door.

"Where is he Ray? Over," Det. Sgt. Guerin radioed.

"He is in a taxi, gold-coloured Toyota Avensis, Taxi plate number NB212121TTZ. Over."

As soon as the taxi pulled away and out of our view, we ran from the airport and jumped into the Ford Mondeo.

Det. Sgt. Guerin shouted: "I will drive."

Ray sat in the front; Billy and I were in the back.

"Bourkie follow us in the Ford Focus," she radioed. "Are you receiving? Over."

"Yes Sgt. Over."

We followed the taxi out of Dublin Airport and onto the M50 motorway. He drove at speeds in excess of 90mph.

"This taxi driver thinks he is a cop," Det. Sgt. Guerin said. "Ray you'll have to talk to him when we catch up with him."

Ray laughed and nodded.

The taxi then turned onto the M7 Naas motorway, which leads to Kildare.

"I bet you he is staying in Naas or Sallins," Ray said.

"Yes it looks that way," I agreed.

The surveillance was difficult as the M50 was busy and the taxi driver was driving at dangerous speeds.

The taxi eventually turned off at the exit for Sallins. He drove onto the Main Street and then turned left into the Sallins Woods estate.

We pulled in on the main street and Det. Sgt. Guerin picked up the radio.

"Bourkie drive into the estate and see what is happening. Over."

I knew she was concerned that Harrison or the taxi driver might have been suspicious of our Ford Mondeo car as we had been following them for about 35 miles.

Detective Bourke turned left into the estate. Detective Carrick appeared totally at ease as he sat beside me in the car.

"Are you not nervous he will be detected?" I asked

"Bourkie and I do this surveillance all the time and we have not been spotted," he said calmly.

A few moments passed as we waited for an update. I was comforted by Billy Carrick's words but I was still anxious.

"Subject is on foot, walking towards a house … opening the door with a key and has gone inside. Over," Detective Bourke radioed.

"Well done everybody. Good job, Bourkie. Hold your position. Over," Det. Sgt. Guerin radioed as she drove into the car park of a local pub. "Don't know about you three but I need the toilet!"

I sat in the bar and ordered four coffees.

"Well did you enjoy being a cop today Andy?" Det. Sgt. Guerin asked as she sat down beside me.

"Yeah, I was really impressed by it all. Tell me how did you spot him?"

"Years of practice and your photographs were a great help, but it was Billy who spotted him."

"So what happens next?"

"Well we know he is due to fly home tomorrow afternoon, so we'll watch him until then and see what he does."

"He is only in Ireland for 24hrs, so he must be here for a reason, maybe another passport?" Ray suggested as he rejoined us.

"Yes, I would say another passport," she agreed.

"So you are going to watch him all night?" I asked.

"Not us; we have two surveillance people who will monitor his movements and call us if anything happens," Det. Sgt. Guerin replied.

"So Ray are you going to tell me how you knew he was on the flight? And what name is he travelling under?"

"I guess we can tell you now," Ray smiled. "He is travelling under the name of Shay O'Brien, which is a name we did not have, but the eejit used the email you gave us to book the airline ticket; we had alerted the airlines to watch out for it."

"We also got some assistance from Interpol on the other side, so we knew he had boarded the flight," Det. Sgt. Guerin said.

"Very clever," I laughed, feeling a real sense of satisfaction.

"You look as if you have just won the lottery Andy," Detective Carrick said, back from his smoke.

"Yes it is a good feeling, but we have not got him in custody yet."

"Andy is right – come on lads, time to get another update," Det. Sgt. Guerin said.

We left the pub and sat in the car.

"Bourkie, come in. Over."

"Sgt. all OK out here, no movements from the house. Delta 1 surveillance unit have just arrived — over."

"Roger that."

"Sgt. Guerin to Delta 1, you have the ball. Over."

"Roger, Delta 1 has the ball. Over."

"OK Bourkie, good job. Let's call it a day. Delta 1 will contact me with any developments. Over."

Det. Sgt. Guerin drove Ray and I back to our cars in Kealy's pub. Detective Carrick had gone with Detective Bourke.

"Guys I can't thank you enough for including me on the surveillance."

"You're welcome Andy, even if you nearly got arrested!" Det. Sgt. Guerin laughed.

"What's this?" Ray asked.

"A good-looking Ryanair girl had her eye on Andy, didn't like his responses to her questions and called in the Airport Police!"

"Good man Andy, a real ladies man," Ray laughed.

"Yeah, yeah, yeah, but thanks Sgt. for getting me out of that mess. My phone will be on all night so please call me if there are any developments, even if it's 3.00am."

"Relax Andy, get some sleep. Delta 1 will not let us down."

That night, I might as well have been on surveillance with Delta 1 as I did not sleep for a single minute.

CHAPTER 32

❧

The following morning I was rather anxious about the ongoing surveillance and hoped that everything was still going well. I knew that Det. Sgt. Guerin, who has to be one of the best detectives I have ever worked with, was correct in saying we needed to gain further intelligence on Harrison's activities in Ireland but it was a potentially expensive exercise if he managed to get away once again. I wished sometimes that fraud investigation was not such a risky business. I would compare it to a game of poker as you simply do not know the cards that your opponents are holding and what tricks they may have up their sleeves. Fraudsters also flaunt the laws of all jurisdictions, whereas investigators and detectives have to work within the parameters of the law.

I dropped the kids off at school and was driving towards the office when I suddenly turned around and headed for Sallins, Co. Kildare. I had been thinking about the surveillance operation all night and I needed to try to establish the current situation. I knew this was risky and that Ray and the Sgt.

would not be impressed. However my car was not known by Harrison or the Delta 1 surveillance team, so I was sure a quick drive-by would not cause any problems.

I drove into the housing estate and checked the address where Harrison was staying. It was just after 10am and all the curtains were drawn back in the house and the Delta 1 vehicle was gone. I checked all over the area but could not locate the surveillance vehicle so either Harrison was on the move or Delta 1 had lost him and the cops had called off the surveillance. There was nothing more for me to do, so I drove to our Dublin office, feeling tense.

I wanted to telephone Ray or Det. Sgt. Guerin to find out what was happening but I did not want to get in the way of the complex surveillance operation. Instead I sat down at my desk to try to do some work. It was almost impossible. My mind was completely focused on the Harrison case.

None of my team was in the office; they were all working in the field on different cases and Denton had gone to Spain on his vacation. Sitting in the office alone reminded me of the early days when I was the only person employed in the company as a fraud investigator. Although I was pleased that our unit was bigger I sometimes missed the old days, when I didn't have people reporting to me and I was on my own. There were five of us now — it showed that the global insurance industry had come a long way when it came to dedicating funds to combating fraud. If Harrison had succeeded in his case against Dallast, then he would have received a payment of around €1 million. Harrison was so successful at making false insurance claims he was making a good living from his tax free earnings.

I read through my emails, looking for something of interest that would hold my attention. There were all sorts of emails however I just could not get my mind off the surveillance operation which was hopefully still ongoing. My mobile was glued to my shirt pocket in case there was any news.

As I sat drinking a coffee it finally rang. Looking at the displayed number it was so long it had to be from a foreign country. I quickly answered.

"Hi Andy, it's Joe Peleg here."

"Hi Joe, how are things? You're not calling me from London are you?"

"I am great Andy. I am on vacation in Atlanta. I am calling you about that passport in the name of Luke Wilson."

"Yes Joe, you got anything?"

"I am not sure Andy. I have run a few checks with some Secret Service colleagues in Arizona. I have a copy of the Wilson passport that was issued in 2002 in Los Angeles, California."

"Los Angeles, California, is that not strange for somebody who lives in Arizona?"

"No, not really Andy. Americans move around a lot so maybe he moved afterwards. I am not sure what I am looking at Andy, so tell you what I will email you a copy of it."

"Are you sure? Thanks so much Joe."

I could hear him tapping away as I called out my email address.

Within a few moments the email arrived. I quickly opened it and looked closely at the attached passport image. I was amazed. I was looking at a United States passport in the name of Luke Wilson, but the photograph was that of John Harrison. The Cowboy had managed to get an official United States passport through identity theft. His actions were a serious threat to the safety and security of the United States, especially after the 9/11 terrorist attacks.

I was sure I now had a good reason to telephone Ray.

Unfortunately his phone was switched off. I decided not to try ringing Det. Sgt. Guerin's phone as she was possibly involved with Delta 1.

Instead I quickly phoned Joe back on his mobile in Atlanta.

"Joe I got your email thanks, but the guy on the passport photograph is not the owner of the passport."

"Great; who is it Andy?"

"His name is John Harrison from Dallas, Texas."

"This is a little over my head Andy. I will talk to our head of section and come back to you for more information."

"Thanks Joe or feel free to pass over my number as I have no problem talking to anyone."

I was hoping that Joe's Head of Section in the United States Secret Service would contact me directly as an investigator needs good sources for gathering intelligence and I always tried to make new ones whenever I got a chance.

I left the office early and drove home, with my mobile still my shirt pocket. I had tried calling Ray several times but his mobile remained switched off. I was starting to get anxious and was thinking that maybe the cops had lost Harrison again and possibly Ray did not want to tell me.

These thoughts were racing through my head when my mobile suddenly rang and the Bluetooth kicked in. It was Det. Sgt. Guerin.

"Hello Sgt," I said quickly

"Hi Andy, just wanted to give you an update. We are following him at the moment," said Det. Sgt. Guerin.

"Thank God! I thought you had lost him."

"Have some faith Andy," she laughed. "We have been on him since early morning. He did not go out last night."

"What has he been doing? Where is he now?"

"Slow down Andy, he is currently in the passport office in Dublin City."

"The passport office; not again!"

"Yes — he is applying for another passport. Looks like he is about ready to leave. Gotta go."

The phone went dead.

My heart was beating with excitement — at last the noose was starting to tighten around Harrison's neck.

I was still driving when my phone rang again. It was Det. Sgt. Guerin

"Andy I think he is heading for Dublin Airport, as his Ryanair flight is due to depart in 90 minutes and he has just got into a taxi. We will lift him at the airport."

I was in Santry, only a few miles from the airport. I drove fast and was entering the airport car park within minutes of receiving her call.

There was no way I was going to miss out on Harrison's arrest. This was going to be the culmination of all my work. I had been on his trail for over two years now and at last the end was in sight.

I knew he was flying Ryanair, so I quickly ran into the airport and found their check-in desks. Then I sat down and waited for the action to unfold. I hoped that Harrison had not checked in online like the majority of Ryanair passengers.

The airport was unusually busy with passengers checking in for the many flights to the UK and the rest of Europe. Locating Harrison with this amount of passenger traffic would be difficult. All I could do was hope that Det. Sgt. Guerin and her team still had him under covert surveillance.

My fingers-were sore as I had bitten my nails almost into oblivion by the time I spotted Harrison walking towards the Ryanair desk. He was wearing the same clothes as the day before and carrying a small bag and brown folder. He stood in the queue waiting to check-in. I looked around but could not see Det. Sgt, Guerin, Ray or anybody else from the surveillance team.

Recognising Harrison was the easy part, I just hoped the detectives were still there somewhere in the background, following his every move. I couldn't even contemplate the idea that they really had lost him and he would be gone out of Ireland and our jurisdiction in less than an hour. He checked-in and started to walk towards security. I stood up and walked after him. Harrison was walking in a slow, relaxed manner and appeared not to have a care in the world.

He stood in the line waiting to pass into airside. I could see he was holding his Ryanair boarding card in his right hand, along with his passport, waiting to display them to airport security. Harrison looked totally calm, a true professional fraudster and conman. If it had been me or any other law-abiding citizen waiting to board a flight, using a false identity, we would have been shaking with nerves. Not Harrison, he was almost smiling, clearly laughing at the Irish authorities.

I could not believe what I was seeing. He was about to walk airside, board an airplane and depart our jurisdiction. Harrison handed his boarding pass and passport to security. The officer examined the documentation and gave them back to him, gesturing for the Cowboy to move forward.

Harrison had joined a long queue for X-ray machines when a man tapped him on the right shoulder and gestured for him to move aside. He looked like a detective. I walked close enough to hear his words.

"John Harrison, I am arresting you …"

The detective continued talking but his words did not register on my brain. Those four words: "I am arresting you," sounded like the sweetest music to my ears. At last we had him.

"Yes!" I said as I turned and jumped about two feet into the air.

The waiting passengers looked at me as if I was mad as I watched the detective and another police officer escort Harrison out of view.

I ran back to my car and just sat there for a few moments. I was trying to concentrate on driving out of the airport car park, but I was too excited and felt a real sense of exhilaration.

My mobile rang. It was Ray.

"We got him Andy!"

"That's great news Ray, well done," I said, pretending to be surprised.

"We will hold him for questioning for two days. I'll contact you in the morning."

I started my car and drove from the airport; I was happy, really happy. All I needed now was to get him convicted.

I arrived home and told my wife the great news.

"We got him honey, we got him"

"I assume you mean the American ... John Harrison?"

"Yes of course! Yes, and I was there; I saw him getting arrested."

"Where did they arrest him?"

"At Dublin Airport as he went past security to board a Ryanair flight."

"Oh Andy, that is great news I am so pleased for you, especially after all your long, hard work"

I sat down for dinner but how could I eat? I was making a start when my phone rang. It was Det. Sgt. Guerin.

"Hi Andy, you heard the good news then?"

"This is not good news; it's great news! Well done to you and your team."

"You gave us so much of the investigation all we had to do was catch him. It was a great example of financial investigators like yourself working with the Gardaí."

"Thanks Sgt. So what happens next?"

"I go and get some sleep," she laughed. "I worked with the Delta 1 surveillance team all night, so I am dead tired. We will start the interrogation and questioning next."

"What Garda Station have you taken him to?"

"He is in Santry Station. He will be appointed a legal aid lawyer."

"Why are you holding him in Santry?"

"Most of the arrests made in Dublin Airport go to Ballymun or Santry Garda Stations. The lads are out doing organised searches on the addresses we have for Harrison in Sallins and Naas. I will ring you in the morning with an update."

Det. Sgt. Guerin's words had given me a new appetite. I enjoyed my dinner and had a large glass of Scotch to celebrate and to help me sleep. I was looking forward to hearing what the house searches turned up. I was also curious to know how long Harrison would get in jail. I wanted to telephone Ann Wall but Det. Sgt. Guerin had asked me to keep the arrest confidential for a few hours as the searches needed to be completed. I should be able to tell her the next day.

That night the Scotch did its job as I slept like a baby.

CHAPTER 33

The following morning I was congratulated by many of my colleagues who knew how important the Harrison case was to me. Yes success was enjoyable, and I was glad I had put in the hard work; I felt like a student who had just achieved a 1st Class Honours degree. But, although I was happy with the result, I knew that we still needed to succeed in the court case. We had plenty of evidence against him but the next step was to obtain a conviction. It was going to be a difficult process and as my experience was with civil law and not criminal, I was not sure how long it was going to take. Like everybody else, Harrison would be presumed innocent until proven guilty in a court of law but at least he was at last going to face justice, Irish justice, and I was happy about that.

Later that day I got a call from Ray.

"Things are going well Andy. Harrison is co-operating — up to a point."

"Has he mentioned anything about the insurance claims?"

"To be fair Andy, we have not asked him yet. We are concentrating the questioning on the passports."

"So what's the next step Ray?"

"We will keep him here in Santry Station for another few hours. We carried out searches on the addresses in Naas and Sallins but did not find anything incriminating."

"Did you retrieve the passports?"

"He is telling us that the passports are in Poland."

"That's good he is talking at least. We need those passports returned."

"Getting the passports would be ideal, but I don't hold out much hope at this stage. However we have informed Interpol who will alert all border crossings to watch out for passports featuring any of the names on the list we've given them."

"How long more can you hold him?"

"We should only be able to hold him for another few hours but we have an extension from the Detective Superintendent. We'll wait and bring him before the District Court tomorrow morning."

"Is that a public court?" I asked quickly.

"Yes Andy, you can be in the public gallery if you want to see him. He will be in District Court 44 at about 10.30am."

"Tomorrow is Saturday — will the courts not be closed?"

"Court 44 is a special sitting for criminal cases."

"Thanks Ray; I will see you in the morning."

Even though it was a Saturday, I would not miss the court case for a €100,000. I had worked long and hard on this case, along with Ray and Det. Sgt. Guerin, and now it was time for justice to take its course.

I managed to keep my mind busy doing some routine work for the rest of the day. Although I consider myself a good investigator, I had luck on my side as well because even though my mind had been on the Texan case for the past two years I was still pulling in good results, with record financial savings.

I was packing up to leave when I saw Courtney walking towards me. I noticed a large smile on his face, something I was not used to seeing. He put out his right hand and gave my hand a vigorous shake.

"I hear you got your man," he smiled.

"Yes Dan, he was picked up in Dublin Airport yesterday."

"That's a fine job you did son, a fine job; good work," Courtney said, patting me on the back.

"Well Dan, it was a team effort and I could not have done it without your assistance in Poland," I winked.

"The less said about that the better! Good job Pebble."

"Not Stony today then Dan?"

Courtney simply waved his right hand as he walked away.

I was happy to get the praise from him and left work looking forward to the court case the next day.

The following morning I arrived outside the District Court in Dublin city centre. I was about an hour early. It was cold and raining, normal weather for a January morning in Dublin. Ray had told me that the door opened at about 10.15am. With the exception of the District and Circuit Courts sitting around the country, which heard some small criminal cases, I had never been in a criminal court before. I was feeling impatient, looking forward to the prospect of finally seeing Harrison before a judge.

Eventually the doors opened and I walked into the small public gallery of the courtroom. The court was almost deserted and nobody was around, other than the security officer. There was a solid silence in the place; all I could hear was the traffic as it passed by the windows outside.

In front of the judge's bench was a wooden staircase that I later found out led down to the holding cells. There was no room for a jury in this court, only a District Court judge who decided if a person was released or sent back down the stairs into what I could only imagine as a dungeon-styled cell.

As I sat in the gallery the musty smell reminded me of my school days and my old classroom.

The door to the courtroom opened and in walked Ray.

"You're here already Andy," he said.

"I am. I would have camped outside the court if I could as I wanted to get a good seat."

"He will be here in a few moments, just waiting on the prison van. Come and have a look," Ray said, as he urged me to walk outside into the courtyard.

I saw Det. Sgt. Guerin talking to a man who looked like another detective. She saw me and walked over.

"Well, we got him," she said, just as a large prison van pulled into the yard. Unfortunately it drove into a secure area so I was unable to view Harrison getting out.

I turned back to Det. Sgt. Guerin who was reviewing her file notes as she would have to give evidence of the arrest.

"Sgt. Guerin, according to Ray Harrison has co-operated with your interviews do you have new evidence?"

"Not really, but it's early days yet. I have to go and check another case I am running, see you inside."

She walked off and Ray grabbed my arm.

"She is busy, let's leave her to it," he said, as he pulled me back to the courtroom.

We sat back down in the gallery and watched the courtroom start to fill up. I spotted uniformed cops, detectives and a few young journalists who were obviously just learning their trade and had been dumped with the Saturday morning shift. There was also a group of men and women in suits, talking in the corner.

Ray nodded at them commenting: "And they say crime doesn't pay; that lot make a fortune from it."

"What are they barristers?"

"Yep they sure are, barristers and solicitors, and every prisoner in the cell will get free legal aid to pay for that shower of lawyers. And we know who pays for that, you and me Andy, from our taxes. We keep that lot in a job."

Sitting in the courtroom chatting to Ray made me very aware of the amount of tax money that was spent on crime, especially when I considered all the police, judges, prison wardens and legal people involved, particularly the fat cats; not to mention the upkeep of the prisons themselves.

As we sat talking, the judge's clerk entered the courtroom and placed a glass of what I assume was water on the judge's bench. He also placed a large book on the desk and a couple of pens. A few moments later a large, aggressive looking Garda walked up the stairs in the centre of the courtroom. I noticed he had rank of Sergeant. He stood at the top of the stairs, holding a clipboard, with paper clipped to the front of it.

"Won't be long now," Ray said, leaning towards me. "That's Sgt. Mick; he is the jailer responsible for the prisoners."

"He looks a hard man."

"He sure is Andy, only has another couple of years before he retires. You know there is a story that six prisoners attacked him one day and after the fight he was the only one standing."

"A modern day 'Lugs' Brannigan," I smiled.

The courtroom was now almost full. It was difficult to see the staircase leading down to the cells, as uniformed police and detectives stood leaning over the banisters, all deep in discussion about their cases. To the right of the courtroom stood the legal brigade, standing in an orderly queue waiting for their clients. The public gallery was full of the young journalists all anxiously holding their notebooks and pens. Recording devices and cameras are not permitted in Irish courts, so pen and paper are the only way to record the notes of the day.

I checked my watch; it was just after 11am and the day's proceedings were about to commence.

A door to the side of the judge's bench opened and the court clerk re-appeared.

"All rise," he shouted.

As I stood up the judge entered the room and took his seat, like a king sitting on his throne. He was not wearing a wig, just a dark suit and a black cloak. The judge started to speak, however, due to the amount of people in the room who were still talking, nobody could hear him.

Sgt. Mick who was standing at the top of the stairs suddenly stood up straight. "Silence in court … shut up," he shouted.

Almost immediately a silence fell. I was accustomed to the phrase "silence in court" but not so accustomed to "shut up!".

"Thank you Sgt," the judge said.

Sgt. Mick gave a slight grin and a nod of his head.

"How many do we have today?" the judge asked.

"Sixty-two your honour," the clerk responded.

"That's 62 prisoners Andy, who have been arrested in the past couple of days," Ray whispered.

"Is it in alphabetical order?" I asked, thinking that Harrison might be in the first batch called.

"Don't know," Ray shrugged.

The clerk called out the name of the first prisoner: "Thomas Flynn."

"Thomas Flynn," Sgt. Mick shouted down the stairs

Within moments a prisoner walked up the stairs and was jostled by Sgt. Mick into a standing position in front of the judge. A Garda entered the witness box, took the oath and informed the judge that the man had been arrested for being drunk and abusive in a public place.

"What have you to say for yourself?" the judge asked Flynn.

"I am very sorry Judge," the man trembled.

"€100 for the poor box and don't let me see you before me again."

Sgt. Mick reached out, grabbed the man by the arm and pushed him towards a door to the rear of the court.

The clerk called the next case: "John O'Neill."

Once again Sgt. Mick shouted down the stairs: "John O'Neill!"

He arrived and was jostled in front of the judge but this time one of the solicitors walked over and stood beside him.

Another cop walked into the witness box and took the oath.

"This man was arrested for stealing a car last night," the officer stated.

The judge then sanctioned free legal aid and the solicitor and prisoner walked towards the same door at the rear of the court.

This process continued for at least 30 minutes. It felt like a conveyor belt of criminals all waiting for a two minute turn in front of the judge. My mind started to drift as I thought about Harrison sitting in the holding cell under the court-room and how he must be feeling.

After another 30 minutes the courtroom was starting to empty.

"Let's get a closer look," Ray said, standing up.

I followed as he walked over to the stairs and leaned on the rail beside the other cops. I stood near the top of the stairs, beside Sgt. Mick. He was still bellowing out names, down to another officer at the bottom of the stairs. I wondered why they didn't use a radio or intercom system.

Some of the legal crowd were talking rather loudly to each other again and it was disturbing the judge. He looked over and said: "Silence in court please."

The voices lowered but they continued to talk.

Sgt. Mick caught the judge's eye and a loud bellow of "shut up or get out" echoed around the courtroom.

There was instant silence.

"Thank you Sgt., next case please."

The clerk looked down at his list and called: "John Harrison."

Sgt. Mick leaned down the stairs and once again bellowed out a name, only this time it was John Harrison.

I anxiously leaned over the top of the banisters but I couldn't see anything as the stairs were dark at the bottom. As a result of the sudden silence in the court it was now possible to hear some words being said from the bottom of the stairs. I distinctly heard: "up the stairs" and with that I could hear shoes on the staircase and Harrison walked into view. He stood there in a pair of blue jeans and a light-coloured shirt, holding a coat under his right arm.

The guy looked terrified, which was understandable as being in custody must have been bad enough without it happening in a foreign country. Although, having watched programmes about American jails on TV, I think I would prefer to serve my time in an Irish jail and we had far more lenient sentencing.

Sgt. Mick tried to do his usual jostling trick but Harrison confused him by trying to hand him his coat

"Please Sir, will you hold on to this?" he asked, in a strong Southern American accent.

Sgt. Mick pushed him out in front of the Judge and did not answer.

Almost immediately one of the waiting barristers walked over and stood beside Harrison. Det. Sgt. Guerin took her place in the witness box and swore the oath on the Bible. She then gave a brief summary of the surveillance operation, the arrest at Dublin Airport and advised of the ongoing investigation into fraudulent activity.

"The GBFI request that bail be denied as we consider he is a flight risk."

"No objections Judge," the barrister responded.

"Sgt. I will deny bail on this matter. I am not used to having GBFI detectives before me on a Saturday morning; this must be a special case"

"Yes Judge it is special," Det. Sgt. Guerin replied.

"Very Good Sgt. Mr. Harrison you are remanded in custody until your trial date."

Sgt. Mick pulled Harrison by the arm and moved him back towards the stairs to the cells below. He was followed by his lawyer.

"Time to go," Ray whispered in my ear.

I felt exhilarated as we walked outside the court and into the small hall.

"Phew, he did not get bail, thank God."

"Yes it's good news Andy," Ray smiled.

"You must be mad Andy, working on a Saturday morning!" Det. Sgt. Guerin said, as she joined us outside.

"Perhaps I am," I smiled. My wife had also suggested I needed medical attention when I'd set off at 8.00am to attend court but it was worth it. "Thanks Sgt., you did a great job. Now that he is behind bars I can relax."

"Come on Ray, we need to go build our case. We will be in touch shortly Andy."

I waved them off and as I walked back towards my car, gave Shirley Sleator a quick call.

"Shirley, great news, we got Harrison."

"Thanks fantastic Andy, well done. You will have to drop by and fill me in on the details of his arrest."

"I will Shirley. Thankfully he has not made bail so he's off to one of the local remand prisons, most likely Cloverhill."

"He won't like that Andy."

Cloverhill Prison was the main remand prison, used for holding prisoners awaiting their criminal trials whose bail applications had been refused.

"You know if he appeals the decision on bail in the High Court and succeeds, he will most likely abscond out of our jurisdiction before his trial date," she added.

"You're right Shirley. If he did make bail he would disappear out of Ireland, especially considering the fact that the passports are missing."

"Call around sometime and we'll talk about it … anyway Andy I have to go, playing golf with the girlies so talk to you soon and well done again, great result."

I felt a shiver of reality as I hung up. Harrison making bail was still a real concern. We needed him to be kept behind bars. This was going to be a difficult task and I hoped that Det. Sgt. Guerin would be up to it.

CHAPTER 34

❦

I spent the weekend researching possible sentencing and hoped that Harrison would not get bail. If he did he would be gone. The sentencing in Ireland was most lenient than other jurisdictions, such as the United States of America. Many of my police friends were sick of the system. In the Irish justice system, suspects are convicted and sentenced to a year in jail, only be free again after three months because of good behaviour. When I worked in the southern states of America, convicted criminals were working at the side of the road, all chained together under the supervision of armed prison officers. If a convict tried to escape, they would face a blast from the shotgun and certain death. I am not advocating this system, but we should remember that people who are put in jail are there for a reason, mainly punishment and to protect our society and that's what Harrison deserved.

As I logged on to my computer, a message from Denton popped up. He was out on the road investigating a large burglary claim with Denise. Lesley had phoned in sick and the two new staff members were both on training courses, so not much was happening in the office.

"Andy, any news on Harrison?" Tanya asked when I met her at the coffee machine.

"Yes I was in court with him on Saturday morning. He has been remanded in jail for further questioning."

"Saturday morning... "

I interrupted Tanya before she could complete the sentence.

"Yeah, yeah ... I know working on a Saturday, I must be mad!"

"Will he make bail Andy?"

"There is a possibility but let's hope not as he will leave Ireland and escape justice if he gets it."

"We have got to keep him in jail. Is there anything I can do to help?"

"No I don't think so Tanya. Just make sure you have all your notes of conversations with him and that your file is in order, as we will need them."

"I will get onto it right away," Tanya said, quickly walking back to her desk.

Tanya had given me great assistance throughout the investigation. I was glad she was handling the claim. Most likely I would not have gotten this far without her help. She was a true professional.

I was shifting through my many emails, wondering why somebody who sat ten feet from my desk felt the need to email me a question, rather than walking over and asking me in person. It's a most impersonal way of communicating. Then again that's the modern office — productivity and getting the job done were all important, friendship was not such an issue.

My mind drifted back to the case and I wished I was part of the Garda interrogation team. If it wasn't for my problem with learning Irish maybe I'd have been working for the GBFI by now. An old school friend, Gareth Harmon, had been accepted into the Gardaí and I'd felt very envious. Sadly a few years after joining up he was killed in the line of duty, with his colleague Garda Conor Griffin. They were chasing a stolen vehicle and lost control of their Garda car and crashed. It was a horrendous accident and to this day I wonder if it might have been preventable if they'd had better equipment.

I have been in a few American police cars and they are well-equipped, with standard safety equipment including air bags, roll bars and reinforced doors and bumpers. I recall being in Los Angeles with a good friend of mine Shay. We met up with a few cops in a bar, one of whom I had known previously. Shay, who was on holidays, had always had an ambition to drive a US cop car. This was not permitted, however on an early evening patrol they agreed to let Shay sit in the rear seat, with me in the front passenger seat. We responded to several calls, including the armed robbery of a convenience store, two car crashes and also stopped two cars for suspicious activity. The police car was super-fast and yet there was so much protective equipment fitted it must have been extra heavy. However the main difference between the Irish and US cop cars was the shotgun positioned directly in front of the passenger seat. It's very different in Ireland where the Gardaí use normal everyday cars, like the Ford Mondeo I'd been in during the surveillance operation and most of them are unarmed. Whenever I think of Gareth and Conor I'm sure that we should give our police the same protection as the US cops. It would be better than wasting our taxes paying fat cat lawyers to provide free legal aid for criminals.

The phone on my desk rang, bringing me back to reality and interrupting my grim thoughts. It was Reception.

"Andy a Detective Sergeant Guerin is here for you in reception."

"I will be down straight away!"

I stood up immediately and started walking. I was very curious to know why she was looking for me, especially as Ray or Sgt. Guerin usually phoned me before calling over. I felt sick in the pit of my stomach — had Harrison been released after all? Did he somehow get bail?

"Nice offices Andy; so this is where you rich insurance boys live," she smiled.

"Somebody may well be making money but it's not me, especially with all the tax I pay! Well how can I help you? Harrison's not free is he?"

"No don't worry he is not going anywhere. I just need some advice and I think you can help me."

"You want to buy some insurance?" I joked.

"No I don't thanks," she said looking serious. "This is something very different Andy and I need your advice."

"Please continue Sgt. Guerin," I said soberly, feeling intrigued. I wondered how I could be of assistance to her.

"Andy, please call me Sinead, Sgt Guerin is too formal."

"OK Sinead sit down," I said, as I gestured for her to sit down in one of our customer consultation rooms, located off reception.

"I need some advice about how to deal with the parents of the dead babies. I know that you lost your son Andrew, so I'm hoping that maybe you can give me some guidelines to follow."

I wasn't sure what to say for a moment.

"Why do you have to talk to the parents?" I finally asked.

"I need to interview them and obtain statements, giving me full details of what happened to their babies," she said.

"Not a nice task, especially as these children died in 1975 over 35 years ago. Will you even be able to find them?"

"We have located the parents of three of the children and they are all still living in Ireland."

"I am not so sure if I can help you as Andrew died in 2003, but I know somebody who you should talk to. Ron Smyth Murphy is the Chairwoman of the Irish Stillbirth and Neonatal Death Society (Isands), which is now known as A Little Lifetime Foundation. They are a charity and give great support to bereaved parents."

"That sounds like the place. Do you have a contact for them?"

I checked my mobile but I could not find their number. It made me realise that although I was still a member of the organisation, I was not as active as I used to be.

"Let me get a number from the internet," I said as I logged onto the computer and found the website www .alittlelifetime.ie

I wrote down the contact details and handed them to Sinead.

"Please wait until tomorrow to call as I would like to talk to Ron first."

"Thank you Andy. I know this is not easy for you either but we do need to talk to the parents."

We stood up and as usual she said: "I will be in touch soon."

I returned to my desk and immediately telephoned A Little Lifetime. The answering machine kicked in, so I left a message asking for Ron to give me a call as soon as possible and I tried to put it out of my mind for the rest of the day.

The following morning I received a call on my mobile.

"Hello Andrew, this is Ron from A Little Lifetime."

"Thanks for calling me back. I need to talk to you about something important," I said.

I explained some of the basics of the case and that she should expect a call from a Det. Sgt. Sinead Guerin.

"I have already spoken to Det. Sgt. Guerin and she's meeting me at my house at 2.00pm. Sgt Guerin asked me to phone you as she would like you to attend the meeting."

"I'll be there," I agreed quickly.

It was just after 9.00am and I was running late for my meeting with Denton and Denise.

"Hi Denton, Andy here, is Denise with you?"

"Yes we are on our way; we will be with you shortly."

"Tell you what, meet me in Starbucks and we will have our meeting there."

"Starbucks OK, as long as you're paying."

Our meeting commenced just after 09.15 which was not so bad. Denton and Denise had both achieved a lot and were now making serious financial savings as a result of their investigations.

I returned briefly to the office after the meeting and then headed to Castleknock, following Ron's detailed directions. Arriving with ten minutes to spare, I saw Sinead's Ford Mondeo in the driveway.

The front door was open and just as I was about to knock, a voice said: "Come in Andrew; we are in my office."

I closed the door behind me and walked into a large office area, with a traditional coal-fire blazing.

Ray and Sinead were sitting on the sofa.

"You must be Andrew," a woman who was sitting behind a large, oak desk said.

"Yes I am Andrew Stone," I replied, moving forward. "Good to meet you."

We shook hands as she replied: "I am Ron Smyth Murphy. Good to meet you at last Andrew. Please have a seat."

I sat on a large leather chair.

"I am sorry for the loss of your son Andrew," Ron said.

"Thank you Ron and to the charity; they really helped me through that difficult time in my life."

"Yes a horrendous time for anyone which makes it so much worse to think of what John Harrison is doing. You know we lose about 900 children a year at the time of their birth."

"I have given Ron a full brief on the case and what we have uncovered," Sinead said. "I've explained that we have traced the parents of the dead babies whose identities Harrison has stolen and now we need to go and meet them, to obtain statements."

There was an uneasy silence as we all imagined the parents' reactions. Ron stood up.

"This is a very sad and problematic task. Would you like me to accompany you when you interview the parents?"

"Yes, we would like you to be there Ron, but sadly the law will not permit this, only Garda officers can be present," Sinead replied.

"But that's not right," I said. "The poor parents are going to have to relieve the nightmare of losing their sons, some 35 years ago!"

"I didn't write the law Andy and the parents are entitled to confidentiality."

Once again there was a tense moment.

"OK, here is what we can do," Ron said decisively. "We can provide you with information packs and I will give you my personal phone number to pass on to the parents. I can provide a support service, if they want to talk."

"That is very kind of you Ron," Sinead said, looking more relaxed.

This did not sound fair to me.

"Surely Ron or another support person from the charity can attend. She is an expert in counselling bereaved parents."

"Andrew, this is the law. We must respect what the Gardaí are saying," Ron said. "Now come and help me prepare some packs for the parents, or better still you go and make some coffee and I will get the information packs. The kitchen is the first door on the right. Now Sergeant how many will you need?"

"We will need five packs," Sinead said.

"Why five packs? I thought there were only three parents affected," I queried.

Ray stood up and nudged me out the door: "Come on Andy, I will help you with the coffee."

"Ray what other names have you found?"

"Well aside from Thomas Taylor we now know of one other name we believe Harrison also used but we are not totally sure of the seventh name," Ray said.

From my experience when Gardaí used the words "we believe" it normally meant they were 100 per cent certain. In one sense I was delighted as it was evidence that the police were taking the file seriously and still investigating the stolen identities. But in another way I was horrified that the detectives had confirmed that the Cowboy had stolen the identities of Sean Moran, Kenneth Smith, Gary O'Neill, Shay O'Brien, the US citizen Luke Wilson and Thomas Taylor; and now there was another victim. It made me realise that John Harrison was a true professional criminal. I was hoping he'd get 20 years in prison.

We made the coffee and were walking back into the office when Ray grabbed my arm.

"Can you run Shay O'Brien's name through your Insurance Link system?"

"Sure Ray, you want me to make your lunch as well?"

I was annoyed he hadn't told me about the seventh name. I'd thought I was part of the investigating team and yet Ray was holding out information on me.

"Ah Andy, come on you know what the Sgt. is like about confidentiality and doing it by the book!"

"OK Ray I will run the name but I want to be kept posted on developments on it and on the new name."

Ray nodded as he held the door open for me.

Ron was standing in the midst of five bags of material dealing with the loss of a baby – teddy bears, telephone numbers for the charity, pens and notepads; there was even a cook book in each bag.

I drank a couple of sips of coffee, made an excuse, said goodbye and left Ron's house. There was no need for me to be at the meeting and I was finding it difficult to listen to them talking about meeting the parents when Ron couldn't go along. The law was truly an ass.

I was feeling annoyed and also a bit shocked. I had done all the grunt work, obtained leads and evidence and provided it all on a plate to the Gardaí. This was the first time in my life that I really regretted not being a member of the force. I was effectively a civilian investigator, without any powers or protection. Det. Sgt. Guerin was a professional and I understood her decision not to tell me about the new name they had found but all I could think about was how many more names Harrison had used. I felt a deep sense of sadness for the parents of the babies. Can you imagine losing your baby 35 years ago and then a police detective calling to your house and telling you that the baby's identity was being used for fraud? I was hoping that Ray would let me know how the meetings went with the parents.

CHAPTER 35

I spent the few days after the meeting in Ron's house running the name Shay O'Brien through Insurance Link and our other IT database systems. Nothing of any interest came up; there were no matches at all on the various systems. It looked like Harrison might have only recently obtained Shay O'Brien's identity and he had not yet put it to fraudulent use.

I was still annoyed with Ray and Sinead for not telling me about the developments in the case. However I decided to give Ray a call, but just as I picked up the phone, I got a tap on the shoulder. I turned and noticed a large grin on the face of my former manager Dan Courtney.

"Hi Andy, you still working on that old case then?" Dan asked.

"Yes we still have him in custody but plenty of loose ends to be tied up."

"Well I am sure you will get your day or two in court. Can you meet me in Starbucks in about 20 minutes? I want to run something past you."

"Sure no problem."

As Dan walked off I wondered what he wanted to talk to me about.

"Hi Ray, Andy here," I said quickly dialling the number. "I ran those checks for you on Shay O'Brien and got nothing."

"Thanks Andy, it was only on the off-chance because Harrison used his passport to fly over this time."

I jumped into questioning mode.

"And what about Thomas Taylor? He is another baby, right?"

"Yes he died in 1976. Thanks for your help the other night and for putting us in contact with Ron and the charity Andy."

"How did it go with the parents?"

There was a silence for a moment.

"In general it was fine. The parents just listened to what we had to say but one or two of them were upset and one guy wanted to kill Harrison, which is totally understandable. I suppose grief affects us in many ways."

"It certainly does," I muttered, thinking back to when my son had died.

Ray then surprised me.

"Sinead found it difficult talking to the parents; she is not as hard as she appears."

"Yes I would say it was really difficult for you guys."

"Yeah it was Andy. I'll be in touch if anything new comes up."

I hung up the phone thinking of how hard it must have been for Sinead and Ray, having to give such bad news to the parents.

I was thinking about it so much I almost forgot about meeting Dan. I quickly dashed across the road. I was in such a rush I didn't even grab a jacket and must have looked ridiculous walking along in my shirt in the Dublin rain.

"I have ordered for us Andy," Dan called over as I walked in.

"Sorry Dan – got held up."

"No problem Andy. That was a great job you did on the Harrison case and I hear you even have plenty of change left over from the €20,000 investigation budget."

The investigation had only cost about €3,000, mainly thanks to Dan's CIA friends in Poland.

"Thanks Dan," I smiled. "You know financially we did make substantial savings in the non-payment of the fraudulent insurance claims, but above all stopping Harrison from using the dead babies' identities for criminal activity, that was the true saving."

"You're right Andy. That was the real victory. Tell me are you still a member of the Association of ... what is it again of International Special Investigators?"

"The International Association of Special Investigation Units (IASIU) — yes I am."

The waitress dropped off our coffee and Dan handed over a €10 note, with his usual "keep the change". Then he continued: "I hear they are having a conference in San Antonio, Texas, next month."

"Yes all the top insurance fraud investigators, the FBI and some other law enforcement people will be attending — should be interesting."

"Well now Andy, I think it would be good for the company if you attended the conference and took your wife with you. Enjoy a break and have a little fun. What do you think?"

"Yes that would be great, but two small problems — money and kids!"

Dan smiled and opened his jacket pocket. Before I realised what he was doing he'd handed over two Delta Airline tickets. I opened them up and saw my wife's and my name were printed on return flights to Atlanta, with two free internal flights.

"Here you go Andy it's covered and the company will pick up your hotel costs, just no staying in the Ritz!"

I was shocked.

"Thank you Dan, I can't believe it. How did you get the tickets?"

"I called in a few favours, from a friend."

I looked at the tickets. They appeared to be official Delta Airline tickets, not from a travel agent. I wondered about Dan's friend. Before I could ask him anything he stood up and shook my hand

"I am going off on a holiday with my wife today Andy so you say hello to Texas for me."

I thanked Dan and he walked from the coffee bar, leaving me stunned.

I was delighted; free tickets to Atlanta — I was sure my wife would be happy with this development in the Harrison case!

When I passed on the good news she was absolutely thrilled. It had been a long time since we'd had a break without the kids and getting away for a few days on our own was just the tonic our marriage needed, especially after my two-year obsession.

"I will check with my Dad to see if he will take the kids. I am sure it will not be a problem. Oh Andy, I am so excited. It's been a long time since we have been in America."

"Well go check with your Dad. Then we can make some plans!"

That evening after confirmation that my father-in-law would take care of our kids, we worked out our route. We decided to fly into Dallas via Atlanta and drive to Oklahoma, which according to my Texas IASIU contacts was about a three-hour drive. We would then drive to San Antonio for the conference. It was about six hours from Oklahoma. It sounded like a long drive to an Irishman, but I was sure driving in the States, when there were no screaming kids in the car, would be enjoyable. The conference was only on for three days so we'd have another seven to explore Texas. I had been in Dallas about 12 years before at an American Society for Industrial Security (ASIS) conference, so I knew that my wife was going to enjoy the beautiful city.

The next few weeks flew by. I checked in with Ray and he assured me they were still interrogating Harrison, researching his activities, trying to find the passports and any more identities he'd stolen. I got stuck back into my day job with renewed enthusiasm, especially when I thought about Dallas. It was good to catch up.

Denton and Denise had been working hard but there were a few large files requiring my attention and another identity theft case had been referred from our underwriting department. I managed to sign off on it the day before our flight out.

We arrived at Dublin Airport and as we checked-in, the lady smiled and said: "Mr. Stone you are in the wrong queue; these are business class tickets, but I can check you in anyway."

I have never seen such a big grin on my wife's face.

The flight to Atlanta, Georgia, from Dublin was about nine hours. Flying in Delta Business class made it feel like an hour. It was the first time I didn't want a long-haul flight to end; it was real luxury.

We landed in Atlanta, had a one hour wait and then boarded our Dallas flight, with a journey time of around two hours. Again the flight was perfect as we were in Business Class once more.

"This is really nice of Dan," I said.

"Yes Andy, how many bosses would organise a trip like this for an employee? We will have to get him a present"

"A present? But what the hell should I get him?"

"I don't know Andy, sure we have plenty of time so let's just wait and see."

I decided not to worry about it.

That night we stayed in a small airport hotel in Dallas Forth Worth Airport.

The following morning I collected our Ford Mustang Convertible from the car hire company. It was a dream of a car to drive and within no time at all we were on the open road, heading for Oklahoma. We stopped off at the most famous house in Dallas, Southfork Ranch, for lunch. As a child I used to have to watch the TV show *Dallas* every Saturday night with my mother and it felt like punishment. However actually being on the ranch was incredible and a cowboy hat seemed like an ideal present for Dan! One thing we had not prepared for however was the Texan heat. It was only 11.30am and already it was over a 100°F.

We arrived in Oklahoma that afternoon and I drove straight to the District Attorney's office. I had contacted Detective Mark Keating and arranged to meet him for a few beers. He was waiting in his office and greeted us with Southern charm and true friendship.

"Welcome, my friends to Oklahoma."

"Thank you. It's been a long drive."

"Did you drive straight here from Dallas Forth Worth?"

"Yes, well we stayed in Dallas last night and then drove there this morning. It's amazing to think that here we are thousands of miles from Ireland and the reason I'm here is we both share an interest in catching John Harrison."

"We certainly do Andy, only you have got him in jail!"

After a bit more small talk I presented him with a bottle of Jameson Irish Whiskey and I thanked him again for his assistance with the case. Mark introduced me to his small team and his boss the District Attorney. He then pointed us in the direction of a good hotel and we arranged to meet for dinner.

"I'll collect you from the hotel at 5.30pm."

"I bet he'll be right on time," I warned Jackie as we drove off.

As expected Mark and his wife Debbie collected us from the hotel at exactly 5.30pm.

They took us to a restaurant with a distinctly Native-American theme.

"You know Debbie is a Choctaw Indian and there is a significant connection to Ireland," Mark commented, after we were seated.

"Choctaw, is that like Apache Indians?" I asked.

"Well you're kind of right," Debbie laughed. "Choctaw is a tribe located here is Oklahoma."

"Mark, please continue, what has the Choctaw tribe got to do with Ireland?" Jackie asked.

"Well as I understand it around 1845 there was a real bad famine in Ireland, which claimed the lives of about a million Irish people. During this time, news travelled to North America of the famine and the desperate needs of the Irish people. A group of Choctaw Indians collected circa US$170 and sent it to Ireland to help the starving people."

"I have never heard that story, it's truly fascinating Mark," I said. "I have to ask the question Debbie, why did the tribe help the Irish people?"

"Well Andy about 15 years before your famine the Choctaw people were put off their land by the then American president. They were forced to walk over 500 miles to Oklahoma. As a child I was told that of the 21,000 Choctaw Indians who started the walk, nearly half of them died. This walk became known as the Trail of Tears. I guess the Choctaw people could relate to the Irish people and the problems your country had with the British."

"Well thankfully there is peace in Ireland now," I stated. "That is an incredible story."

"Say Andy did you know your former Irish President Mary Robinson visited Oklahoma in 1995 and met with the leaders of the Choctaw tribe?" Mark asked. "There was a public speech by President Robinson who addressed the Choctaw nation and she thanked them for their charity and compassion for the Irish People."

"No I didn't know that," I said feeling embarrassed. I could tell Jackie felt bad too that we'd had no idea about the connection between Ireland and the Choctaw people.

"Ya know Andy, the reason I am looking for John Harrison is because he wrote some bad paper in a couple of stores which are owned by the Choctaw people."

"What's bad paper?" Jackie asked.

"Bouncing cheques," I said quickly. "How much were the cheques made payable for Mark?"

"Not a large amount. If memory serves me correct it's less than $1,000."

"That's really interesting that the police would go to the trouble of placing a 'Wanted' advertisement and photograph on the internet for less than a $1,000," I said. "I don't think that would be the case back in Ireland."

I was also interested to hear that John Harrison had ripped off the Choctaw people. Knowing that he was in jail in Ireland, gave me a small sense of achieving something for them too.

That night we slept like babies as the alcohol mixed with the jet lag in our exhausted bodies. The following morning we woke early, as Texas/Oklahoma time is six hours behind Ireland. We discussed our plans for the day and checked the driving route to San Antonio, Texas.

Mark rang and invited us to come out for some breakfast before we continued on our journey. My wife declined but I agreed and met Mark in the hotel lobby.

We walked out to his standard issue detective car. It was possibly a Ford. On the police radio a woman's voice called out instructions to other officers who responded in turn.

"Do you not have to respond to these calls?"

"No, they are local police and sheriff's department calls. I only get involved when there is a serious call, like an armed robbery."

"Armed robbery – it's strange for me to see so many guns here as our uniformed officers do not carry guns in Ireland."

Mark looked at me with horror.

"No way! How do they do their job? We all carry guns, I got my sidearm and I have a 12 gage shotgun in the trunk."

"Well ordinary citizens don't carry guns in Ireland. It's illegal."

Mark shook his head in obvious disbelief as he parked the car. We entered a small diner and ordered coffee. Neither of us ate anything as we were both still full from the previous evening.

He then drove me around Oklahoma and showed me some interesting parts of his community.

"This store is owned by the Choctaw," he said as we drove past a large hardware store. "It's one of the stores that Harrison bounced a cheque in."

He also took me to the Sheriff's Department, introducing me to several of the deputies. Whilst we were in the

Sherriff's office I observed a man sweeping the floor, with leg irons attached to his legs.

"That is one of the boys from the local lock-up," Mark explained.

"You get them to work in here?"

"Just the good ones; it gets them out of the hold for a few hours, helps reform them."

Harrison was lucky he was in an Irish prison – he would have a much easier time there than if he'd been caught in Oklahoma or Texas.

Tour over Mark dropped me back to the hotel. I really appreciated him and his wife taking the time to meet with us.

We shook hands and Mark said: "Let me know if you need any more assistance with Harrison and please keep me posted on the court case."

I waved him off and walked up to our room. Jackie was ready to go so we checked out and started the long drive to San Antonio. It took us approximately six hours, at speeds of mainly 70mph along the motorway, the legal speed limit in Texas. After watching the show *Cops* on TV, I was not going to have any issues with Texas law enforcement.

We arrived in San Antonio and checked into the hotel, the Westin La Cantera Resort. Dan Courtney had arranged it and it was a truly beautiful place, located on the hills overlooking San Antonio. The only problem was the heat. For most of the drive we'd had to keep the hood up on the convertible, with the air conditioning on full power.

The following day I attended the IASIU conference and enjoyed meeting with the many insurance fraud investigators, mainly from around America. There were also a few investigators from Europe, Australia and Asia Pacific. There was much interest in the Harrison case, especially from the Texas investigators, who found it amazing that a Texan had travelled to Ireland and obtained multiple Irish passports. I attended several of the IASIU workshops, which were real value for money, a great way of learning and making new contacts and friends. Needless to say whilst I attended the conference my wife enjoyed the facilities of La Cantera and shopping in San Antonio, which was not very healthy for her credit card!

Before we left I visited The Alamo. I don't think it is possible to visit San Antonio without taking a look at this 300-year-old building. I was interested to learn that of the 189 defenders, 12 of them were Irishmen. I wondered just how and why these men who were born in Ireland ended up in San Antonio, Texas. I guess it was a good example of the history and long connections between Ireland and America, connections that the Cowboy had tried to exploit but thanks to people like Detective Mark Keating in Oklahoma he hadn't got away with it.

A few days after we got back to Dublin, I visited the Mansion House, where a plaque is placed on the wall to honour the Choctaw people. It reads: 'Their humanity calls us to remember the millions of human beings throughout our world today who die of hunger and hunger-related illness in a world of plenty.'

CHAPTER 36

It was 26 April, the final court date or at least that's what I hoped. Det. Sgt. Guerin told me that Harrison had decided to enter a guilty plea. But the question was to what was he pleading guilty? Either way Sinead told me to be prepared to give evidence, just in case Harrison had a change of mind. The case was listed for 11.00am in the Circuit Criminal Court, Dublin.

I arrived into the office around 7.00am. I needed to run over my evidence and cross-check some points, just in case I was faced with a tricky question from the defence. As I read through all my notes, I was relieved there were no distractions. Working at a large insurance company was great in many ways but the big disadvantage was working in an open-plan office environment. Only the senior managers had private offices. There were times when I was dealing with fraud investigation, when having the privacy of my own office, to talk to confidential sources, was essential. It was one of the things I missed from my days working at Pinkerton in America.

A few hours later I'd double checked all my evidence and exhibits, so I grabbed a coffee and headed to the courts.

The Circuit Criminal Courts were located just off Parkgate Street, in the centre of Dublin. The courts were built just at the end of Ireland's Celtic Tiger, in 2009. Driving up I thought they looked like a modern airport terminal. They have private security officers, X-ray machines and walk-through metal detectors. This might be considered normal practice for courts in other countries, such as America, but it was most unusual for Ireland. Most of the Irish courts have a single police officer for security but the criminal courts are different. They sit for serious criminal cases, including organised crime, drugs, fraud and murder trials.

I entered the courtroom with plenty of time to spare. It was 10.35am. The court was busy with police and legal personnel, reviewing their evidence. The judge was not yet sitting so there was time for me to once again recheck my notes. To the right of the courtroom was a glass partition behind which prison officers were talking and laughing like children in a school playground. A solitary chair was also located behind the glass partition. This was 'the dock' where the accused would sit. I got a shiver down my spine as I looked at the chair and could not help feeling sorry for Harrison. But then I reminded myself that we are all born innocent and without sin or guilt and Harrison had chosen his own road — he had chosen the criminal route and now it was time for him to pay the price and for justice to be served.

Sinead entered the court and walked straight over to me. I immediately noticed that she was wearing a new suit and looked great and really confident as she marched through the court. Det. Sgt. Guerin reminded me of a female version of Clint Eastwood's character Detective Harry Callaghan in *Dirty Harry*.

"Hi Andy, do you know your evidence then?" she asked.

I answered with a sheepish smile: "I hope so."

"Well sorry but you will not be needed today," she grinned.

I breathed a sigh of relief.

"Thank God! I hate giving evidence. So if I am not needed as a witness he must be going ahead with the guilty plea."

"Yes, I have spoken to his solicitor and barrister. He is going to plead guilty to most of the charges, including the frauds against the insurance companies."

I was delighted.

"Victory!" I smiled.

Just as I was about to continue Ray entered the court, also looking dapper, in a dark suit and shining shoes.

"Hi guys, we're on then," he said.

"Yes things are looking good," I grinned.

"Andy, we need to double-check and confirm the payments from the insurance companies and the related costs and expenses," Sinead said.

I quickly checked my notes and calculations.

"Dallast and Starling payments and associated costs are €55,000. Mustang is also running at €55,000. There are additional associated legal and medical costs which total €8,375 so all in it's about €118,375."

"Thanks Andy," she said just as the court clerk called: "All rise" and the judge entered the court.

The judge sat down at the bench and stated: "Good Morning everybody. I am going to deal with the sentencing first of the individuals who have entered guilty pleas."

"This is good for us with Harrison's guilty plea, he will be sentenced and we should be out of here by lunchtime," Ray said in a soft whisper.

Sinead nodded in agreement.

I started to relax and to enjoy the spectacle of justice being served. Looking around, I suddenly realised that I was sitting on a bench surrounded by uniformed police officers and detectives.

Sinead realised I was looking uncomfortable and asked: "Are you OK?"

"I don't think I'm allowed to sit in this area."

"Relax Andy, they will think you are one of us, just sit back and enjoy it."

I smiled and felt great that I was accepted as being on the same team as the police. With the amount of time and energy I had spent on the file, I appreciated the acknowledgement.

A few prisoners came and went, with the judge passing sentences for varied crimes, all of which were jail terms; the lowest handed down so far was six months, the highest five years.

I leaned towards Sinead and whispered: "What do you think he will get?"

"It's hard to say, at a guess maybe three to five years, but then again he could be set free today."

"Free! No way," I muttered. "He has only been in jail for a little over a year. How could that happen?"

I was about to ask another question when the judge called out: "Next case."

With that the clerk announced the case we had all been waiting for: "DPP v John Harrison."

One of the prison officers opened a door at the side of the glassed area and in walked Harrison. He appeared to have put on some weight since I'd last seen him. He was still wearing the same shirt and blue jeans he'd been wearing the year before in the District Court. I thought of my own children and wondered why his parents or a relative had not visited him in jail and at a minimum provided him with a suit of clothing. If one of my children was in a foreign country, facing criminal charges, I would have been there with them, even if they were guilty of the offences.

My heart skipped a few beats with excitement as he sat down in the dock and I also felt some sympathy for him. However as the clerk stood in front of the judge and commenced reading the charge sheets that pity soon turned to feelings of anger and rage.

"Mr. John Harrison of no fixed abode in Ireland, with addresses in Dallas Texas and the state of Arizona USA, you are charged with the following offences:

1. "That you carried out insurance fraud against Dallast Insurance making a false claim enticing a financial payment to you. How do you plead?"—"Guilty."

2. That you carried out insurance fraud against Magnum Insurance making a false claim enticing a financial payment to you. How do you plead?" – "Guilty."

3. "That you obtained a false identity in the name of Sean Moran. You presented yourself in a Garda station as Sean Moran and made application and obtained an Irish passport in the name of Sean Moran. How do you plead?" – "Guilty."

4. "That you obtained a false identity in the name of Kenneth Smith. You presented yourself in a Garda station as Kenneth Smith, made application and obtained an Irish Passport in the name of Kenneth Smith. How do you plead?" – "Guilty."

5. "That you obtained a false identity in the name of Thomas Taylor. You presented yourself in a Garda station as Thomas Taylor and made application and obtained an Irish Passport in the name of Thomas Taylor. How do you plead?" — "Guilty."

6. "That you travelled on international airline flights under the above false identities using the Irish passports. How do you plead?" — "Guilty."

7. "That you opened bank accounts in all the above false names and in the name of Kenneth Smith, knowing this to be a false identity. How do you plead?" — "Guilty."

The clerk continued and I lost count as he must have read out over 20 charges with Harrison answering "Guilty" at the end of each one. It started to become a little repetitive but at least his answers were keeping me out of the witness box.

Eventually the clerk sat down and the barrister for the DPP called Det. Sgt. Guerin to the witness box. She was sworn in, taking the oath on the Bible. She was a true professional, no fear in her eyes or quiver in her voice, just pure confidence at its best.

As she answered questions, Harrison stared at the ceiling and briefly glanced at his audience, the police and the court reporters who were anxiously writing down notes. His face was motionless, although I did catch a brief hint of a smile as it he was showing appreciation for all the attention he was getting.

The barrister for the DPP asked some basic questions to confirm Harrison's identity. Then he asked about Harrison's previous criminal convictions in North America.

"Detective Sergeant, can you inform the court of what you know of Mr. John Harrison's criminal history outside of Ireland?"

"Yes, I am aware of outstanding warrants for his arrest in Texas and Oklahoma in the United States of America. He also has several previous convictions for fraud within that jurisdiction."

The Judge intervened.

"This is a most extraordinary case Detective Sergeant. Are we satisfied that this man is in fact John Harrison?"

"Yes Judge, we obtained the assistance of the Federal Bureau of Investigation in America and they have confirmed his true identity. We got a match on his fingerprints."

"Excellent Sergeant; truly, truly an extraordinary case indeed," the judge said as he adjusted his glasses and scratched the side of his forehead.

"Det. Sgt. Guerin you made contact with the parents of the dead babies – how have they been affected by Harrison's actions?"

"Yes we traced and met with all the parents of the dead babies whose identities Mr. Harrison had stolen. The parents were horrified and very upset."

"Det. Sgt. when Mr. Harrison was arrested in Dublin Airport, attempting to board a flight to Poland, was he travelling under a false name?"

"Yes, he was booked onto a Ryanair flight under a false name and was using an official Irish passport in the name of one of the dead babies. He was also in possession of the birth certificate of that same dead baby."

"One final question Det. Sgt. what was the cost to the insurance companies in payments for these false claims?"

"The total cost was €118,375"

"That is a very exact figure Sgt.," the judge commented.

"I had some assistance Judge," Sinead said and looked in my direction.

"Thank you Det. Sgt.," the DPP's barrister said as he sat down.

Harrison's barrister then took to his feet.

"Det. Sgt. Guerin is it true that none of the parents of the dead babies are in court today and the reason for this is because my client has entered a guilty plea?"

"That is correct," she agreed.

"My client was co-operative and effectively held his hands up when arrested – would you agree?"

"He co-operated," she replied dryly, sounding non-committal.

I was getting ready for a war of words, but to my amazement the barrister sat down saying: "No further questions."

The judge thanked Det. Sgt. Guerin for her assistance and asked her to stand down.

Harrison's barrister then addressed the judge, commencing with a plea for leniency and fairness for his client.

"My client Judge has spared the pain the parents would have felt if they had being required to give evidence in this case. I noted from the Book of Evidence presented by the Gardaí that if Mr. Harrison had pleaded not guilty there would have been some 46 witnesses called. My client has saved the court and indeed these witnesses a large amount of time. He accepts that he has done wrong and wants this put behind him so that he can re-join his wife and children. I would ask you Judge to be lenient with my client," he concluded sitting down.

The judge coughed, clearing his throat and took a sip of water before starting to speak.

"Before I give my judgement in this case and pass sentence I want to thank the Gardaí for this investigation and for clearly stating the facts of the case and also to thank the insurance investigator, who detected irregularities with the claims and called in the Garda Bureau of Fraud Investigation. Taking the identity of a dead baby for the intention of committing criminal fraudulent activity is a serious matter. Having the ability to effectively cloak one's true identity from Irish financial institutions is also a serious matter. When Mr. Harrison was arrested he was found in possession of a false passport and documents to further advance his fraudulent activities. There are outstanding illegal Irish passports still in existence. I do not believe they have been destroyed. Passports are valuable documents, important to all citizens of Ireland. We must protect the identity of our citizens and our country. I must also consider the poor unfortunate parents who had to deal with Garda detectives informing them of the theft of the identities of their dead babies. The identity of any baby, living or who has sadly died at birth is important. Indeed the very constitution of Ireland states that we should cherish all the children of the nation equally. This man Mr. John Harrison has stolen the identities of these Irish children and visited terrible pain on their parents.

I should and will also take into account the fact that Mr. Harrison has co-operated with the Garda detectives and did enter a guilty plea. However the insurance companies have paid out monies on fraudulent claims to the tune of €118,000. I understand that no restitution or indeed effort has been made by Mr. Harrison to repay this money."

The judge then looked directly at John Harrison who was standing in the dock.

"Mr. Harrison you are from the State of Texas, is that correct?"

"Yes Sir I am."

"Well Mr. Harrison, do you know what sentence you would be given if you were in Texas?"

"I don't ... I don't know Sir," Harrison said with a tremble in his voice.

"Well let me see now, obtaining a United States passport in order to commit fraud. Using said passport to commit insurance fraud, money laundering through the opening of bank accounts with false identities, using illegal passports to fly on civil aircraft. Now Mr. Harrison I think you would be looking at a custodial sentence of a minimum of 25 years."

"Oh my God," Sinead muttered.

"He is going to throw the book at him," Ray hissed.

The judge continued: "I think you saw Ireland as a soft touch Mr. Harrison and that you decided to commit your crimes in Ireland, knowing that if you were caught you would receive a lighter sentence, than the one you would receive in the United States of America."

There was complete silence in the court.

The judge once again cleared his throat and took a sip of water.

"Taking all this into account I feel that this matter warrants a serious custodial sentence. A sentence then will act as a deterrent to stop what I will term criminal tourists from repeating the efforts of Mr. Harrison. I am hereby sentencing Mr. John Harrison to 12 years in custody."

Immediately the barrister for the defence jumped to his feet.

"Judge, I must protest. My client has co-operated, Judge he has pleaded guilty."

"I have given my judgement."

The judge stood up and the court clerk announced: "All rise."

I was stunned, speechless at the harshness of the sentence.

We all stood and watched as the judge walked towards his private chambers. When I'd first seen Harrison I'd wanted to speak to him. Seeing my chance I walked over to the glass partition and stood in front of Harrison's chair.

"Goodbye John," I smiled.

"Who are you?" Harrison asked, staring at me.

"No John, the question is who are you?"

The prison officers then escorted Harrison back towards the holding cells. As I watched, I felt a hand on my left arm.

"Let's go Andy, the job is done," Sinead said, as Ray came up beside her.

"I can't believe it's over and he has been convicted," I said as we walked out.

"Couldn't have done it without you Andy; you built the case and got the result," she said.

Ray nodded in agreement.

"Are you happy with the sentence?" I asked.

"All things considered it is the correct sentence," Ray said.

"Sinead, Ray, thanks for your assistance with this case," I said, as we turned to go our separate ways. I continued on walking through the foyer of the court house towards the car park.

"Hey Andy," Sinead shouted after me.

"Yes?"

"If you have any more suspect files, send them my way – you have my number!"

"Have you not got enough cases?"

"Yes but your referrals are great, as you do all the work," Ray laughed.

I waved them off but turned again at the sound of my name.

"Mr. Stone, can we have a comment on the case?" a young woman who looked like a reporter asked.

I was tempted to give a comment, but I felt a bit emotional so I decided to stay quiet in case I said something that I would later regret.

"No, not from me but you can call Dallast Insurance's marketing department, or talk to those two detectives," I smiled, pointing at Ray and Sinead.

I was owed some time off work, so I decided to head home. I listened to the radio and checked the newspapers that evening but there was no coverage of the case. I found this strange, as surely a Texan cowboy, obtaining Irish passports by stealing the identities of dead Irish babies would have made the papers. There was nothing on the television news that evening either.

The following morning I dropped the kids off at school and stopped off to buy every newspaper available in Dublin. There was absolutely no coverage, not a single mention of the case, which was disappointing. It would have been nice to read an article about it, but then none of us had talked to the reporters.

I entered the office and got a few "well done" comments from my own team and from my immediate manager. Kenny was delighted with the result, smiling: "That's one up for the good guys."

The news of the result soon travelled to my other colleagues in Dallast and also to other insurance companies and I got more congratulations. Although the insurance companies are competing for business the various fraud departments work well together as we share a common goal — to defeat the menace of fraud.

But a few hours later I sat at my desk feeling deflated. It was hard to take on board that the case I had been working on for the past three years was finally completed. I didn't feel like working on any of the ordinary fraud cases. As I was waiting for my computer to load, my mobile rang with a strange number that looked American.

"Hello," I answered cautiously.

"Andy, it's Dan Courtney. Just heard, well done, good job son. You saved the company a lot of money, so my pension is good and safe!"

"Thanks Dan. This is a strange number for you, where are you?"

"I am in Palm Springs, California, and I won't be coming back. My wife and I have a nice place out here. You should come out some time."

"Palm Springs ... I have never been and it sounds great but it must be about 5.00am over there right now?"

"It's 5.10am to be precise. I gotta go get some sleep, so you take care now."

I was delighted that Dan had returned to the States now that he was fully retired. I was sure it was what he wanted.

I forced myself to select a file and throw myself into investigating it. The first step was an interview in North Dublin, not far from my home. I immediately had a plan and felt more positive — do the interview, make some enquires and be home for about 5.00pm. Well at least that was if everything went smoothly but in the insurance investigation business you never know what is going to happen next.

That afternoon I did the interview, completed my investigation and was satisfied it was a genuine incident. I started the drive home, switching on Newstalk 106. It was almost 5.00pm and George Hook was interviewing some sports' star. The traffic was light as I drove along the back roads behind Dublin Airport.

George announced: "Over to the Newsroom for the 5 o'clock news."

As I half-listened to a lady with a stern voice reading the news headlines, I almost missed the second item: "Texas man steals dead babies' identities for insurance fraud."

I went from feeling bored to feeling like I was on top of a roller-coaster in a matter of a second. Suddenly I was back reliving the case which was now public information.

I listened closely: "An American citizen from Texas, John Harrison was sentenced to twelve years at Dublin's Circuit Criminal Court, for the identity theft of dead babies, the obtaining of illegal Irish passports and submitting false insurance claims."

As she went on to the next item I immediately telephoned my wife, who had also heard the news. I felt excited by the fact that my work had finally paid off. Yes there was the court case and the sentence but somehow hearing it reported on the radio was giving me a real sense of achievement and victory.

It was a great feeling to know that the case was finally over and we had won.

The following morning, my poor kids were rushed through their breakfast and pretty much thrown into the car. I was determined to get a newspaper as I was sure that there would now be some coverage of the case.

As it was early the only shop open was our local petrol station. The manager, Mohammed, knew me as I called in most mornings.

"Morning Andy," he said.

I was so focussed I completely ignored him, walking straight for the newspaper stand. I frantically scanned the first newspaper I picked up and there it was on page 2: 'Texan Fraudster used Irish Passports for Insurance Fraud'

I read the article and was delighted. To read about the result of three years hard work in a national newspaper was a fantastic feeling.

"Are you going to pay for that?" Mohammed asked smiling, bringing me back to reality.

"Sorry, thanks."

I handed him a €5 note and walked for the exit, engrossed in the rest of the article.

"Andy – your change!"

"Keep it!" I said.

I sat back into the car and showed my daughters the article as I drove to their school.

I was listening to the radio when, *Second Hand News*, by Fleetwood Mac came on. It was strange hearing it again as three years previously when I'd started the case it had been playing as I drove to Naas. It was like the theme music to the opening and ending of a movie but it was much to the disapproval of my daughter Olivia who would be more of a Beyoncé fan.

As I drove in through the school gates, a man was handing out copies of the free paper the *Metro Herald*. Olivia opened her window and asked for a copy and he handed her two.

"Oh my God, look Dad it's … it's the front page news," Olivia said, as she ran out of the car, with Sarah my younger daughter following her. They were so excited they ran off without even saying goodbye.

I read the headline: 'Modern Day Outlaw from Texas Stole Irish Identities for Fraud.' and quickly scanned the rest of the article. All I could think of was the poor parents who had lost their children so many years ago, the pain they must be feeling now, reading the newspapers and listening to the news on the radio. I felt a huge sense of hurt and pain and started to cry.

I think that when you suffer the pain of losing a child, of any age, that a part of you becomes more sensitive and aware of your feelings and of the feelings of others. The only small consolation I have found in Andrew's death is that it has made me more sensitive in my career and has improved my gut instincts and my ability to detect inconsistencies.

I was really upset. It was Wednesday morning and I needed to get to the office but I was a complete mess. I was feeling the pain of my son Andrew's death all over again. I did not want to call my wife or my mother but I needed to talk to somebody. I decided to phone Ron from A Little Lifetime. The minute she answered I started crying.

"I'm sorry; I'm sorry Ron. It's Andy."

"I was waiting for your call Andy. There is nothing to apologise for or to be sorry about."

Ron continued to provide words of comfort and wisdom, which somehow improved how I was feeling. After a few minutes she had given me the strength to drive on towards the office. This is why the charity A Little Lifetime is so important. It provides a support service for bereaved parents where you can talk to other parents who have also lost a child; Ron had an immediate understanding of the pain I was feeling and it made all the difference. I put a reminder in my phone to send them a donation as like so many charities it relies on donations from the public. If you can spare anything at all please log onto www.alittlelifetime.ie and know that any money you donate will go towards a great cause.

As soon as I entered the office I was greeted with more "well done" and "congratulations" comments from my co-workers. I really appreciated it as I must have bored the socks of these guys for the past three years, as all I could talk about was the case, my personal obsession. It was one of those cases that had demanded the use of all the abilities and skills I had learned over the past 23 years working in the investigation business.

The following day I rang in sick as I had been up most of the night. I simply could not sleep. My mind was racing and I was unsure why. I was due some annual leave so I took a day's holiday which was not an issue for my manager.

I decided to go and visit my son's grave. After I'd said a prayer at his grave I went to the Angels plot in Glasnevin Cemetery, in North Dublin, resting place of such famous Irish people as Michael Collins, Eamon de Valera and Daniel O'Connell. The old Angels plot is a burial place for babies and children and it was completely renovated in 2005 by A Little Lifetime or Isands as they were known then. Ron had told me about it and I would urge you to go and visit. It was obviously a sad and solemn place but there was also a feeling of life and fun. After all there are over 50,000 babies buried there, so why would there not be a sense of play? I stayed there for about two hours, exploring my thoughts.

Leaving the cemetery, I felt renewed and ready for the next challenge in my life. I was ready to continue the battle against fraud, thankful for having two beautiful children and also thankful that for whatever reason I had been chosen to investigate the Harrison case.

Perhaps my friend the retired Garda Chief Superintendent was right: "The case found me, rather than me finding the case."

"Mission completed Andrew"

Someone Has Taken My Place

I did not die Young
I lived my span of life
Within your body
And within your love
There are many
Who have lived long lives
And have not been loved as me
If you would honour me
Then Speak my name
And number me among your family
If you wound honour me
Then strive to live in love
For in that love I live
Never ever doubt
That we will meet again
Until that Happy day
I will grow with god
And Wait for you

© *Christy Kenneally*

A Little Lifetime Foundation
A Registered Irish Charity
Number: CHY 11507

"An Angel in the book of life wrote down my baby's birth. And whispered as she closed the book "too beautiful for earth."
~Author Unknown

"And whosoever shall offend one of these little ones that believe in me, it is better for him that a millstone were hanged about his neck, and he were cast into the sea."
Jesus Christ — Mark 9:42 — King James Bible

A Little Lifetime Foundation (formerly Isands) is a voluntary organisation, founded in 1983 by a group of bereaved parents whose babies died before or at birth (stillbirth) or some time after birth (neonatal death).

Each year in Ireland approximately 500 babies die around the time of birth. As a result a large number of parents, brothers and sisters, grandparents and friends are bereaved.

Up to 15 years ago, parents who experienced the death of a baby were given no recognition or acknowledgment. Parents coped with unbelievable pain and sadness and only now, years later have the courage to come forward for support.

In recent years there has been a much better realisation of the tragedy it is when a baby dies and the loss that it is for parents, brothers and sisters. Thankfully, there is also a better understanding of this loss by the Medical Profession and in general, parents and families are encouraged to be part of and create precious memories in their baby's short life.

A Little Lifetime Foundation (formerly Isands) produce and distribute a booklet called A Little Lifetime to all maternity hospitals and units in the country. This booklet has helpful and important information to help and support parents at the time they are told the sad news that their baby has died or is expected to die shortly after birth. If you are a parent reading this who has just been told that your baby is expected to die, then if you have not received a copy of A Little Lifetime, please make sure to ask for one from the Health Care Staff or make contact with A Little Lifetime Foundation and we will make sure you get a copy as soon as possible.

A Little Lifetime Foundation's aim is to provide information, services and support based on other bereaved parents' and families' experiences which can be different but there is a common link that is recognised — the loss of a son or daughter, brother or sister.

Fund-Raising

A Little Lifetime Foundation are always in need of funds!! The general running costs for all charities has increased enormously. The charity is run by volunteers but we need funds to continue the services we provide and develop new ways to provide information and offer support. Our literature is a life line for families and we need to ensure the publication and distribution of - A Little Lifetime and our twice yearly Newsletters.

We also want to continue to provide Facilitators (who are volunteers but need to be trained and supervised) and venues for our Parent Support Meetings and offer support on the phone. We also hope to continue to develop links with Health care Professionals and interested others and provide updated publications like our A Little Lifetime Foundation Guidelines Professionals.

You can help by

Making a donation, buying Christmas cards and Memory Collection cards, participating in sporting events like — the mini marathon or organised events (sponsorship cards available from A Little Lifetime Foundation all year round). Some families also organise small fundraising events in their own area in memory of their baby. If you have any ideas for a fund raising event please let us know.

How to Contact A Little Lifetime Foundation
A Little Lifetime Foundation, Carmichael House, 4 Nth Brunswick Street, Dublin 7
Telephone 353 1 8726996
Email - info@isands.ie

Message from the Author:

Sadly in 2003 I required the services of A Little Lifetime, when my son Andrew died at the time of his birth. This charity is an excellent organisation which is totally funded by charitable donations. In purchasing this book you have made a contribution to this charity. If you would like further information or would like to make a further donation then please log onto www.alittlelifetimefoundation.ie

Thank You
David Snow

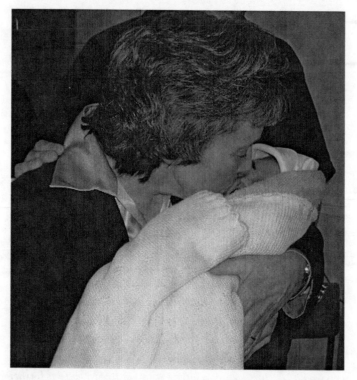

Figure 1: My Mother Mary and son Andrew in 2003

Figure 3 The Old Angels Plot, Glasnevin, Dublin, Ireland, Over 50,000 Irish Babies are buried here

Figure 4 My daughters Olivia & Sarah

Figure 5 Ron Smith Murphy of A Little Lifetime Foundation & The Author at a presentation for his efforts in detecting the identity theft of Irish babies

CPSIA information can be obtained at www.ICGtesting.com
Printed in the USA
LVOW131054130113

315503LV00001B/9/P